More Early Excitement for
Pandemic

"*Pandemic* is a totally compelling novel, one of those rare thrillers that lays out a scenario that is not only possible, but terrifyingly probable."

Douglas Preston, author of *Relic* and *The Codex*

"*Pandemic* is fast, fierce and frightening. Kalla delivers a shot of adrenaline in a medical thriller that really thrills."

Don Winslow, author of *California Fire*
and *The Life and Death of BobbyZ*

"At last! A new thriller writer worthy to join the Ludlum, DeMille, LeCarre club. Not just a great read, a real treat."

—Beverly Swerling, author of
*City of Dreams: A Novel of Nieuw Amsterdam
and Early Manhattan*

**By Daniel Kalla
From Tom Doherty Associates**

Pandemic
Resistance
Rage Therapy
Blood Lies
Cold Plague*

*Forthcoming

PANDEMIC

DANIEL KALLA

TOR®

A TOM DOHERTY ASSOCIATES BOOK
NEW YORK

This is a work of fiction. All the characters and events portrayed in this book are either products of the author's imagination or are used fictitiously.

PANDEMIC

A Tor Book
Published by Tom Doherty Associates, LLC
175 Fifth Avenue
New York, NY 10010

www.tor.com

Tor® is a registered trademark of Tom Doherty Associates, LLC.

ISBN-13: 978-0-7653-5994-0
ISBN-10: 0-7653-5994-4

First Edition: February 2005
Second Edition: October 2007

Printed in the United States of America

0 9 8 7 6 5 4 3 2 1

For my girls . . . Cheryl, Chelsea, and Ashley

Acknowledgments

It's a long and occasionally bumpy road from glimmer of idea to published novel, but I can't imagine a more fun ride. Along the way, so many people have generously lent their time, ideas, and moral support that I haven't the space to name everyone, but I do need to recognize a few in print.

I am fortunate to be blessed with several good friends-cum-readers, but I would like to single out the most dedicated and burdened of the bunch, including Dave Allard, Rob King, Duncan Miller, Geoff Lyster, Kirk Hollohan, Bin Lim, Jeremy Etherington, Jeff Jacobs, Alisa Weyman, Chiara Hnatiuk, Brooke Wade, and Alec and Theresa Walton. For the medical background, I relied heavily on the advice of an excellent microbiologist, Dr. Marc Romney. And I am so grateful to have found terrific mentors in Beverly and Bill Martin (of agentresearch.com) and Michael McKinley, whose generous advice proved invaluable. Of all the readers in my corner, though, the one who went farthest above and beyond the call was Kit Schindell. Her tireless reading and re-reading, insightful feedback, and gentle steering ensured that I got the story as right as I could. Thanks, Kit!

I would like to acknowledge Susan Crawford for bringing my manuscript to Tor, where thanks to people like Paul Stevens, David Moench, Seth Lerner, and especially Tom Doherty—a publisher whose hands-on approach exceeded all expectations—I was made to feel very much at home. A special thank you goes to my marvelous editor, Natalia Aponte, who has patiently guided this neophyte through the process of publication while helping to make the novel that much better.

Finally, I could not have done this without the unwavering support of my family. My wife Cheryl's honest feedback and resolute belief in me kept me balanced and focused as I wrote. My brother Tony has been a key advocate for this book. My brother Tim and sisters-in-law, Becca and Tammy, along with the rest of my extended family and in-laws all provided much needed encouragement and support. And none of this would have been possible without the guidance and love of my parents, Judy and Frank.

PROLOGUE

The SUV rattled along the dusty road, twelve miles south of Jiayuguan's city limits. There was little to see in the unvarying dirt hills rolling past. Besides, Kwok Lee was too agitated to take in the scenery. He cringed with each rock that pinged off the windshield, and he cursed every pothole that rocked his precious new vehicle. Where was all the money the State Council promised for infrastructure? In their pockets, Lee thought miserably, never considering that as an inveterate black marketer he fueled the province's systemic corruption. He consoled himself with the thought that in a few hours he would be able to replace this vehicle with ten more like it. Not that he needed a fleet of SUVs, just one for his girlfriend. Maybe that would quell some of her nagging, the way it had his wife's.

Lee glanced in his rearview mirror at his two backseat passengers. Since loading into the car, neither had spoken.

Two hours driving, and not so much as a word out of them in Mandarin or even their native tongue, which they had claimed was Mongol though Lee knew better. Dressed in cheap suits, the men had darker skin, rounder eyes, and broader noses than the local Chinese. They could have passed for brothers, except the one who answered the questions was half a head taller than his colleague. Lee considered the possibilities, concluding they must be Malays. He guessed they were reporters. Why else would they want to see the godforsaken place? But their identity was of no concern to Lee. What mattered were the wads of crisp American bills that he'd seen in the briefcase of the shorter one.

In the distance, a building burst through the dust cloud. A bleak concrete structure, fenced and gated, it could have been one of a million such in China. It wasn't until Lee slowed for the approaching gate that he noticed a difference. If not for the semiautomatic rifles slung over their shoulders, the soldiers manning the gate could have passed for surgeons. All three wore gowns, plastic caps, gloves, and surgical masks.

One of the soldiers leaned his head through the open driver's window and eyed Lee's passengers suspiciously.

"Missionaries," Lee explained cheerfully. "They've come to pray for their brother." He laughed and waved his documents in the soldier's face. "Like prayers will help the poor bugger!"

The soldier grunted a humorless chuckle, and then grabbed the documents. A few moments later, Lee slid his filthy car into a parking spot in the gravel lot. Outside the building's entrance, Lee and his passengers went through a similar security screen. And again one hundred meters down the corridor, but this time their papers were more thoroughly scrutinized by soldiers who wore lab hoods. At each checkpoint closer to the patients, Lee sensed a higher degree of disquiet among the guards. Inside the building, the tension in the air was palpable.

A guard led the three of them up the stairway to an office, where a small, balding, bespectacled official sat at a huge desk, which accentuated his diminutive size. He introduced himself only as Dr. Wu, but Lee knew he was the associate director of the regional hospital.

Wu studied Lee's silent companions for a few moments. "You are aware of the risks?" he finally asked.

Both men nodded.

"And yet you still want to see the patient?"

More nods.

"To pray for him?" Wu said with a raised eyebrow.

"He is our brother, sir," the taller man said in halting Chinese, leaving it unclear whether he meant the patient was a blood relative or a member of the same religious order. "We can't offer our blessings unless we see him in person."

"I see." Wu nodded, but his frown questioned the man's sanity. "By protocol, no one, not even family, is allowed to visit."

Lee shifted in his chair. What is this nonsense? he thought. Was this tiny bureaucrat renegotiating his price at the eleventh hour? Lee reached into his case and pulled out the thick envelope. "Doctor, I think these papers explain everything." He slid it across the desk allowing the envelope's flap to flash a glimpse of greenbacks.

In one motion, Wu swept the envelope into an open drawer and pushed it shut. He rose from his desk without gaining much height. "You will have five minutes. No more. Do not touch anything. You will wear full protective gear. You will need to decontaminate—" Seeing the confusion on their faces, he rolled his eyes and said, "You must shower after the visit."

The men nodded. Lee bowed his pudgy form toward the

associate director. "Thank you, Dr. Wu. You are most accommodating."

Wu's eyes narrowed in disdain. "Five minutes," he reminded them. "One of my men will stay with you. He will tell you when—"

The shorter of Lee's customer, though much taller than Wu, spoke up for the first time. "No. Doctor. This is between our brother and God," he said in near-perfect Mandarin. "We need a few minutes of privacy."

Before Wu finished violently shaking his head, the man had his hand extended, offering another fat envelope from his briefcase.

Wu hesitated. For a moment it seemed as if he might refuse the offer, but he snatched the envelope and scrambled back to his desk. He dropped the envelope as if it were on fire in the same drawer he'd deposited the other. "Five minutes, not a second more," he said.

Another guard led them into the changing rooms. After gowning and gloving, they passed through two sets of doors that served as a makeshift hermetic seal. On the other side, they changed into yellow biohazard suits before donning particle-filtrating hoods. Lee thought they resembled three misplaced beekeepers, but he kept the thought to himself. He was gripped by sudden foreboding.

Following the soldier, they walked through another set of airtight doors and onto the hospital ward. The similarly garbed staff paid little heed as the three men headed down the dingy corridor, but with each step Lee's anxiety rose. He struggled to breathe in the suffocating hood. Beads of sweat ran down his face and pooled at his collar. No one had told him that he would have to join the others in the patient's room!

Their soldier escort stopped at the last door in the hallway. He knocked. A nurse emerged from inside and shut the door behind her. After a brief exchange, she nodded and walked off down the hallway. The soldier held up five fingers to the others.

The tall one entered first. Lee hesitated, but the crisp shove from behind left him little choice but to follow. Inside the cramped room, surrounded by machines and IV drips, a patient lay on the bed. At least, Lee thought he was the patient but wasn't certain since the form on the bed was entirely swaddled in plastic bundles. The beeping machines and the occasional rustle of the plastic sheets suggested someone might be alive under the sheets. The whirring from the life-support system's ventilator by his head obscured most other sounds. But the longer he stood, the more aware Lee became of a harsh gurgling sound. Appalled, he realized it emanated from the patient, not the machine.

No one moved. Then both Malays fell to their knees. Lee experienced a fleeting moment of relief. Maybe they had come to pray for their brother after all?

But the relief was short-lived. They weren't praying. They jumbled at their legs, eventually withdrawing packages from inside their boots.

Lee's chest thumped. Sweat drenched his neck. He felt unsteady on his feet. Even before the taller man pointed the gun at him, he knew everything was wrong.

The shorter Malay approached the patient. He began to unwrap the protective plastic. Soon the patient's face appeared. He might have been anywhere from twenty to eighty, but his face was so swollen and bruised Lee couldn't place his age. His eyes puffed out like apricots. His lips swelled out farther than his nose. The line of his jaw was lost in the unnatural folds of his neck. Between his sausage lips, a clear plastic tube led to the ventilator.

Lee stared transfixed as the Malay leaned over the creature's neck. With obvious expertise he inserted a needle into the ill-defined skin folds. Then he attached a test tube to the other end. A stream of dark red blood shot into the glass tube. Satisfied, he detached the test tube from the needle, shook it in his gloved hand, and laid it on the bed. He repeated the steps until he'd filled five large test tubes. He pulled the needle out of the patient's neck and then turned to his partner with a quick nod.

The taller Malay handed the gun over to his partner. Then, almost casually, he unlatched his hood and removed it. He walked over to the other side of the bed and leaned close to the patient's bloated face. With both hands he uncoupled the ventilator tubing, leaving an unattached endotracheal tube, which looked more like a toilet paper roll, sticking out of the patient's mouth.

The gurgling amplified, and drool formed at the open end of the tube. The patient writhed on the bed and the plastic covers shook as he struggled to breathe. He coughed in frequent spasms. With each cough, bloody sputum sprayed from the tube's end.

Out of reflex, Lee took a step back and closer to the door, but the gun waving at his head halted his retreat. Horrified, he watched the taller Malay stoop forward and without hesitating place his mouth over the open end of the tube and suck from it like a snorkel.

Nausea swept over Lee. It was all he could do to stop from vomiting into his hood. He had never believed the sick brother story, but only now did Lee realize what the two maniacs had in mind. For the first time in weeks Lee thought of his daughter and son, My Ling and Man Yee, who were at the state school not ten miles away.

Watching the stranger inhale breathfuls of the deadly saliva Lee realized his own fate had already been sealed. The panic vanished, replaced by calm remorse.

One thought reverberated in his head: what have I done?

CHAPTER

1

The sharp, red point zoomed around the screen, before settling on the spiky gray structure in the center. "Ugly little bastard, isn't he?" the lecturer said. "Looks like something a junkyard dog ought to wear around his neck."

The remark was met by scattered laughter in the packed auditorium; Dr. Noah Haldane's lectures were always a huge draw. Among the medical students, the infectious diseases specialist and world expert on emerging pathogens had a reputation as a hip and irreverent speaker whose lectures managed to cut through the esoteric bullshit and get to the meat of the matter. There was another factor, too. At thirty-nine, without a trace of gray hair in his short uncombed hair, he stood six-two and still fit into his college jeans. His blue-gray eyes, sharp features, and readily amused smile helped pull in several women and even a few men who weren't even registered for the course.

Haldane ran the laser pointer around the circumference

of the structure on the screen, following the spikes of the outer ring. "But this particular virus"—he tapped the crystal with the laser pointer's light—"he caused us no end of grief the year before."

"Please, no letters to the dean's office." Haldane held up a hand in mock disclaimer. "I refer to all viruses as male." He shrugged, unapologetically. "Maybe it's because they're so basic. So incomplete. So dependent on others to sustain their existence." He paused. "Like my couch potato of a brother-in-law, it's unclear whether viruses even represent a true form of life." He waited for the laughter to subside. "Whereas I think of bacteria, which are far more complex, independent, and beautiful, in the female sense."

"How about parasites?" someone called out. "What sex are they?"

Haldane squinted through the dimness until he spotted the questioner in the fifth row. "Mr. Philips, I don't think of parasites in terms of gender."

"Why not?"

"Because they remind me too much of med students."

More laughter. Haldane circled the bug on the screen again with his pointer. "Does anyone recognize our ugly friend?"

"SARS-associated coronavirus?" a young, thin woman tentatively ventured from her front row seat, where she hunched over her notebook, scribbling madly even as she spoke.

"Exactly, Ms. Tai." Haldane nodded. "Or coronavirus TOR2."

Haldane clicked a button in his hand. The sterile electron microscope's image disappeared, replaced by a blood-spattered female cadaver whose eyes were blacked out by a solitary bar. Without comment Haldane tapped the button again. A human lung sat perched on a steel gurney. Another click. The screen sprang to life. A pair of gloved hands grasped the lung. One hand steadied the lung, while the other sliced into it with a scalpel. Bloody fluid spurted out as if a wineskin had been slashed open.

As he let his students absorb the images of an anonymous pathologist dissecting the pus- and blood-filled lung, Haldane wondered how lecturers in the age before Power Point and multi-media managed to make any impact. "Four days before the video was shot, this lung belonged to a perfectly healthy forty-two-year-old nurse . . ." He clicked the button and the black and white viral crystal reappeared. "Then she breathed in a few particles of SARS-associated coronavirus.

"Like all self-respecting coronaviruses, he has an affinity for the human nasal mucosa. He easily penetrates the epithelial barrier and replicates inside the mucosal cells." The scientific sketches on the screen changed in rhythm with Haldane's explanation. "That's when the body's armed forces, the immune system, mobilizes. Think of the phagocytes and neutrophils as the infantry in this battle. Doing the dirty work—the cell-to-cell combat. While the lymphocytes are more like the artillery, lobbing their ammo, in this case viral-specific antibodies, from afar.

"With most other coronaviruses this isn't exactly a level battlefield. Kind of like Luxembourg invading the U.S. Most of the damage comes from friendly fire—namely, the patient's own immune system, not the virus, producing the muscle aches, fever, and runny green sputum. After a couple of days the viral invader is inevitably wiped out."

The SARS virus reappeared on screen. "But this guy is tougher. In a significant percentage of cases he moves past the nasal mucosa and down the trachea into the pulmonary tissue. There he crosses the alveolar membranes of the lungs." He flashed up the images of the blood-filled lungs being slashed open again. "Resulting in a diffuse pneumonitis. And, as seen in this video, often pulmonary edema. In five percent of SARS cases, despite maximal therapy, the patient dies."

Pens throughout the auditorium flew to keep pace.

"But for those of you who consider SARS one of the horsemen of the Apocalypse, think again. It has killed less than a thousand people since its inception. In infectious disease terms that's as devastating as a fart into a headwind." He shook his head. "Or looking at it another way, a thousand dead isn't even a global day's work for malaria, HIV, or cholera to name but a few." He slashed through the image of the viral particle with his laser pointer. "SARS-associated coronavirus is nothing more than a cold virus with attitude."

Haldane dropped the pointer on the lectern and stepped away. He walked across the floor until he stood a few feet from the students in the front row. "I was as scared as the next guy—no—way, way more scared when SARS first broke. After all, this bug was targeting health-care professionals. Clearly not playing by the rules. And I witnessed firsthand the havoc the little bastard could wreak." He shook his head. "But in the long run SARS has been good for us."

He scanned the quizzical young faces in the audience, allowing a few more seconds of confusion before expanding. "SARS put global infectious disease control measures to the test. And guess what? Not one country came up smelling like a rose. In fact, most stunk. Take Canada. Despite boasting one of the world's best health care systems, my colleagues in Toronto didn't react fast enough to the first case of SARS. And the city ended up paying dearly for it." Haldane pointed at the audience. "But at least now the world has been warned. We have the chance to fine-tune—in some cases revamp completely—our public health measures. In that sense, SARS was a good dry run for the real McCoy."

Haldane clicked a button and the screen filled with a grainy black-and-white still, depicting an old hospital ward packed so tightly that the stretchers touched. It was difficult to tell whether the patients (some of whom were doubled up on stretchers) were alive or dead. If alive, none were well.

Haldane stretched his hand out to the screen. "Ladies and gentlemen, meet the real McCoy."

"Fall of 1918. As World War I is winding down, something even worse is sweeping through the battlefields, military hospitals, and cities of Western Europe." Haldane stepped back to the podium. "The Spanish Flu," he said with his back to the audience. "And in the soldiers returning home following the armistice of November eleventh, this virus found the perfect vector for global dissemination."

More old snapshots of hospitals and morgues. More black and white devastation.

"In the winter of 1918–1919 this mutated influenza virus killed twenty million people. Which in today's terms is the equivalent of eighty million dead in less than six months."

Someone in the crowd oohed.

"Well put." Haldane nodded solemnly. "And we're not talking about twenty million ancient nursing home residents or mutilated war vets aching for deliverance. In fact, the opposite. For reasons unknown, this virus selectively killed young healthy adults. People would go to bed at night and not wake up the next morning . . . or any morning." Haldane eyed a student in the second row who played on the varsity baseball team. "Not even pro athletes were safe. The 1919 Stanley Cup had to be halted because two of the Montreal Maroons dropped dead in the middle of the series.

"And if you think all hell broke loose because of primitive infection control and treatment measures, you would be wrong again. Granted, public health was limited in 1919, but we wouldn't fare much better today facing such an outbreak. We still have no specific treatment. And with every single person in the world connected by three or less commercial flights, it might spread even faster.

"It was probably *only* because of the draconian public health measures—people were quarantined in jails and some countries made it illegal to shake hands—that the epidemic was controlled at all.

"But the strangest part of the whole story?" Haldane allowed himself a theatrical pause. "There was nothing particularly unique about the Spanish Flu. Each winter the latest incarnation of influenza rolls around from Bangkok or Hong Kong or Melbourne or some other exotic locale I can't afford to visit." No one laughed. "It opens up beds in nursing homes, keeps temp agencies busy, and makes life an achy hell for those of us unlucky enough to stand in its path. But it does not decimate the population." He scanned the audience, satisfied he held their rapt attention. "The reason influenza only kills the old and the infirm is, flu shot or not, the virus is old news to our immune system. It's just a slightly modified—a protein here, an organic ring there—version of an antigen our immune system has seen before. So our bodies can mount a strong defense."

Haldane thumbed at the screen. "Not so with the Spanish Flu. It represented a brand-new genre of the virus." He shrugged. "But that's what viruses excel at, right? They mutate. In fact, up until 1919 every forty years, like clockwork, the latest version of a new and devastating influenza virus surfaced.

"So, the weirdest thing about the Spanish Flu is that we haven't seen a similar pandemic in over eighty years." He shook his head. "Not to put a damper on your bright futures, Doctors, but the killer flu is way overdue!"

Noah Haldane chuckled to himself on the drive back to his office. Sure he'd offered up a little ham with his lecture, but he believed it critical that his students—and all future physicians—hear the message: they were the front line against the next wave of epidemic, which almost certainly would be viral. It was vital that they recognized the signs early. And judging from the cacophony of questions after his lecture, hear him they did.

In those dark days of spring 2003, when he'd spent his time shuttling between Hong Kong, Hanoi, and Singapore, he wasn't as confident that SARS would just be a flash in the pan. None of them at the World Health Organization were.

Haldane hadn't exaggerated when he told the students that he'd been touched by the destructive power of SARS. It had claimed the life of a close friend and colleague, Dr. Franco Bertulli, in a Singapore Intensive Care Unit. Wearing full biohazard gear, Haldane had sat at Bertulli's bedside until the end and watched helplessly as his friend suffocated in his own secretions. Nothing in all his medical, virology, or epidemiological training prepared him for that. And the vision still visited him regularly in the form of a recurring nightmare.

But over a year had passed since the last travel advisory was issued. Haldane was home, and reveling in the relative quiet of the infectious diseases world. He had time to catch up on his research and clinical work. Best of all he had time to reconnect with his three-year-old daughter Chloe. Enough time even to take a stab at resuscitating his crumbling marriage.

Lost in plans for a family getaway for the upcoming weekend, Haldane breezed through the door of his research office in Georgetown. "Karen, hi," he said as he dropped off a cup of coffee on his receptionist's desk and then strode past her into his office.

When Haldane ignored his receptionist's hailing, she jumped up and followed him into the office. At twenty-seven, Karen Jackson had taken the job as Haldane's secretary so she could entrench herself in the academic milieu while she worked her way through graduate school. An African American full-figured beauty, she was bright, able, and defiant to a fault.

"Noah, did you hear me?" she said with her hands on

her hips, as if talking to a toddler who had just covered the walls in ink.

Haldane leaned back his chair and rested his own Starbucks cup on top of the shortest of the tall piles that covered his desk. "What's up, Karen?"

"You forgot your pager and cell phone, again, didn't you?" Jackson chastised.

Haldane shrugged. "I was lecturing."

"Oh, yeah, that explains it," said Jackson with a roll of her eyes at her absentminded boss.

Haldane slid a hand in his drawer and pulled out his phone and pager. "Who is looking for me?"

"Exactly." Jackson chuckled, pulling her hands off her hips. "The WHO is looking for you. Dr. Nantal. Said it was urgent."

As the WHO's Executive Director of Communicable Diseases, Dr. Jean Nantal was responsible for all global hot spots. He had no time for social calls, especially "urgent" ones. Haldane rubbed his eyes and sighed heavily. "You were supposed to tell him I died."

"Noah, haven't I been telling you for months to give up this globe-trotting gig with the World Health Organization?" she demanded. "It's a job for single people. Not old married folk with a young child like you. That old smoothie, Dr. Nantal, could charm a starving lion out of his kill, but you should tell him 'no' this time."

Haldane marveled at his young finger-wagging secretary. She must have been mothering people since she could talk. Maybe before. Besides, her point was moot. Nantal's urgent phone call could only mean that something nasty was brewing somewhere on the planet. As the WHO's expert on emerging pathogens, Haldane knew Nantal wasn't asking.

Haldane was being summoned.

CHAPTER

2

Bleary-eyed, Dr. Gwen Savard had trouble focusing on the screen. As Department of Homeland Security's inaugural Director of Counter-Bioterrorism (or the "Bug Czar" as some of her colleagues had taken to calling her), she chaired the Bioterrorism Preparedness Council meeting, through which she now struggled to stay awake. She tried to convince herself that it had nothing to do with Peter moving the last of his belongings out the previous sleepless night and everything to do with the dull speaker in front of her.

Oh, how the man droned! Savard was tempted to cut him off. Or to scream. Everyone in the room knew about anthrax. How accessible it was in the former Soviet Union, the Middle East, and even in the U.S. How deadly it could be in the perfect aerosolized form. He wasn't enlightening a soul when he explained how a thermos full of anthrax spores spilled on a windless day over Manhattan could kill hundreds of thousands.

But Gwen didn't intervene. Instead, she conceded that maybe she was a touch hard on her poor subordinate. And she grudgingly realized she might even be a tad run-down, physically and emotionally, this morning.

It wasn't so much the departure of Peter—who as her mother had predicted early in the relationship was a decent guy but all wrong for Gwen—as the implication of his leaving. The end of her marriage dealt an unexpected blow. Failure was foreign to Gwen. And it meant that at forty-two, she had to start over. Not that attracting other men would pose a challenge. Year in, year out, she maintained her size four figure. Her face with its high cheekbones, full lips, and upturned nose had aged well. The crow's-feet at the corners of her striking green eyes softened her features; those little imperfections of time had made her less intimidating, more accessible to men. She drew more attention in her forties than she had in her twenties. Still, she shuddered at the thought of one day facing the "dating scene" again.

Savard was relieved when Alex Clayton, the Central Intelligence Agency's Deputy Director of Operations, interrupted both her unhappy ruminations and her subordinate's endless rambling. "Yeah, Dr. Graves, fascinating stuff," Clayton said, but his stifled yawn belied the remark. "Can you get to the part where you update us on the powder trail from the anthrax mail out?"

Oblivious or indifferent to Clayton's condescension, Dr. Clive Graves responded in the same nasal monotone. "We know the powder is consistent with what was developed in Baghdad in the late 1980s, but we haven't matched it with any of the U.S. control samples. We've tested the known substrate from the labs and universities with legal access to anthrax in every state. We're in the process of subtyping—"

"So the trail's gone cold, Doctor?" Clayton cut him off.

Graves pushed his glasses back up his nose. His shoulders sagged. "Um, I'm not in the detective business, so those aren't the, er, terms I would choose . . ." he stammered.

Always protective of her staff, Savard stepped in. "Even in ballistics, a far more traceable science, you need to find the gun before you can match a bullet to it. Short of what we've known for some time—that the powder on those letters was consistent with what the Iraqis and Soviets were producing in the eighties—we will never be able to narrow down the origins until you and your colleagues find us some source material to compare it to." She leaned forward in her seat and eyed Clayton steadily. "Find us a smoking gun, Alex, and we'll tell you if it's the right one."

Clayton chuckled. "I'm not packing today, Gwen."

Though Savard maintained a healthy suspicion for anyone associated with the CIA, Clayton's ability to laugh at himself and his organization—an exceedingly rare characteristic among the spies she'd met—endeared Clayton to her. In spite of his brash, reckless demeanor, she liked the guy. Not quite enough though to ever accept one of his offers for coffee or a movie.

"So, in summary, you've made no progress on the anthrax case," Moira Roberts interjected with a heavy sigh. In just a few months on the job, the Deputy Director of the FBI had already cemented her reputation as a humorless and brusque bureaucrat. In her early forties like Gwen, Roberts was one of the youngest deputy directors in the FBI's history, but with her gray hair and formless matronly wardrobe, few realized she was still on the young side of middle age. "Dr. Savard, is there any possibility we can move on to *variola major*?"

Gwen Savard resisted the rising ire. Who was this woman trying to impress by tossing around esoteric phyla names? Even the people in the know, and Roberts wasn't one, always referred to it as smallpox. But Gwen refused to let Roberts draw her into another confrontation in front of the whole committee. She wasn't about to give the oth-

erwise male group more locker-room fodder with another
demonstration of alpha females butting heads.

"No problems with smallpox," Gwen said, realizing the
irony of her remark but choosing not to rephrase it. "Vaccine production is on schedule. We should have 300 million doses available by spring. The logistics of the
vaccination program are still being hashed out. Public
Health estimates a minimum of one year to inoculate the
majority of the population."

The group discussed the smallpox vaccination program
a few minutes longer, before moving on to monkey pox.
Every week the committee covered all the communicable
big hitters of bioterrorism: anthrax, botulism, smallpox,
Ebola, cholera, the plague, Q fever, typhoid, shigellosis,
brucellosis, and tularemia. The panel cut across all government and scientific agencies. Aside from CIA, FBI, and
Homeland Security, there was at least one representative
from the Centers for Disease Control, Department of Justice, Department of Health and Human Services, Department of Energy, and the Department of the Environment.

The last item on the agenda led to a sobering discussion
on the vulnerability of the East Coast's water reservoirs to
tampering, one of the committee's favorite topics. And
with good reason.

Clive Graves pushed his glasses up the bridge of his
nose again and sorted through the notes in front of him.
"It would not necessarily involve a significant amount of
the botulism toxin either. If they could push the water concentration to a level in the neighborhood of one nanno-
gram per milliliter, we are talking about thousands,
potentially hundreds of thousands, of fatalities," he said in
a delivery so flat that he managed to make one of Gwen's
greatest fears sound tedious.

Moira Roberts nodded somberly. "We can only provide
so much security for every reservoir in the country," she

said. "This is another example of why it is so vital that we have better information on terrorist activity abroad."

"Of course, Moira, if only the CIA did our job better we would be worry-free." Clayton laughed facetiously. "Let's not forget how long the last batch of terrorists was operating on our soil before they acted," he said calmly.

Roberts eyed him coolly. "There's no reason to finger-point, Mr. Clayton. I am merely suggesting that local security alone will not remove the threat."

"And I am telling you," Clayton said, matching her clipped tone, "that the CIA cannot track every person on the planet with a petri dish and a hate-on for the States."

Rubbing her temples, Savard sat back and allowed the heated debate to rage on concerning the level of security at water reservoirs. While Clayton and Roberts squared off, the rest of the group fractured into its usual factions—the scientific and environmental types on one side, the security and military types on the other.

After about fifteen circular minutes, Savard reluctantly cut Clayton off in midsnipe at Roberts. "We've only got a few minutes left for roundtable discussion," Gwen said.

Clockwise, they went around the long oval table. After allowing each of the fifteen members to raise issues and concerns, which in most cases led to venting about budgetary limitations and overstretched resources, Gwen spoke up. "We spend most of our time and energy at this table anticipating terrorist threats from laboratory-generated or artificially acquired agents."

Gwen scanned the table and noticed several *no-shit* expressions, but a few faces creased with curiosity. "The most devastating of these pathogens—smallpox, Ebola, and so on—are secured in a very few select labs," she pointed out. "Moreover, they're fastidious agents, exceedingly difficult to work with. Now granted, it's not difficult to get your hands on some of the other organisms in question—anthrax, for example. But those agents are not person-to-person transmissible. And thus far, the distribution methods have been, thankfully, primitive and limited."

Gwen noticed Roberts fidgeting with the papers in front of her. Clayton leaned back in his chair with hands folded behind his head, but his half smile suggested he might step in with a "get to the point" comment at any moment.

"The recent SARS epidemic got me thinking," Gwen said. "If I were a terrorist, why would I go to the effort—in most cases futile—of trying to breach lab security?"

"Oh?" said Roberts, skeptically. "What would you as a terrorist do, Dr. Savard?"

She scanned every face at the table before answering. "During the SARS outbreak, imagine how easy it would have been to go to Hong Kong, infect yourself, and then intentionally spread it elsewhere." She paused before turning to the FBI Deputy Director. "Man-made propagation of a natural epidemic. That, Ms. Roberts, is where I think the terrorists will get the best bang for their buck."

CHAPTER
3

Hazzir Al Kabaal sat in his thirty-second-floor office, gazing out the window. The smog was less of a factor than usual and the Nile wound resplendently below, but the publishing magnate was too preoccupied to notice.

As he had every five minutes for the past two hours, Kabaal hit the "send/receive" icon again on the computer in front of him. Like each time before, all he saw in response was the same frustrating "no new messages" reply.

What is the hold up? he thought for the umpteenth time as he dusted away imagined particles on the sleeves of his navy silk jacket. Vanity was one sin Kabaal had yet to overcome. He rationalized away his hand-tailored Italian suits and hundred-dollar haircuts as necessity, arguing that Mohammed would have understood the need to assimilate among the enemy. But Kabaal worked hard at maintaining his Omar Sharif-like good looks. At fifty, he was still in top physical shape. And he made a point of pride to never be seen publicly unless immaculately dressed.

He tapped the "send/receive" button again. The lack of response was taxing the patience of the man whose patience and resolve had grown to legendary status after he transformed a series of obscure Arabic newspapers into a publishing conglomerate, one paper at a time. As a result, Kabaal wound up controlling a huge sphere of influence in the Arab world while amassing a personal fortune.

Though his papers' readership was fiercely loyal, running an Islamic newspaper within Egypt's corrupt autocracy posed a daily challenge. Tacitly, most government officials agreed with his Islamic Brotherhood's beliefs. Denunciation of Israel was accepted, even encouraged, but the officials showed far less tolerance of similar condemnations of the U.S.A. or Europe. And retribution for criticism of the Egyptian government was swift and harsh. After publishing what authorities perceived as an attack several editors had learned firsthand the brutality of the Egyptian judicial system. Not Kabaal. He had a sixth sense for knowing how far he could push. Or at least, he thought, he used to.

Kabaal tapped the key again, but the screen offered nothing in return. Discouraged, he leaned back in his seat and mulled over the details of his initiative. As he pictured the fallout, he felt the unwelcome twinges of doubt stir inside.

Kabaal knew that few would have considered him capable of militancy. Most people saw him as a progressive Arab businessman. His extravagant wardrobe aside, he'd spent much time in the West. He completed his master's degree at the London School of Economics where he had experimented with alcohol and Western women who were easy prey for his exotic good looks and worldly charm.

But things had changed since those halcyon student

days. Kabaal had reconnected in a far deeper sense with his Islamic roots. And, as he had learned from Sheikh Hassan, with commitment came obligation. Obligation to disseminate the word of God. Obligation to strive for a state where religion and life weren't forced asunder as they were in the hedonistic West or corrupt Arab monocracies. The Sheikh made it clear that it was Kabaal's duty to push his brothers, by force if necessary, toward a nation like the Prophet Mohammed's Al Madinah, where the Shari'ah (or Islamic law) ruled supreme.

Still, Kabaal had been slow to reach for the sword. When the twin towers fell in New York he even allowed a few of his papers to criticize the action. But then Kabaal watched with a sense of bitter betrayal as the West mounted a savage retaliation—Afghanistan, Palestine, and finally Iraq. The last aggression galled him the most. When the supposed weapons of mass destruction never materialized, "democratization" became the catchphrase. What hypocrisy! Kabaal knew it was always about the oil. And now the U.S. was already eyeing Syria and Iran with her gluttonous insatiable appetite for oil and power.

Sheikh Hassan had predicted it all. In a voice that trembled with passion when the cleric spoke of the degenerate West, the Sheikh argued that the Crusades had never ended. In every country where Islam met Judeo-Christianity, war was ongoing. A war in which Islam was the victim. And as the Sheikh pointed out, when facing the bombs and airplanes of the infidels, what choice did the outmatched righteous have? Guerilla warfare was the only option. When Islam was under threat, no weapon—regardless of its unorthodoxy or lethality—was beyond consideration.

While the Sheikh's arguments moved Kabaal, until recently his involvement in the cause had been limited to financial support. And he supported it generously. Through murky, circuitous trails, his funds found their way to coffers across the globe. From the Hezbollah in Lebanon to the Abu Sayyef in the Philippines, Kabaal's *"endowments"* allowed The Brotherhood to pursue the cause.

The time had come for Kabaal to jump into the operational field. He intended to do so with an eruption that would reverberate around the globe.

If only he heard back from the Malays.

He clicked the "send/receive" button again. This time, a bar popped up as the antivirus software scanned the message. A moment later the message opened on his screen.

Shipping update. Items: Religious Texts.

Unavoidable delay with Chinese customs. One container damaged beyond repair.

Discarded prior to shipment. Other container arrived with all the books intact.

Awaiting further distribution instructions.

Yours,

I.S.

Kabaal smiled. The Malays had done well. Very well.

He deleted the message and turned off his computer. "And so it begins," he said to no one.

CHAPTER

4

Had Noah Haldane waited another millisecond before yanking his leg out of the aisle, the drinks cart would have steamrolled over his foot.

"Sorry, sweetie," the chunky middle-aged flight attendant chirped in a southern drawl. "Almost crushed your little piggies, there."

"No. My fault," Haldane said as he shifted in the seat and repositioned his pillow to no avail. In spite of his fatigue and the relative comfort of the first-class surrounds, he wasn't any closer to sleep.

"You look so uncomfy, hon," the woman said, flashing her teeth and gums in another huge smile. "Anything I can do to help?"

"Can you make the last twenty-four hours of my life disappear?"

The flight attendant laughed so vigorously that her voluminous, dyed blond hair shook. "Honey, I absolutely can." She leaned forward and rummaged through the cart before emerging with three minibottles, each one squeezed between neighboring fingers of her right hand. "Vodka? Gin? Or is this a job only Johnny can handle?" She shook the miniature Johnny Walker whiskey bottle between her thumb and forefinger as if it were a small bell.

"I'll start with vodka."

Haldane nodded his thanks as he sat up in his seat and accepted the glass of vodka on the rocks. Conceding that sleep wasn't an option, he reached for the stack of printouts that the WHO had e-mailed him.

He forced himself to focus on the different pages. Lab reports, medical consults, and bureaucratic memos were mixed willy-nilly in the pile. Déjà vu overwhelmed the emerging pathogens expert. The rural Chinese origins, the pattern of dissemination, the inconsistent care—he had seen it all before with SARS. But sifting through the patient records, Haldane reached the same conclusion the local authorities had. This was not the rebirth of SARS. This had the potential to be far worse.

Haldane understood that time was no longer a luxury for the WHO or him. He had so much to do in the upcoming days and hours, but his mind kept drifting back to the scene shortly before his departure at his Washington suburb home in Glen Echo Heights, Maryland.

Chloe Haldane had yet another ear infection. A month shy of her fourth birthday, she had already suffered through a lifetime's worth of ear infections. With an insider's knowledge of side effects and complications, Noah Haldane viewed his daughter's antibiotic dependency dimly. He wasn't much more excited about the prospect of the myringotomy, or drainage tubes, that loomed in Chloe's near future.

Like many men, Haldane had entered fatherhood without much in the way of expectations, aside from the presumption of sleepless nights. But he took to the role with a passion he never imagined possible. From the moment he had first held her, Chloe became the focal point of his life. When not working or traveling, he happily dedicated the rest of his time to his daughter. In spite of his hectic schedule and the forced time apart, he still changed more diapers and attended more Baby Dance and Gymboree classes than most of his male counterparts. Chloe made it easy for her dad. His bias aside, she had a joyful temperament. So much so that when she was eight months old her parents took her to a pediatrician, concerned that she never cried. With a laugh, their doctor reassured them that time would soon rectify the deficiency; and with the onset of her ear infections, the tears did come. Even then, it only put a temporary dent in her otherwise sunny disposition.

Haldane lay beside Chloe in her bed. Cramped as he was, almost hanging off the side of the single bed, he loved the chance to snuggle in tight while reading her favorite stories. With their heads touching, he could feel the warmth from her brow. Her fever had yet to break. But after the fifth story, her disproportionately loud snore assured Haldane she had nodded off. Realizing that this would be his last chance for weeks, maybe months, he lay beside Chloe for half an hour longer before rising, kissing her on the forehead, and heading downstairs.

When he walked into the living room, he found his wife sitting sideways on the couch with knees bent and bare feet drawn up on the gray fabric. She nursed a mug of tea in her hand. With her other hand she brushed away a few strands of the long dark hair that drifted over her eyes. "How's she doing?" Anna asked.

"Still feels warm," Haldane said as he joined her on the couch. "But she's asleep."

Anna nodded, but her eyes focused on the coffee table beside him. "Will you be back in time for her birthday?"

Haldane shrugged. "I don't know."

Anna didn't respond.

"It's not like I'm heading off on a golf trip, Anna."

"No, you're off to save the world," she said with a trace of bitterness.

"You can drop the melodrama," Haldane said. "I didn't ask to go."

She looked up at him, her face softening. "I know, Noah. You never do."

He reached over and laid a hand on her knee. She didn't respond to the gesture, but neither did she withdraw from it as he had half expected she would.

They sat for several silent moments on the couch. Recognizing how much intimacy had been lost between them, Haldane felt a pang of remorse.

Free of makeup and wearing a loose hooded sweater, Anna struck him as painfully beautiful. Barely five feet, she had a slight figure, a ballerina's form. Her large brown eyes, high cheekbones, and slightly crooked smile aside, Anna possessed a fragile porcelain-doll quality that only enhanced her attractiveness.

He squeezed her knee. "When I get back—"

She shook her head. "Noah, there's no point in talking about it until you *are* back."

"I think we need to talk about it now," Haldane said. "This is about more than just you and me."

Anna stiffened in her seat. She pulled his hand off her leg and put her mug down on the coffee table. "You think I don't know that?"

"Sometimes, you don't *act* like you know it," he said.

She grunted a humorless laugh, and eyed him stonily. "You disappeared for over four months. Besides, you were gone before you left. Remember?" she said, referring to the stormy few months when Noah, by his own admission, had withdrawn from their marriage.

Haldane knew better than to let it escalate, but he

couldn't help himself. "And that was reason enough to fall in love with someone else?"

She crossed her arms. "I wasn't looking for an excuse to. I was very lonely. It just happened, Noah."

"Bullshit, Anna," he snapped. "It doesn't just happen. I know I left you and Chloe, but there was a crisis going on, remember? I was needed over there."

"I needed you here," she said softly, looking down at her feet.

"*Me*?" He grunted. "Or just somebody?"

She shook her head without looking up. "You don't get it, do you?"

"No, Anna, I don't. But you had better make up your mind soon. I'm not sharing you with another partner." He paused for a deep breath. "You are going to have to choose between her and me."

WHO HEADQUARTERS, GENEVA, SWITZERLAND

Despite the sunshine and cloudless blue sky, the autumn chill brought a shiver to Haldane who, expecting warmer weather, was jacketless. Nonetheless, he welcomed the crisp Geneva air, which provided a partial reprieve from the exhaustion, jet lag, and slight hangover that were blending into a throbbing headache.

He stood with his suitcase slung over one shoulder and his laptop the other—there had been no time to stop at his hotel on the way in from the airport—while he surveyed the familiar WHO headquarters. In the foreground fluttered a big blue WHO flag, which consisted of the UN flag with a superimposed caduceus (staff and serpent). In the background rose the imposing main building whose waffle-style design looked a little more dated with each visit. What caught his eye this time was the never before seen show of force. Armed guards shouldering automatic rifles were posted on the street and at the entryways. An incongruent sight for peaceful Switzerland, but since the lethal bombing of a UNICEF meeting in Baghdad the UN wasn't taking chances. Haldane found all the security measures a depressing reminder that the world was a little less safe than it used to be.

He lingered for a few more breaths of the refreshing air before heading up the main pathway. After flashing his credentials for two sets of guards, he entered the foyer where an assistant met him, stored his suitcase, and shepherded him up to the tenth-floor conference room.

The meeting was already in progress when Haldane stepped inside. With his usual French flourish Dr. Jean Nantal rose from his seat and rushed over to greet Noah with a hug and kiss on each cheek. "Ah, Noah, how good of you to come."

Impeccably groomed, lean with a long narrow face, Dr. Jean Nantal appeared the epitome of a distinguished European professor. In his mid-sixties, Nantal was a legend in Public Health circles. In his youth, he had been one of the architects of the wildly successful international smallpox eradication program of the '60s and '70s. With his ready smile and soothing French accent, the WHO's Executive Director of Communicable Diseases had a gift for putting people at ease, which helped explain his enormous popularity and his ability to draw Herculean effort and self-sacrifice from his staff.

"Hello, Jean," Haldane said. "Sorry, I couldn't get over any sooner."

Nantal waved his hand as if it were a bird taking flight. "Nonsense, Noah. We appreciate you coming on such short notice." He indicated the others in the room with a sweep of his hand. "I think you know everyone here, NON?"

Noah nodded to the three people at the table. "Hello, Helmut," he said to Helmut Streicher, the stern young Austrian epidemiologist with blond hair and brooding grayish blue eyes. "Milly." He smiled at the petite shy Tai-

wanese microbiologist, My Li Yuen, who called herself
Milly, if she spoke at all. But he saved his warmest welcome for Duncan McLeod, the gangly Scottish virologist
and fellow emerging pathogens expert who, personality
aside, made an unforgettable impression thanks to his
flaming red hair, scraggly beard, and lazy left eye. "Duncan, how the hell are you?" Noah asked.

"Great! Shite! Couldn't be better," McLeod bellowed
with typical loud irreverence. "The Chinese have finally
done it this time, Haldane. Unleashed unholy Armageddon on us from one of their overcrowded farms. And the
best part? Jean's going to drop us into the eye of the hurri-
cane like a couple of ill-fated palm trees!"

"Ah, Duncan, always so colorful." Nantal laughed. "I
think you are getting ahead of yourself." He turned to Haldane. "Have you had a chance to peruse the material we
sent?"

Haldane rummaged through his carrying case, pulling
out the e-mail printouts, before sliding into the seat beside
Yuen. "I read through what you sent, Jean, but there are a
few holes in the picture."

"No shite!" McLeod piped up. "You could drive a tank
through them."

Nantal flashed his unflappable smile. "Let's review
what we do know, shall we?" He looked over at Streicher.
"Helmut, for Noah's benefit, do you mind reviewing the
fascinating details you've just shared?"

Streicher frowned before reaching for the open laptop
computer in front of him. "Please." He pointed at the
screen on the far wall. He clicked the mouse and a map
of China appeared. He tapped a key and the map zoomed
in on northern China. An area in the screen's center,
roughly the shape of Florida, turned light pink. "Gansu
Province."

Streicher clicked the mouse again. A small red "X"
appeared north of the largest regional center, Jiayuguan

City. "First known infection was documented on a farm fifty miles north of Jiayuguan City."

"Same old story, Haldane," McLeod cut in. "Pigs, sheep, ducks, and Farmer Chan all drinking out of the same water supply. Common waste system, too. Shite! The whole farm probably ate with the same pair of bloody chopsticks. Their viruses allowed to—no, hell, encouraged to—mingle, share DNA secrets, and superinfect each other's hosts. Lo and behold we get the second coming of the plague."

McLeod waved to My Li Yuen in a belated "no offense" gesture, but his diatribe had no visible effect on her. His acknowledgment, however, caused her to flush. "I know, Duncan," she said in a slight high-pitched voice with only a trace of an accent. "You don't hate *all* Chinese, right?" she giggled.

"Very true. Especially the Taiwanese. Marvelous folks. Shite, Milly, truth be known, I've got a gigantic crush on you." He blew her a kiss, which drew another giggle and a deeper shade of red from the microbiologist.

"As I was saying," Streicher said, unamused. "According to the authorities the first four cases, two adults and two children, developed symptoms just over three weeks ago."

"Has the Chinese government played ball so far?" Haldane asked.

Nantal nodded. "Noah, it seems they've learned from their last experience," he said, without specifying the SARS outbreak. "They're the ones who invited us to come."

"Fucking great!" hollered the redheaded Scot. "I was wondering where to send the thank-you card!"

Like a child whose story had been interrupted one time too many, Streicher huffed and raised his voice louder. "Over the ensuing two weeks we see direct spread to neighboring farms. Eighty infected, twenty dead. The notable feature in this pocket of infection is the very short incubation period. Two to three days."

Streicher tapped the button and a few more Xs appeared in a cluster around the first one. "From these index cases," he said, using the medical term for the first patient or patients responsible for local outbreaks, "we see spread to the towns north of Jiayuguan. Hundreds more infected. Same rapid incubation."

"Mortality rate?" Haldane asked.

"The early figures suggest roughly twenty-five percent." Streicher ran a hand through his thick blond hair. "Apparently, the young and the healthy are worst affected."

"Oh . . ." Haldane muttered. "That sounds familiar."

Jean Nantal read the recognition on Haldane's face. "Ah, yes. We've been wondering about that, too. Maybe the Spanish Flu has come back to visit, NON?" Nantal grinned in his disarming way. "It's a bit premature to know."

"The first case was documented four days ago in Jiayuguan City," Streicher said. "According to local authorities they've only had a handful of cases in the city itself, but it is early."

"Very." Haldane nodded. "And the hospitals?"

"Coping quite well." Nantal clasped his hands and shook them in a victorious gesture. "They've been doing better so far than with the SARS outbreak. No documented spread of the infection within hospitals. You see, Noah? There is a silver lining."

Not much of one, Haldane thought, but he nodded without comment.

Nantal turned to Yuen. "Milly, can you share a little background on the microbiology?"

Yuen shuffled through her notes. Though she wasn't reading them, she kept her eyes fixed on the pages as she spoke. "We've only had the blood samples for under a week, but the bacterial and viral cultures are negative thus far. We're running standard phenotypical and molecular viral diagnostics. We have run PCR, polymerase chain reaction, to every common viral family . . . so far nothing conclusive."

Haldane picked up on her hesitancy. "What, Milly?" he asked.

Yuen looked up from the papers and caught Haldane's gaze. "It's not hard science or anything, but some of the RNA probes were weakly positive for influenza."

"So it's a strain of the flu?" Haldane asked.

"We can't say that," Yuen said and dropped her eyes to her notes again. "All we're testing for is viral DNA and RNA. The source patients might have all been exposed to an influenza outbreak ten years ago, and we're just seeing the remnants of the dead virus in their blood."

"No causality." Haldane nodded. "I understand, but what does your gut say, Milly? Is this the newest strain of the flu?"

"No," Yuen said, but then her voice wavered. "I can't say for sure, but it's more like this microbe cross-reacts with the influenza on testing."

"Close but no cigar, huh?" Haldane said.

Yuen nodded enthusiastically. "That's my hypothesis. This isn't any known influenza A or B, but a closely related virus. Probably one we've never seen."

Haldane wasn't so sure. He leaned back in his chair and looked over at Nantal. "What do the Chinese expect from us?"

"Noah, they only want what every government that comes to us wants." Nantal held his arms wide open in front of him and smiled. "To find the cause and wipe out the disease."

"Right," McLeod said. "And do it yesterday. And let them take the bloody credit."

"They can keep the credit," Haldane said. "This bug sounds a bit too familiar. Short incubation. Related to influenza. Hemorrhagic pneumonia. Targeting the young and the healthy . . ." He paused and caught the eye of each of his colleagues in turn. "As you know the Spanish Flu— a form of Swine Flu—disappeared in 1919 just as quickly as it came. They've only ever found remnants of the actual virus. Thus, only part of the virus's genome has ever been sequenced. We wouldn't recognize it for sure if it had resurfaced."

"Ah, Noah, it's early to make that leap," Nantal said.

"Yeah?" Haldane said. "But if it is the Spanish Flu, or some descendent of the same, it would be catastrophic to overlook the possibility."

"Understood." Nantal nodded. "But you know the rules, my friend. Until we isolate a pathogen, we only refer to it by the syndrome it produces."

"Which is?"

"'Acute Respiratory Collapse Syndrome.'" Nantal pointed proudly to Yuen. "We have Milly to thank for the acronym. ARCS."

The term sounded to Haldane as innocuous as the other viral acronyms, like SARS and AIDS, which had surfaced in the past few decades. But hearing it spoken aloud sent a chill through him as if he had just stepped out into the cool Geneva air.

He wondered, grimly, if ARCS was going to make the world forget about all other viruses.

CHAPTER

5

With Peter's possessions gone, their spacious three-bedroom condo felt empty to Gwen Savard. Not in a heartsick, if-only-we-had-one-more-chance way. Just barren. Peter had wanted to divide the furniture equally, but Gwen had insisted he take most of it. Now she regretted it. Guilt, she realized in retrospect, was not a helpful emotion when it came to dividing assets.

What did she have to feel guilty about? she wondered. She hadn't been unfaithful. She had never treated him with malice or cruelty. She had cooked her share of meals and had done more than her share of the laundry. She even attended most of his firm's insufferable socials, ever the lawyer's dutiful wife. Though Peter cited her consuming career as the cause, it was not the reason their relationship had derailed. Neither was the infertility issue. At painfully introspective moments like these, which only came after the breakup, Gwen realized her heart hadn't been in the marriage from the outset. As hard as Peter tried, one person cannot carry a romance. After he finally threw his hands up and walked away from their pleasant but passionless relationship Gwen assumed the lion's share of the blame.

Unwelcome childhood memories stirred. Gwen could picture her mother's face. Not the current surgically pulled and heavily painted version, but the youthful stunning face of Gwen's childhood. How Savard remembered her mother's pained half smile that failed to conceal her disappointment when the A wasn't an A+ or when the silver piano prize wasn't gold or when the state scholarship wasn't a Rhodes scholarship. Gwen imagined her mother's youthful face, lips locked in that letdown grin, reassuring her how much better off she would be without Peter. Gwen's stomach tightened. Like every day since Peter had left, she decided it best to put off telling her mother for another day.

The unadorned walls amplified Savard's sense of emptiness until it became oppressive. She needed to escape the reminders of her failed marriage, which explained why the country's Bug Czar packed for a business trip that could have been handled over the phone.

New Haven, Connecticut

Gwen arrived in the early evening feeling rested. A self-confessed '70s music addict, she had passed the six-hour drive—which accounted for the longest stress-free stretch in Gwen's recent memory—listening to her favorite CDs, including Elton John's *Captain Fantastic*, Fleetwood Mac's *Rumors*, and Supertramp's *Breakfast in America*.

Driving through New Haven she was flooded with nostalgic memories of her postgraduate days at Yale, especially when she passed by her old apartment block. In sixteen years nothing had changed from the outside. Slowing to a halt at the front door, she could practically smell the exotic flavors that permeated her cramped studio apartment year round thanks to the thick hallway carpets, which absorbed her multi-ethnic neighbors' cooking, magnified the aromas, and then released them. Gwen wondered if her unit still had the same blue and pink pastel-colored walls, which she and her friends had impulsively slapped on one day and regretted thereafter.

Her career since graduation had been so demanding that in retrospect the four years spent completing a PhD at Yale while working two part-time jobs struck her as carefree by comparison. By college, Gwen had accepted her driving ambition as part of her makeup; neither good nor bad, but as much a part of her as her passion for travel or her tireless work ethic. Most of her fellow students kept the goal of their PhD as their primary focus. Not Gwen. She planned her life well beyond the degree. But she never envisioned a career within government. As a student, she assumed she would get her own lab and a national health research grant. To one day have a shot at a Nobel Prize like her mentor, Dr. Isaac Moskor.

Savard was surprised to realize that she hadn't seen Isaac in almost four years. He never left New Haven. And she rarely found time to make it back. They had kept in touch by e-mail and phone, but Isaac wasn't much of a phone-talker and even less of a social writer. Professionally, Gwen tried to keep abreast of Moskor's research because many considered him *the* leading researcher into antiviral antibiotics. Though fiercely secretive with his work, he trusted Gwen enough to share breakthroughs with her.

Driving by her favorite student haunts, Gwen meandered her way across New Haven. Eventually she reached the sleepy middle-class neighborhood at the edge of town where Moskor lived. She pulled up to the curb in front of his modest, fifty-year-old beige bungalow. Like her former student residence, the house had not changed in the past twenty years.

Isaac Moskor met her at the front door. At least six-four and 250 pounds, he had a square face, slanting forehead, and a protuberant jaw that one might associate with professional wrestling, not academia. In his late sixties, his posture was still bone-straight and age had not diminished his mass. Though Savard was taller than average at five-eight, Moskor still had to stoop down to hug her. He held her in a tentative, awkward embrace, as if afraid of crushing her in his massive arms. Acts of physical intimacy were the only times Gwen ever sensed uncertainty from her mentor.

Moskor stood back and sized her up from toes to hair. "Still too skinny, but otherwise you look okay, kid," he said with his deep Jersey accent.

Gwen smiled warmly, realizing how much she had missed the man. "Can you still be a kid at forty-two?"

"To a sixty-nine-year-old? Absolutely." He spun with surprising speed for a man of his age and size. "Don't stand there like a potted plant. Come. Come."

Gwen followed him through the small foyer and into the living room. With two worn gray corduroy sofas, a frayed throw rug, and a few charcoal abstract prints, the room was as utilitarian as the rest of his house. Gwen knew that to Moskor and his wife houses were for sleeping and eating. The lab was where one lived.

"Where's Clara?" Gwen asked, sinking into one of the surprisingly comfortable sofas.

Moskor shrugged. "Who knows? Maybe at the lab. Maybe at our daughter's." His face crumpled into a half grin, the deeper creases of which displayed the first evidence of his having aged since their last meeting. "The secret to our forty-plus-year marriage is a deep and abiding indifference to one another's whereabouts."

Gwen laughed. "I don't know why Clara puts up with you."

Moskor shrugged again. "My movie-star good looks, I suppose." He dropped into the sofa beside Gwen. "If you want anything after your trip—like a beer, soda, bite to eat, or whatever—you know where the kitchen is. Nothing's moved. I'm too old to wait on anybody."

Realizing how parched she was from the trip, she got up and walked into the same kitchen where she had spent so many evenings helping Clara prepare dinner. "Want anything?" she asked Moskor.

"Wouldn't say no to a beer."

Gwen returned in under a minute with two opened beer bottles, knowing better than to bother with glasses in this house.

"How's the lawyer?" Moskor asked as Gwen sat back down on the couch beside him.

"Peter moved out a couple of days ago," she said. "We're getting divorced."

Moskor nodded, showing as much surprise as if Gwen had told him that Peter was out parking the car.

"Best for both of us, Isaac. We tried, but it hasn't worked for a long time. We're night and day, really."

Moskor shrugged helplessly. "Look, kid, viruses I understand. People I don't."

Gwen smiled again. God, she had missed the man. And even though he showed no sign of interest in her domestic tribulations, it felt good to finally unload on someone. While Moskor slumped back in his seat, sipping his beer and once that was finished teetering on the brink of sleep, Gwen poured out her heart. She filled in the details of the terminal months of her marriage, from her ambivalence about the failed fertility drugs to the travel schedule she deliberately calculated to increase time apart from her husband.

When she had finished, she wasn't sure if Moskor was still awake. Just as she leaned closer to peer into his half-mast eyes, he said, "Kid, I don't do personal advice. You know that. But I will say this again. Apart from being too skinny, you look okay."

Gwen felt a weight lift off her shoulder. In her role as a top-level government scientist, who at times reported directly to the President, few people held sway over her, but Moskor's acceptance provided the absolution she sought.

He stretched his long arms over his head. "Hope you didn't drive all the way up here just to announce you're single again," he said. "Because the only single guy in my lab is gay."

Gwen smiled. "I appreciate you listening, Isaac. It helps."

Moskor shrugged, looking slightly embarrassed.

"I came up here to hear about your latest research."

He sat up straighter in his seat. His face lit up, shedding years. "Gwen, it's showing some real promise."

Gwen leaned forward and cocked her head in curiosity. "How so?"

"A single-stranded RNA virus like influenza. Nothing to the bug, really. Can't even reproduce without invading a host cell. But, damned if it doesn't offer one of the most complex defenses known to nature!" Moskor was suddenly more animated, like a jock at a party where the topic of conversation had just shifted from ballet to football. "With our earlier drugs, A35321 through 348, we saw some promising early results with the chimps, but the bug mutated so quickly they were as good as useless in a couple of life cycles."

Moskor stood up and hurried out of the room. He jogged back in moments later, carrying a binder under his arm and wheezing slightly. He flopped back onto the sofa and opened the binder in front of him. The page showed a schematic drawing of an organic molecule with multiple limbs, some ending in circular chains. "Here's the original A35321. The beauty is that she doesn't target DNA transcription, like most antivirals. No. She blocks the ribosomal RNA translation of the genes. Shuts down the whole protein-producing factory. Influenza can't replicate without that. Ergo, end of infection." He exhaled heavily. "But the whole A35 series was flawed. Within a few life cycles the microbe kept developing a resistance to it. We kept making minor adjustments, lopping off a chain here or throwing in another there." His finger flew over the complex structure, pointing to the rings and chains. "But at the end of the day, we were fighting a losing battle. We'd run out of fingers to plug all the leaks that kept springing, you understand?"

His lips curved into a proud grin. "Forced us back to the drawing board. Truth be told, it was Clara's idea. 'Why not make it simpler?' she said." His hand cut across the sketch, pantomiming the act of cleaving the molecule in half. "Sometimes less is truly more!" His voice rose joyfully. When he flipped a page, the next diagram showed a much more compact molecule. "Meet A36112. Same mechanism of action—we've tested several strains of the bug in primates—but so far no resistance documented. As of yet the little devil doesn't know what hit her."

"Is it a pill?" Gwen asked.

Moskor nodded. "We're using one hundred milligrams twice a day, but it's likely that once a day would do the trick."

"Do the results depend on the stage of the infection?"

Moskor grinned. "Ah, kid, I taught you well, didn't I? The curse of most antivirals is that unless given early— the first forty-eight to seventy-two hours of infection— they don't work worth a damn. Of course earlier is always better than later, but A36112 seems to work at any point of the infection." His grin grew wider. "Eighty percent of our chimps lost their fever within twenty-four hours of treatment."

Swept up in Moskor's enthusiasm, Gwen rose from her seat and hovered over the diagram as if it were a treasure map. "What about human trials?" she asked.

Moskor nodded. "Took us a while to steer through Ethics and get FDA approval, but phase one trials have begun on volunteers."

Gwen nodded. She knew that phase one trials weren't

used to prove much more than the drug wasn't more dangerous than the disease it was trying to treat. "Preliminary results?" she asked.

"So far, so good." Moskor shrugged. "Ten to twenty percent get diarrhea, just like our poor monkeys. But give sugar pills to people and ten to twenty percent will get explosive diarrhea, too."

"Where would we be without the old placebo effect? Makes snake oil so damn effective." Gwen smiled. "You don't have any industry sponsorship on this, right?"

As soon as it left her lips, Gwen knew it was a dumb question; Moskor's contempt for pharmaceutical companies bordered on hatred.

His brow furrowed until his hairline pulled forward. His eyes darkened. "The only parasites I work with are those of the microbiological variety." He almost spat the words. "Those drug company sons of bitches don't care one whit for the people the research might help. Look at what they've done in Africa. They'd rather encourage genocide than lower their profits on the HIV anti-retrovirals. Makes me sick to even talk about them."

Savard didn't hold the same belief, but they had argued the point too many times for her to raise it again. She just nodded. "Isaac, I know how you feel, but with phase two and three trials looming, you need resources . . ."

"We've got NIH funding. We'll get whatever resources we need."

Gwen leaned in closer to Moskor and rested a hand on his. "Isaac, I can help."

The anger dissipated from Moskor's face. He let out a familiar, low-pitch chuckle. "The federal government is interested in finding a cure for the flu?"

"Especially if I make it a matter of national security, Isaac."

CHAPTER

6

Money. In a country without government or law, money is both, Hazzir Kabaal thought. And his had served him well.

The gray tin-roofed complex, which consisted of a two-storey building with a single-storey annex, could have passed for a warehouse from the outside. It stood eight miles outside of the impoverished northern Somali town of Hargeysa, the capital of the disputed region of Soma-liland. Warlords, clans, secessionists, and foreign powers like Ethiopia all fought unsuccessfully for control of the region. As a result, leadership and allegiances varied from street to street. This might have posed a problem for some-one assembling a covert guerilla operation, but Kabaal's deep pockets allowed order to prevail within the anarchy.

The local militia secured access to all roads leading to and from the facility. Their machine guns and shoulder grenade launchers kept the curious and the nosy at bay. And they oversaw the safety of the steady stream of unmarked trucks, which transported in the lab equipment and medical supplies that made the precarious journey up from Mogadishu. Aware that all movement in Somalia was monitored from the sky by U.S. satellites, the drivers followed a similar route and schedule as the drug runners and other supply trucks in the area. Perimeter security of the complex fell to Kabaal's men, who were a far better trained and equipped group of Egyptian fighters than the Somali militia. The Egyptians were faithful above all to The Brotherhood and the man who had handpicked them, Major Abdul Sabri.

In a traditional robe but clean-shaven and wearing six-hundred-dollar desert boots, Kabaal met Dr. Anwar Aziz and Major Abdul Sabri at the entryway. Stepping inside, Kabaal was again reminded what a good choice he had made in his two lieutenants. The unlikely pair had managed to convert an old military hospital complex, abandoned for over ten years and likely not much to begin with, into an impressive camouflaged laboratory facility.

Short and stout, Dr. Anwar Aziz had a round expressionless face with small bespectacled eyes and a closely cropped beard. From his brisk gait to his perfectly ironed white lab coat, everything about the fifty-year-old Jordanian microbiologist emanated scientific precision.

Major Abdul Sabri stood silently beside Aziz. In contrast to the scientist, Sabri's speech and movement were unhurried to the point of languid. Despite his simple galabiya, the traditional Egyptian workingman's floor-length robe, Sabri was still an intimidating sight. Tall and muscular, his large head boasted a beardless face with jarringly delicate, almost feminine features accentuated by light blue eyes—rare for an Arab. Kabaal couldn't separate Sabri's daunting physical presence from the man's history. As a member of the Egyptian Army's Special Forces, Sabri had seen extensive action, fighting primarily on native soil against Islamic rebels. Despite the highly classified nature of these operations, Kabaal had heard of Sabri's legendary reputation within the military for getting the job done at any cost. After leaving the army at forty, for reasons unexplained, Sabri had thrown his lot in with those who were once his bitter enemies.

Though Kabaal knew that both Aziz and Sabri were devoutly religious, he had little illusion about their motives. Aziz was above all a scientist, and Sabri a soldier. The operation was an excuse for both of them to exercise their passions, but motives didn't concern Kabaal; only loyalty and results mattered.

After exchanging brief pleasantries, Aziz and Sabri toured Kabaal through the facility. They started in the main building on the second floor, which once was a large open hospital ward and had since been divided into a series of offices and storage rooms. When they reached a set of sealed metal doors leading to a locked area, Aziz jabbed a stubby finger at them and said, "Subject evaluation." Kabaal did not require further explanation to know what went on behind the doors.

Aziz led Kabaal and Sabri down a different set of stairs from which they had come up. They walked out of the stairwell, through a small corridor, and into a large open laboratory on the main floor of the annex. The room buzzed. Everyone was in motion. No one stopped to acknowledge the visitors. White-coated technicians busied themselves at computers and workstations. Others worked under vented lab hoods, their arms slipping through holes in the glass and into long, orange rubber gloves that allowed them to manipulate the test tubes and containers inside without risking self-contamination.

Following Aziz around the makeshift virology lab, Kabaal tried to digest the stream of rapid-fire information, but much of the jargon-laden explanations sailed over his head. Still, he felt giddy, delighting in the technological trappings his money had assembled. Centrifuges, freezers, incubators, vented lab stations, and computers were everywhere. The sight filled Kabaal with a sense of purpose. Silently he thanked Allah for choosing him for the pivotal mission.

After finishing the tour, Aziz, Sabri, and Kabaal met in Aziz's office on the second floor. Aside from the wooden desk and chairs, two bookshelves stuffed with medical texts, and the prayer rug covering a small portion of the tile floor, the room was empty to the point of austere. Aziz insisted that Kabaal assume the seat behind the desk. The scientist took the chair across from him, but Sabri remained standing.

Hazzir Kabaal made a circular waving gesture with a finger, indicating the complex. "Dr. Anwar, Major Abdul, I am most impressed by what you have accomplished here."

Sabri nodded distantly while Aziz kept his eyes fixed on the tabletop and shrugged, either embarrassed by or indifferent to Kabaal's praise.

"How are the experiments proceeding?" Kabaal asked.

"So far very promising, Abu Lahab." Aziz called Kabaal by his Arabic honorific that literally meant "father of the flame," a reference to his handsome features.

"Promising?"

"Our facilities have been more than adequate to preserve the virus," Aziz said, his eyes never leaving the desktop. "The original Asian serum samples have not lost any of their infective potential."

Kabaal shrugged. "I am sorry, good doctor. 'Serum'?"

"Serum is what is left of the blood once you remove the cells and clotting factors, Abu Lahab," Aziz explained. "So far, we have injected eight subjects with the serum of the original Chinese patient."

"Subjects," Kabaal repeated, realizing that Aziz meant his own men. "And?"

"Every one of them has acquired some degree of infection."

"How many are dead?"

"Two."

Kabaal nodded solemnly. "And the others?" he asked, willing away the twinges of doubt.

"Four have recovered fully. To be truthful, three showed only a slight increase in temperature but otherwise had little more than colds. And two others are still symptomatic but showing signs of recovery."

Kabaal leaned back in his chair, ignoring the tip of the screw that pressed into his back. "So, this virus kills twenty-five percent of those infected?"

Aziz's head shot up and his eyes fixed on Kabaal's. "We don't have close to enough of a sample size to make that assertion. Besides, we have selection bias. We've only infected healthy men, ages seventeen to twenty-nine. We do not know what effect it would have on the rest of the population."

"Of course, Doctor." Kabaal waved away the scientist's quibble. "But it is safe to say that early figures suggest one in four young adults would die from this infection."

"That's what the very preliminary results would suggest," Aziz hedged.

"You have had no problem passing the infection through blood," Kabaal said. "But what about through the air. In the . . ." He struggled for the words.

"Respiratory droplets," Aziz offered.

"Yes," Kabaal said.

"This virus is not smallpox." Aziz sighed, sounding almost disappointed. "I would classify it as only moderately contagious."

Kabaal leaned forward again. "Can you elaborate, Dr. Anwar?"

Aziz chewed his lower lip, thinking. "We chose an index case who was at day two of symptomatic infection, when we estimated he was carrying the highest viral load—" When Kabaal shrugged, Aziz explained further.

"When we assumed him to be most infective. We put this man who was actively coughing in a room roughly the size of a large elevator with ten other subjects for thirty minutes. Three days later, only two of the subjects showed signs of infection."

"Allah be praised." Kabaal smiled.

Aziz frowned. "But had this been a virus like smallpox all of them who were not immune would develop infection."

Kabaal's smile broadened. "It is enough, good doctor."

Aziz nodded, but disappointment lingered in his small eyes. There was too much microbiological imperfection in the statistics.

A knock interrupted them. A compact, muscular Malaysian man stood at the open door. He wore a loose white robe along with an ornate green and gold *kopiah,* the traditional Malaysian skullcap.

"Ah, Ibrahim Sundaram, welcome, welcome," Kabaal said, and he rose to greet the young man with a warm handshake.

Dr. Aziz nodded once to Kabaal and then rushed by Sundaram without acknowledging him.

Kabaal put an arm on the Malay's shoulder. "Come, let's walk," he said. He waited for Sabri to saunter over before leading Sundaram out of the room.

They walked down the stairs and out a back door into the dusty hot daylight. Kabaal directed the others over to a patch of shade offered by the tin overhang. He was disappointed how little relief the shade provided from the equatorial heat, but he wanted to have the conversation outside and this spot was as private as any Kabaal knew of.

Kabaal and Sabri stood side by side at the edge of the shade, facing Sundaram whose back almost touched the wall of the complex. "You wanted to see me, Abu Lahab?" the Malay asked in perfect English.

"I wanted to thank you, Ibrahim," Kabaal said with an accent that was a soothing hybrid of Queen's English and

Egyptian, which had been so irresistible to the female students at the London School of Economics. "Without your help, none of this would be possible."

The man who had single-handedly transported the virus from China to Africa shrugged humbly. "I was only a courier. And without my good friend, Farouk Ali, I had no chance of success."

"Of course, of course. Brave Farouk," Kabaal said solemnly. "What happened to him?"

"He became sick before we reached the Chinese border. It was far too risky to cross with Farouk showing signs of the illness." Sundaram looked down at the dirt. "I shot him and the Chinese black marketer before I crossed. Farouk died a martyr's death."

"Allah be praised," Sabri said softly in Arabic, though he clearly understood the English conversation.

"A glorious death," Kabaal said. He narrowed his gaze at Sundaram. "And you, Ibrahim? How are you feeling?"

Sundaram dug at the soft ground with his shoe. "Better, Abu Lahab. Much better."

"What was it like?" Kabaal asked.

Sundaram considered the question for a moment before looking back up. "At home, when I was thirteen and working on my father's farm, I came down with malaria. For twenty hours a day, I felt fine. But twice a day my fever would spike. The pain was unbearable. I felt so weak, I couldn't lift my arm to bring water to my lips. With this illness, for three days, I felt like that every moment. I was certain I would die. But then it was gone quicker than it came. And now I feel well again."

"I am glad you are well, Ibrahim," Kabaal said.

Sundaram's lips broke into a smile. Then he began to chuckle. It was an infectious laugh. Soon Kabaal joined in, while Sabri watched them impassively.

When he stopped laughing, Kabaal asked, "How is your Arabic?"

Sundaram shrugged. "I speak several languages, but I am sad to say my Arabic is not very good. I can read the Koran, but I have trouble conversing."

"A pity," Kabaal sighed. "Most of the men here speak nothing but Arabic."

Sundaram nodded.

"And there is the issue of your presence in East Africa," Kabaal said. "You don't exactly blend in. You understand?"

"Of course," Sundaram said.

"If the wrong person were to see you they might make the connection," Kabaal continued. "And you know how people talk. Even my people."

"Unavoidable," Sundaram said.

Sabri took a few steps back until he stood in the sunlight.

"It comes down to loose ends," Kabaal said, trying to convince himself more than the young man with the relaxed shoulders who stood in front of him. "This operation is so fragile. We cannot afford loose ends."

Sundaram held his hands open in front of him. "It is God's way."

"Which is sometimes the hardest way," Kabaal said. He glanced over his shoulder at Sabri and nodded, then turned back to Sundaram. "Of course, it will be a martyr's death."

"A martyr's death," Sundaram repeated with conviction.

"Paradise awaits you," Kabaal said as he took a few steps to his side and away from Sabri.

The major withdrew the semiautomatic handgun from underneath his galabiya. In one deliberate motion, he raised his arm until it was level with Sundaram's face.

He fired.

Sundaram's head snapped back against the wall of the complex. A momentary pause, then his legs crumpled and he dropped like a detonated building. When his head hit the ground, his kopiah rolled off as if leading the stream of blood that followed close behind it.

Kabaal glanced at Sabri who stood motionless with his gun by his side. His face was so devoid of expression that it could have been cast in wax. Staring into Sabri's pale icy eyes, Kabaal fought off a shudder. Partly because he had never seen an execution before, but mainly because he was looking at one of the most fearsome men he had ever encountered.

CHAPTER

7

Jiayuguan City was named after a section of a wall. Not just any wall. The Great Wall of China. And in the fourteenth century, the Jiayuguan Pass, or fortress, was the westernmost point of the Great Wall. A formidable structure, it was once called the "The First and Greatest Pass Under the Heaven."

Haldane had learned all this from the guidebook he had tried to read, between bouts of nausea and Duncan McLeod's incessant nervous chatter, on the turbulent China Airlines flight. When too green to read, Haldane mulled over what little he knew about ARCS, dejectedly deciding they would need the epidemiological equivalent of the Great Wall to keep it from spreading beyond the Gansu Province.

Thirteen hours after leaving Geneva, with their internal clocks turned upside down, the WHO team—Milly Yuen, Helmut Streicher, Duncan McLeod, and Noah Haldane—

touched down at the Jiayuguan City airport. They were met by a sea of bureaucrats and military personnel laden with gifts varying from flowers to local carvings and silks. Everyone was smiles and gratitude. A sharp contrast to the chilly welcome Haldane received on his previous visits to China during the heyday of the SARS uproar. As Jean Nantal had assured, the Chinese government appeared to be taking a different approach from their disastrous policy of secrecy and denial when SARS swept the Guangdong Province.

After an impromptu receiving line of introductions, handshakes, and bows, the Chinese officials led the WHO team out of the terminal to a waiting stretch limousine, which sat in the middle of a row of escort cars. UN flags flew prominently from the antennae on either side of its trunk. With lights flashing, police motorcycles led the procession from the airport.

With their backs to the driver, Haldane and McLeod sat across from Yuen and Streicher in the rear seat. McLeod pointed out the window at the motorcycles flanking either side. "Shite, when exactly was I crowned Queen?" he commented in his Scottish lilt.

Yuen giggled, but Streicher sighed. "Dr. McLeod, must everything be a joke to you?"

"Not everything, Helmut." McLeod stroked his patchy red beard. "But don't you find it a tad curious that we're here to investigate the plague and we get welcomed like we were the Spice Girls . . . before Ginger left?"

"Ginger?" Streicher frowned, bewildered by the reference.

"If you ignore him, Helmut, he eventually stops," Haldane advised. He pointed out the window. "Duncan's got a point. The government is making a big show of us."

McLeod stretched out in the plush leather seat. "Then again, it's about damn time we got the recognition we deserve."

"Why now?" Milly asked quietly, without making eye contact with anyone.

"Exactly." Haldane nodded. "Last time we were pariahs, now we're heroes. And we haven't done anything except show up."

McLeod shrugged. "The locals know they're going to be under the spotlight soon. They're readying themselves for the circus."

Haldane nodded distractedly. "Yeah. Makes sense."

Streicher fixed his intense gray-blue eyes on Haldane. "You're not convinced." He stated it as fact.

"I'm a born skeptic when it comes to government motives." Haldane shrugged. "Whenever I see them roll out the red carpet, I wonder if it's out there to cover up some serious dirt."

McLeod laughed and slapped the seat beside him. "Haldane, you're a cynical bastard! But I like the way you think."

The procession wound through the streets of Jiayuguan City. With Yuen translating, their driver acted as tour guide, tossing out tidbits of history and geography along with a hefty dose of local political gossip.

With a population of less than two hundred thousand, Jiayuguan was a small city by Chinese standards. Modern and industrial, it was built in the sixties to support the local steel industry. As a result, it had all the gray uniformity of communist construction from the peak days of the Cultural Revolution. But it lacked the ethnic charm seen in the temples, palaces, and other features of more historic Chinese cities that Haldane had seen.

After driving for ten minutes through the heart of Jiayuguan, the scenery was so repetitive that Haldane felt as if they were circling the same block. Just as he turned to McLeod to voice this suspicion, the limo pulled up to the front of the Great Wall Hotel. Stepping out of the car, Haldane suddenly felt uneasy. He didn't know if it was the gray clouds, the oppressively similar buildings, or the specter of the unspecified epidemic that hung in the air, but he experienced a sense of unsettled urgency.

Walking into the hotel's bland lobby, what had been niggling at him since the moment they arrived came into focus—the scarcity of people. Granted, it was a cold Sunday evening in a remote western province, but this was China, the most populous country in the world. During his brief layover at the Beijing airport Haldane saw firsthand the smothering congestion of urban China. Now, not even 8:00 P.M. local time, Jiayuguan City was a relative ghost town. Suddenly the excitement surrounding their arrival made sense to him. The welcoming committee wasn't trying to impress the WHO delegates so much as reassure the local residents that the cavalry had arrived. Judging from the emptiness of the streets, Haldane decided their attempt had been in vain.

After another outpouring of smiles and handshakes in the hotel lobby, the WHO team parted ways with their welcoming party and fled to their rooms. Though clean and quiet, the rooms were small and dimly lit in the three-star hotel. Haldane had to agree with McLeod when the Scotsman bellowed from down the hallway: "Some guidebook's being awfully generous handing out stars!"

Haldane's seventh-floor room looked out onto a central plaza, which was as deserted as the rest of the street. Though the view was prettier than anything he had seen from the limo, he had little interest in the scenery. He headed straight for the nightstand phone.

Maryland was thirteen hours behind China (which officially maintains one time for the whole country despite spanning five time zones from east to west), but Haldane couldn't wait. By the time the operator connected him, it was just before 7:00 A.M. at home.

Anna answered on the second ring. "Hello?" The line crackled.

"Hi, Anna, it's me. I'm in China," Haldane said, hearing his own voice echo in his ear from the delay.

"Oh, Noah," she said in a monotone. "Everything okay?"

"Everything's fine. I didn't wake you, did I?"

"No," she said softly. "Been up for a while."

Haldane knew what that meant. Normally, Anna and Chloe were sound sleepers in the morning. "Her ear?" he asked.

"Yes," Anna said. "She crawled into our bed around 3:00 A.M., but you know."

He did. It was a common occurrence at their home.

Lying back on the firm unfamiliar mattress, Noah could picture his wife wearing one of his T-shirts that fit her like a nightgown, curled up in their queen bed with Chloe squirming in her arms. Chloe would be in constant motion, writhing, sobbing, and sweating in turn, unable to find comfort despite the Tylenol. And Anna would lie still beside her, clinging to Chloe and whispering reassurances in her daughter's ear.

The visual brought a stab of guilt and loneliness. "Can I speak to her?" he asked.

There was a rustling noise on the line, then heavier breathing and a snort. "Chloe?" he said.

"Hi, Daddy." In spite of the static, her voice sounded nasal.

"Chlo, are you okay?"

"It hurts, Daddy," she sniffed.

Another stab. "Oh, sweetheart, I know. I wish I were there with you. I miss you so much." When she didn't reply he added, "I'm coming home soon."

"For breakfast?" her voice perked up.

"No, Chlo," Haldane sighed. "But soon as I can. I love you so much."

"Bye, Daddy," she said. He heard a thud as the phone dropped.

After a moment, Anna was back on the line. "You brought the first smile I've seen in a while," Anna said with new warmth.

"I wish to hell I could see it in person," Haldane said.

No answer.

"How are you?"

"A little lonely." She hesitated. "A lot confused."

Haldane sat up on the bed and squeezed the receiver tighter. "You haven't worked things out, huh?"

"Not exactly," she said.

They were both silent. Haldane felt every mile of the twelve thousand that separated them.

His mind wandered back to the scene in their living room a few months earlier. After weeks of having evaded questions about her withdrawn nervousness, Anna waited until her mother took Chloe for the afternoon before sitting him down for a "discussion".

Unsuspecting, Haldane had sat beside her on the living-room couch, enjoying a rare moment of intimacy as she caressed his hand in hers.

The tears came before the confession. Haldane sat silently clutching her hand, not out of support but utter shock, as she told him how her relationship with Julie, the single dentist who lived two doors away, had progressed from growing friendship into budding romance. Haldane wasn't floored by the same-sex angle; he knew that Anna spent two of her college undergrad years romantically involved with her female roommate. On first meeting their attractive neighbor with the short brunette hair and piercing brown eyes, Haldane sensed she might be gay, but he never suspected that his wife's moodiness or remoteness might be attributable to her having fallen for this woman or anyone else.

While Anna fluctuated between apologies and rationalizations, Haldane said very little that afternoon. But as days passed, he couldn't stop talking about it with her. He wasn't looking for the contrition Anna offered, or even the energetic sexual solace she seemed to need from him. He wanted guarantees. And while Anna was adamant she had cut off all contact with Julie, she would not give Noah what he sought: assurance that she was, or would soon be, over Julie. Instead, she maintained that she was in love with both of them.

The crackle of static brought him back to the moment. He took a deep breath. "Have you seen her since I left?" he asked. Julie was always "she" or "her" to Haldane.

"No." Anna wavered. "Not face-to-face."

"But you talk to her regularly?" he snapped before his brain could catch up to his mouth.

"She e-mails me."

Haldane resisted the urge to break the receiver in his hand. "And you write her back?"

"They're poems, Noah. Beautiful." She was silent for a long while. "Yes, I write back."

He swallowed. "Anna, I don't want you to write to her."

"I know," she said almost imperceptibly over the static.

Haldane heard his daughter crying in the background. "You better take care of Chloe."

"Okay," she said. "Noah, promise me you will be careful over there. Please."

"Bye, Anna."

He lay back on the bed, staring at the ceiling, ruminating about this last fruitless conversation and all the others that preceded it. Again he felt lost, unsure of how to hold up the crumbling walls of his domestic life. He thought of his daughter suffering through another ear infection without her dad around to comfort her. He thought of his wife. Her large brown eyes. The fragile smile. The bulky T-shirt that only hinted at the smooth, responsive body hidden underneath. And in spite of the torrent of mixed emotions, he realized how aroused he was. He longed to see her face, smell her hair, and clutch her flawless back as her legs wrapped around his waist.

Haldane shook away the conflicting thoughts, jumped off the bed, and grabbed his laptop. He moved the phone out of the way and flipped it open. With a tap of the built-in mouse, data regarding Acute Respiratory Collapse Syndrome filled the screen. Jotting notes as he reviewed the documents, graphs, and charts, he succeeded in distracting himself by studying a world even more chaotic than his own.

The next morning, the WHO team separated. Streicher and Yuen, the nonclinical specialists, went off to review the regional laboratory while McLeod and Haldane headed off to see the front lines in the battle against ARCS.

Walking out of the hotel to the waiting unmarked government sedan, Haldane noticed the first of several Jiayuguan residents sporting surgical masks over their faces. It was an eerily familiar sight from the SARS days.

"People very panicky," their translator and guide explained away the phenomenon from the front seat of the car.

"People very sensible," McLeod aped from the backseat.

They drove past the city limits and continued southward.

"Haldane, I have to tell you," McLeod said, "I don't like this bug."

Haldane laughed. "Are you partial to any microorganism?"

"Not particularly, but I really don't like this one."

The smile left Haldane's lips. "How come?"

"The short incubation period. The rapid respiratory failure in otherwise healthy people. The hemorrhagic pneumonia . . . Reminds me of only one other I've seen before."

Haldane shook his head. "Duncan, this is not Ebola."

McLeod nodded. "I know. And it's a bloody shame."

"Oh?"

"Nice and clean killer, Ebola." McLeod nodded in admiration. "But its ruthless lethality is its shortcoming. Kills everything in its path. If this were Ebola, we'd have a few hundred dead farmers and some very cheap farmland on the market, but the disease would burn itself out for lack of new victims."

Haldane nodded, picking up on McLeod's logic. "Whereas ARCS only kills the significant minority of its victims, allowing the virus to propagate and spread beyond the site of the index cases."

"And spread rapidly."

"That is yet to be determined, Duncan," Haldane said, but he was unconvinced by his own argument.

The car slowed before turning off the main road and onto the driveway of Jiayuguan's regional hospital. They passed through two checkpoints, manned by masked soldiers, and drove into the gravel parking lot in front of the hospital. A cold spitting drizzle fell as Haldane and McLeod hopped out of the car, bundled their jackets, and strode for the front entrance.

Once they cleared the internal security measures, McLeod and Haldane were led into the change room. Haldane had slipped into too many biohazard, or HAZMAT, suits to feel the slightest alarm. As he stepped out through the two sets of sealed doors and into the clinical area, he actually felt relief to be among the appropriate high-level, scientific protective measures and away from the irrational fear he had seen on the streets in the eyes behind the surgical masks.

A hospital guide, fully suited in blue HAZMAT gear like the rest of the staff behind the doors, acted as their

translator. The chubby man led the two emerging pathogens experts to a hospital room on the second floor. Haldane was surprised to see that the door was locked. They
had to wait for a security guard to let them in. "Why the
guards?" Haldane asked the translator.

The translator spoke to the security guard and then
turned to Haldane. "The men might still be contaminated,"
he said in a voice that was muffled by the spacesuitlike
hood he wore. He pointed to the guard opening the door.
"They take no chances."

Inside, with the door locked behind them, they stood in
a bleak windowless hospital room befitting a second-
world country. Two beds were hidden behind drawn curtains. On the other side of the room, two men wearing
masks, gloves, and shower caps along with standard hospital pajamas sat across from one another on narrow cots
and played mahjong with small white domino-like tiles.

"Why are they still here?" McLeod pointed at the
healthy-looking men.

"Still might be contaminated," the translator replied.

" 'Infectious' ", Haldane corrected distractedly. He
waved to the two men, who responded with friendly nods,
and then he asked the translator. "When did they become
sick?"

The translator spoke for several minutes to the two
patients in their native Mandarin.

"Watch," McLeod said, shifting impatiently from foot
to foot. "I've seen translators do this a thousand times
before. They'll gab back and forth for half an hour and
then the guy will turn to us and say 'yes' or 'no.' "

Haldane had witnessed the same frustrating happening,
but in this case, McLeod was wrong.

"Both men live in the same town fifty miles north of
Jiayuguan," the translator said. He pointed to the smaller
man on the cot nearest them. "Seven days ago, Xiang got
a high fever. In a day, he started to cough. Then he

became very, very sick. The oxygen did not help him. He was suffocating on his own mucus." He put both hands on his own throat and pantomimed a choke. "The town's doctor arranged to bring Xiang here, but he told his wife it was probably no good. Here at our hospital, the doctors put Xiang on a life-support machine. After three days, he got much better." The translator snapped his finger to indicate the rapidity of his sudden improvement. "Now, he waits for two days until the doctors say he is no longer *infectious*." The translator glanced at Haldane with a proud nod.

Haldane chuckled and nodded back. "And the other man?" he asked.

"Tan," the translator said, thumbing at the tall, thin man. "He also got sick a week ago. He never became as very sick as Xiang. Only a heavy cough. But . . ." The translator cleared his throat. "Tan's sister died from the virus three days ago."

"Oh," Haldane said. "Please tell him how sorry we are."

The translator and Tan spoke for a moment. Tan raised a hand and waved it at Haldane, leaving him confused as to the intent of the gesture.

"We want to ask some questions about their illness," McLeod said to the translator.

Through the translator, McLeod and Haldane focused their questions on the early symptoms of the infection. Neither patient had the classic sore throat or vague aches that are the harbingers of the common flu. Their symptoms began with a sudden fever and weakness, followed within hours by agonizing muscle pain, cough, and some degree of respiratory collapse.

Haldane had heard enough to know that whatever caused ARCS was one scary pathogen. It hit quickly. And it hit hard.

After thanking the patients for their time, the translator banged on the door. Released by the security guard, they headed into a stairwell and up to the fourth floor. Haldane had to twice catch the railing when he tripped on the stairs walking in his bulky rubber suit.

On the fourth floor the contingent passed through another set of sealed doors. Though Haldane couldn't read the Chinese lettering, from the bustling activity of the staff at the nursing station he recognized the ward for an Intensive Care Unit. Not as sleek or modern as the North American or European ICUs Haldane had seen, the air was taut with the same sense of urgency. Maybe more so.

After consultation with the nurses, their translator led them to one of the closed rooms that surrounded the nursing station like the spokes of a tire. But this door wasn't locked. As soon as they opened it, Haldane understood why. The patient wasn't going anywhere soon, except possibly the morgue.

As they approached the bed, the translator explained, "This is the doctor. Dr. Zhao Fung."

"Which doctor?" McLeod asked.

But Haldane answered before the translator. "He's the town doctor. The one who looked after the two men we just interviewed."

The translator nodded his head vigorously.

"Shite!" McLeod said. "I thought they told us there hadn't been any intra-hospital spread."

The translator waved his gloved hand. "No hospital in that town. Only the . . . clinic . . . where he worked. He used the best precautions he had, but . . ."

Haldane nodded absentmindedly. He was thinking of his colleague, Dr. Franco Bertulli, dying of SARS in a similar room in Singapore after following all the recommended precautions. He remembered how Bertulli joked about his mother encouraging him to go into medicine because she thought it was so much safer than his alternate choice, the police force. In the case of both Bertulli and Fung, the viruses managed to circumvent their protective measures. In the end, medicine turned out to be a very unsafe choice for both doctors.

Dr. Fung looked older than fifty. Behind a deathly pallor, his face was swollen and contused. His oozing lips were as thick as the endotracheal tube sticking between them and leading to a ventilator, or artificial life-support system. Bloody sputum fluttered inside the transparent plastic tube, flapping back and forth with each breath the ventilator forced in and out, like a piece of paper trapped at the opening of a vacuum hose. Bruises covered his flaccid arms. A blanket shrouded the rest of his skin from his chest down, but Haldane knew that he would see similar welts and bruises on any exposed surface. Haldane made the diagnosis from the foot of the bed: disseminated intravascular coagulopathy or DIC. The inflammatory reaction instigated by the virus was chewing up the clotting factors in the patient's blood. As a result, he was bleeding spontaneously under his skin; thus the bruises.

Haldane experienced the same helplessness he had felt in Singapore. The local specialists had done all they could—all anyone could—for their colleague. Standing at the bedside in his rubber suit, Haldane felt embarrassed, as if he were a nosy bystander gawking at the sight of a fatal car crash. He was of no use to the doomed physician. All he could do was try to prevent others from following down the same road. He silently vowed to do just that.

He'd seen enough. He spun and walked to the door. McLeod and the interpreter followed behind. Even McLeod was silent as they headed back to the change rooms where guards supervised their showers to ensure proper decontamination steps were followed.

Once they were dressed their translator led them into a modest gray office, which smelled of herbal tea, on the main floor. The associate director, Dr. Ping Wu, jumped up from his desk and walked around to meet them. Wearing thick glasses and a crisp white lab coat, the middle-aged doctor stood chest-high to his two Western colleagues.

The translator made the introductions, but the diminutive administrator addressed Haldane and McLeod in a slightly accented English. "My English is most poor, but I think I can manage," he said with typical Oriental humility. "I studied four years at UCLA." He waved to the interpreter who turned and left the room.

Haldane and McLeod sat down across the desk from Wu. "My deepest apologies, Doctors," Wu said. "The director, Dr. Huang, is at the provincial capital Lanzhou reporting to the governor. He very much wanted to meet you."

"We appreciate you taking the time to meet us, Dr. Wu," Haldane said.

Wu bowed his head. "It's an honor."

"Likewise," Haldane said. "Dr. Wu, I understand your hospital has had the most experience of any facility with this disease."

"Very true, Dr. Haldane," Wu said. "We have treated 146 cases at this hospital. As many as the other hospitals combined."

McLeod rubbed his beard roughly. "How many dead?"

"Twenty-seven." Wu cleared his throat. "I fear that number will rise to thirty by day's end."

"Including Dr. Fung?" McLeod said.

"Yes."

"It would be very helpful for us to hear about your firsthand experience with this virus," Haldane said.

"Certainly." Wu looked down at his desktop. "It began twenty-three days ago. A farmer from the north was sent to us with a high fever and complete respiratory failure. He died within twenty-four hours of arrival. We were concerned about the possibility of the Bird Flu or even SARS."

Haldane frowned. "Did SARS ever reach Jiayuguan?"

"No. Not anywhere in the Gansu Province. Still, we exercised precise pulmonary protocol with our patient. We did not know until the blood tests came back negative for the SARS coronavirus. Soon more patients arrived with the same symptoms. Abrupt onset of high fever followed by respiratory symptoms, pneumonia, often associated with hemoptysis." Wu used the technical term for coughing up blood.

"Followed by respiratory collapse," McLeod said.

Wu shook his head. "Not in all cases, Dr. McLeod. Over half the patients never became short of breath. Just a cough, fever, and severe weakness. Prompt recovery in less than four days in all cases. We believe there are still others who have a subclinical form of the illness and do not require treatment."

"And in those who did become critically ill," Haldane said. "What treatments have been tried?"

Wu sighed. "Everything our infectious disease specialists can think of steroids, ribavirin, acyclovir, amantadine, even the HIV antiviral medications."

"And?"

Wu held up his little hands in a helpless gesture. "We have seen no benefit from any of them. The only intervention that seems to make a difference is the ventilator. The support of the artificial life-support system has helped some patients stay alive long enough to recover." He shrugged. "If the patient lives for four days, then it seems he or she will recover. But our resources are limited. All the ventilators are in use. We have to guess who has the best chance of surviving. And the others . . ." His shoulders sagged. He looked down at the table, as if personally responsible for the lack of resources.

"Understandable," McLeod said. "How about the town doctor? How long has he been on the ventilator?"

"This is only Dr. Fung's second day. We will remove the life support in the next few hours." He glanced away in embarrassment. "We need it for one of the others who might have a chance."

Haldane nodded sympathetically. His heart went out to Wu and the rest of the staff, knowing this kind of life-and-death rationing of resources was the worst kind of decision health-care professionals ever had to face. "Dr. Wu, what measures have you instituted to prevent spread within the hospital and beyond?"

Wu stiffened in his chair. "I don't understand what you mean by the question, Dr. Haldane," he snapped. "We have not had any spread away from this hospital."

Haldane was taken aback by the administrator's abrupt defensiveness. "Dr. Wu, we appreciate the excellent work you and your staff have done. What I meant is, can you describe your infection control program?"

Wu nodded, but he still eyed them guardedly. "We implemented the same precautions the hospitals in Beijing used with SARS. In this hospital, we now only accept patients suspected of having the virus. Other patients are diverted elsewhere. All patient care areas in the hospital have negative pressure airflow and filters. The rooms and wards are sealed behind airtight doors. All staff wear bio-hazards suits in patient care areas. So far we have not had a single incident of transmission to a staff member within the hospital."

"I thought Dr. Fung followed the precautions, too," McLeod pointed out.

Wu crossed his arms over his chest. "He was infected at his clinic. He only wore a surgical mask, gown, and gloves. This was proven during the SARS outbreak to be inadequate, especially if the masks were not fitted properly."

Haldane noticed that Wu's attitude had subtly shifted from that of deferential collegiality to bureaucratic wariness. While he didn't understand the reason for it, Haldane realized that they would learn little more from the associate director. He rose from his chair. "Thank you, Dr. Wu. You have been most helpful," he said.

Before rising, McLeod looked at Wu and asked, "Between us, how much does this bug scare you?"

Wu looked away, as if ignoring the question. Finally, he said, "I never saw a patient with SARS, but I believe this virus is worse. I think this is the worst thing to ever strike Gansu."

"Will it stay in Gansu?" Haldane asked.

Wu's eyes narrowed to slits. Then, slowly, he shook his head.

Dr. Ping Wu stood at his window and watched until the car carrying the two WHO physicians pulled out of the driveway. Then he turned down the window shutters, locked his door, and returned to his desk. He left instructions with his administrative assistant that he was not to be disturbed under any circumstances.

He cleared the papers off his desk, cleaned his glasses with his handkerchief, and then folded his hands on the desktop. He sat perfectly still, trying to compose his thoughts before proceeding.

The two WHO doctors had struck Wu as sincere, but he had his doubts. Their questions and innuendoes about the virus spreading from the hospital and beyond Gansu hadn't come out of thin air. Maybe they already knew?

How did it come to this? He tried to retrace the steps in his mind.

For four years of residency at UCLA in the 1970s, he lived below the poverty line, ever the good communist. Never complaining or wanting for the material wealth that was everywhere around him. Returning to China, he continued to live a life of virtual asceticism, forsaking a family of his own to work harder than all his colleagues and subordinates while he watched lazy party officials grow rich from graft and corruption. He practically built the hospital in which he now sat, but when the time came to appoint a director, an underqualified party hack, barely out of his teens, was placed ahead of him. None of it softened Wu's rigid ethical conduct, until his eighty-year-old parents became too frail to live in their own hovel. In order to help them, he needed to supplement his income. So he did what he had to. What he was entitled to do, for all his years of service.

It had begun harmlessly enough. He accepted small gratuities for providing priority access to diagnostic services like lab tests or X-rays for people who might have otherwise waited months. In that first year, the money barely covered the expense of the homecare worker he hired to help his parents. From there, his services expanded. For a larger fee, he would move people to the top of elective surgical waiting lists. Soon surgeons began to pay for more operating time to work on their own "private" patients. For a substantial fee, Wu would even "doctor" disability and other pension applications.

When he first heard Lee's offer in exchange for allowing two "relatives" to visit a dying infected patient, he balked at the idea. But the black marketer offered more than Wu had ever seen before. In spite of huge misgivings, Wu could not resist. The moment he laid eyes on the foreigners, he knew they were not honest in their intentions. He tried to convince himself that they were just reporters, capitalizing on a sensational story and that they needed privacy to capture the virus's victims on film, but in his heart he never believed that. He knew something more sinister was at work.

When hours after their visit, a nurse discovered that the dying patient had puncture marks over his jugular vein, Wu managed to cover it up. However, he could lie to himself no longer. They had stolen the man's blood and with it the virus. And he had facilitated the theft.

Wu had long since quelled the stirrings of self-recrimination about his acts of petty corruption. It was understandable, even expected to some degree, within the system he lived. But his life had been dedicated to the practice of medicine. Never before had his profiteering been undertaken at the patients' expense. His role, inadvertent as it was, in disseminating the virus beyond Gansu was beyond rationalization. Or forgiveness. And in the week since the men had stolen the virus, he barely slept at night.

Satisfied his thoughts were in order, he put his glasses back on, reached for the computer keyboard, and began to type. He addressed the e-mail to his immediate superior, the hospital's young director, Dr. Kai Huang.

Dr. Huang,

I am writing to inform you of a critical breach in hospital security that occurred seven days ago.

I accepted money from a man, Kwok Lee, whom I know to be a black marketer. In return for the bribe, I arranged for Mr. Lee and two of his accomplices to see one of the afflicted patients. Mr. Lee claimed the two men were relatives of the dying man, but I knew differently as they appeared to be of Malaysian or Indonesian descent. I assumed they were reporters, but I did not dwell on their identity or intentions.

They spent five unsupervised minutes with the patient. The patient died an hour after the men left. While preparing the body, one of the nurses discovered recent puncture marks over the left jugular vein. No medical procedures had been performed at that site. My only possible conclusion is that the men withdrew vials of venous blood.

From our experience, we know that body fluid of infected patients is highly contagious. Since he was suffering from overwhelming sepsis, this patient's blood would have had a particularly high concentration of the virus.

I have no knowledge of how they mean to use this

infected blood, but I can only assume that it involves criminal intent. And I cannot exclude the possibility of terrorism or the use of the virus as a weapon.
Yours,
Ping Wu

Wu reread the e-mail, satisfied. He intentionally left out
any attempt to minimize his role or justify his actions. He
did not owe them that. Without hesitating, he tapped the
"send" button. As soon as the e-mail left his screen, he felt
a weight lift off his shoulders. He had done his part to
warn others.

He reached down and opened the same desk drawer
where he had twice deposited those dirty envelopes that
had ruined his life and, possibly, countless others. The
money was gone, but he pulled out the two bottles from
the drawer. One was a popular Chinese wine, the other a
pill bottle containing one hundred tablets of a major seda-
tive.

He popped the lid off the pill bottle. Bringing the hard
plastic to his lips, he tasted the bitter-salty flavor as he
stuffed as many pills as would fit into his mouth. He
choked them down with a gulp of wine. He had another
sip of wine, but the medicinal taste lingered. He took a
deep breath, and then swallowed the rest of the tablets.

CHAPTER

8

It was an ominous name: "Carnivore". The software system electronically spies on e-mails from across the globe, trying to sniff out criminal activity and threats to U.S. national security. Among the several hundred million screened that day, Dr. Ping Wu's final e-mail piqued Carnivore's interest because it contained the words "terrorist" and "virus". After translating it into passable though grammatically questionable English, Carnivore graded the e-mail as "moderately suspicious", meaning it required review by human eyes.

As did 68,435 other e-mails sent the same day.

The overburdened CIA staffers who ran Carnivore were forever falling behind in their attempt to find the needle in an electronic haystack. Eavesdropping on the entire world was a challenge that the CIA had yet to master. Another "backlog debulking" loomed in the near future. The term was classic CIA-speak—a euphemism for a random, massive hard drive purge of all but the most suspicious of the unread e-mail backlog. The espionage world's equivalent of Russian roulette.

Even if Wu's e-mail wasn't destined to be lost in the "backlog debulking," no one at Langley would have a chance to review it for a minimum of seven days.

HARGEYSA, SOMALIA

A southern breeze stirred up flakes from the dirt road. It carried with it the faint smell of food that drifted in from the cooking fire of the militia posted a half mile down the road.

Hazzir Kabaal and Abdul Sabri stood out front of the laboratory complex in the windy but warm dusk. Minutes earlier they had said prayers together with mats almost touching. Neither had spoken a word since.

Kabaal had a knack for reading people, which helped explain his unfettered success in the cutthroat world of print media. But after four days spent in Sabri's company, Kabaal still read nothing behind the man's pale eyes and placid expression. From that alone, Kabaal realized that Sabri was a man to be reckoned with. Having witnessed the dispassionate and unhesitating manner in which Sabri executed the Malaysian—one of their own men—Kabaal knew he had chosen well.

His choice was not made in haste. Kabaal had screened several candidates before settling on Sabri. He was not the only candidate with a history distinguished by ruthlessness. However, one report from the major's thick blood-stained military file tilted the balance in his favor.

Six years earlier, Sabri had led an elite team of Egyptian soldiers against an insurgency in the south of the country. After a bitter standoff, with heavy casualties on both sides, the government soldiers captured a rebel leader. Major Sabri was entrusted with interrogating the man to uncover the whereabouts of his fellow fighters who had

melted away into the nearby hills. The rebel leader with-
stood twenty-four hours of torture without divulging a
word. So Sabri changed tactics. He had the man's wife led
into the room. Chained to a chair beside the bed, the rebel
was forced to watch as three of Sabri's men viciously
raped the woman. When the leader stayed mute, despite
his wife's screams, Sabri's men brought in the man's
youngest daughter and strapped her to the bed. That was
the breaking point. Sabri had the rest of the rebels
rounded up and summarily executed within twelve hours
of the incident.

After hearing this account from the mouth of an eyewitness, Kabaal knew Sabri was the man he sought. A man of
single-minded focus and unflinching violence capable of
doing whatever necessary to achieve their goal: the
preservation of Islam, at any cost.

Why? Kabaal wondered again. Why had this secular
enforcer swapped sides and become a defender of Islam?
Kabaal mulled the question over, more out of curiosity
than concern. Sabri was foremost a fighter, a man of
action. The cause was secondary. Kabaal would, and in
fact had, bet his life on this belief.

Lost in his thoughts, Kabaal didn't notice the woman
until she was standing in front of them. At first, he didn't
recognize her in the dwindling light. He had only ever
seen Khalila Jahal wearing a haik, the loosely fitted one-
piece Moroccan robe that covers the head and body. Now,
as instructed, she wore jeans, sandals, and a tightly fitted
white blouse.

Large brown eyes, perfect tawny skin, and long shiny
black hair complemented Jahal's hourglass figure. Most of
the devout at the complex would have found her dress
intolerably immodest, but Kabaal had spent enough time
in the West to appreciate her sexiness without condoning
her attire. In spite of his reinvigorated faith, his old habits

died hard and he couldn't resist a compliment: "Ah, Khalila, in the privacy of your home you would please a husband with your exquisiteness."

She met his eyes confidently. "My husband is dead, Abu Lahab."

"He is in paradise, now," Kabaal said, knowing that the twenty-three-year-old's husband had died in the caves of Afghanistan, fighting alongside the Taliban.

Abdul Sabri eyed Jahal with clinical detachment. "You will draw the attention of many Western men dressed that way."

"Even better," Kabaal said. "More importantly, she will pass for a Western woman dressed like that."

"I will," Jahal said with certainty.

Kabaal nodded at her solemnly. "Khalila, you do not have to go, you know that?"

"I will go," Jahal said.

"There are others," Kabaal said. "You do not have to."

Jahal shook her head defiantly. "I will go, Abu Lahab. My husband would want this. I want this. It is my duty." She bit her lip, and then smiled sadly. "It is my opportunity to serve."

Kabaal felt a pang of melancholic nostalgia. She had such obvious intelligence behind her alluring brown eyes. And her confidence and selfless faith only enhanced her attractiveness. Under different circumstances, he gladly would have done the honorable thing and married this widow.

"Are you familiar with the plan?" Sabri asked of her, his pale blue eyes seemingly indifferent to the loveliness of the woman.

"Yes, Major." Jahal nodded, showing the first hint of intimidation in his presence. "I will be inoculated in the morning. The truck will pick me up immediately following. I will fly out from Tangiers. I will pick up my new papers in Paris."

"Do you know all the rendezvous points?" Sabri's eyes narrowed, still not convinced.

"Yes, Major," Jahal said. "I once spent several months in Paris. My French is impeccable. I could pass for a local," she said without a trace of conceit.

"And from there?" Sabri pressed.

"My transit is all arranged," she said. "I will wait for the fever and cough to develop before I go out. I have gone through the routine a thousand times in my head."

Again, Kabaal was struck by her confident poise in the presence of two men; a rare trait for a young female Islamist. Had she grown up in the West, Kabaal decided she would have been a feminist. He was struck by another wave of nostalgia. He had bedded a few self-described feminists in London in the seventies, happily discovering that their passion wasn't limited to gender politics.

Major Sabri studied the Moroccan woman for a long while. "Good." He finally exhaled, appearing satisfied but not pleased.

"You understand what is at stake?" Kabaal asked her.

"As I said, Abu Lahab, I know the plan to—"

Kabaal cut her off with a wave of his hand. "No. No. No. Do you understand why we must do this?"

She nodded calmly.

"We are under siege, Khalila," Kabaal went on though Jahal did not appear the least doubtful. "*They* have all the conventional weapons. Their army is camped at the gates of the Tigris. Their tanks and planes are within miles of Mecca. You understand, Khalila?"

"I do," Jahal said.

"I am not a madman." Kabaal looked away from her, pained by her lovely resolute face. "If there was another way." His shoulders sagged and his head drooped. "I don't want you to die. I don't want others to die."

She reached out as if she might touch Kabaal's shoulder, but her hand stopped short. Instead, she ran her hand through her hair like she meant to brush it all along. "It is what must be done," she said.

"It is the only way." Kabaal cleared his throat. "We cannot let them take our holy sites . . . take our way of life . . . take our God." He held his head up higher. "They will learn His vengeance for trying. They will learn it from you, Khalila."

He looked from the expressionless Sabri to the nodding Jahal.

"And there will be no mercy for those who stand in His way," Kabaal predicted.

CHAPTER

9

Dr. Kai Huang sat silently at his desk and trembled with rage.

At thirty-two, Kai Huang was one of the youngest medical directors in all of China, and he had no intention of stopping there. But now his career teetered on the brink of ruin. All thanks to the now-deceased associate director.

He read Ping Wu's e-mail again, and the trembling increased. Huang had always sensed that the bitter little man would somehow be his undoing. That Wu had done it from beyond his grave only made Huang that much angrier. He would never have the satisfaction of wringing Wu's neck. *If only I had acted sooner!* Huang thought bitterly.

Huang was aware of how much Wu resented being overlooked for the director's position. In the five years since the hospital opened, Huang had always kept a watchful eye on Wu. When Wu inexplicably jumped from self-righteous communism to shady profiteering, Huang opened a file tracking his under-the-table dealings. Huang would have intervened sooner, but Wu's tireless and efficient work habits had come in very handy for the young director during his long absences on career-building trips to Lanzhou and Beijing.

When the hospital had become the epicenter for treating the mysterious viral outbreak, Huang had to concede that Wu had responded well in his absence. Returning from the capital, Huang had stepped back and allowed Wu to continue managing the crisis, knowing that his career stood to gain a huge boost if Wu succeeded. And if Wu failed, it left a convenient scapegoat and a simple solution to his problem with this unlikable little man.

Animosity aside, Huang was still shocked by what Wu had allowed to happen. Especially as the man had seemed determined to single-handedly control the outbreak. Huang never dreamed that Wu would actually try to profit from an epidemic.

Even in his state of panicky self-preservation, Huang understood that Wu's treachery impacted far beyond his own career. But as he stared at the message taunting him on his computer screen, he realized that he was the only recipient specified in the e-mail's "To" field. Unless Wu had written separately to someone else before his suicide or sent blind copies to others, which seemed unlikely considering the man's basic computer skills, Wu had left Huang as the sole caretaker of his dirty secret.

Huang sat for a long time, considering the implications of his next step.

Whoever stole the virus was either dead or long gone, he rationalized. Aside from signing his own death warrant, what possible good would come from sounding the alarm to his superiors?

With a shaking hand, Kai Huang reached for the keyboard and tapped the "delete" key.

DEPARTMENT OF HOMELAND SECURITY, NEBRASKA AVENUE CENTER, WASHINGTON, D.C.
Gwen Savard's ankle ached even after she sat down at her desk. She blamed it on the colder weather, not willing to accept it as a sign of aging. D.C. had taken a turn for the colder in mid-November. Even her Lycra suit, gloves, and lined hat couldn't keep her jogs warm, when she headed out daily at 5:30 A.M. And this morning, she had tweaked her ankle again in the predawn darkness. The time had come to move inside to the gym for the winter, which meant twenty more minutes of commuting. So be it, thought Gwen. Her directorship of the counter-bioterrorism program with its demanding and unpredictable schedule had already cost her her spot on her women's soccer team. She wasn't about to give up her morning workout ritual, despite the ever-mounting workload.

Gwen willed away her ankle pain as she scanned through her massive list of e-mails. Once she answered the most pressing of the messages, she logged onto the password-protected highest security zone of the Centers for Disease Control Web site.

Gwen spent the next fifteen minutes, as she did every morning, reviewing the CDC's global surveillance of the "hot spots." A shigella epidemic had hit West Africa, but she was relieved to see that the reported outbreak of possible Ebola in Nigeria turned out to be no more than Dengue Fever; no walk in the park, but still no Ebola.

Scanning the catalogue of infections sweeping the planet—antibiotic-resistant tuberculosis among New York's drug addicts, syphilis in the San Francisco gay community, chloroquine-resistant malaria in the Philippines, and so on—she was reminded of the forest fires that had burned out of control in California. Just as one pocket of flames was doused, ten others would spring up around it. And so it was for the CDC and WHO in their attempts to contain the uncontainable.

Savard shook her head, thinking of how twenty-five years earlier, in the days before HIV and bacteria resistant to all known antibiotics, some scientists had declared the war on infectious diseases over—a knockout victory for medical science. How wrong they were. Now microorganisms had the doctors against the ropes, not vice versa.

Gwen clicked on the headline concerning the new virus in western China. She had kept a close eye on the story ever since the scattered reports of farmers developing atypical respiratory infections had surfaced two weeks earlier. She was not surprised to read that the virus had reached a small city in northwest China, but she knew it meant trouble. Urban spread was the epidemiological equivalent of flashpoint.

She decided it was time to speak to someone closer to the forefront of the outbreak. A name danced around the back of her head, but refused to surface into consciousness. She reached for the old-fashioned Rolodex on her desktop. She had to flip through it twice before her brain and fingers connected. There it was: Dr. Noah Haldane, professor of infectious diseases at Georgetown and WHO emerging pathogens expert. She had met him only once, six months earlier, when they were both lecturing at a conference. Though his talk was funny and irreverent, she most recalled his chilling description of how ill prepared the planet was for the pandemic, which he guaranteed was on its way. She couldn't picture his face, but she remembered him as handsome. When they chatted afterward, he refused to accept any of the credit people ascribed to him for halting the SARS epidemic in the Far East.

If anyone at the WHO had an inside track on this latest outbreak, she thought it would be Haldane. A knock at the door stopped her just as she reached for the phone. "Come in," she called out.

Alex Clayton, the CIA's Deputy Director of Operations, strode in as assuredly as if Gwen had been expecting him all morning.

Savard hit a button on the keyboard to close the CDC Web site. The screensaver she had been meaning to change—a picture of Peter and her with a number still pinned on her chest, hugging at the finish line of the Washington Marathon—popped up. She rose from her desk. A stab of pain shot up from her ankle, but she suppressed her wince out of reflex. She had been conditioned to believe that as a woman in the upper echelons of the D.C. power structure, she was not allowed to show any hint of weakness or fallibility.

"Was I expecting you?" Gwen asked.

"Can't say," Clayton said with a wide flirtatious smile. "But we weren't scheduled to meet."

He wore a three-button, black suit with an olive green shirt, collar open, which highlighted his dark green eyes and Mediterranean complexion. With gelled hair, Armani suit, and perfect accessories, he struck Gwen as the consummate "metrosexual"—a straight, male urbanite with all the vanity and fashion sense of a stereotypical gay man.

Gwen knew Clayton had inherited his brooding good looks from his Greek father. When she had once asked him about his baseball-and-apple-pie surname, he explained that his immigrant father had anglicized their last name from the original Klatopolis in a failed attempt to better fit into the small Pennsylvanian town where he had grown up.

Gwen sat back down on her chair, thankful for the opportunity to take the weight off her ankle. "What's up, Alex?"

Clayton slid into the seat across from her desk. He unbuttoned his jacket and crossed a knee over his other leg. Once he made himself comfortable, he asked, "Got a minute?"

"No," she said with a laugh. "But what's up?"

"I've been thinking about what you said at the meeting last week."

"Oh?"

"About terrorists getting their hands on SARS."

"And?"

The smile left Clayton's lips. "It disturbs me."

"Good." Savard nodded. "It damn well should."

Clayton made a clicking sound with his tongue, before speaking. "Gwen, we've been picking up a lot of cellphone chatter lately."

"Terrorists?"

"We think so."

"Who?"

Clayton shrugged. "Not sure."

"That's not very helpful, Alex."

"Christ, Gwen, it's not like they get on the phone and say, 'Hello, terrorist X speaking,'" he snapped.

Savard leaned back in her chair, unperturbed. "Your job wouldn't be much of a challenge if they did."

Clayton chuckled. "Golf and dating are challenges enough. Who said I needed my job to be one?" His expression darkened. "You know, everyone expects us to be watching what goes on in every nook and cranny of the planet, but we can't. We're spies, Gwen, not fortune-tellers."

"You can't be everywhere at once, huh?"

"It's not so much that." He shook his head in disgust. "Today's enemies have become like the bugs you study under your microscope."

She cocked her head and frowned. "How so?"

"When I joined the CIA in the mid-eighties, there was a definable enemy. The Soviet bloc and a few other rogue states." He sighed, sounding to Gwen like one of those

CIA relics who truly missed the Cold War and its constant threat of nuclear annihilation. "Sure, they had operatives around the world up to what we considered no good. But at least they were linked, albeit obliquely, into a command structure. You could take down an entire operation by cracking one piece of the puzzle."

"Not now?" Gwen asked.

"Take Al Qaeda," he said. "Those fanatics multiply like bacteria into their own 'cells.' But colonies might be a better word, sticking with the micro analogy. Each colony functions entirely independently from the others. None of the traditional hierarchy of the KGB or any state-sponsored insurgency," he said with another melancholic sigh. "These colonies are totally self-sufficient with their own finances, operations, and leadership. You take one down, you still have nothing on the others. It's so damn frustrating. Like cutting off a head of the Hydra only to have two more spring up in its place."

Gwen wasn't used to such intensity from Clayton. Normally, he favored the cavalier, unflappable "superspy" routine salted with a trace of charming self-parody. She felt a rush of genuine empathy for Clayton, realizing that in spite of his pretense none of this was a game to him.

"Gwen, no one remembers our success in dismantling cells from New Jersey to Pakistan," Clayton sighed. "Everyone remembers the misses."

Gwen knew he was referring to 9/11, but she didn't comment. "What does the chatter have to do with the concerns I raised?" she asked.

"Nothing, maybe." Clayton shrugged. "But we overheard pieces of conversations concerning lab equipment and transport. At least, that's what we think they were talking about. It's hard to be sure."

Savard nodded. "Anything else?"

Clayton nodded. "Last week, we tracked a shipment of high-tech laboratory equipment—incubators, centrifuges, hoods, and other supplies—from Germany to Algeria. But our sources in Algeria can find no record of any hospital or lab ordering any of it. What's more, the stuff seems to have disappeared after arrival."

"Disappeared?" Gwen bit her lip. "Sounds like a lot of equipment. How would it just disappear?"

"Gwen, are you kidding me?" Clayton leaned back in his seat and laughed bitterly. "This is Africa we're talking about. With enough money and connections you could make Kenya disappear without a trace."

Savard stared at the video screen's picture of herself locked in a hug with her estranged husband. Without looking up she said, "What now?"

"We're focusing resources on Africa. We're even sending agents in to see what they can dig up." He adjusted the collar on his shirt. "We're surprisingly well connected in Algeria and northern Africa."

"But?"

"East Africa . . ." He held his hands up, as if to say that half of the continent was a write-off.

"We should tell the Secretary," Gwen said.

"Mine already knows," Clayton said, referring to the CIA Director. "What you want to tell the Homeland Security Secretary is up to you."

Gwen nodded distractedly.

"Do we take this to the weekly council meeting?" Clayton asked.

She shook her head. "Why? Not much to tell them now, is there?"

"Fine by me. The less I have to say to Moira and the rest of the happy-go-lucky gang at the FBI, the happier I am." He grinned as his placid self-confident demeanor resurfaced. "You know, I'm sure we could work this whole thing out over a plate of sushi and a couple of sakis."

Gwen smiled in spite of herself. "There's a high potential for all kinds of nasty bugs in uncooked fish."

Clayton rolled his eyes. "Right now, I get the feeling uncooked fish is the least of my worries."

"I suppose," she said. "But I've barely gotten used to the emptiness of my condo. Alex, I don't know if I'm ready for sushi and saki just yet."

Hopping to his feet, he slapped his forehead in mock embarrassment. "What am I thinking? I completely forgot about the minimum-six-months-before-having-Japanese-after-a-breakup law." He headed for the door. "The offer stands, though," he called over his shoulder without turning back.

After he was gone, Gwen sat and stared at her embracing image on the screen. What was the harm in going out for dinner with the handsome spy? she thought. She reached for her mouse and scrolled through the options until she chose a new screensaver: an image of a robin's nest in which baby birds were breaking free of their shells. Maybe a little heavy on the schmaltz, but what the hell, she thought. She needed it now. Barring a catastrophe befalling them during the rest of the week, she resolved that she would call Clayton and accept his offer.

She clicked back open the CDC web site. She read the rest of the CDC's failing report card on global infection control, but she couldn't concentrate. The similarities between the coverage of this new Chinese virus and the early days of SARS were uncanny. But last time, there were no laboratory supplies missing in Africa to compound her concerns.

CHAPTER

10

Sergeant Achmed Eleish of the Cairo Police sat in a housecoat on his living-room sofa reading the Sunday paper. His wife Samira and he had just returned from Fajr, the morning prayers, at the mosque. Their two adult daughters, both teachers, had gone "for a quick shop," which meant Eleish would not see them again before the evening. Sunny but not too hot outside, Eleish decided it was shaping up to be a perfect lazy Sunday.

Aside from the homeless and the ultrarich, the rest of Cairo's eighteen million residents lived in apartments. The Eleishes were no exception. Leaving a smaller one-bedroom apartment, they had moved into their modern nineteenth-floor, two-bedroom apartment in the heart of Cairo two years earlier when, with the help of his daughters' savings, Eleish scraped together a down payment. Their home was Achmed Eleish's pride and joy. His castle. He often told his wife and daughters that if Allah smiled upon him, He would let Eleish live in the apartment until the day he died.

Still dressed in her black dress from the prayer service, Samira Eleish stood across from her husband, ironing his shirts for the week ahead. "What's new in Cairo, Achmed?" she asked.

The detective looked up from the newspaper. Again, he was struck by her warm large eyes and aristocratic face, which had aged so well in the thirty-two years since they wed. Even her gray hair seemed to complement her mature beauty. And unlike her husband, Samira had maintained the same slim figure her entire adult life.

Eleish shrugged and flapped the paper in his hands. "Corruption. Cost overruns. Minor scandal. In short, absolutely nothing is new in Cairo."

"No news is the best news of all," Samira said as she hung a shirt and then reached for the next one in the pile.

"Hmmm." Eleish mumbled his agreement as he turned the page. The headline caught his eye immediately— "Publishing Mogul Re-defines Arab Newspapers." Below it, a picture of Hazzir Kabaal occupied a third of the page. Staring at Kabaal's smug smile and expensive Italian suit, Eleish felt his stomach knot. He wanted to flip the page and forget about Kabaal on his day off, but he couldn't peel his eyes from the article. It described how with his latest newspaper acquisition Kabaal had claimed a monopoly over the conservative print media in much of the Arab world. Suddenly Eleish's perfect day clouded over.

"Achmed?" Samira asked, recognizing the frown on her husband's face.

"Hazzir Kabaal," he said softly.

Samira shook her head slowly and sighed. "Let's not talk about him today."

Eleish held up the paper for his wife. "He's right here on page two," he said.

"What is he up to?" Samira asked calmly without taking her eyes off her ironing.

"He bought another newspaper." He flapped the paper in his hand. "Can you imagine, Miri? Soon, his will be the only opinion the man on the street reads. Then what?"

"People are not fools, Achmed." Samira stopped ironing. She fingered the pendant hanging from her necklace. "His kind may make the loudest noise, but he doesn't speak for the people."

"He will soon enough," Eleish grumbled.

Ever since he had been shot, Eleish harbored an interest in Kabaal that bordered on obsession. Eight years earlier, Eleish and other police officers had raided the home of a fundamentalist who was part of a plot to assassinate members of a visiting European Union delegation. Bursting through the apartment door, Eleish was blown back against the wall by a shotgun blast discharged from five feet in front of him. Only the Kevlar vest and his proximity to his would-be-killer—which prevented shrapnel from spraying into his head—saved his life. Two of his colleagues and all four of the terrorists were killed in the gunfight.

Several weeks later, when he could finally take a breath or a step without feeling like a chainsaw slashed at his chest, Eleish investigated. He discovered three of the four terrorists worked for newspapers owned by Kabaal. Eleish refused to accept it as coincidence. While he never connected Kabaal directly to the assassination plot, he discovered that Kabaal and his papers had links to several extreme Islamist elements, including Sheikh Hassan's Al-Futuh Mosque.

"Miri, he won't stop until he has shamed our religion in front of the whole world," Eleish sighed. "Or worse."

"I know, Achmed," Samira said patiently.

"There I go again, right?" Eleish chuckled with a flash of self-insight, but he couldn't help himself when it came to Kabaal. "He embodies the worst of these extremists and their so-called Muslim Brotherhood," he said.

Samira closed her eyes and nodded. Eleish knew she had heard the speech a hundred times before, but he had to get it off his chest.

"They are so few in number, but thanks to them people around the world associate the name of Islam with bombings and terror." He shook his clasped hands in front of him. "The Kabaals of the world are the worst of the lot! From the comfort and safety of their homes and palaces, they fan the flames of bitterness and violence among the poor and downtrodden. Then they send the brainwashed fools out to kill themselves along with all those innocent people." His voice grew quiet, and he looked down at the sofa. "They defame our Faith, Miri. Making Islam look to the rest of the world cruel and vindictive when it is anything but."

"It's just another right-wing newspaper," Samira said tenderly.

"One paper at a time. Soon he'll have all of them," Eleish murmured as he turned back to the article. Reading the last paragraph, a sentence caught his eye. "Listen to this, Miri," he said to his wife and waved his paper again. " 'Hazzir Kabaal was not available for comment as he has been out of Egypt on vacation for the past week.' "

Samira put her iron down. "So?"

"In eight years, I've never known Kabaal to take a vacation," Eleish said. "The man is a workaholic."

Samira eyed her husband for several seconds. "There's something else, isn't there, Achmed?"

"I make it my business to know whenever Kabaal leaves the country," he confessed sheepishly. "And I hadn't heard about him going anywhere."

Samira's lips broke into a smile that Eleish recognized as part admiration and part exasperation. "What do you intend to do, Achmed?"

Eleish shrugged. "Find out where he is."

She stared at him without comment.

Eleish folded the paper and put it down on the couch beside him. "Miri, I have been a detective my whole life. It's all I know. And it's the only thing I've ever been good at."

"Come, now." Samira's brown eyes twinkled. "You're a pretty good father, and not so bad a husband."

Eleish smiled, but when he spoke his tone was serious. "I have a feeling that Hazzir Kabaal is up to something. Something bad. I cannot tell you why, but you know my hunches are rarely wrong."

The smile left Samira's lips. She nodded. "Go find out where he is and what he's up to. But, Achmed . . ." Her voice trailed off.

"Yes?" Eleish said.

"Never forget what happened the first time you crossed his path. Our girls need their father. And I do not want to be a widow." Her face creased and her eyes bore into his. "Achmed Eleish, you be careful with this man."

HARGEYSA, SOMALIA

Though she had to rise in a few more hours, Khalila Jahal was no closer to sleep than she had been the rest of the night. Even more than her apprehension about her looming predawn viral inoculation, the continuous soft sobs of her neighbor kept sleep at bay for Jahal.

Unlike the men's section of the complex, which was an open dorm, curtains partitioned the women's side into rooms so small that the women had to sit on their beds to finish dressing. More than twenty women stayed at the complex. Khalila had been given the spot next to Sharifa Sha'rawi. In Cairo Jahal and Sha'rawi hardly spoke, but their friendship blossomed in the Somali wasteland. Khalila had naturally assumed the role of a protective big

sister to her emotionally fragile neighbor with the round
face and wild, black curly locks.

When Sharifa's weeping showed no sign of abating,
Khalila slipped out of her bed and peeled back the curtain
separating their rooms. She knelt down by her friend's
bed. "Sharifa?" she asked gently.

"Oh, Khalila, I am sorry." Sha'rawi sniffed, but then
broke into an even louder cry.

Khalila reached out and squeezed Sharifa's arm. "May
I lie with you?" she asked.

Sharifa nodded her assent, and Khalila climbed onto
the bed. Though neither woman was particularly large, the
wooden cot was so narrow that they had to lie on their
sides to both fit. Even snuggled against Sharifa's back,
Jahal could feel the rough edge of wood digging into her
buttock and shoulder. And she felt the dampness on her
cheek from where Sharifa's tears had wet the sheets.
"What is it?" Jahal asked.

"You are going, tomorrow," Sha'rawi sobbed.

"It is time."

"How come you are not more frightened?" Sha'rawi
asked.

"I am." Jahal rubbed the other woman's shoulder,
thankful for the human contact. "But what can I do? It is
what God has chosen for me."

"But it is men who have chosen this for you," Sha'rawi
said. Then she grabbed Jahal's hand on her shoulder. "I
didn't mean that!" she said fearfully. "You know, it's just
that sometimes—"

"I know, Sharifa." Jahal reassured Sha'rawi with a
squeeze of her shoulder. "Sometimes men are fools." She
paused, then added in a quieter voice, "And sometimes
they are hateful and very dangerous."

Sha'rawi giggled nervously.

"But not Abu Lahab," Jahal continued. "Sheikh Hassan

explained it to me. Abu Lahab is fighting the only way he can to preserve our faith."

"But you, Khalila." Sha'rawi sniffed again. "It is such a waste . . ."

"It is our duty—our honor—to serve God." She paused. "Zamil would agree. I know it."

Sha'rawi looked over her shoulder. Though Jahal couldn't see the other woman's face in the near darkness, she could feel and smell her warm, garlicky breath. "I should go in your place, Khalila," she said earnestly.

Khalila stroked Sharifa's cheek, feeling the slight pocks of old acne scars. "I want to do this," Khalila said.

"But, Khalila, you are so beautiful and intelligent," Sha'rawi said and her voice cracked. "I am the slow orphan girl that no man would marry. I have no husband or children to live for."

"Hush, Sharifa. I don't like to hear you talk this way." Jahal removed her hand from the girl's cheek. "Women do not need to live for men or children. You are very special. You serve God here." Then she spoke in a near whisper. "Besides, my husband is dead."

"Please, Khalila, tell me more about Zamil," Sha'rawi said.

Jahal shook her head slowly.

"Is it too painful?" Sha'rawi asked.

Jahal shrugged, but pain had nothing to do with it. Every waking moment she carried the pain of his loss like a knife in her side, but she had decided not to discuss the memories of their perfect life together with anyone else. She had learned that protecting the privacy of those memories helped maintain their lingering sense of intimacy.

Sha'rawi groped for Jahal's hand and squeezed it tight. "I had no right to ask—"

"Zamil never wanted to go to Afghanistan, but he felt duty bound," Jahal said calmly. "He was a scholar not a fighter." She had a vivid mental picture of her scrawny, beautiful husband packing up his heavy books to drag to a dark cave in the middle of a war. "The night he crossed the border from Pakistan into Afghanistan, I found out I was pregnant."

Only when Jahal heard Sha'rawi's sobs did she realize that tears had begun to run down her own cheeks. "Ten days later, I miscarried," Jahal said slowly. "Everyone wondered why I mourned so hard for a baby I had only carried for weeks, but I knew."

"Knew what?"

"It was a sign," Khalila said. "A week later I heard Zamil had been killed by an American bomb that destroyed his cave on the same day I lost my baby." Her voice went hoarse. "The very same day."

Sha'rawi squeezed her hand even tighter but said nothing.

"I accepted the Fate God had chosen for me," Jahal said, feeling the resolve cement inside her. "I vowed to make myself useful. To commit the way Zamil had. Then Sheikh Hassan introduced me to Abu Lahab. And now here I am beside you."

Sha'rawi sniffed several times. "But you will leave in the morning. And without you . . ."

"Listen to me, Sharifa." Jahal let go of her friend's hand and placed her hand on Sharifa's cheek again. "You will be fine without me. Abu Lahab will take care of you."

Sha'rawi swallowed. "I will miss you so much."

"As I will miss you." Jahal tapped the woman lightly on her cheek. "Sharifa, I want you to promise me something."

"What?"

"That you will stay away from the Major."

"Major Sabri? Why?"

"He is not like the rest of us." She paused. "He is no fool but . . ."

"But?"

"Remember what I said about some men?" Jahal asked.
Sha'rawi nodded. "That they are full of hate?"

"And very dangerous," Jahal said wistfully. "Just like
the Major."

CHAPTER

11

Like everything else he had seen from the Cultural Revolution era, the box of a boardroom struck Noah Haldane as austere. He decided that if the bank of windows lining the wall behind him were even half the size of the dour black-and-white portraits of the Party functionaries hanging on the other walls, the room might have come across as a little less oppressive.

Noah sat between Duncan McLeod and Milly Yuen at the large, rectangular board table. Helmut Streicher sat on the other side of the table beside the city's chief health officer, Yung Se Choy. A blueprint-sized, detailed map of Jiayuguan City covered the tabletop in front of them. In his late forties and skinny to the point of swimming in his navy-blue suit, Yung Choy had a mop of thick hair and a wispy mustache that failed to hide the scar of a repaired cleft lip. Dr. Kai Huang, the regional hospital's young director, sat on the far side of Choy and fidgeted distractedly with his pen. Both Choy and Huang spoke passable English, but Milly Yuen filled in as translator where necessary.

Streicher ran a finger over the map. "Here," he barked in his crisp Germanic accent. "All known cases of viral transmission have occurred among people living in these zones in red." He pointed to the north corner of the city, where several blocks had been circled in red. "And the blue lines represent the buffer zone," he said of the single blue rectangle that enclosed all the red zones plus a buffer of several city blocks.

"Fucking great, Streicher!" McLeod hollered. "No doubt all those potential Typhoid Marys knew better than to walk past the little red and blue lines."

Streicher adjusted the Lennon-style round eyeglasses, which highlighted his striking blue-gray eyes. "You understand, Dr. McLeod, about sectorizing outbreaks, no?" he asked with a hint of condescension. He circled the red zones with a finger. "There have been no confirmed cases outside of these. Correct, Mr. Choy?"

Choy nodded vigorously.

Streicher pointed at the blue line. "As of yesterday, the local authorities have quarantined this entire zone within the blue."

"Quarantine, of course," McLeod said. "I remember the wonderful quarantine in Toronto during SARS. Suspected cases were told to stay at home and wear masks, but some of them went to work anyway."

The health officer shook his head. "No one leaves," Choy said emphatically. "Army guards against it."

"Lord love a repressive dictatorship during an epidemic!" McLeod said. "Makes our job so much easier."

Streicher nodded as if McLeod were serious. "The quarantine should contain the spread within the city. The incubation period is estimated at three to five days. We will know in seventy-two to ninety-six hours whether there has been spread beyond the blue."

"When was the first case seen in Jiayuguan City?" Haldane asked.

"Five days ago," Choy squeaked in a high-pitched voice.

"And how many cases so far?"

Dr. Huang spoke to Yuen in Mandarin. "Seventy confirmed, forty-five suspected, and twenty-six dead," she translated for him.

"Five days and less than two hundred cases," Haldane thought aloud. "With the short incubation period, I would have expected greater spread by now. It's a safe bet that this virus does not exhibit airborne spread."

Even after the translation, Choy stared blankly at Haldane. With Yuen acting as the go-between, Haldane explained. "For all infections, there are three routes of potential spread. First, direct contact. HIV or Hepatitis B are examples of viruses requiring intimate contact. Second is droplet spread like with the common cold or flu. When an infected person sneezes or coughs, large mucous droplets carry the virus from person to person. However, these droplets are relatively big and fall to the ground quickly so you need close and immediate contact. The final and most feared route of spread is airborne. Smallpox and measles are viral examples. By coughing or sneezing, people aerosolize tiny particles. These particles can linger in the air for hours or spread remotely via ventilation systems and so on. It means that people can be infected without direct contact to a contagious person."

"*Ja*," agreed Streicher. "Airborne spread is an epidemiological catastrophe. But this ARCS looks only to have droplet spread."

Eyes wide, Choy asked in English, "This is very good?"

"Bloody marvelous," McLeod said. "As it stands, we might not die for weeks."

Haldane glanced sidelong at his colleague. "Not helping, Duncan."

Milly Yuen held up a hand tentatively. "I have something to report."

"Please, Milly . . ." Haldane held out his palm.

"I heard from the WHO Influenza Surveillance Lab in Hong Kong an hour ago," she said quietly. "They've isolated the virus in the serum samples."

Two hands on the table, McLeod pushed himself up out of his seat. "Don't keep us hanging, Milly!"

"As we assumed, this virus is closely related to influenza," Yuen said.

Haldane folded his arm across his chest. "But it's *not* influenza?"

Yuen shrugged so imperceptibly that her shoulders barely flickered. "It is a subtype, but it is not influenza A or B."

"What other kinds of influenza are there?" Streicher asked.

Kai Huang dropped the pen and looked up at the others. "The Spanish Flu," he said in English.

Haldane shook his head. "I wondered about that, too, but I don't think this is the Spanish Flu. At least, not the exact same virus that caused the 1918 pandemic."

"How can you be so sure?" Streicher asked.

"Because that pandemic swept the planet in four months in an age before commercial air travel," Haldane said. "One billion people were infected. Greater than fifty percent of the world's population at the time. If we were dealing with the same bug, the genie would already be out of the bottle. Clearly, ARCS is not as contagious."

"How do you know that the infection control measures haven't been better this time?" Streicher asked.

"Or maybe the last time, the Spanish Flu banged around some remote Chinese province for a few years before going global." McLeod pointed a bony finger at Haldane.

"Could be the same with ARCS? Like some Australian teenager, it might just be chomping at the bit to head out and party around the world."

Haldane shook his head slowly. "It's already been in this city for almost a week and they've seen fewer than two hundred cases. The Spanish Flu would have swept the city like wildfire by now." He tapped the table. "What's more, even in 1918 the mortality rate for the Spanish Flu was only two percent. Whereas ARCS is far deadlier. It's killing twenty-five percent of its young, healthy victims." He shook his head. "Twenty-five percent!"

"So ARCS is not the Spanish Flu?" Streicher asked.

"Could be closely related, though." Haldane shrugged.

McLeod nodded. "Maybe this is the Spanish Flu's long-lost meaner but antisocial sister."

"I think we can find out," Yuen said quietly.

"How so?" Haldane asked.

She looked down and shuffled the papers in front of her, needlessly. "The U.S. military pathology labs have saved tissue samples from the 1918 Spanish Flu victims. We have a partially sequenced genome for the virus. Now that we know ARCS is a member of the influenza family, we will be able to sequence this virus with DNA probes. Then we can compare the two."

"All good and bloody well, Milly," McLeod said with a sympathetic smile to her. "But sequencing the virus doesn't help the people who are dying of it today, or those who will acquire it tomorrow."

People around the table nodded.

Haldane snapped his fingers. He whirled to face the two Chinese health officials. "How are you controlling the spread in the countryside?"

Huang looked away. He picked up his pen and started twirling again.

With Yuen translating, Choy answered for them. "We have the same strict quarantines in place in all the towns and farms for two hundred miles around the city. There is no travel allowed into or out of any areas that have had an active case within the last ten days."

"But the livestock!" Haldane said.

Choy shrugged, confused.

"As with the Spanish Flu, ARCS is almost certainly a product of zoonosis, or species intermixing." Haldane leaned forward in his chair, tapped the table, and spoke so urgently that Yuen had difficulty keeping up with the translation. "The pig is the usual mixing vessel. Inside the porcine bloodstream, viruses from birds like chickens meet their human equivalent and mutate. We call it a 'massive reassortment of genetic code.' Since pigs are the usual intermediary, most of these mutated viruses are forms of swine flus."

"I see." Choy nodded. "But what does that mean in terms of our quarantine?"

"It means," Haldane said, "that you have to slaughter the livestock. Like they did last year in Vietnam and Korea for the Avian Influenza outbreaks."

"Just the pigs?"

Haldane shook his head. "No. Birds are the natural carriers of influenza. They develop the most profound viremia, or highest blood levels, without becoming sick. The chickens—in fact, all the livestock—must be sacrificed."

Choy glared at Haldane and his face crumpled in dire concern. Yuen translated Choy's frantic, squeaky response. "But farming is one of the province's essential industries. Gansu's economy would be devastated if we slaughtered all the livestock."

"And the alternative?" Haldane held his hands out in front of him. "Imagine what would happen to the economy if ARCS broke free of here and stormed across China and beyond, killing one in four of the healthy people who stood in its path?"

Haldane glanced around the table. The others, even

Choy, nodded in agreement, but Dr. Kai Huang refused to meet his gaze. Instead, he stared at the table and frantically twirled the pen in his hand. Haldane wondered why the youthful hospital director looked more fearful than anyone else at the table.

Haldane grappled with the door to his small hotel room. Once opened, he took two strides and lunged for the ringing phone. "Hello?" he said, hearing his breathless anticipation echo back in his ear.

"Noah?"

He felt a pang of disappointment, recognizing that it wasn't his wife's voice. "Oh, Karen, hi," he said.

"Well, hello to you too, stranger," said his secretary, Karen Jackson.

"What's going on, Karen?"

"Tell me everything," she said excitedly. "How's China? What's the Great Wall like?"

"I don't have a clue," Haldane said irritably. "I'm not over here on the AAA's Great Chinese Bus Tour. We're kind of working against the clock."

"Excuse me," Jackson murmured. "I forgot how busy saving the world must keep you."

Haldane chuckled. "Sorry, Karen, I haven't caught up from my jet lag yet. But in all honesty, all I've seen so far is the hotel, the hospital, and city hall. None of which are anything to write home about."

"No, it was a boneheaded question." She laughed. "Of course, you're too busy for all that." Then she asked in a hushed voice: "What is it like over there, Noah? Scary?"

"Yeah. A little."

"You keeping safe?" Jackson demanded with her usual maternal protectiveness.

"It's not me I'm worried about," he said, sitting down on the bed and resting his back against the headboard. "This virus is some piece of work."

"That's what they say," Jackson said.

"Who's they?" Haldane asked.

"The news folk," she said.

He hit the bed with a fist. "Damn it. This has made the news?"

"Small print, back page stuff so far," she said. "I came across a small article in the *Post*. Wouldn't have even seen it if I wasn't looking for the crossword."

"That's better, I guess," he said. "Is that what you called to tell me?"

"No," she said. "Someone is looking for you. She said it was important."

"Who?"

"Dr. Gwen Savard."

"Why is that name so familiar?"

"She sounds like a bigwig," Jackson said. "Her title's a mouthful, anyway. Director of Counter-Bioterrorism for the Department of Homeland Security."

"Sure. I met her at a conference." He remembered her fiery intensity as much as her California-girl good looks. "What does she want?"

"She wouldn't tell little old me," Jackson said. "But she left about forty numbers for you to call her at."

Haldane patted around the nightstand until he found a pen and a pad. "Give me the first two," he said.

After she recited the numbers, she asked, "When are you coming home?"

"Soon as I can, Karen."

"Good," Jackson said. "I know that little girl of yours is missing her daddy."

Not as much as her dad is missing her, Haldane thought as he hung up. With the phone still in his hand, he dialed the operator.

On the second ring, someone answered. "Hello, Haldane residence."

He experienced another rush of disappointment as he

realized he was talking to his mother-in-law, Shirley Dolman, not his wife. "Hi, Shirley, it's Noah."

"Oh, my goodness, I'm talking to China," Dolman said as if the entire country had called her. "How are you, Noah?"

"Fine," he said. "How is everything back home?"

"Things are well," Dolman said in her syrupy tone. "Chloe is asleep. And I'm afraid Anna is out with a friend."

"With a friend," Haldane repeated. He checked his watch, and recalculated. It was after 10:00 P.M. in Maryland. "Did she say whom?" he asked.

"No, matter of fact she didn't," Dolman said. "But she said she wouldn't be home until after midnight. They were going to a late movie, you see."

"Oh."

"She left her cell phone on in case of something with Chloe. I'm sure you can reach her on that, Noah."

"Great, thanks, Shirley. You take care."

Haldane dropped the phone back on the cradle. He had no intention of trying his wife's cell. Why interrupt her movie? he thought. Not that he believed she was at the theater, but movie or not, Haldane couldn't shake his absolute conviction that Anna was with *her*.

It was near dusk by the time the officials arranged for a car to take Haldane and McLeod out to the site of quarantine in the northeast section of Jiayuguan City.

Staring out the window of the car, images of Tiananmen Square from the student uprising in 1989 popped to Haldane's mind. The sight turned his stomach. He had once dabbled in student activism during his undergrad days. While the students at Tiananmen had to face firing squads or the caterpillar tracks of tanks rolling toward them, all Haldane got out of his activism was a security escort back to his dorm.

There were no tanks in Jiayuguan, but trucks and military vehicles were plentiful. Masked soldiers patrolled the streets, rifles slung prominently over their shoulders. Several muscular German shepherds strained at leashes. A barbed-wire fence snaked around the far side of the street, isolating an entire section of the city.

"These lads don't mess around when it comes to quarantining," McLeod said, his wide eyes surveying the scene outside the window.

"What the hell are they doing?" Haldane said.

McLeod nodded. "They're doing it right, Noah."

Haldane frowned at his colleague. "You don't honestly believe that?"

"How else do you stop it from escalating?" McLeod pointed out the window, as if identifying individual viral particles standing behind the barbed wire.

"You set up a real quarantine with reasonable checks and balances," Haldane said. "You don't create a concentration camp for victims!"

Their driver waved a hand and pointed ahead as the car approached a break in the barbed wire. "See, the people come in and out through there."

With a makeshift hut, a swing gate, and numerous masked guards, it resembled a sci-fi version of one of the old Cold War checkpoints between East and West Berlin. Their car pulled up across from the checkpoint. Before the driver had switched off his engine, Haldane and McLeod hopped out of the car and headed for the action.

With back doors wide open, two empty ambulances had pulled up in front of the gate. Among the official personnel milling about, Haldane recognized the chief health officer, Yung Se Choy. His uniform resembled something the police or fire brass back home wore to formal occasions. It changed Choy's appearance, filling him out and making him look more important than the nervous bureaucrat he had earlier seemed. But the tousled mop of hair and barely concealed cleft lip scar were unmistakable.

Haldane caught up with Choy in front of the gate. "Hello, Dr. Haldane," Choy said with a slight bow.

"Mr. Choy, what is all this?" Haldane indicated the barbed wire and guards.

McLeod and their driver joined the two of them at the gate. The driver began to translate Haldane's question, but Choy answered in English before he could finish. "A quarantine." Choy shrugged, appearing amazed that it wasn't self-evident.

"This is not a quarantine." Haldane shook his head angrily. "This is a siege."

The setting and uniform had influenced Choy's attitude, too. Though he spoke through the translator in Chinese, his high-pitched voice was more authoritative and certain. "We are doing what your own WHO team recommended. What is necessary. We are controlling the spread of this virus. The people inside"—he pointed beyond the barbed wire— "are being looked after. We are sending food and supplies. And our doctors and nurses are monitoring them. If they require medical attention, we transport them to hospital."

As Choy spoke, two ambulance attendants in HAZMAT suits appeared at the gate. Once the arm of the gate rose, they pushed their stretcher unhurriedly toward him. The attendants moved without any urgency. As soon as they passed by, Haldane understood why. The patient on the stretcher was wrapped in a black body bag.

Haldane nodded his chin at the corpse on the stretcher. "This is what you mean by looking after the people?"

Unfazed, Choy answered through the translator. "This woman was found dead in her apartment. Apparently, she refused the neighbors' help. She was too scared to go out even after she became sick."

"I wonder how many others are going to be scared to death in there," Haldane grunted.

Choy held up his hands. "What is the alternative, Dr. Haldane?" he asked through the translator. "Would you rather we allow this virus to escape from here and sweep across China and beyond, killing one in four who stand in its path?"

CHAPTER

12

From her toenails to the roots of her hair, every inch of Khalila Jahal throbbed. She didn't know it was possible to ache so badly. She tried to move, but her limbs seemed to pay no heed to the will of her brain. They were deadwood.

Her sheets were soaked with sweat, but she had never felt colder in her life. Her body shivered uncontrollably under the wet sheets. The cough that had started as a tickle in her throat last night now racked her body with predictable waves of spasms. With each paroxysm, it felt as if a pillow had been stuffed down her throat.

The light streaming in between the vertical blades of the blinds told her she had overslept, though she wasn't clear whether what she experienced overnight was sleep or a coma. She tried to move again, managing to roll onto her side, exhausted from the effort.

Please God, give me the strength, she prayed.

She cursed herself for not heading out last night, when

her arms and legs still worked. Dr. Aziz had instructed her to wait until the fever peaked. As of yesterday evening, her temperature hadn't broken through the 102 degree Fahrenheit barrier, hovering instead in the 101 range. Still, she knew she was ill enough to venture out, but she had chosen to wait. She risked the entire mission. She could have died overnight. Then where would they have been?

She no longer had the luxury of time to continue the moral wrestling match with herself that had seen her vacillate through the previous evening. It was not her place to judge, but to act. Still, the idea of releasing this thing that consumed her body—to the point where it felt as if she were being boiled from the inside out—gnawed at her as much as the pain did. How could this be God's way? she wondered as she struggled to lift her legs off the bed.

The shivers subsided and she knew from the sudden suffocating heat that her temperature had peaked. Her husband's bearded face floated in front of her. She was happy for the hallucination. She missed Zamil desperately.

They had played together as young children in their village, nestled in the shadows of the great pyramids on the Giza plateau. By the age of eleven, boys and girls were forbidden from mixing, but Khalila refused to accept the decree. And she convinced Zamil to risk beating or worse to explore with her the Nile riverbed and the desert beyond. Knowing better than to act upon the hormones that raced inside them, they maintained a platonic but clandestine relationship throughout those teen years, while the sparks between them built steadily into a white-hot flame.

When they were both seventeen their fathers, ignorant of the pair's preexisting relationship, decided they should wed. Khalila and Zamil were overjoyed. Khalila considered every moment of their time together blissful, even the year away from their friends and families when Zamil studied at the mosque in Paris. Zamil shared with Khalila his studies in the strict Wahhabi sect of Islam. In the privacy of their cramped bedroom under his parents' roof, he tolerated, even encouraged, her thoughtful skepticism. With tender eloquence, Zamil won her mind and soul over. She grew into as devout a believer as he was.

Then came 9/11 followed by the American offensive in Afghanistan. When the call came to join the Taliban brethren in their defense, Khalila begged Zamil not to go. She knew what awaited her peaceful scholarly husband. Though he pretended otherwise, he knew it too, but he refused to shirk what he viewed as his duty.

Her heart ripped in two by her husband's death in an Afghani cave and her nearly simultaneous miscarriage, Khalila accepted the path God had chosen for her. She would never bear Zamil's or anyone else's children, but she pledged to make herself useful to Him. She dedicated her life to Zamil's cause. And she sought out the guidance of one of his teachers, Sheikh Hassan. Through the Sheikh, she met Hazzir Kabaal and his people.

During all the training and planning that followed, she never once questioned the mission. Not until she grew feverish to the point of delusional in her dank London hotel room did the doubts of whether the means justified the end creep into her conscience.

Zamil's hovering face vanished. Without her husband around to explain it, everything seemed unclear. The room darkened. She fell back to sleep.

Six hours later, she awoke trembling with vicious shivers. The fever was spiking again. She felt as if a heavy rock had been lowered onto her chest. She had to breathe twice as fast to avoid suffocating. The coughing spells grew longer and more frequent. But at least her arms and legs responded to her commands. She looked at the clock, which read 4:28 P.M. Time was running out.

Without allowing herself a chance to reconsider, she dragged herself out of bed. As per the plan, she didn't shower, but instead changed into the provocative Western clothing that she had debuted for Kabaal and his henchman in the Somali desert. She staggered to the mirror. Her tawny complexion had whitened, and what was once alluring now came across as sickly. With a shaky hand, she applied extra blush and lipstick in an attempt to mask the pallor.

She forced down two glasses of bottled water followed by two glasses of orange juice, convinced she might vomit with each sip, but knowing she needed the fluid and sugar to give her enough strength to make the trip. She didn't vomit, but a coughing fit overcame her. She kneeled over the toilet and gasped for air, until she coughed up a wad of bloody sputum. Finally she caught her breath and pulled herself to her feet.

She was relieved to see a row of taxicabs waiting in front of the hotel. She hobbled over to the first one, mumbled her destination to the driver, and collapsed across the backseat.

The driver didn't say a word to her, but she caught his concerned glances in the rearview mirror. By sheer will, she propped herself upright, scared that otherwise he might drop her off at a hospital. She forced her lips into what she hoped was a flirtatious smile for the sweaty, smelly cabdriver as she breathed heavily but quietly through her nose.

The taxi pulled up in front of the lobby of the Park Tower Plaza. A recently constructed five-star hotel, the Park Tower Plaza was a favorite among affluent businessmen, especially Americans.

Jahal paid the driver with a twenty-pound note. Clutching the door with two hands, she pulled herself out of the car. She had to pause for another coughing fit to pass. A tall, heavyset man in a cowboy hat, waiting for her cab, leaned forward and offered his arm, but she refused him with a shake of her head. She caught her breath and headed for the entrance.

Inside the hotel, her staggering gait drew a few glances from the people in the crowded lobby. She smiled and waved away anyone who offered his or her assistance.

According to the original plan, Jahal was supposed to have been at the hotel before 8:00 A.M., waiting for the morning exodus. But inadvertently her timing had worked out even better. At 5:00 P.M. on the nose, the bankers, lawyers, and other businesspeople were returning to their rooms from meetings and conferences all over London.

Standing amid a group of American businessmen, she swayed on her feet waiting for the elevator with them. She let the throng of people carry her into the spacious elevator. Unsteadily, she elbowed her way to the buttons and pressed the top floor. As instructed, she ran her germ-filled hands along the surfaces of the buttons and surrounding walls.

When a wave of coughs began, she covered her mouth but deliberately left a hole between her thumb and index finger, which allowed the now-bloody mucus to spray free into the air and onto the men surrounding her. Most of the men paid little attention to her, but a few of the ones nearest her stepped backward in an attempt to put as much distance between them and her coughs.

Khalila rode the elevator to the top floor and disembarked with the few people remaining on the ride. As they headed for their rooms, she pressed the "down" call button and waited. She felt so weak. She had to rest against the closed elevator doors to stop from collapsing. When the doors opened, she staggered back into the empty elevator. She smeared her hands over all the buttons. She descended with the elevator, as more unsuspecting people boarded on their way down to dinners, shows, sightseeing, and for a few of them, a relatively imminent death.

She repeated the pattern, riding the elevator up and down with groups of hotel guests, growing weaker with each trip. On her fourth trip back up, the door opened on the second floor. A striking young woman stepped into the elevator with her two small girls. The pretty sisters wore matching pink bathrobes. Their hair was wet, and each one held a pool towel. They were close in age; the older couldn't have been more than six.

Jahal watched in horror as the mother moved her two girls toward her and the elevator control panel. "I promised they could press the buttons," the mother explained to Khalila with a warm smile.

The room spun. Jahal felt another coughing spasm building. She turned her head to the wall and covered her mouth as she hacked, desperate to keep the bloody virus-soaked sputum from the two little girls.

Jahal backed away from the mother and girls, making her way to the far side of elevator. She wanted to scream at them to leave the contaminated buttons alone, but she knew better. Tears welling in her eyes, Jahal watched as both girls took turns pressing the same button for their floor. And when the youngest daughter reached for the alarm button, her mother's hand shot out and brushed against the steel panel, pulling her daughter's hand away. The mother leaned forward and spoke in a hushed tone to the little girl. Scolded, the little girl's lip began to quiver. And then, for comfort, she stuck the same thumb that had just touched the buttons into her mouth.

CHAPTER

13

Sergeant Achmed Eleish patted the pockets of his jacket, desperate for a smoke. After an anxious moment, he remembered tossing the pack in the bottom drawer of his desk—his halfhearted stab at giving up smoking. Ever since the long night he'd spent in hospital with crushing chest pain, later diagnosed as angina, the detective had been under attack from all sides. Samira, his two daughters, his doctor, and even the mosque's imam had been haranguing him to quit. While the others were concerned with Eleish's health, the imam focused on what he perceived as a breach of Islamic law—according to Mohammed it was a sin to deliberately harm your health or to waste money.

Eleish had to admit they were right. At age fifty, he already carried fifty pounds too many on his tall frame along with his family's propensity for coronary artery disease. But as a dedicated family man, policeman, and otherwise good Muslim, Eleish believed he had the right to one vice, even if it meant smoking himself into a premature grave. So he rummaged through the drawer until he found the pack. He slid a cigarette out and tucked the pack back into the pocket of his rumpled gray suit jacket, knowing that he would need another soon.

He lit the smoke and savored two long puffs before turning his attention to the pile of "open case" files in front of him. As he was reaching for the top file—the tragic, but familiar story of an unsolved rape and murder of a fourteen-year-old prostitute in the slums of Cairo—his phone rang.

"Eleish," he said into the receiver. It was an unusual manner of salutation for a Cairo Police officer, but he had borrowed the idiom years earlier from one of his favorite detective novels, and it had stuck.

"Sergeant, it's me," Bishr Gamal said in a hushed tone.

Eleish could hear traffic noises in the background of the public pay phone, from where Gamal usually called. He could picture the little informer whispering nervously into the phone while constantly checking over his shoulder. He took another drag from his cigarette, then asked, "What is it, Bishr?"

"I am getting back to you about the mosque," Gamal said, referring to the Al-Futuh Mosque. A well-known hotbed of Islamic fundamentalism, the mosque's charismatic cleric, Sheikh Hassan, had enough political cunning and popular support to ward off the local authorities' attempts to rein him in.

"And?" Eleish asked.

"Very interesting things, Sergeant."

"Bishr, I don't have time for mind games," Eleish said, though secretly he enjoyed the drama that Gamal always infused into their conversations.

"But, Sergeant, this is worth more than our usual arrangement," Gamal said.

"Gamal, you always say that! And more often than not, your tips aren't worth anything." Eleish paid Gamal out of his own pocket on a tip-by-tip basis. "But tell me what you know," he sighed. "If it's useful, I'll pay you double."

"Triple," Gamal said.

"Double and a half." Eleish smiled to himself. "Not a piastre more!" He could imagine himself in a raincoat and fedora, speaking the line Bogey style. He suppressed a laugh.

"Okay, Sergeant, okay," he said. "Your man disappeared."

Eleish's smile vanished. He dropped his cigarette into the ashtray. "What do you mean he disappeared?"

"He usually comes for prayer twice a day, but no one has seen him in over eight days," Gamal said. "I asked others at the mosque. No one knows where he's gone."

"Hmmm," Eleish grunted. "Okay, Bishr, what else?"

"He's not the only one missing," Gamal whispered, as if spies surrounded his phone booth.

"Who else?" Eleish asked impatiently.

"A number of other regulars, men and women, have been gone for the same time," Gamal said.

"And you've heard nothing about their whereabouts?"

"No," Gamal said. "I've been going to prayers regularly. I did overhear two men discussing a 'desert base,' but I couldn't make out the rest of their conversation. And it's not safe for me to be asking too many questions."

"Okay," Eleish said, reaching for his cigarette. "Good work, Bishr. I will pay you triple for this. But I want you to stick close by the mosque. Report back to me if you hear anything new."

"I will, Sergeant Eleish, I will," Gamal said in a solemn, hushed voice.

Eleish hung up the phone. Distractedly, he reached into his desk drawer looking for the snack that his wife always packed for him. Then he realized that it was the middle of

Ramadan. Like every day during the Muslim holy month, he had to fast until sunset, when he would say the evening prayers, or Taraweeh, with his family at their mosque. He was supposed to have forsaken smoking during Ramadan's daylight hours, as well, but he had long decided he couldn't manage both and opted for what he considered the lesser sin.

His stomach rumbling, he reached for the file that he kept separate from the open cases. On the flap, "Hazzir Al Kabaal" was written in pencil. He flipped it open and scanned his own scrawled handwriting from the past eight years.

Gamal's information fit with what Eleish discovered earlier in the morning. When he checked with Kabaal's newspapers (under the pretense of buying substantial advertising space) no one had seen or heard from the publishing magnate in over a week. "On vacation," he was told. Eleish realized that it still wasn't a crime in Egypt to take a vacation, but he didn't believe for a moment that Kabaal was lounging on a beach. Though he'd only met the man twice, after years of studying him Eleish knew Kabaal inside and out. He was a creature of habit. And vacations—at least ones where he left his mosque during Ramadan and dropped out of contact with the newspapers that he oversaw with a mother's devotion—were not Kabaal's style.

Achmed Eleish stamped out the butt in the ashtray and reached for another cigarette through the smoke wafting in front of him. He had no proof of any wrongdoing. When it came to Kabaal, proof was something he always lacked. And Eleish believed this recurring issue damaged his coronary arteries as much as the cigarettes.

Compounding his frustration, Eleish had so little time to dedicate to his pursuit of Kabaal. Rarely had Eleish ever fallen so far behind in his caseload of unsolved murders and other crimes. And like the rest of the police force, he was under constant pressure from above to intensify the crackdown on Egypt's homosexuals. He found it an insulting and laughable waste of time to harass Cairo's underground, but thriving gay community.

Eleish closed the file on Kabaal. He tapped his nicotine-stained fingertips on the back of the manila folder as he weighed his options. True, he had more pressing official matters than locating a missing mogul who was not known to have broken any laws, but Eleish felt a sense of criticalness that he could not readily explain. A voracious reader of detective novels, Eleish had long believed in the "hunch". His hunches had solved many cases over his twenty-five-year career. One of those same hunches told him that finding Kabaal, and soon, was an issue of great urgency.

Whatever Kabaal was up to, Eleish suspected it would only serve to further shame his beloved Islamic faith. And he intended to prevent that from happening at any cost.

Park Tower Plaza Hotel, London, England

Malcolm Ezra Fletcher III—Fletch to any of the boys back in Arkansas—couldn't shake his nagging cough. The hulking, fifty-five-year-old oil company executive was damned if a little head cold was going to ruin his first trip to London. Just my luck, Fletch thought, my first day clear of interminable meetings and I wake up with a fever and cough.

The cough reminded him of the young woman he'd seen getting out of his taxi in front of the hotel. He remembered that the pretty little thing had been hacking up a lung, too. Maybe that was where he picked up his cold? Wherever it came from, it was a doozy!

Still, lying around feeling sorry for himself was never Fletch's style. He hadn't missed a day of work in thirty-two years due to illness, and he wasn't about to miss his only chance to sightsee because of it either. He pushed himself out of bed and headed for the landmarks.

At the Tower of London he signed up for a tour. Climbing the winding staircase inside one of the Tower's turrets, he empathized with the medieval prisoners the tour guide mattered on about. Even though Fletch was a history buff, especially of the dungeons and dragons variety, he was too winded to concentrate on the guide's words. And with each step, Fletch felt as if his legs and arms were in the same shackles the prisoners once wore.

Exhausted and short of breath, Fletch had to drop out of the tour halfway through. He stumbled his way to the exit. Fulfilling a promise, he stopped at the gift shop to load up on keepsakes—toy swords and replica crown jewels—for his two little grandsons. Though made of plastic they felt like lead as Fletch dragged the bag toward the exit.

After staggering out of the taxi, he had to stop five or six times on the short walk to the elevator and then again on the way to his room. He felt so short of breath that he wondered if he was having a heart attack, but he knew that wouldn't explain his spiking fever.

Ten minutes passed and Fletch still sat huffing and puffing on the queen-sized bed. He reached for the bedside phone, thinking of calling 9-1-1, not even certain if that was the right number in England. But in spite of how horrible he felt, he opted to stick with his mother's tried-and-true remedy: brandy and sleep.

After swallowing a little bottle of Courvoisier from the minibar, he crawled under the covers, convinced that a good nap would set him right.

CHAPTER

14

They had played phone tag for the last four days. Sitting back on the double bed and listening to the phone ring a fourth time, he resigned himself to another day without hearing his daughter's voice. Then he heard a click. "Hello?" Anna said.

"Hi," Haldane said. There was a pause, which Noah didn't know whether to attribute to phone delay or to Anna.

"How are you?" she asked stiffly.

"Fine," Haldane said. "How about Chloe and you?"

"Chloe's much better. The fever is gone. She's back to her old self." Anna paused. "She misses her daddy, though."

Haldane waited, but Anna didn't mention whether or not she missed him, too. "Looks like things are stabilizing here in China," he said. "I hope to be coming home in the next couple of days."

There was another brief silence. Long enough for Haldane to realize that it had nothing to do with the phone connection. "That's great, Noah," she said, but her words rang obligatory.

"Yeah," Haldane said distantly. "Can I speak to Chloe?"

"Sure."

He tapped the receiver against his ear while he waited for his daughter. Finally, he heard breathing on the line.

"Chloe?" He felt butterflies. "Is that you?"

"Hi, Daddy."

"Chlo, it's so good to hear your voice."

"Where are you, Daddy?"

"I'm in China, honey."

"At a tea party?" she asked excitedly.

It took Haldane a moment to make the connection. Then he laughed, remembering Chloe's miniature china tea set at home. "No, Chlo. Not that china. I'm in the country China. Remember? The place where we tried to dig to last summer."

"Daddy, did you dig a big hole?" she asked him sternly.

"No, I flew in a plane, honey."

"Daddy?"

Haldane pictured his daughter cradling the relatively oversized phone against her ear. His heart ached. "Yes, Chloe?"

"It's my birthday party tomorrow."

Her birthday was ten days away, but in Chloe's vocabulary "tomorrow" meant anytime in the future. "Very soon, sweetie," Haldane said.

"Will you bring balloons?"

The previous year, Haldane bought a huge bouquet of balloons for her party, and Chloe had forsaken all her other gifts to play with the balloons until the helium drained and they lay as deflated sacks on her bedroom floor. "I promise you'll have balloons," he said. "More balloons than clouds in the sky."

She giggled with glee. "And cake?"

"And cake," he said.

"Bye, Daddy." Then Haldane heard Chloe yell to her mom, "Daddy says I am going to get balloons and cake for my birthday!"

"I love you, Chlo," Haldane said, but from the sound of the phone hitting the table, he knew Chloe was already gone.

After a moment, Anna picked up the phone. "Noah?"

"Where did Chloe go?" Haldane asked.

"The playroom," she said. "Looks like she's gone to bake you another cake."

"Hope not." Haldane forced a laugh. "Those imaginary cakes are murder on my hips and thighs."

Anna cleared her throat. "Noah, listen, we should talk."

"Not now, Anna," Haldane cut her off. "I have to get to an evening meeting. Like I said earlier, I am going to be home soon. We can talk then."

"Okay . . . good," Anna said.

"Bye, Anna," he said, hanging up the phone without waiting for her reply.

After dropping the receiver into the cradle, he sat on the bed and massaged his temples. He had lied to Anna about the meeting—there were no more that evening—but he was not prepared to discuss separation or whatever else she had in mind over the phone.

How did we screw it up? he wondered. He increased the pressure of his thumbs against his scalp even after it began to hurt, because he knew where most of the blame lay.

Noah would never forget the day they met two days before his thirtieth birthday at a house party, to which both of them had been reluctantly dragged by friends. They ended up spending his entire birthday and as many subsequent days as their schedules allowed together in bed. Haldane had just completed his infectious diseases' residency while, at twenty-five, Anna had just begun her master's in languages, in Italian. They wed a year later. For the next six years, they stayed the best of friends, sharing mutual ambitions and an insatiable passion for one another. After Chloe's birth, their home life grew more idyllic. As with most couples, the sex life diminished in those sleep-deprived breast-feeding days, but their intimacy heightened. In Chloe, they shared something even more important than their deep romance.

When Chloe was only two, Haldane woke up one morning in a black cloud. At first, he didn't know what had hit him. He attributed his burnout to the constant fatigue and pressures of juggling his clinical and academic commitments, his WHO obligations, and his devotion to his daughter. Thinking it would soon pass, he took a few weeks off work, but the rest didn't help.

Determined not to let his funk affect his relationship with his daughter, he dedicated even more time to Chloe. He attended as many classes with her as possible. He took her to almost every playground in the city. But Noah found it impossible to try to fill the role of perfect father, doctor, and husband. Something had to give. And Anna wound up bearing the brunt. Not that he wasn't around as much or more than before, but their time together lacked the previous closeness. He had grown uncharacteristically irritable. He shared less of his work life. He stopped taking her out on regular dates. And he made so little effort in the bedroom that their once active and imaginative sex life dried up almost completely.

For eight months, Anna stomached his detachment in silence. One day, she sat Haldane down in their living room. With arms folded across her chest and tears welling in her large brown eyes, she pointed out that he had stopped being a husband and had become merely a co-parent. She told him that she could not and would not continue to live like that.

It was the wakeup call Haldane needed. Though aware

that he had withdrawn from their marriage, he never realized the extent it had reached or how badly he had hurt his wife. The threat to his family hit him like a bucket of ice water. He resolved to right things. And while there were no easy fixes, he put energy into improving their relationship. Over the ensuing months, slowly but surely Anna and Noah reclaimed some lost ground. Then SARS hit, and Haldane was summoned to China to help deal with the crisis.

He had only been home for a few months when Avian Influenza, or Bird Flu, surfaced in the Far East, and he was sent back to help investigate.

At some point during his long absences, Anna fell in love with Julie.

Papers spread out over the bed and his notebook computer still on his lap, Haldane drifted off without intending to. The ringing phone woke him with a start. Sitting up, he knocked his laptop onto the mattress beside him.

He grabbed for the phone, hoping to hear from a more conciliatory Anna. "Hi," he breathed.

"Dr. Haldane?" the female voice said.

"Yes . . ." He cleared his throat and tasted the staleness in his mouth. "Who is this?"

"Gwen Savard, Department of Homeland Security."

Haldane positioned the computer on the nightstand. "Sure. I remember. We met at that conference on the end of the world."

Savard laughed. "You were the only one claiming the end of the world was near."

"Isn't it?" Haldane wet his dry lips.

"I've been trying to find that out from you, but you're a hard man to track down."

"One of the drawbacks of being in remote China, I guess . . . or maybe it's an advantage." Then he added, "Nothing personal, Dr. Savard."

"Gwen," she said. "None taken. I need to be unreachable for a month just to begin to catch up. Do you have a few minutes now?"

He looked at the clock, which read 10:18 P.M. He had the rest of the night. "What's on your mind, Gwen?"

"The Gansu Flu," she said.

He grimaced at the receiver. "Which genius came up with that name?"

"Some reporter," she said. "It's better than their other choice, the 'Killer Flu.' I don't know if you've noticed, but this virus is getting a lot of press coverage in the wake of SARS and the Bird Flu."

"Luckily, I'm also sheltered from most of the media, but I've seen some stories on the Internet," he said. "We call it Acute Respiratory Collapse Syndrome, or ARCS, because the syndrome was identified before the virus."

"What's it like, Noah?"

Haldane sighed, considering the question. "It's bad, Gwen."

"Worse than SARS?"

"Yes and no."

"Meaning?" She spoke with such confident authority that Haldane was grateful to share the privileged information with her, as if unloading a secret he didn't want to bear alone.

"The clinical syndrome is worse than SARS," he said. "Infected patients develop a sudden severe pneumonia often leading to multi-organ failure and death in a couple of days. Sometimes faster. And it's an ugly death, too. Not all that different from the philoviruses like Ebola, except without as much hemorrhaging. The mortality rate of ARCS is at least four or five times that of SARS."

She didn't reply for a moment. Haldane thought he heard the sound of her teeth tapping. "So how is it better than SARS?" she asked, her voice monotone.

"It's so damn fast. The incubation period is only a few

days, maximum five. And once sick, the patients either die or recover fully in under a week."

Another pause, more tapping. "That doesn't sound so much better."

"From an epidemiological point of view, it's a big advantage," he said. "It makes for a much shorter quarantine period than with SARS. Five days versus twelve. And we don't have to worry about latent spread. Unless of course the virus mutates again."

"I suppose," Savard said, sounding unconvinced.

"But the biggest advantage is this bug's relatively low contagiousness," Haldane said. "Unlike SARS we've seen minimal spread to health-care workers. And if this were a common influenza strain, it would have escaped Gansu by now. We would never have been able to contain it."

"You have contained it?" she asked pointedly.

He didn't answer right away. "It seems to be contained in Jiayuguan City," he said, hedging. "There have not been any new case reports in over forty-eight hours. It's too early to tell about the more rural regions."

"That's great news, Noah."

"Maybe for you," Haldane said. "You haven't seen what it's like here."

"So tell me."

"The government set up a quarantine that looks more like a ghetto. They fenced in ten thousand people behind guns and barbed wire. So far 276 people have died, most of them young adults or children. It's like something out of a nightmare. Ambulances rush in, body bags are dragged out. The fear is so thick in the air you can almost touch it. It's awful."

"Sounds awful," Gwen said with genuine empathy. "But also necessary. Imagine those same ghettos in cities all over the world, if you hadn't stopped the spread in China."

Haldane grunted a laugh. "I didn't have much to do with it."

"Jean Nantal tells me otherwise." She forced the praise on him. "He says that you convinced the officials to sacrifice the local livestock. And he says that was the key to stopping this virus."

"I wish I were as confident as you." Haldane sighed. "I am not so sure we've seen the last of ARCS or the Gansu Flu or the Killer Flu or whatever the hell you want to call it."

"Why?" Savard asked.

"Maybe I'm just being dramatic." Haldane rubbed the rest of the sleep out of his face. "But we have been incredibly lucky not to see any spread beyond this province. Almost too lucky. You understand?"

"Not necessarily," she said. "Maybe the Chinese have learned from the SARS experience."

"Clearly." He stood up with his phone to his ear and stretched. "With the way they run the farms around here they're going to need to learn a lot more if they don't want to be responsible for Armageddon."

She swallowed. "Noah, my biggest concern lies in the potential for weaponizing this virus."

"I wouldn't recommend it."

She ignored the quip. "How easy do you think it would be for someone to get their hands on the virus."

"You mean from a lab?" he asked.

"From anywhere," she said.

"I don't imagine it would be too difficult," he said. "Who would want it? No. Don't answer that. I have enough trouble sleeping." He sighed. "Okay, your question would be better answered by our microbiologist Milly Yuen, but let me take a stab at it. This virus is more fastidious than most influenza, which explains the delay in identifying him. But at his core he is a member of the same family. Influenza is easily incubated in chicken eggs or for that matter live animals like pigs and certain primates. I imagine you could use the blood or other body fluid products of an infected patient to propagate the virus. From there . . ."

She didn't comment, so Haldane added, "If it makes you feel any better, I haven't bumped into Osama bin Laden on the streets of Jiayuguan City."

"That's a big relief," she groaned. "When will you know for sure whether the virus is contained in Gansu?"

"If there are no new cases, *anywhere*, in the next week, then I will sleep a whole lot better."

"Me, too."

They said their good-byes, promising to touch base with updates and any new developments, but Haldane suspected that she no more intended than he did to follow up on their conversation.

After giving up on the prospect of sleep, Haldane headed down to the small dark bar in the lobby of the hotel. Someone was playing an Elton John tune passably enough on the baby grand piano, but he butchered the words in his heavily accented nasal voice.

Haldane saw Duncan McLeod sitting alone at the far booth, sipping from a highball glass with another empty glass on the table in front of him. As soon as McLeod spotted him, he hailed him over with a flailing arm. "Haldane, over here! Come listen to 'Someone Shaved My Wife Tonight' the way Sir Elton *meant* it to be played."

Haldane sat down across from McLeod. "Vodka on the rocks?" the Scotsman asked.

Haldane nodded. McLeod waved three fingers in the air until he caught the attention of their waiter.

"I'm a little behind," Haldane said, indicating the glasses on the table.

"I've no intention of letting you catch up, Haldane," McLeod said with a slight slur.

Haldane had never seen McLeod drink as heavily before. Normally, McLeod looked ten or fifteen years younger than his forty-seven years. Not tonight. The creases around his mouth and eyes seemed deeper. His red hair was even more askew than usual. And there was something melancholic behind his asymmetrical eyes.

"What's wrong, Duncan?"

"Don't know if you've noticed, but I've spent my last week trapped in the capital of Nowheresville, China. Home of the Grim Reaper."

"We're going home very soon."

"Maybe, maybe not." McLeod shrugged his whole upper body. "Doesn't matter much. I don't even remember what home looks like."

The white-coated waiter arrived at their table. He picked up both of McLeod's glasses and replaced them with two fresh vodkas for McLeod and one for Haldane. "A man could die of thirst waiting for a second drink around here," McLeod explained away his simultaneous drinks with an unsteady finger.

"So you're homeless?" Haldane asked.

"In a manner of speaking." McLeod took a large sip from the first glass. "We've got a cute little hovel in Glasgow, but I'm hardly ever there. With this WHO job, I live out of a suitcase." He heaved a sigh. "Do you know I haven't seen my boys in almost three months?"

Haldane knew that McLeod had twin teenaged boys, but he hardly ever spoke of them or any personal aspect of his life. "How old are they, Duncan?"

"Fourteen. Both in their 'O' levels. What you'd call high school. Smart kids, too." He shook his head as if their age surprised him. "Fourteen!"

"Do they look like Dad?"

"Christ, no! Thank God. I think the missus started sleeping around before the boys came along. Even if they got some of my genes, luckily they got her looks."

"That is lucky." Haldane tasted his drink for the first time.

McLeod glanced at Haldane askance. "You've never seen my wife."

"Doesn't matter."

McLeod howled with laughter and slapped the table. "Haldane, thank God you're on this miserable adventure with me." He took another long tug from his glass. "I spoke to Alistair tonight, but Cameron was too busy to speak to his old man."

Haldane nodded sympathetically. "Teenagers, huh?"

"Nah." McLeod sucked at the first empty glass, as if the ice cubes were hiding precious drops of vodka. "I can't blame them. Their old man hasn't been around much. Too busy chasing little bugs around the world. Now I'm not much more than a stranger to them. Like the dad from that 'Cat's in the Cradle' song.'" McLeod turned to the piano player and yelled, "Hey, Elton, you know that song 'Dogs on the Table'?"

"You're still their dad," Haldane said.

McLeod shrugged. He turned his attention to the second glass on the table.

"When this is through, why don't you take some time off to catch up with your kids? Get to know them again," Haldane suggested. "No doubt the WHO owes you some vacation time."

McLeod stared at Haldane for a moment. Then he nodded slowly. "And the others all say you're dumb as a post." He nodded again. "Truth be told, I've been thinking about it. Maybe I will, Haldane. It's been too long since I've seen ugly old Glasgow. And for years now I've been talking about taking the family on a ski trip."

"Couldn't hurt," Haldane said.

"Apparently you haven't seen me ski," McLeod slurred. "And you, Haldane? You have to abandon your wee little one for long stretches, too."

Haldane took a bigger sip from his drink. "Too long."

"Ah, don't beat yourself up. It's not like she'll remember any of it at her age."

Haldane didn't want to talk about Chloe. "Duncan, how

does your wife deal with all the time you spend away from home?"

"Fine." He shrugged. "Let's face it, Haldane. Maggie never liked me that much in the first place." His mischievous smile betrayed his obvious affection for his wife. He looked down and swirled the ice in his drink. "You know? Today's our anniversary."

"Congratulations."

"Great. And here I am in a little backwater Chinese wasteland, which Chairman Mao probably didn't even know existed, getting pissed by myself."

Haldane punched McLeod playfully on the shoulder. "You got me now, buddy."

"Fucking excellent, Haldane! But unlike those vacuous weak-kneed lasses back in Geneva, your movie-star looks are wasted on me." He burped. "I'd trade ten of you in a heartbeat for Maggie."

Haldane laughed. "How many years?"

"Twenty-four. We were just children, Haldane." McLeod looked over to him. "Still, no regrets. She's great, my Margaret. She raised the boys and put up with this"— he thumbed at his chest—"without ever complaining. And we can still laugh about it all. You can't ask for much more than that in a marriage."

Haldane shrugged.

"I can't anyway." McLeod squinted at Haldane, and then he pointed a swaying finger at him. "But you and your wife live the fairy tale, don't you?"

Haldane didn't reply. Instead, he reached for his glass.

"What?" McLeod's wild eyes went wider. "Trouble in Camelot?"

"Maybe," Haldane said noncommittally.

"Another man?" McLeod asked.

"Sort of," Haldane said, deciding not to elaborate.

"Ach, shite!" McLeod dismissed it with a wave of his hand. "Affairs aren't usually the problem."

"Oh, really?" It came out a touch more defensively than Haldane had intended.

"It's a symptom, Haldane. Like a bad sneeze from a virus," McLeod said, nodding in agreement with himself. "You don't treat the symptom, you treat the disease."

Haldane shook his head, less than delighted at the comparison of his wife's infidelity to a sneeze or a head cold. He drained the last of his vodka and changed the subject. "Duncan, they're calling it the 'Gansu Flu.'"

"Catchy."

"A bigwig from the States just phoned. She wanted to know if we had contained it."

McLeod put his glass down. "What did you tell her?"

"I told her it was too early to say, but it looks like the spread has stopped. In this city, at least."

"You know what, Haldane?" McLeod said as he held up three more fingers for the waiter. "I know we have to wait a few more days to find out, but my gut tells me it's contained here."

Haldane stared at his colleague. "So you think we've seen the end of ARCS?"

"Haldane . . ." McLeod ran a hand through his tangled spears of red hair, then he put the glass down and eyed Noah with a deadly sober expression. "God help us if we haven't!"

CHAPTER

15

Staring down at her unconscious four-year-old daughter, Alyssa, the lump cemented in Veronica Mathews's throat. Tubes and lines hooked Alyssa to machine after machine as if suspending her from a nightmarish, high-tech spider-web. Her bluish-tinged skin had grown translucent. Her angelic face had gone sallow. Her cheeks seemed to have lost their padding, inverting to hollows overnight. Under the sheets and blankets, her little chest heaved up and down with each breath the ventilator wrestled to push in and out of her waterlogged lungs.

Garbed in mask, shower cap, gown, and surgical gloves, Veronica sat as she had for most of the last forty-eight hours hunched over the railing of her daughter's bed, clutching Alyssa's cool hand. She had stayed at the bed-side since the moment Alyssa was rushed into the Royal Free Hospital's Accident and Emergency, the British version of an E.R. In the past two days, Veronica had slept for only minutes at a time. She hadn't eaten at all. But she had no intention of moving. She was not going to leave Alyssa. Ever.

It had happened so quickly. Alyssa had developed a fever and a cough two days earlier. Just a run-of-the-mill cold, Mathews had thought at the time, but within twelve hours of the first cough, her four-year-old was gasping for air. Then she turned dark blue.

Now her baby lay comatose in a pediatric ICU bed, struggling for life with a double pneumonia that left the specialists bewildered. At first they had thought Alyssa might have SARS, so unusual were the many blotches on her chest X-ray. But the blood tests had ruled it out. The doctors told Veronica that they suspected Alyssa might be suffering from severe complications of the flu, but they admitted that they did not know with certainty. As a result they were taking no chances, insisting that all staff and visitors use the same precautions as had been employed with the SARS outbreak.

The sterile physical barriers between Veronica and her daughter—her only allowable physical contact was through two pairs of latex gloves—compounded her helplessness. Veronica was tempted to rip off her mask, cover her daughter's brow in kisses, and rub noses the way they had the other times one of the girls was sick. It was only the warning that such contact might lead to spread of the infection to her five-year-old daughter Brynne that stopped Mathews from breaking the strict contact precautions.

Veronica Mathews had grown up three miles from the picturesque Hampstead Heath—an oasis of natural parkland in the middle of London's urban sprawl—at the corner of which the Royal Free Hospital stands. She had played in the heath often as a child. Since moving to New York, whenever she visited London the twenty-nine-year old former model always found time to return for a stroll or jog with one of her childhood friends. She had planned to bring her two girls to the heath on this trip, had the November rain ever lifted. But none of them would be visiting it this November. Alyssa might never see Hampstead Heath, or any other park, again.

Mathews felt another stab of guilt at how her thoughts had drifted from Alyssa to a patch of grassy moorland. Guilt had plagued her ever since Alyssa had been rushed to hospital. Veronica could not forgive herself for dragging the girls back to London in the middle of flu season, with people everywhere—on the plane, in the underground, and at the tourist attractions—hacking and sneezing all around them. The trip was Veronica's idea, a pathetic attempt to salvage her marriage to her twenty-year older disinterested banker husband. Aside from saving face by proving to the world that she wasn't just another trophy wife, what was the point of even having tried? she wondered bitterly. No marriage was worth risking her daughters' health for, least of all hers.

Veronica didn't understand most of the readouts and displays that flashed numbers and colored graphics on a large monitor at the head of her daughter's bed. The one number that she fixated on was the oxygen saturation. A doctor had explained how the oxygen saturation, which normally ranged from ninety-five to one-hundred percent in healthy people, reflected her daughter's lungs' ability to absorb oxygen and pass it on to the tissue. In Alyssa's case, even with the help of the jet ventilator and high flow oxygen she was barely able to maintain the number in the high sixties. Despite Veronica's constant monitoring and her endless promises and threats to a God to whom she hadn't prayed since childhood, the number refused to budge.

My baby can't die, the thought repeated like a loop of tape in her head. It's not possible! Only the week before Veronica had marveled at how big and independent Alyssa had grown, but now nestled in all the machinery she looked as tiny as a doll and even more helpless. "Please God," Veronica implored aloud, "take me instead!"

The oxygen saturation dropped a percentage point to sixty-six.

HARGEYSA, SOMALIA

Like most things Kabaal touched, he had managed to infuse opulence into the once-utilitarian room, which had become his office, on the complex's second floor. Ornate Moroccan rugs hung from the freshly painted walls. Even larger rugs adorned the floors. The massive antique oak desk behind which he sat had been shipped in pieces from France and painstakingly reassembled to perfection.

Like the six-hundred-dollar shoes he wore in the desert hideaway, he believed these material comforts brought with them a soothing constancy that enabled him to better focus on his sacred mission.

He flipped open his laptop computer and waited for it to link up to the satellite. Once he saw the little blue interlocking computers icon in the corner of the screen, he tapped a button and the new mail message downloaded. Moments later, it popped up on the screen. Written in English, it read:

Dear Tonya,

Arrived in London with all our baggage. Dropped off the present. Everyone was surprised. We had a lovely time, but we couldn't stay. I'll be in touch soon.

Love, Sherri

Kabaal felt a rush of joy, tempered by bittersweet melancholy. It was the second such message "Sherri" had sent. The only difference being that the first one had been written from Hong Kong. Otherwise the wording was identical. He wasn't surprised. After all, he had composed the message himself.

The e-mails indicated that the operation had proceeded without complication in two cities on two different continents. He could only infer one conclusion from the good fortune required for such flawless execution: God had to be on their side.

Now it was time to wait and see whether the virus claimed a beachhead.

The cosmopolitan cities were not chosen at random. Political retribution, expedience, and necessity all factored into the choice. But the superiority of the health-care systems and, in the case of Hong Kong, recent experience with the SARS epidemic, were the overriding factors. For now, Kabaal wanted cities that would react swiftly to an outbreak.

The e-mails also implied that his female couriers were already dead, fallen by bullets from their brothers' guns; their bodies safely disposed of. Kabaal was saddened by the loss of the Hong Kong courier, but Khalila Jahal's death hit him much harder. As inevitable as it was, the confirmation of her death still evoked an unexpected sense of loss.

Kabaal looked up to see Abdul Sabri filling his doorway and thoughts of Khalila slid from his mind. Kabaal wasn't surprised by the major's sudden stealth presence. He had grown to expect the abrupt appearances. When he chose to, the hulking man could move with the speed and silence of a tiger. "Major Abdul, please come in," Kabaal said.

In a plain white robe, Sabri sauntered across the room and sat in the leather chair across from Kabaal.

Kabaal was struck again by the paradox of Sabri's delicate features born on his dangerous frame. "The news from abroad is good," Kabaal said.

Sabri shrugged as if there was no other possible outcome.

"Both operations were successful," Kabaal added,

annoyed that Sabri did not seem to share his pride in the news.

"It might be premature to label the operations a success," Sabri said emotionlessly.

Kabaal shook his head. "Major, I've learned in my business that it is important to celebrate all victories in life. They are at times few and far between."

Sabri shrugged again. "And I've learned from my business that premature celebration can cost you victory."

"Not if you keep your guard up," Kabaal countered.

"Always advisable," Sabri agreed.

"Speaking of which, I heard from our people in Cairo this morning."

When Sabri didn't respond, Kabaal continued. "Someone at the mosque has been asking questions as to my whereabouts."

Sabri leaned forward in his seat. His blue eyes narrowed. "Who?"

"His name is Bishr Gamal."

Sabri shook his head.

"I have not heard of him either," Kabaal said. "Apparently, he is not a man worthy of much respect. And I am quite certain he has no legitimate reason to be looking for me."

Sabri nodded. "I will take care of it."

"Personally?"

"Yes."

"Good," Kabaal said.

Sabri stood from the chair. He took two steps toward the door before he turned and eyed Kabaal intently. "When will you let them know?"

"Not yet," Kabaal said.

Sabri tilted his head, questioning.

Kabaal held his palms open in front of him and smiled mischievously, as if letting Sabri in on an inside joke. "We will let them think nature has taken its own course."

"Why?"

"When terror is your weapon, the unknown adds to its potency." Kabaal stopped smiling. "We will let the panic simmer. That way, when we are prepared to announce ourselves, we will have their absolute attention."

CHAPTER
16

Five nail biting days had passed without a new case of ARCS reported in Jiayuguan City or anywhere else in the Gansu province. With the tacit approval of Noah Haldane and the WHO team, the provincial authorities declared "absolute victory over the Gansu Flu." They intended to trumpet their triumph to the whole world. The provincial governor had flown in from Lanzhou, while the Deputy Premier had come from Beijing. Scores of party officials and dignitaries had collected from all across China for the occasion. And the international press, who had been barred from the region during the epidemic, was welcomed to the celebratory gala dinner where the members of the WHO team were the guests of honor.

Haldane was itching to get home. He hadn't seen Chloe in almost three weeks, and he hated the idea of another day passing without seeing his daughter. He wouldn't have delayed his departure one minute for the self-congratulatory feast, but there weren't any flights leaving until the morning. Along with a navy sports jacket, a blue casual shirt, and black cotton pants, he put on a brave face and headed down to the banquet.

Any concern of being the most underdressed at the event evaporated when he laid eyes on Duncan McLeod. The redhead had tamed his hair with at least one pass of a brush, but he still carried deep bags under his eyes from the bender of three nights before. Wearing rumpled wool pants and a tattered sweater, he stood out even more than usual among the formally dressed crowd.

Haldane sat between McLeod and Jean Nantal, the WHO's Executive Director of Communicable Diseases, who had flown in that morning from Geneva. The silver-haired Frenchman wore a natty four-button black suit along with a beaming smile that he hadn't shed since arriving. For the third time that evening, he raised his wineglass and individually toasted each of the four WHO members at his table. "You have made me so proud." He beamed.

"I'm not toasting me or anyone else," McLeod said, leaving the full wineglass untouched in front of him. "I'm through with drink."

Helmut Streicher put down his own glass and let out an uncharacteristic laugh. "*Ja*, for a Scotsman, you don't hold your alcohol so well. Hah!"

"Ah, there's that wonderful Germanic sense of humor," McLeod grunted sarcastically.

Milly Yuen, who had turned beet-red after two sips of wine, giggled at the exchange.

Haldane tipped his glass to Nantal. "Jean, the Chinese didn't need us this time. They were going to contain the virus at any and all cost."

"Not necessarily, my humble friend," Nantal said in his buttery smooth French accent. "After all, who helped coordinate their quarantine?" He raised his glass to Streicher. Then he turned to Haldane with a proud, paternal nod. "And was it not you who initiated the livestock slaughter?"

Haldane shrugged.

Nantal looked around the indifferent faces at the table. "Your modesty aside, *mes amis*." His smile broadened. "It does not hurt for the WHO to get a little credit and positive press now and again. Downplay it all you want, but you've earned this." His hand swept fluidly across the sea of dignitaries and cameras in front of them. "The WHO has earned it. And I for one won't shy away."

"Glad to hear you say that." McLeod pointed at his chest. "Means you won't have any problem with me taking the next three months off."

"Duncan? You're asking for vacation time?" Nantal laughed. "This truly is a day of marvels."

As McLeod was about to respond a waiter tapped Nantal on the shoulder. After a brief whispered exchange, Nantal rose to his feet. "Excuse me, I must take a phone call."

After Nantal left, the speeches began. For the benefit of the WHO team, the deputy premier spoke in English. Haldane had heard the same type of political speech a hundred times before—pure rhetoric and revisionist history. The deputy premier commended the local medical personnel's "heroic battle" against the virus, and hailed their success in halting its spread. He praised the people of Jiayuguan City's bravery as if they had chosen to be fenced in behind barbed wire. He often used the term "we," even though he had kept three thousand miles between himself and the epidemic. And finally, he lauded the WHO team for coming to offer their expertise to the local specialists "where needed," implying that while they had appreciated the help it wasn't actually required.

During the protracted standing ovation for the WHO doctors that followed the speaker's remarks, the same waiter who had pulled Nantal away from the table came for Haldane.

Nantal sat behind the desk in the borrowed office, speaking urgently in French into the phone's receiver. When he saw Noah at the door, he waved him over to the chair across from his.

When the Frenchman hung up the phone and looked up at Haldane, his face was fixed in a disconsolate frown. Haldane couldn't ever remember seeing Nantal fazed before. His boss looked as if he had aged ten years in the thirty minutes since he'd left the dinner table. "What is it, Jean?" Haldane asked.

Nantal spoke in a quiet subdued tone. "A little girl in a London hospital has tested positive for the virus."

Haldane shook his head, refusing to make the connection. "What virus?"

Nantal just stared at him.

"You're not serious, Jean!" Haldane leaned forward and gripped the edge of the desk. "The Gansu Flu has shown up in London, England?"

Nantal nodded.

Haldane stood without even realizing it. "Has the girl been over here in the last month?"

Nantal shook his head. "She's not Chinese. Neither she nor anyone else in the family has ever been to China."

Haldane lowered himself back into his seat. "Then why do they think it's the Gansu Flu?"

"A PCR probe. Our European Influenza Surveillance ran the blood test. It matched."

Haldane shook his head, unwilling to accept the lab's verdict and its implications. "Then someone in the lab screwed up!"

Nantal stared at Haldane for several seconds. "Noah, there are others," he said softly.

"Others!" Haldane's heart slammed against his rib

cage. He took a deep breath. "Okay. Back up, Jean. Tell me what you know."

"There have been five cases reported in London," Nantal said. "They all came from the same exclusive hotel, the Park Plaza Tower, in London's business district. One of the victims has already died."

Haldane gritted his teeth. "The little girl?"

"No. A fifty-five-year-old American oil company executive. He was found dead in his hotel room."

The fact that it wasn't the little girl brought a sense of irrational relief to Haldane. The shock subsided. His mind raced, already planning steps ahead. "Do we have the index case?" he asked.

Nantal ran a thumb and a finger along his eyebrows and then shook his head. "None of the victims have traveled to China in the last three months."

"So someone else brought it over," Haldane said. "All right, who was the first to become sick?"

"We will never know when the oil company executive first developed symptoms, but the four-year-old girl was the first to be hospitalized."

"When?" Haldane demanded.

"Three days ago."

"One more day and she'll make it," Haldane mumbled to himself.

Nantal tilted his head. "I'm sorry, Noah, I do not follow."

"Nothing." Haldane tapped the desktop in front of him. "The other cases, Jean. When were they first reported?"

Nantal consulted the notes written in flawless script on the pad in front of him. "Two of the cases showed up within twelve hours of the little girl. The other two just declared themselves this morning. They were guests at the same hotel. As soon as they developed fever and cough, they were immediately isolated."

"So we have a two-day gap between the initial cases

and the last two. Those two must be the result of collateral spread from the first set," Haldane said, describing the phenomenon of secondary spread of the virus from one "generation" of victims to the next.

"I agree," Nantal said.

"And none of the hospital staff who treated the victims have shown signs of infection?" Haldane asked.

Nantal shook his head. "Thankfully, the hospitals have been very responsible in instituting early precautions, but several of the nurses and doctors are in quarantine."

"Good," Haldane said. "Five days should be long enough. What about the staff and guests at the hotel?"

"All of them are in quarantine," Nantal said.

"Voluntary?"

"We're talking about England, my friend," Nantal pointed out graciously. "I don't think they erect barbed-wire fences. But from what I have heard people are cooperating."

"They had better," Haldane said. "Are they getting word out to the public, Jean?"

"I don't yet have those details," Nantal said. "I hear that the media in London is spreading the news, but the authorities are concerned about the public's response. They are worried about causing wide-scale panic."

Haldane threw up his hands. "If they don't get on top of this thing now they'll see wide-scale panic, and with damn good reason!" Realizing he was "shooting the messenger," Haldane lowered his voice. "Jean, they need to immediately set up screening clinics like we did with SARS. It's the only hope of containment." He paused. "If that still even is a hope."

Nantal reached over and patted Haldane on the hand. "We helped contain it in Jiayuguan City, Noah. We can do the same in London."

Haldane looked down at the liver spots on his mentor's hand. The sight dejected him. Even the great Jean Nantal, a pillar in the struggle against nature gone awry, wasn't immune to the inevitability of biology. "We need to find that index case, Jean."

"You'll go to London then?"

Haldane closed his eyes and exhaled heavily. Then he nodded.

Nantal squeezed Noah's hand once before withdrawing his hand. He studied Haldane, hesitating, before he finally spoke. "Noah, I know you won't want to hear this now, but we have suspect cases elsewhere. Not confirmed yet microbiologically but clinically very suspicious."

"Outside of London?"

"Quite a ways." Nantal smiled halfheartedly. "Two people in *Hong* Kong have developed classic symptoms."

The sense of déjà vu slammed Haldane like a punch. It was SARS all over again, but with a far more vicious bug. "We have to get out of here, Jean. Tonight!"

HEATHROW AIRPORT, LONDON, ENGLAND

The flights were a blur. Emotionally drained by the catastrophic developments and the subsequent phone call home to explain his further delay, Haldane dozed in and out of a restless nonrestorative sleep for much of the eighteen hours and three transfers it took to get them to Heathrow Airport in London.

The whole team had been rocked by the news of the spread, but Duncan McLeod seemed to take it hardest. "The son of a bitch has decided to visit my miserable island. I'm not going to take that lying down!" he said when he first heard the news. He had hardly spoken since.

At the Beijing Airport, the team had separated. Nantal, Streicher, and Yuen boarded a flight for Switzerland, while Haldane and McLeod headed directly to London.

Through the throngs of people standing at the arrival gate of Heathrow—which struck Haldane as a microcosm of cultural and global diversity—he spotted a thin woman holding up a placard reading: "Drs. Haldane and McLeod." He nudged McLeod with an elbow, and the two of them walked over to meet her.

"Doctors, I am Dr. Nancy Levine, the Assistant Director of the London Health Commission," she said without smiling as she met their handshakes. "I can explain further once we are on the road. Please follow me." She headed for the exit. Of average height but skinny to the point of bony, Levine had black hair tied in a tight ponytail, thin lips, and sunken brown eyes. She wore no makeup. Her humorless expression was consistent with her abrupt to-the-point disposition. Haldane suspected it long predated the current crisis.

Outside, London's gray skies spat a cool November drizzle. Walking to the car, Haldane wondered if he was ever going to see the sun shine again. Once they had loaded into Levine's Land Rover—Haldane in the passenger seat, and McLeod in the back—she explained the command structure of the city's public health system. "The Commission coordinates six separate government agencies under one umbrella organization," she said in her clipped, upper-crust English accent. "We are responsible for overseeing all aspects of Londoners' health, including management of infectious outbreaks and epidemics."

"Sounds incredibly busy," Haldane said. "Thanks for taking the time to pick us up."

"It's a matter of expedience," she said with a shrug of her narrow shoulders. "This is the ideal opportunity for you to describe to me your firsthand experience with the Gansu strain of the influenza virus. And more specifically, to explain how the Chinese managed to arrest its spread."

"We wouldn't be here if they had managed that!" McLeod grunted from the backseat.

"Clearly," Levine said. "What I meant is how they contained it locally. That is what I need to know from you."

"Dr. Levine, Jiayuguan is a remote community. A small

city in the middle of nowhere," Haldane said. "It bears no comparison to London."

"That aside, Dr. Haldane . . ." Levine harrumphed.

"They put a section of the city under siege, Dr. Levine," Haldane said. "In a democracy you could never get away with the kind of cold military offensive the Chinese government used."

Levine stared ahead silently for a moment. "Are you familiar with our Emergency Health Act?"

"Not the specifics," Haldane said.

"Enacting it would be the equivalent of imposing martial law," she said. "You would be surprised by exactly what we could do."

"Martial law," McLeod echoed. "That's what you'll need, too."

Levine glanced at Haldane. "Can you please describe your clinical observations?" she said. It was a command, not a request.

Staring out the window and watching suburban London give way to the more congested metropolitan areas, Haldane painted an overview of the Gansu outbreak, coloring it with his eyewitness perspective. McLeod muttered the occasional clarification or facetious remark.

After Haldane finished, Dr. Levine asked a few pointed insightful questions. Once she had fielded her queries, she lapsed into silence. Haldane got the feeling that having exhausted her passengers' usefulness, Levine would have been pleased to pull over and let them off at the side of the road.

"Where are you taking us now?" Haldane asked.

"To the Commission's head office," she said. "The others are expecting us."

"They will have to wait," Haldane said.

"Pardon me?" she asked indignantly.

"I want to talk to the surviving victims."

"In good time, Dr. Haldane."

"No, Dr. Levine. Now."

"Dr. Haldane, this is not China," she said quietly. She kept her eyes straight ahead, but her tone could have frosted the windshield. "You are here at the WHO's request. Not ours. Ergo, you are here to observe, not lead our process."

"Welcome to friendly London, Haldane!" McLeod piped up from the backseat.

Haldane looked over at Levine with an intentionally condescending smile. "Dr. McLeod and I have spent the last few weeks in the epicenter of this epidemic. We know it inside and out. I think it's safe to assume that we have more experience with emerging pathogens and viral hot zones than the rest of your Commission combined." He let his barbs hang in the air for a few moments. "But, Dr. Levine, if you don't see the sense of listening to our advice then perhaps your director will."

Her head didn't move, but the corner of her lip twitched. "We are closest to the Royal Free Hospital where the pediatric patient is," she said evenly. "We will begin there."

Dr. Nancy Levine had already cleared their presence with the Royal Free Hospital's administrators. After she flashed her identity card at the main desk, the three physicians were directed up to the Pediatric ICU on the tenth floor.

Outside the nursing station, a matronly middle-aged woman in a white uniform and headgear, which looked to Haldane like something from a black-and-white movie, introduced herself only as "Sister."

"Sister, we're looking for the patient Alyssa Mathews."

The woman shook her. "I am sorry, Dr. Levine, but she has already gone."

"Oh," Haldane sighed, assuming the worst. "When did it happen?"

"It?" The sister's face crumpled in confusion for a moment. "Oh, no, no!" She shook her head again. "Alyssa has not died. On the contrary, she has shown signs of stabilizing this morning. Today is the first day her doctors have deemed her stable enough to go downstairs for a CT scan of her chest. She only just left ten minutes before."

By the time Haldane, Levine, and McLeod reached the Radiology Department, Alyssa was already on the procedure table having her scan performed.

A radiology clerk led them to Veronica Mathews who paced nervously in the department's waiting room. Veronica wore hospital greens. Her long black hair was frizzled at the flyaway ends, and she only had speckled remnants of her blue eyeliner inside the dark circles encasing her eyes. Even still, Haldane had no trouble picturing her on a runway in New York or Paris, because her sharp features and tall graceful body were so striking.

They sat down at a bank of chairs in the far corner of the waiting room. Haldane sat directly across from Mathews, while McLeod and Levine sat on either side of him. During the introductions Veronica stared blankly over Haldane's head, appearing as sedated as a postoperative patient. Only when he explained how he had just come from China and had seen several other cases of the Gansu Flu did Veronica snap into focus.

Her eyes pleaded with Haldane. "You saw people who recovered from this *thing*, right?" she said in an accent that seemed to fluctuate between New Yorker and Brit on every second syllable.

"Yes, Mrs. Mathews." He nodded. "We saw people who had hovered on the brink of death and then rebounded. They were fine by the time we talked to them."

She reached out and grabbed his arm. "And children?"

"Yes, children too. Most of the children in China survived the virus."

She squeezed his arm and her lips formed a tentative smile. "But Alyssa has been so sick . . ."

"But she has hung on for four days."

Mathews shrugged helplessly and shook her head. "So?"

"Four days was the magic number in China," Haldane explained. "All the patients who survived for more than four days went on to recover fully."

Mathews's fingers dug into Haldane's arm. Her eyes went wide. "Alyssa will recover?" she demanded frantically.

Haldane donned a reassuring smile. "I expect so, Mrs. Mathews."

She loosened the grip on his arm. Tears began to pour from her eyes. "Thank you, Dr. Haldane. Thank you so much . . ."

"Not me," Haldane said. "The staff here at the hospital."

"Of course," she sniffled, but still clung to his arm.

Haldane allowed her a moment, and then asked, "Mrs. Mathews, do you have any idea where Alyssa picked up this virus?"

The sleeplessness caught up to her again. Her eyes glazed over. She waved a hand carelessly around the empty waiting room. "There are bugs everywhere. People sneezing and coughing, it's an insane time to travel—"

"Veronica," Haldane cut her off. "We're confident that Alyssa picked it up at the hotel. Probably five to seven days ago give or take. Do you remember seeing anyone who looked particularly sick at that time?"

She shook her head wearily. "I've seen so many red and runny noses . . ."

"Think, Veronica, please. It's very important."

Haldane's request didn't appear to register on her blank face. "I tried to keep the girls away, but they're everywhere. In the lobby, at the restaurants, by the pool. Some places you can shield them a little, but what can you do when you're stuck on an elevator with someone who—" She stopped in midsentence. Her eyes narrowed. She began to nod.

Haldane leaned closer to her. "What is it, Veronica?"

"About a week ago, we were riding the elevator just before supper. We had just been at the swimming pool, the girls and I. They loved that pool . . ." She smiled her first openmouthed smile in their presence, exposing perfect white teeth. "A woman was on the elevator. Standing by the buttons. She was coughing."

Levine cut in. "What did she look like, Mrs. Mathews?"

"Not well." Veronica shook her head. "She looked as if she needed the elevator wall just to keep her upright. When the girls headed for the buttons—they love to press the buttons—she backed away from them, as if scared."

"Can you be any more specific in your description?" Levine asked, her tone slightly critical.

"She was younger than me. I'd say, early to mid-twenties, at the most. Her thick sandy brown hair was a mess, but she was pretty. Big eyes. She looked pale, but I think that was because of her illness. To me, she looked Mediterranean. Italian? Spanish? Maybe even Greek, but I don't think so . . . Spanish would be my bet."

"Anything else?"

Veronica thought. "She was dressed a little"—she searched for the word—"seductively, considering."

"Considering what?" Haldane asked.

"That she obviously wasn't well," Veronica said. "She wore a tight blouse and jeans, along with a fair bit of makeup. It struck me as out of place for someone fighting a rotten cold. Especially in November."

"Did she speak to you at all?"

"No," Veronica said. "When I apologized for the girls crowding her at the control panel, she smiled nervously and stumbled back away from the girls." Veronica's eyelids drooped again from fatigue. She looked at Haldane, sadly. "The poor woman just sort of wilted in front of my eyes."

"That was the only time you saw her?" Haldane asked.

Before Veronica could answer, a man emerged from the CT scanning room, wearing the gown, mask, and gloves. Once outside, he pulled off his mask and walked over toward the bank of chairs.

As soon as Veronica saw him, she leaped to her feet and ran over to him. "What did it show, Dr. Mayer? How is my baby?" She reached out to touch him.

CHAPTER

17

Hobbling into the conference room, Gwen Savard couldn't conceal her gimpy ankle from Alex Clayton, the CIA Deputy Director of Operations, or any of the other members of the Bioterrorism Preparedness Council. Gwen had no one to blame but herself. She had continued to run on the treadmill at the gym for days after her injury, and now she paid the price. Maybe Peter had been right when he'd once jokingly described her as a dog with a bone and a bad case of lockjaw.

All fifteen members of the council were already around the oval table when Savard took her seat at its head. After she made a few brief remarks, the meeting unfolded predictably. They discussed the old standards of bioterrorism—smallpox, anthrax, the plague, and so on—recycling data they had seen before without shedding new light. They reviewed the sixth draft of the generic urban centers' Emergency Response Plan to Biological Attack, known by most of them as ERPBA, without reaching consensus.

Savard had difficulty concentrating on the debate. After her conversation earlier in the week with Haldane, she had filed the Gansu Flu into the recesses of her mind; worthy of no more than a mental footnote. Now with its sudden reemergence, she could focus on little else.

After the committee covered the agenda items, Gwen said, "No doubt, everyone here has heard that the Gansu strain of influenza has shown up in London. At last report there are at least fourteen cases and three deaths. And in Hong Kong, there are now five confirmed infections and several more suspect cases."

Halfway down the table Moira Roberts, the Deputy Directory of the FBI, leaned forward and squinted at Gwen. "And this has to do with bioterrorism how?"

In a plain black suit and gray blouse, which matched her prematurely gray hair worn in an outdated bob, Roberts struck Gwen as the epitome of frumpy. "No one seems to know how the virus got to England or Hong Kong," Savard said.

"Have you considered travelers from China?" Roberts asked in a tone that made it unclear whether or not she meant to be facetious.

"It did occur to me." Savard matched Roberts's tone. "But unlike SARS where the index cases were easily traceable, they have found no link in London or Hong Kong to the Gansu outbreak."

"Which means it must be bioterrorism, right?" Roberts said, no longer bothering to mask her sarcasm.

"Which means," Gwen said slowly, suppressing her mounting irritation, "we cannot discount the *possibility* of terrorism."

"It might be a while before you can discount any possible explanation for the outbreaks," Roberts pointed out.

Gwen didn't doubt Roberts's intelligence, but her agitative personality made it impossible to warm to the woman. "So in the meantime we just ignore it?" Savard said.

Roberts folded her arms and sighed. "That's not what I'm trying to say."

Annoyed, Clayton cut in. "What are you trying to say, Moira?"

"I remember we had similar discussions around SARS," Roberts replied, talking to the table instead of Clayton. "Some people were convinced it was a biological weapon dreamed up by Al Qaeda. That didn't exactly pan out, did it?" She sighed. "No doubt this new virus poses a potential major public health risk to the United States. I don't discount that for a minute. What I suggest is that we wait to learn more before we overreact and waste precious resources chasing phantom terrorists when other departments, like Health and Human Services, will have more pressing priorities to address."

A few of the members around the table nodded, but none spoke up, appearing content to sit on the sidelines.

Ignoring Roberts, Clayton turned to Savard. "Gwen, how do we find out where this virus came from?"

"Finding the index case or cases is the key," she said.

"And if we don't?" Clayton asked.

"That would concern me," Gwen said gravely. "With almost every epidemic of this magnitude, the index case is readily identifiable. The person usually seeks medical attention just like any other victim. And if they don't then you have to wonder if he or she is deliberately avoiding detection."

"But, Dr. Savard," Roberts said, "I understand from the newspaper that this bug is only twenty-five percent lethal."

"Only!" Gwen said. "That's a devastating mortality rate. Most flus run at a mortality rate of far less than one percent. And those influenza strains kill only people at the extremes of age. This bug is killing otherwise healthy children and adults at a rate of twenty-five percent. That is up there with smallpox and flesh-eating disease!"

"And people recover quickly from it," Roberts continued as if Gwen hadn't spoken. "So the index case might have already recovered without thinking he ever had anything more than a bad flu. Or conversely, he might have died somewhere and no one has connected his death to the outbreak."

"So two people carry the virus over from China to London and Hong Kong, simultaneously, and then both die in obscurity? What are the chances?" Savard held out her hands, palms up.

"I'm simply suggesting that there are several reasons aside from terrorism for the index cases not to have materialized." Roberts nodded to Gwen, as if mollifying an irrational child.

"Moira, Moira, Moira," Clayton said with an exaggerated sigh. "I've heard the Tony Robbins tapes too, but wishful thinking isn't going to make everything okay this time."

Several people laughed. Even Savard had to bite her lip. Roberts glared at Clayton with undisguised contempt.

"Correct me, if I'm wrong," interjected Jack Elinda, a weedy balding man from the Department of the Environment. "But this is a form of influenza, true?" He cocked his finger and thumb into an imaginary gun at Gwen, which he had a tendency to do whenever he was trying to make a point.

"A mutated form," Savard said. "One that has undergone massive reassortment of its genetic code. Effectively, it's a virus that man has never seen before."

"Still, if it's an influenza virus we should be able to use a vaccine, true?" Elinda pressed.

"The current flu vaccine would be useless," Savard said.

"But we could manufacture a new vaccine for this particular strain, true?" Elinda cocked his finger at Gwen again.

"Theoretically." Savard nodded. She turned to the Assistant Secretary of the Department of Health and Human Services. "Any thoughts, Dr. Menck?"

Dr. Harold Menck was an epidemiologist in his early sixties. Of medium build with a slight paunch and a tight crew cut, he always wore the same blue suit and white shirt with a rotation of bland ties. He rarely spoke at the Bioterrorism Preparedness Council meetings. Gwen had the suspicion that in spite of his high-profile appointment Menck was biding time while awaiting the golden parachute of retirement.

Leaning back in his chair with his hands folded on top of his head, Menck said, "I tend to agree with Ms. Roberts."

"That wasn't the question," Savard said.

"I know." Menck shrugged. "But I have no idea how long it will take to create a vaccine. I hear scientists have started to look into it, but remember they are still nowhere near a SARS vaccine."

"This is influenza, though," Savard said.

"That should make it easier," Menck said with as much interest as if they were talking about genetically altered peaches. "But even if they had already developed the vaccine, it would take several months to produce enough of it to immunize the country. And I think we should be careful not to overreact. Young lady, you probably don't remember the Swine Flu fiasco, but I lived through it."

"I remember, Dr. Menck," Savard said coolly.

"Well I don't." Clayton shot her a playful smile. "Then again I'm way younger than Dr. Savard."

Gwen rolled her eyes, but chuckled in spite of herself.

"In 1975, a nineteen-year-old recruit died on a Louisiana army base after developing flulike symptoms," Menck said. "Tests confirmed he had acquired a strain of Swine Flu, thought to be closely related to the original Spanish Flu. Everyone panicked. The then president, Gerald Ford, authorized production of 150 million doses of vaccine against Swine Flu. Six months later no one else had died of the virus. They even began to wonder if that first soldier had died of heatstroke. But by then, Ford was into an election year and he didn't want to admit a costly mistake. So he listened to the CDC advisors and let them proceed with a mass-scale immunization. Problem was the vaccine started to kill people. A couple hundred people died of vaccine complications before they stopped. It turned into the most costly class-action lawsuit in medico-legal history. And for what?"

"No offence, Dr. Menck." Savard shook her head. "Three hundred people in China did not die of heatstroke in November."

"I understand," Menck said, resuming his disinterested pose with hands on top of his head. "I am merely suggesting we should consider all options, but balance our response. No point in people throwing on gas masks and climbing into backyard bunkers, like we did in the fifties every time the Soviets got out of sorts."

"With all due respect, Dr. Menck," Savard said evenly. "A man-made pandemic is the one occurrence that could make a nuclear event look tame by comparison."

After the meeting broke up, Clayton lagged behind with Savard. Standing at the doorway, he asked, "What happened to your foot?"

Gwen shrugged. "Just a little sprain."

Clayton flashed his openmouthed *GO* smile. "I was kind of hoping you had broken it on the ass of a certain unnamed deputy director of the FBI."

She laughed. "Who knows? Maybe, she's right," Gwen said, taking the weight off her foot by leaning against a chair. "Maybe I am overreacting."

Clayton shook his head. "You're doing your job, Gwen."

She nodded. "Something very strange is going on with this bug, Alex. I know it. I wish I were closer to the action."

He laughed. "Hey, that's my line! You sound like a washed-up ex-field operative."

"I just wish I had more to go on." She frowned. "Speaking of which, anything new on that missing lab equipment in Africa?"

"Our people are still looking into it, but I wouldn't hold my breath." He snapped his fingers. "I think it's gone."

"I don't like the sound of that," she said. "Any more cell chatter?"

"Just the usual." Clayton reached forward and brushed his hand against her wrist. In spite of the light contact, Gwen sensed his strength and confidence. She couldn't deny the sexiness of the gesture. It had been too long since she experienced anything akin to physical warmth.

"We still on for tonight?" he asked.

"Alex, I would love to—"

"Oh, no! You're canceling, aren't you?" Clayton covered his face in mock mortification. "It's prom night all over again. I'm going to wind up taking my mom out for sushi, aren't I?"

"Alex, I want to," she said. "But I'm not going to be in town tonight."

"I should have guessed." He shook his head and laughed. "You're flying to London, aren't you?"

YALE UNIVERSITY, NEW HAVEN, CONNECTICUT

Clayton had it almost right. Gwen was going to London but not until the next morning. In the meantime, she had one interstate trip to make before heading overseas. The Lear jet flew her from Ronald Reagan Washington National Airport to Tweed-New Haven Airport in less than thirty minutes. The waiting car drove her directly to the Yale campus.

It was after six o'clock when the car pulled up in front of the pharmacy research laboratory, but even in the dark the sight conjured up a wave of memories. Gwen hadn't been back to the lab in more than fifteen years, but like everything else she had seen of Dr. Isaac Moskor's life the building hadn't changed in the interim.

Most of the building was dark, but behind the top row of translucent windows, the lights of Moskor's lab burned brightly. After clearing security at the front door, Gwen headed up the stairs to the fifth-floor lab. She rang the doorbell. The metal door opened, and on the other side stood her mentor, looming larger than life. His white hair was tousled, and his thick-framed glasses askew. His lab coat had black streaks and patches on it. He looked as if he had just slid out from underneath a car whose transmission he had been adjusting. Gwen recognized the disheveled appearance and the burning determination in his eyes. It meant Moskor had been wrapped up in an experiment of one kind or another. It meant he was happy.

"I get to see you twice in a month?" he grunted in his low-pitched Jersey accent. He shot her a crooked grin. "You get yourself fired or something?"

She stepped forward and wrapped her arms around the bear of a man. "Isaac, it's always a pleasure to see you."

"You too, kid," he said, breaking off the embrace. "Come see the old lab."

She followed him down a corridor into the main room of the laboratory. Along the back wall a row of cages rattled when she stepped into the room. Gwen remembered how the male rhesus monkeys always used to hoot and shake the cages when strangers, especially females, entered the room.

She might as well have stepped back into her postgraduate days of the late eighties. Most of the equipment was the same—lab tables, fridges, animal cages, and incubators—but there were new computers and other high-tech pieces of equipment scattered through Moskor's large lab. The sights, sounds, and smell of the place made Gwen realize how much she missed the milieu. The rewards of being a top-level government scientific administrator suddenly paled in the presence of the indescribable rush that came with the search for scientific truth, or even just the possibility of it, palpable in the air of her old research lab.

Moskor led her over to a row of microscopes on the table. "Gwen, you got to see this!"

Gwen leaned over the first microscope. She peered through the eyepieces and rolled a knob until the slide came into focus. The field lit up like a fluorescent green fireworks display. Between the luminescent areas were several dark cells. "African green monkey kidney cells?" Gwen asked without looking up.

"Yup."

African green monkey kidney was one of the best culture mediums for growing viruses in the lab. She recognized the bright green as direct fluorescent antibody or DFA staining, which meant that fluorescent-labeled antibodies had latched on to virally infected cells and lit them up in radiant green.

She stood up from the microscope and pointed at the slide. "Influenza?"

Moskor nodded. "An overwhelming infection, as you can see. Now look at the next slide. Same DFA stain. Same source blood."

Gwen moved down one microscope and looked into the eyepieces. The color was gone. Only the dark kidney cells floated in the field. She glanced up at Moskor. "What happened?"

"That blood came from the same monkey forty-eight hours later. Difference was he had been treated with our new drug," he said with a hint of pride. "A36112."

She leaned forward and wrapped her arms around Moskor again, catching him off guard. He stumbled back a step before regaining his balance. He laughed. "I'm not willing to take a hug even from a beautiful girl like you if it's going to cost me a broken hip."

Gwen released her grip. She gaped at him with a huge smile. "That's amazing, Isaac! No trace of infection at forty-eight hours."

"Not all of the subject cases turn out this well," he said. "But this is fairly typical of what we've been seeing with A36112."

"Do you know what this means, Isaac?"

"Yeah." He shrugged. "It means we've got a decent treatment for the flu in lab monkeys."

"C'mon, Isaac," she pressed. "It means a lot more than that."

"Don't get ahead of yourself, kid," Moskor said. "I'm as excited as a boy who just got the complete set of Yankees' ball cards, too. But I've learned better than to assume you can take this"—he pointed at the microscopes—"and replicate it in the real world."

"There's no reason to think you can't," Savard said.

"We're only in phase one testing on humans," Moskor pointed out.

"And?"

"So far the side effects have been mild, like with the monkeys. A bit of diarrhea. Not much else."

Savard nodded. "See."

"Gwen, even if everything goes off without a hitch," Moskor sighed. "You know how it works. We're minimum five years away from commercial production."

"Unless you're talking about compassionate release," she said, referring to the Food and Drug Administration clause that allows drugs to be released before finishing clinical trials in cases where the prognosis is otherwise hopeless.

"Compassionate release for the flu?" Moskor's face crumpled into a grimace. Then his eyes went wide with realization. He shook a finger at her. "You've come about that Gansu strain of influenza! That's why you're here, isn't it?"

"It's spreading, Isaac. London and Hong Kong."

"And I'm genuinely sorry about that," Moskor said. "But you're not seriously thinking about treating real patients with A36112."

"Why not?"

"Gwen, have you lost your mind?" he said. "This is a research lab drug. Nothing more as of yet."

"Isaac, we don't know of any currently available drugs to treat this infection."

He shook his head so vehemently that strands of his white hair fluttered above his head. "No. No. No."

Gwen put a hand on her hip. "Isaac, do you know what this Gansu strain is capable of? It's an indiscriminate killer."

Moskor sighed. "I don't doubt it, but that doesn't change anything."

"Twenty-five percent of its victims die," Gwen continued. "Most are under fifty So far, sixty children in a remote area of China died in one month, Isaac. Imagine what will happen if it sweeps the States?" She paused. "And we would have no treatment to offer."

"So you're willing to throw some untested drug at everyone and just hope for the best?" Moskor glared at her. "What of the seventy-five percent people who recover without treatment?"

"What of them?"

"What if my drug kills some of them?" he demanded. Then he added in a hushed tone, "That would be a fine legacy for my life's work."

"You said yourself that the side effects were mild in phase one testing," she countered.

"In a hundred healthy volunteers!" Moskor said. "We have no idea what it would do to thousands of already sick patients."

Gwen reached up and rested a hand on one of Moskor's thick, slumping shoulders. "Isaac, what if your drug saved thousands of lives instead? That would be a very fitting legacy for your life's work."

He shook his head, but with less vehemence. "It's too early, Gwen."

CHAPTER

18

Twenty miles south of Vancouver, Canada, Glenda and Marvin Zindler sat in their pickup truck in one of the six lanes at the Peace Arch Border Crossing, waiting to cross into the States. The dark gray skies threatened to erupt in rain at any moment. Only a white sedan stood between them and the customs agent, but it had been idling at the booth for over ten minutes while the agent leaned through the open window and interrogated the car's occupants.

"This would have been the fastest lane for sure!" Marvin growled, his round face flushing and his jowls shaking as he tapped the steering wheel like a bongo.

"What's the hurry, Marv?" Glenda asked, recognizing the familiar signs of escalation in her husband. "Seattle is less than three hours south of here, and the wedding isn't until tonight. We'll cross the border when we cross."

"That's not the point, Glen!" Marvin snapped.

Glenda noticed that the agent rested a hand on his belt

just behind his holstered gun. Though she had crossed this border often, it was the first time she realized that unlike their Canadian counterparts, American customs agents were armed.

The handsome young agent pulled back from the window. Not only was his blue uniform similar to a state trooper's, but he swaggered like one too as he walked around to the trunk of the car. He tapped on the back window and flagged the occupants inside.

"Oh, for goodness' sake!" Marvin huffed. "We'll be here forever!"

Riveted by the minidrama unfolding in front of her, Glenda ignored her husband's impatience as she watched the doors of the sedan open and a young couple step out.

"Figures!" Marvin heaved a sigh. "Look what we have here. A couple of them."

"Them, who?"

"A-rabs. Now we're going to have a search. Why they let those people come over here in the first place, I will never—"

"Give it a rest, Marv," Glenda said distractedly as she studied the young couple. They both wore jeans and light jackets. The young man was of average build. He stood stiffly immobile by the trunk, and he only removed his sunglasses when the customs agent tapped by the side of his own eyes and pointed at him.

In contrast to her husband—at least Glenda presumed the couple was married—the woman kept in constant motion, looking like someone desperate for a bathroom. Short and squat with a thick shock of curly black hair, she glanced around constantly. The one time her eyes met Glenda's, she dropped her gaze straight to the ground.

"Look, Marv, the poor dear is nervous as a virgin on her wedding night," Glenda said and she reached over and tapped her husband on his fidgeting hand.

"Probably has good reason to be," he grunted. "Bet they have forged papers. Or maybe they're carrying a bomb."

"Oh, Marvin!" Glenda sighed and shook her head.

The customs agent slammed the trunk shut. He signaled something to them with his index finger, and the young couple climbed back into their car. "He's letting them go through after all that?" Marvin said as if it were a personal insult.

But after passing the booth, the white car immediately turned off to its right. Glenda watched as the car circled back and passed them heading in the opposite direction toward Canada. "They're turning them back," Marvin said. "Good."

"Racist." Glenda shook her head at her husband. "Well, I feel sorry for them. That poor girl is going to be beside herself next time she tries to cross the border."

POLICE HEADQUARTERS, CAIRO, EGYPT

Sergeant Achmed Eleish sat at his desk, hidden in a cloud of cigarette smoke, reading the incomplete dossier. Its content was so bland that it could have documented the military career of any undistinguished officer. But from what Eleish knew of Major Abdul Sabri, his career had been anything but undistinguished.

When his informer, Bishr Gamal, had whispered Sabri's name from a phone booth in downtown Cairo, Eleish felt a chill. Gamal had refused to expand much on the revelation, demanding more money and a more secure line of communication. However, he had told Eleish that Sabri had been frequenting the Al-Futuh Mosque and seen often in the company of Hazzir Al Kabaal.

What was a secular army officer with a reputation for ruthlessly crushing Islamic radicalism doing at an Islamic mosque? Eleish wondered. He reached for the file again, hoping to glean a clue.

Even for an Egyptian Army Special Forces officer,

Sabri's file had been censored beyond usual. There were months, even years, missing. And the mentioned postings told very little of his activities. Some of the content was outright contradictory. In Alexandria in the early nineties, it said he had been assigned to port security, which did not fit at all with his Special Forces branch of the army. And after the Luxor massacre of 1997 (where sixty-eight Western tourists were gunned down by Muslim extremists), Sabri had been allegedly entrusted with assuring "tourism safety" for the pyramids of Giza. Eleish couldn't picture Sabri standing outside the Great Sphinx shepherding tourists around like a traffic cop. He could only infer that Sabri played a role in the largely successful hunt to track down and kill the masterminds behind the massacre.

The last entry was the oddest part of the file. Dated six months earlier, a single line stated that Sabri had voluntarily resigned his commission. Eleish did the calculation in his head. It meant that Sabri had resigned after twenty-three years of service, two years shy of the highest level of military pension that all officers sought. It made no sense.

Eleish's stomach rumbled. Thankful that Ramadan had ended, he reached into the desk drawer and pulled out his lunch at 10:40 in the morning. Samira had made him a pita bread sandwich stuffed with the cold lamb kebabs from last night's dinner. His favorite. Devouring the sandwich, he mulled the facts over in his mind trying to come up with a logical link between a publishing magnate, a Special Forces soldier, and a mosque known as a hotbed for Islamic extremism.

A raspy voice interrupted his thoughts. "Sergeant, I have something for you to see."

Eleish looked up from his lunch to see Constable Qasim Ramsi standing in front of his desk. Short and sweaty with beady eyes and an oily smile, the junior detective looked perpetually guilty, which coincidentally he was. Eleish knew Ramsi to be a corrupt officer who spent much of his time extorting money from the dealers, pickpockets, pimps, and prostitutes of Cairo.

"I'm busy, Constable," Eleish said, searching his desk for a napkin to wipe the pita sauce off his hands and face.

"You will want to see these," Ramsi said, and Eleish knew immediately that he wouldn't.

Ramsi pulled out the manila envelope from under his arm. He reached two stubby fingers inside and withdrew a series of black-and-white blowups. He dropped the first one on Eleish's desk.

Eleish finally located the lunch bag under the chair. Inside, he found the napkin his wife always thoughtfully packed for him. Only after his hands were clean did he reach for the photo. It was a snapshot of a murder victim lying on the street in his underwear. His head and face were covered in so much blood that his features were unrecognizable. Huge bruises mottled the upper chest and legs.

"Congratulations, Qasim, you have a murder victim," Eleish said. "It will be even more impressive if you find the murderer."

Ramsi smiled wider. "Not just any victim, Sergeant." He tossed another enlarged photograph onto Eleish's desk. It fluttered in the air, flipping upside down.

Annoyed, Eleish reached down and flipped it over.

It was a close-up of the victim's face after some of the blood had been wiped away. The victim's eyes were swollen shut. His lower lip was filleted down the middle. The nose deviated to the right. An open red sore replaced most of his right cheek. And his right ear was missing. In spite of the mutilation, Eleish recognized Bishr Gamal's face.

"Looks like you'll be needing a new informer," Ramsi grunted.

Eleish suppressed the surge of anger. He stared at the photo for a few moments, composing himself. "Where?"

"In an alley not far from Khan al-Khalili," Ramsi said.

"How did he die?"

Ramsi put a meaty finger on the picture. "Badly."

"This is not an autopsy report," Eleish said through gritted teeth. "Was he shot, knifed, or just beaten to death?"

"Beaten."

"Who?"

"Did you notice the missing ear?" Ramsi asked, patronizingly.

The gesture was the signature of one of Cairo's most notorious gangs, the Muhannad Al Din. Their name meant "sword of the faith," but Eleish had yet to meet a spiritual member of the gang. They were lowlife who trafficked in people, drugs, and firearms. They traded with anyone willing to pay, from Islamic extremists to European drug smugglers. And the price for double-crossing them always involved the loss of an ear before death.

"They didn't kill him quickly, though," Ramsi said. "Some of his bruises had ripened. And see the sore on his cheek. His face was burned with something."

"Tortured?" Eleish said.

Ramsi nodded.

"Why would the Muhannad Al Din torture Bishr?"

"A thousand reasons." Ramsi shrugged. "He was a street rat, Sergeant. Either he stole from them. Or short-changed a prostitute." He snickered. "Or maybe he snitched on them to you, and they wanted to find out what he told you."

Eleish took a slow breath, suppressing the urge to punch his slimy colleague. He swallowed his rage and spoke in an even tone. "Look, Ramsi, I knew Gamal. It will be easier for me. Why don't I take care of this?"

Ramsi shrugged. He dropped the rest of the photos on Eleish's desk. "It's all yours, Sergeant. He was going to the very bottom of my pile, anyway."

After Ramsi left, Eleish sat at his desk and stared at the photos of Gamal's disfigured face. Ramsi was right. Cairo was a violent city. There were a thousand reasons why the Muhannad Al Din might have killed Gamal. Still, Eleish sensed that his murder had something to do with his presence at the Al-Futuh Mosque. The realization stirred the pangs of guilt. It also tangibly reinforced the risks of tracking Hazzir Kabaal.

Eleish moved the black-and-whites out of the way and reached for Abdul Sabri's file. He flipped open the cover, on which there was a half-page black-and-white photo of Sabri. His delicate features stared tranquilly back at the camera.

"You work for Kabaal now, don't you, Major?" Eleish asked the picture softly under his breath and then reached for another cigarette.

CHAPTER
19

After finishing at the Royal Free Hospital and then visiting the headquarters of the London Health Commission, Haldane did not get his first glimpse of his hotel room until after 1:00 A.M. The message light was blinking on his phone, but he opted instead to check his e-mail. Propped on a pillow against the bed's headboard, he rested the notebook computer on his lap and flipped it open. After linking to the hotel's wireless network, he downloaded his e-mails. Several of the 224 messages were marked "urgent," but when Noah noticed his wife's name among the list of senders he went straight for her message. Sent almost twenty-four hours earlier, she had left the subject field blank. He read:

Noah,

I can't imagine a more cowardly way to do this, but I didn't know how else to reach you before you came home.

And I don't think I can look you in the eye and say what I need to say.

Noah, I never thought I could love anyone else the way I have loved you, but I can't deny any longer to you or to myself how deeply I have fallen for Julie. Gay? Straight? Bisexual? I don't know, "selfish" might be the only term that applies.

You've always been loving and decent to me. Even in those dark months when you withdrew from the world, I felt your pain. I know you never set out to hurt me. And it wasn't an excuse for what I did. There is no excuse.

Noah, you are a good person . . . maybe a great person . . . I am not. Still, I have tried to do the right thing. I wanted to turn my back on this consuming passion. Or is it addiction? God help me, I still do! But in the end, I can't.

Love? Lust? Infatuation? I don't know. I've lost my perspective. But whatever it is, I can't help how strongly I feel it.

I know so much more than my feelings are at stake. Chloe and you . . . But right now, I need time and I need space. Noah, I hope you will be willing to give me both though I deserve neither.

Anna.

Haldane sat and stared at the letters on the screen, without reading the e-mail again.

He wasn't shocked by any of what Anna had written. The signs had been building for some time. However, his calmness did surprise him; and even more astounding were the flickers of relief. He had heard patients say that the not knowing was worse than having the worst confirmed, but he hadn't believed them. Now at least in the case of his wife, he understood. The crippling doubt and agonizing second-guessing evaporated, replaced by a heavyhearted sense of purpose. Saddened as he was, at least he could start looking ahead instead of behind.

His cell phone rang, and he absentmindedly reached for it. "Hello?"

"Oh, Noah!" Anna said. "I've been trying to reach you all day."

He sat up over the side of the bed. "Is Chloe okay?"

"She's fine," Anna said. "It's just that I sent you an e-mail yesterday . . . when I thought you were on your way home."

She paused, but when Haldane didn't comment, she continued in her frantic tone. "I never would have sent it if I'd known you were going to London to fight this epidemic. What an awful thing to put on your plate with you already facing so much!"

"Why awful?" Haldane asked evenly.

"It was such a stupid e-mail. All melodramatic and full of impulsive thoughts like something a fourteen-year-old might write." She swallowed loudly. "Noah, please, will you just delete it?"

"Okay," he said.

"And can we pretend I never sent it?" she added.

He considered it for a while, then he said, "Anna, can I speak to Chloe?"

"Mom's got her for dinner. She won't be home for a couple more hours." Anna hesitated. "Noah, the e-mail? Will you destroy it for me?"

"If you like."

"Very, very much," she said with a nervous laugh. When he didn't comment, Anna spoke up to fill in the silence. "Noah, this Gansu Flu. The media makes it sound so dangerous over there!"

"They exaggerate," he said.

"You are being really careful, right?"

"Always," he said distantly.

"Noah, please come home soon," she said, her voice cracking. "Chloe misses you so much, and I . . ."

"Anna," Haldane said.

She swallowed again. "Yeah?"

"The answer is yes."

"Yes?"

"You can have time and space," he said.

"Noah, I told you, it was just an impulsive—"

"We both know that's not true," he cut her off. "You have a lot to sort out. I understand. I want you to. It's important for all of us." He cleared the lump from his throat. "Do what you have to do. Okay, Anna?"

Through the slight static, he heard his wife sobbing softly on the end of the line. "Will you still be there afterward?" she asked in a whisper.

Haldane woke up early the next morning with a slight headache and an ill-defined sense of defeat, like a drunk waking up after a fall off the wagon.

Desperate to avoid thoughts of the train wreck of his personal life, he lay in the warm strange bed and focused his mind on viruses. In spite of their oblivious malevolence, they held such fascination for him. They lived only to reproduce, and yet, they didn't really live at all. Nature's lethal half-measure, viruses were just floating bags of parasitic DNA or RNA, which required the complex machinery of a living cell to reproduce.

In his mind's eye, he imagined the electron-microscope-enhanced images of influenza crystals—perfect spheres surrounded by two proteins, hemagglutinin and neuraminidase, which stuck out of its surface like a ring of open umbrellas. Hemagglutinin and neuraminidase, which help bind the virus to its potential target, were also influenza's fingerprints, allowing scientists to classify strains of the virus by their H and N type. He had heard the previous day from the WHO Influenza Surveillance Lab that the Gansu strain had been identified as H2N2, the same subtype that accounted for the Asian Flu of 1957. But he knew that ARCS was not the Asian Flu. After intermixing with other species' viruses new proteins had hopped onto its surface and new genes had crawled into its RNA creating a superbug that had found its way from the farms of China to the streets of London and Hong Kong. And from there who knew where this minute monster might hit next?

Haldane glanced at the clock. It read 6:32 A.M. Time to move. He dragged himself into the shower. He was changed and in the lobby by 6:45. Duncan McLeod greeted him by the elevator with a steaming foam cup. "Here's a double-shot espresso for you," McLeod said. "You'll need this before Princess Charming shows up."

No sooner had he said it than Dr. Nancy Levine strode across the lobby toward them in a dour gray pantsuit. Her hair was in another tight bun, which served to accentuate the sharp ridges of her cheekbones and chin.

"Speak of the devil," McLeod whispered to Haldane. "Literally."

Haldane nodded to her. "Morning, Dr. Levine."

"Good morning, Doctors," she said crisply. The creases of her frown deepened. "We had best get a move on it. There have been more cases."

Levine started to walk, but Haldane stood his ground. "How many more?" he asked.

Levine stopped and turned to him. "Eight people inside the hotel."

"And outside the hotel?" Haldane asked.

"There are seven more suspect cases in Greater London," she said. "All of them are traceable directly or indirectly back to a tour of the Tower of London where they had contact with the first casualty, an American oil company executive named Fletcher."

"Fucking marvelous!" McLeod hollered in the middle of the lobby. "Some brilliant Yank takes a walking tour with walking pneumonia."

Haldane ignored his colleague. "How geographically spread is this new cluster?"

"A family in North London accounts for four of the cases," she said. "The other three are Dutch tourists staying in a hotel in the city center."

"And their contacts are quarantined?"

"Of course," Levine said coldly. "To the extent that is possible. The victims are tourists. Therefore, they have been visiting all over London."

Haldane digested the information without comment. After they had loaded into the Land Rover and headed out into the morning traffic, Haldane summarized. "So we have at least three distinct clusters of infections in the city now. Most of it among travelers. What sort of screening is going on at the access points like airports and train stations?"

Levine glanced at Haldane with an unfamiliar expression. It bordered on respect. "We immediately instituted our SARS screening plan at the airport. We have used the same questionnaire regarding fever and cough. And we are screening temperatures," she said. "We have tried a similar approach at the train stations. However, we have far less control of the traffic there."

"How many of the guests at Park Tower Plaza have left the country in the last five days?" Haldane asked.

"Several," Levine said. "We have been going through the hotel's checkout lists and the flight logs, contacting affected travelers. So far, no one we have reached has developed symptoms. We have recommended home quarantine to all of them for a minimum of five days."

"Good." Haldane nodded. "There have been no cases reported outside London?"

"No." Then Levine added, "Not yet."

The fatalistic comment brought a lull to the conversation. Haldane stared out the window at downtown London. There were cars and people on the sidewalk, but it looked very different from the bustle he remembered. The sight was eerily reminiscent of the streets of Jiayuguan City. He knew it wouldn't be long before faces everywhere in London were hidden behind surgical masks.

Haldane looked over at Levine. She gripped the steering wheel tightly. She had deep bags under her eyes, suggesting she hadn't slept in days. It occurred to him that Levine's haughty frigidity might have been partly in reaction to the enormous stress she was confronting. Haldane had seen other senior public health officials crumple in the face of lesser outbreaks.

"Dr. Levine," he said, "it would be a good idea to set up screening clinics today in the neighborhoods where there are known cases."

She glanced at him, her face set for an argument, but then her expression softened. "I will suggest it to the others on the Health Commission."

"What about the index case?" McLeod piped up from the backseat.

Levine shook her head. "We've not found her yet."

"Her?" Haldane said. "So you think it is the Spanish woman from the elevator of the hotel?"

"So far, she is the only connection we have uncovered."

"Bloody odd, isn't it?" McLeod pointed out.

"How so?"

"Why hasn't she turned up anywhere for treatment?" McLeod asked.

Levine sighed. "Dr. McLeod, there are countless hospitals and private clinics in London. She may well have presented to one of those before they had been alerted to the existence of the Gansu Flu."

"Or maybe she's dead," McLeod said. "You have checked the morgues, right?"

"Of course, we have," Levine snapped. "None of the cadavers match her description."

Haldane shook his head. "Putting aside the fact that she disappeared into thin air, the question I can't shake is: where? From where would this woman—Spanish, Greek,

Italian, whatever—have caught the virus in the first place?" He looked over his shoulder. "Duncan, did you notice many scantily dressed Caucasian women in Jiayuguan City?"

"Not an abundance, no," he said. "But Hong Kong is a different story."

Haldane shook his head. "The outbreaks occurred simultaneously. The timing would have been all wrong for her to become infected in Hong Kong and then spread it here."

"What about the Chinese government?" McLeod asked.

"What about them?"

McLeod leaned forward. "They lied through their teeth about SARS. Maybe the Gansu Flu is rampant in Beijing or some other city and they've been busy covering their asses."

"Then why invite us to Jiayuguan in the first place?" Haldane asked.

"Christ, Haldane!" McLeod threw himself back against the seat. "You're not under the delusion that governments apply logic or reason to their planning?"

"Dr. Haldane is right," Levine said definitively. "We would know by now if the Gansu Flu had spread to central China."

"So where does that leave us with our index case?" Haldane looked from McLeod to Levine.

"A mystery," McLeod muttered. "The fucking Stonehenge of microbiology, isn't it?"

Haldane didn't reply, but he knew from experience that there would turn out to be a very rational explanation for where the woman and the virus she shed came from. He hoped that explanation would come sooner rather than later. He knew they were just spinning their wheels until they found it.

"How's the little girl doing?" McLeod asked from the backseat. "Alyssa."

"I heard she was weaned from the ventilator this morning," Levine said and her lips formed a hint of a smile. "Apparently they have upgraded her condition to stable."

They drove past the landmark Kensington Gardens at the west end of Hyde Park and turned off onto Pembroke Road in the heart of the trendy Notting Hill district of London. Approaching the entrance to the Park Tower Plaza Hotel, Haldane noticed that the streets were lined with rows of trucks and vans, many of which bore TV channel logos on the side. As the car slowed to a stop, Haldane experienced another jolt of déjà vu.

The street had been barricaded with police cars blocking either end.

"To keep the press away," Levine explained as she rolled down her window for the officers manning the checkpoint. Once she had cleared security, she inched the car past ambulances and other government vehicles and into the hotel's driveway.

Armed police guarded the entryway. They scrutinized Levine's ID before directing her group to a makeshift change room. The three doctors donned gloves, caps, booties, gowns, and special N95 masks, which were designed for protecting against airborne TB particles. Looking like an entourage of misplaced surgeons, they entered the lobby. The posh hotel had been converted into a makeshift clinic. Fully garbed health-care workers milled about the lobby carrying thermometers, charts, and stethoscopes.

Nancy Levine led the others to the elevators. They rode the same elevator where Alyssa Mathews had acquired her life-threatening infection to the twenty-fifth floor. "We're using this floor as a special quarantine floor, specifically for people known to have acquired the virus," Levine explained. "The gentleman we are to meet, Mr. Collins, was in the Royal Free for three days but transferred back here last night to free up space in the hospital once his fever broke."

A fully garbed attendant met them at the doors to the elevator and directed them to the end of the hallway. After three knocks, the door opened. On the other side stood a bald man, wearing a mask and pajamas that looked loose on his thin frame. Because of the man's mask and lack of hair, Haldane had difficulty placing his age. Though he would have guessed Nigel Collins was close to his own age, somewhere in his late thirties.

After introductions, they followed Collins back to the small sitting room. As in the hospital in Jiayuguan City, Haldane found it awkward to conduct an interview with a group of masked people. Without seeing people's faces, it was difficult to read much into their responses.

"Where are you from, Mr. Collins?" Levine began.

"Call me Nigel," Collins said in a thick Liverpool accent, making him sound to Haldane like John or Paul from an early Beatles' interview. "Liverpool originally but live in Birmingham now. One of the local reps. Steelworkers union." He laughed. "Lucky me, name got drawn to come down for the big convention and stay in this swish hotel. Hah!"

"When did you first fall ill?" Levine asked.

"Four days ago!" he said, shifting constantly in his seat. "Hit me like a train. Woke up and couldn't move. Burning up. And the pain! Felt as if my arms and legs had gone through the rolling presses. Then the cough came. Crikey!" He guffawed. "Had me thinking that the smokes finally caught up with me!"

"Were you short of breath, Nigel?" Haldane asked.

Collins hemmed and hawed. "When the coughing spasms came, couldn't stop to catch my breath. Between times, not so bad. No idea it was possible to feel so weak, though. Raising a cup of water took both hands, if I could at all." He blew out so heavily that his mask fluttered over his mouth. "Then yesterday the fever broke quick as it came. By evening time felt almost normal again." He pulled at his pajama tops. "Except skinnier."

"Nigel, where do you think you might have caught this virus?" Haldane asked.

"Not think!" He puffed out his mask again. "Know!"

"And where is that?" Haldane said.

"Lovely little waif of a girl," he said and then looked at Nancy Levine. "Sorry, Doctor, it's just that—"

"Mr. Collins," she cut him off impatiently. "Could you describe her please?"

He offered a similar description of the woman as Veronica Mathews had, and then he said, "Around supper-time. I stood beside her waiting for the lift. Kind of swayed on her feet the whole time. Not well at all. Cough-ing the whole ride up. Still she covered her mouth, polite-like, and she wasn't exactly hard on the eyes." Again, he glanced to Levine. "You know what—"

"I know exactly what you mean," she snapped. "Which floor did she get off?"

"Same as me. Twenty-seventh." He guffawed. "Union boys outdid themselves, getting me a room on the top floor!"

"You rode the whole way up with her?" Haldane asked.

"Yes, sir."

"Did you ever see the woman again?"

Collins shook his head.

"Did you remember seeing a mother and two little girls board the elevator?" Haldane asked.

"Another beauty, right?" Collins asked and then shrugged at Levine apologetically. "I can't help noticing, Doctor."

"Apparently not," Levine said. "Mrs. Mathews is tall with dark hair and large eyes. A former model with daugh-ters aged four and five. Does that sound like her?"

"Exactly like!" Collins said. "Except she wasn't in the lift. I had seen her at the pool with her girls once or twice."

"You sure she wasn't in the elevator?" Haldane asked.

"Not with me or the coughing girl," Collins said. "At least not on the way up. I can't speak for the way down."

"Meaning?" Haldane asked.

"Well, when I got to my room, I turned around for one last little peep," he said sheepishly without looking to Levine. "The girl had sort of collapsed against the wall by the lift. Thought about going back to see if I could help. Then the lift door opened. She stumbled back in." He paused. "Never really thought much of it, but don't know why she bothered going all the way to the top just to turn around and head down. Maybe she missed her floor?"

Haldane rose from his seat, suppressing the urge to jump out of it. "Thank you, Nigel, you've been extremely helpful," he said as he headed for the door.

Out in the hallway, McLeod stopped him. "What's buzzing in your bonnet, Haldane?"

Haldane pointed at his chest. "Explain to me why a woman so sick that she can barcly stand rides the elevator from the lobby to the top and then heads back down."

"Shite, how do I know? Maybe Nigel was right?" McLeod said. "Maybe she was so sick that she missed her floor."

"Then why did she go all the way down to the lobby and ride back up with the Mathews family?" Haldane asked.

"How do you know she didn't take another trip later in the day?" McLeod asked.

"Remember?" Haldane tapped the back of his hand against his other palm. "Both Nigel and Veronica said it was just before suppertime!"

McLeod tilted his head from side to side, wavering.

"And why has she disappeared without seeking help?"

Haldane asked. "And where did she get the virus in the first place?"

McLeod's eyes widened to the point where his lazy one seemed to drift into the midline. "Are you suggesting that this woman was deliberately trying to spread her vile germs?"

Haldane shrugged. "Can you give me another plausible explanation?"

For the first time in all the years Haldane had known him, McLeod's eyes showed genuine fear. "What are we dealing with here, Noah?" he asked softly.

CHAPTER

20

When Nicole Caddullo awoke, for a disoriented moment she wondered if she had fallen asleep in her bathtub. Then she realized her bedsheets were drenched. Confused, the nineteen-year-old assumed her roommates had dumped a glass of water on her in her sleep as a joke. Thanks, guys! she thought angrily, but after the violent shakes set in she began to piece it together. Waking up in the middle of the night burning up from fever, she had thrown the blankets and bedspread off her. She had assumed it was a dream, but the proof in the form of her tangled bedcovers now lay in a heap at the foot of her bed.

Not the flu! Nicole thought. Not today.

She had an oceanography exam to write. And then back to the Vancouver Aquarium where she worked as a guide for her afternoon shift. The Aquarium! She remembered the small woman with the jet-black hair who wore thick-framed sunglasses despite the sunless gray skies. She had stood beside Nicole at the sea otter show two days earlier. Nicole had almost asked the woman to leave because her harsh cough was distracting the trainers and disrupting the show.

I bet that's where I picked this up, Nicole thought bitterly.

Freezing, she sat up and reached for the blankets at her feet. Flopping back on the bed, she couldn't believe how the minimal effort winded her. Lying with her blankets bundled around her she panted and gasped as if she had just broken her personal best time for the three-thousand meter dash.

Rather than easing with rest, her breathing grew more labored with each passing minute. Then the cough started. Her whole chest rattled with each hack. She coughed harder and harder. Then she choked on a gob of phlegm as if it were a chunk of meat before finally managing to spit it into her hand. She glanced down and saw that her hand was full of blood.

The sudden overwhelming panic surfaced as a hoarse scream.

HARGEYSA, SOMALIA

Hazzir Kabaal sat in his sumptuous office, enjoying his fourth espresso of the day. He liked a strong coffee before bedtime; he had trouble sleeping without it. In recent days, it had become a moot point. With or without coffee, he hardly slept.

When the media blitz first erupted, Kabaal had swelled with a prideful sense of accomplishment. It soon turned into a bittersweet victory. Kabaal had forgotten how attached he had become to London in his four years spent there. He remembered Sheikh Hassan's warning: "When the West takes hold inside you it grows like a cancer that is difficult to cut out." He knew the Sheikh was right, but the pictures of the empty London streets and the fear in the voices of TV interviewees had stirred the slivers of uncertainty. If only the Sheikh were here, Kabaal thought, he would wipe away the doubt with his pious reasoning.

"Sometimes God's way is the hardest way," Kabaal reassured himself aloud.

"So I have heard," Major Abdul Sabri said.

Kabaal hadn't realized that Sabri had materialized in his doorway. Kabaal looked down and flushed with embarrassment. He cleared his throat. "Welcome back, Major. I trust you had a safe trip."

Sabri shrugged. He wore another plain white robe, but with his thick shoulders, opaque blue eyes, and an air of certainty he didn't need a uniform or a weapon to establish his dangerousness.

"You met Mr. Gamal?" Kabaal asked.

Sabri sauntered up to the desk, answering only when he reached the foot of it. "We spent time together, yes."

"And?"

"Bishr Gamal was a petty criminal. A thief and a pickpocket." He paused. "But he supplemented his income working as a police informer."

Kabaal put his cup down and leaned forward in his chair. "Go on," he said.

"He was sent to spy on us at the mosque." Sabri looked over Kabaal's head as if already bored with the topic of conversation.

Kabaal tried to emulate Sabri's detached calm, but he couldn't keep the edge out of his voice. "Sent by whom?"

"Sergeant Achmed Eleish. A detective with the Cairo Police Force."

"Eleish!" Kabaal said. "That man has been dogging me for years."

Sabri nodded, displaying neither surprise nor interest in Kabaal's revelation.

"Eight or nine years ago, Eleish was shot by an activist who worked for my paper. Ever since he has been trying to prove my connection to The Brotherhood." Kabaal shook his head and sighed. "I should have taken care of him a long time ago."

"Shall I now?" Sabri asked.

Kabaal weighed the idea. "What exactly did Gamal tell Eleish?" he asked.

Sabri pointed from Kabaal to himself. "That we had been seen together. And that several of us had gone missing in the past weeks." He shrugged. "He didn't know much else."

"Much or nothing else?" Kabaal pressed.

"Gamal had heard mention of a desert base, but he swore he knew none of the details."

"Maybe he knew more than he was willing to tell?"

Sabri shot him a fleeting half smile. "After a couple of hours spent in my company, I don't think Mr. Gamal was capable of lying," he said as matter-of-factly as if the two of them had gone for a stroll.

"Did Gamal know if Sergeant Eleish had told others?" Kabaal asked.

Sabri shrugged.

Kabaal stared at his empty cup. "It would be foolish to assume Eleish is acting alone. If he disappeared now it would only raise suspicions and bring us even more attention."

"So what?" Sabri exhaled. "They couldn't find us if they wanted to."

"And neither will Eleish," Kabaal said. "For the time being, we should just keep an eye on him."

Sabri looked as if he might yawn at any moment. "There are many ways that Sergeant Eleish could go without raising suspicion. Cars crash. Police raids go awry. And the difference between poisons and heart attacks can be very subtle."

Kabaal hesitated, but then said, "Not yet, Abdul."

"As you wish."

Kabaal reached for a small stack of papers on his desk. "Our second wave has landed in America." He sighed. "Not without problems."

Sabri raised an eyebrow. "Problems?"

"Not in Chicago, but Seattle, yes." Kabaal reached for a paper on his desk and waved it at Sabri. "An e-mail from Sharifa Sha'rawi."

Kabaal read it aloud:

"Dear Tonya,

Arrived in Vancouver, Canada, with all our baggage. The line at the border crossing was too long. I never made it across to Seattle. I had to leave the present in Vancouver. We had a lovely time, but we couldn't stay. I'll be in touch. Love, Sherri"

Sabri nodded impassively. "So they turned her away at the border."

"Security is so tight these day. We should have flown her directly to Seattle." Kabaal shook his head. "I could have predicted that the logistics were too complicated."

Sabri shrugged. "Canada, America, what's the difference?"

Kabaal shook his head. "Canada didn't participate in the invasion of Iraq. We never intended to involve them."

Sabri's blank face broke into a slight smile. "Hazzir, you do realize that we have involved the whole world now?"

Kabaal looked down at the e-mail and nodded. "The Western world, anyway."

Sabri laughed bitterly. "You think the virus respects borders or religion? I doubt it will differentiate between the righteous and the infidels. And I know that the American bombs that follow will not."

"That is not the point, Abdul!" Kabaal looked up. "This is not about creating chaos. We will give them the chance to choose. To make amends. And once they do, we can stop spreading this unholy plague."

"God willing," Sabri said, straight-faced, but his eyes were loaded with doubt. "So when do we contact them?"

"Soon. Very soon," Kabaal said calmly. "But first, we must make them realize just how vulnerable they are."

CHAPTER
21

By the time Noah Haldane got back to the hotel, he had reached a slow boil. In his career, he had seen Ebola slaughter an entire village, a close friend die of SARS, and people perish in third-world hospitals for want of antibiotics readily available in any first-world drugstore. He had seen people put politics, stupidity, greed, and self-interest ahead of the welfare of victims, but never before had he suspected anyone of willfully propagating an epidemic.

Lost in his rage, he walked through the hotel lobby with his eyes cast to the ground. At first, he didn't register that it was his name being called out. "Noah?" the voice called again.

He looked up to see a woman striding rapidly toward him despite her slight limp. It took him a moment to place her. "Gwen?"

Gwen Savard shot out her hand. "I've come from Washington to see you."

He met her firm handshake. "Gwen, I am not sure I've ever needed a drink as badly as I do tonight."

"You too, huh?" She turned and headed for the lobby bar.

They chose a corner table by the crackling flames in the huge stone fireplace. They could have picked any seat in the bar. With widespread news of the virus's grip in London, it looked to Haldane as if the city had emptied overnight. While the traffic had seemed light to him yesterday, today the streets were largely deserted on what normally would have been a hectic workday. Of the few people he had spotted on the streets, several wore medical masks and most darted and dodged past as if air raid sirens had blown.

The waiter was at their side before they touched their seats. Haldane was tempted to invoke McLeod's two-highballs-at-once policy, but he refrained, ordering a bottle of Heineken instead. Savard asked for a double gin and tonic.

Once their drinks arrived, Haldane took a long sip of his beer. Placebo or not, the relief was immediate. With the bottle still on his lips he viewed Gwen, appreciating her striking features for the first time. With shoulder-length sandy blond hair, full lips, and the most aqua-green eyes he had ever seen, she was prettier than he remembered. But the steely resolve behind those eyes reminded him of what had struck him the only other time they had met in person: her serene confidence. Considering the circumstances, he found her self-assuredness soothing.

Haldane had little doubt that she had been sizing him up, too, but her placid expression was undecipherable to him. "How are things in London?" she asked.

Haldane exhaled. "Sixty more suspect cases of ARCS were reported today."

"Where?"

"There are three distinct clusters, so far." Haldane described the geographical dissemination of the virus, which followed the oil company executive's tour of the Tower of London. "Most of the infected are tourists."

Savard drained the last of her drink. "Which will make it very difficult to contain the virus to London."

He shrugged. "That's probably a moot point."

Savard spun the glass in her hand, staring at the swirling ice cubes at the bottom. "Oh?"

"ARCS didn't get to London on its own."

She stopped swirling. "No?"

"Someone meant to bring it." He studied her face waiting for a reaction but saw none.

"What makes you so sure?" she asked.

"I don't think you would be here if that weren't the case," Haldane said. "Besides, I've seen enough to know that infections don't just pop up on the other side of the world without leaving a trail." He paused. "And then there's the highly suspicious index case who by all accounts went out of her way to spread her germs." He described what he knew of the mysterious woman from the Park Tower Plaza's elevator.

Savard put her glass down. She stared at Haldane with a look of calm concern. "I agree, Noah. Someone has weaponized the Gansu Flu."

"Who?"

She shook her head.

He pointed the neck of his bottle at her. "No theories?"

"There's always the usual suspects, though we have nothing linking it to them." Her bone-straight shoulders sagged a few inches. "Some sophisticated lab equipment disappeared in Africa, but we don't know if it's related."

"Africa?" Haldane grimaced. "How does ARCS get from China to Africa?"

"It's just conjecture," she said. "The bigger question is where will it go next?"

"Depends on who has their hands on it, right?" he said.

Savard leaned over the table and locked her eyes on his. "Noah, how difficult is it to grow this virus in a lab?"

"You're not asking about WHO or CDC or any other legitimate lab, are you?"

"No."

Haldane nodded. "It would be dead easy. It's a type of influenza. Once you had a sample, you could incubate it in eggs, chickens, primates, or . . ."

"Humans!" Gwen jumped in.

"No lab required." He nodded. "Just people crazy enough to deliberately infect themselves with the Gansu Flu."

Gwen's eyes narrowed. She spoke quietly but with a noticeable edge. "There are people willing to strap bombs to their chests and walk into theaters, malls, and daycares. How different is this?"

Haldane rubbed his eyes. "Viral suicide bombers, huh?"

"Carrying a load more dangerous than any conventional explosive."

"Much," Haldane agreed. He pointed at her empty glass. "Another?"

"I'm okay, but you go ahead."

Haldane waved the waiter over and ordered a second beer. Then he turned back to Gwen. "I don't know if I can be of much more help."

Her smooth brow creased into a skeptical frown.

"Gwen, I deal with emerging pathogens of the natural kind. I have no expertise . . ." He sighed and then grunted a laugh. "Expertise! Christ, I don't have the first clue in dealing with man-made spread. That's your department."

"Man-made or not, we're facing a potential pandemic here." Then she added firmly, "And for that, we need your help."

The waiter arrived with Haldane's second beer. It felt

like ice in his hand, but this time the long sip brought no relief. "I'll do whatever I can," he said. "I'm just saying this is virgin territory for me."

"For all of us." The crow's-feet deepened at the corners of her large green eyes. Her lips parted into a wide smile. "But thank you."

Haldane laid the beer on the table. "So what's the next step?" he asked.

"We deal with each outbreak while we track down the source."

"Or sources," he said.

"Yeah."

"How?" he asked.

She swept her hand over the table. "A coordinated international police and intelligence effort."

"The CIA?"

She shrugged. "And Interpol, MI5, FBI, NSC, CDC, WHO, DHS . . ."

Haldane forced a grin. "Maybe the AAA?"

"If necessary." She laughed. "Whoever it takes." She bit her lower lip and eyed him intently. "Do you have any ideas?"

Haldane hunched his shoulders and grimaced. "For catching bioterrorists?"

"For dealing with this."

"A vaccine should be a top priority," he said.

"Which could take months, if not years."

"But if this virus is going to be used as a weapon, it will always be a threat until everyone is immunized . . . or has already been infected."

"Okay. Fair enough," she said. "Any more immediate suggestions?"

"The single best defense in outbreak control is communication. Especially in this case since the Gansu Flu could hit anywhere next. We need to put the world on notice."

"I think they already are." Gwen bit down harder on her lip.

"They might be aware, but now they need to act," Haldane said. "Every fever or cough on the planet must be assumed to be ARCS until proven otherwise."

Savard whistled.

"Can you imagine if we don't?" Haldane asked. "This bug has ground one of Europe's biggest centers to a halt. And we've just seen the beginnings of it. Wait until it comes to the States." He sighed. "And, Gwen, we both know it will."

His cell phone rang. He pulled it out of his pocket and glanced at the call display, which read "Switzerland." Haldane brought the phone to his ear. "Hello."

"Ah, Noah, it's Jean," Nantal said as warmly as if he were calling to wish him a happy birthday.

"Can I call you back later, Jean?" Haldane said. "I'm in the middle of a debriefing with Gwen Savard."

"No, Noah, I wish I didn't have to interrupt you and the beautiful Dr. Savard, but my news is terribly important," Nantal said. "For both of you."

"What news?" Haldane asked.

"Two people have tested positive for the Gansu Flu in Vancouver," Nantal said.

"Vancouver, Canada?" Haldane said, more for the benefit of Gwen who watched him intently.

"Yes," Nantal said.

"New cases?" Savard mouthed the question at Haldane.

He held up two fingers for her. Then he spoke into the receiver. "Look, Jean, we believe somebody is deliberately spreading this virus."

"So it would seem," Nantal said without a trace of surprise.

"I imagine it will crop up all over the place soon. We need to meet with Gwen's team and set up a pandemic ARCS task force, sooner—"

"Excuse me, Noah," Nantal cut in. "There is something most peculiar about the latest Vancouver case."

"*Everything* about this is beyond peculiar," Haldane said.

"Yes, of course," Nantal agreed. "But aside from the nineteen-year-old girl who died in hospital, the other Vancouver victim was pulled out of a river." He paused. "And she had a bullet hole between her eyes."

CHAPTER
22

Ran Delorme had worked for the Agency for six months, but the twenty-four-year-old doubted he would be able to handle one more day at Langley. He had never expected (though he secretly hoped) to walk off the street and into James Bond's life, but neither had he expected to spend twelve hours a day in front of a computer reading mind-numbingly boring e-mails, which Carnivore had plucked out from the high-tech sewer of global chatter. Words like "terrorist," "bomb," and "hijacking" found their way into the most mundane of e-mails, but Carnivore did not know any better so the piles of "suspicious" e-mails accumulated daily to be reviewed by human eyes; in other words, Delorme and his hapless colleagues.

Delorme glanced at the clock: 11:50 A.M. He figured he could trash twenty more e-mails before lunch. He breezed through the first eighteen. He had scanned two paragraphs of the nineteenth before the red flags went up.

He read the e-mail again, and then printed it out. His hand trembling slightly, he highlighted the last sentence in yellow: "I cannot exclude the possibility of terrorism or the use of the virus as a weapon." He glanced from the name at the bottom of the e-mail to the electronic source. They both read: "Dr. Ping Wu."

Delorme's eyes darted around in search of a date stamp. They locked on to a date in the screen's bottom corner, which proved the e-mail was sent over a week earlier from somewhere in China. He tapped a few keys and the computer spat out a more specific location for the e-mail's source: Jiayuguan City, Gansu Province.

Gansu! He felt butterflies in his stomach. He had just read an article in the morning's paper on how the Gansu Flu was sweeping London.

Forgetting about lunch, his hand shot out in search of the phone.

HARGEYSA, SOMALIA

Hazzir Kabaal, Major Abdul Sabri, and Dr. Anwar Aziz sat in Kabaal's office staring at the tape recorder on the desk.

Kabaal hit the play button. There was a hissing sound, before a voice spoke up in Arabic. At thirty, the spokesman was one of oldest fighters in the compound. Physically nondescript, he had been chosen because of his anonymity and his deep raspy voice. "I am a representative of The Brotherhood of One Nation," the man said. "In the name of God and Jihad, we have struck at the hearts of our enemy. We have unleashed a new weapon in our holy war!" His voice quavered. "We have brought the outbreaks of the Gansu Flu to London, Hong Kong, Vancouver, and Chicago. More cities will follow soon if the fools and infidels do not heed our demands."

A pause was filled by the sound of a page turning. "All American and Coalition soldiers must immediately withdraw from the holy soil of Iraq, Afghanistan, the Arabian Peninsula, and all other observant nations," the spokesman said. "These same aggressors must desist in their threats to Syria and Iran, and withdraw their military and financial support for the Israeli oppressors." He paused again, this time for effect. "There will be no negotiation. If withdrawals have not begun within four days of today, an army of martyrs will be unleashed upon the cities of the West." His tone dropped an octave. "Let the blood be on the hands of that criminal, the American President." He paused one last time. "It is God's way. Allah be praised."

The tape hissed again before Kabaal reached over and hit the stop button.

Sitting stiffly in his lab coat, Aziz did not comment, but he appeared acutely uncomfortable; a scientist who had inadvertently strayed into a foreign world of politics.

Sabri looked at Kabaal inexpressively. "Where will you send this tape?" he asked.

Kabaal leaned calmly back in his chair. "We will courier it to Al Jazeera Network and Abu Dabi TV. We will also e-mail a translation to the Western news outlets."

"When?"

"In a few days, when this next wave of virus has fully taken hold." Kabaal pointed at the tape recorder. "What do you think of the message?"

Sabri rocked his head slightly from side to side. "It is not specific enough."

Kabaal frowned. "I don't understand, Abdul. What more could we say?"

"There is no mention of us," Sabri said.

"Of course there is. He talks about The Brotherhood—"

Sabri stopped him with a raised palm. "You miss my point, Abu Lahab." He pointed his finger from Kabaal to Aziz to himself. "Where are we mentioned?"

Kabaal gripped his desk. "Are you suggesting we tell

the world that Abdul Sabri, Anwar Aziz, and Hazzir Kabaal are behind this?"

Sabri nodded.

Kabaal gaped at Sabri, questioning the major's sanity. "Except for making it easier for them to find us, what possible purpose would that serve?"

Sabri tilted his head at Kabaal. "Why do you think Osama sends videotapes confessing—no—boasting about his involvement?"

"Adulation?" Kabaal shrugged. "What does this have to do with him?"

Sabri shook his head again. "He offers his name so the faithful have a hero to look to. If Al Qaeda had no face, they would not inspire and incite the people the way they do. Osama gives them strength and courage. He gives them a leader. And he draws them to the flame."

Kabaal shook his head. "They already have Osama for inspiration. Our purpose is to achieve a more tangible goal. And now we have the weapon to do it."

Sabri frowned. Coming from anyone else, it wouldn't have meant much. But his impassiveness was so built into his blank face that the slight grimace conveyed a torrent of emotion. "Something else is bothering you, Major?" Kabaal asked.

Sabri looked down. "I want them to know," he said quietly.

"Who?"

Sabri's head shot up, his pale blue eyes burning. "*They* are my former superiors in the Egyptian Special Forces."

"You want them to know you have joined us?" Kabaal's jaw dropped. "Why?"

"For twenty years, I did whatever they asked of me," Sabri said.

Mouth still open, Kabaal shrugged.

"Don't you understand?" Sabri glared at him. "They made me fight my own people. They made me torture, maim, and kill my Muslim brothers for abiding by the word of God." He tapped his chest. "And I was a good soldier. I went along with it."

Kabaal stared at his lieutenant, astounded by the outpouring.

"I became very good at it, too. I did things other people didn't have the stomach, the guts, or the brains to do. And the more I killed, the more they wanted from me." Sabri's facial features looking even more feminine creased in indignant outrage. "And after doing their dirty work for twenty years they chose not to advance me. To keep me at the same measly rank of major. Do you know why?"

Kabaal shook his head. Aziz stared at the desk, avoiding eye contact with Sabri.

"Because I had too much blood on my hands!" Sabri said.

Kabaal didn't comment.

"They said my reputation preceded me. That I had become infamous for my tactics. And now that political winds had changed, they could not afford to alienate certain people by recognizing me for my 'ruthlessness.' " He laughed bitterly. "I gave them my soul. I betrayed my people and my God. And they reward me by telling me I did it too well. And I could never be more than a contemptible major!"

Kabaal didn't reply. Shocked as he was by Sabri's uncharacteristic effusion, the pieces suddenly fit. He finally knew why Sabri had joined their cause. As Kabaal had long suspected, it had little to do with piety. But Kabaal never before understood the real driving force: Sabri was out to wreak his vengeance on those who had overlooked him for promotion.

His face blank, Sabri retreated to a more familiar pose.

Kabaal wondered if Sabri regretted the outburst. Kabaal didn't. For him it came as a relief. It removed the unknown from Sabri's motives, which had hung over

Kabaal as a potential threat. And from his years in the newspaper business, Kabaal knew that motive was often inconsequential to result. Sometimes the people driven by the pettiest reasons, like greed and envy, reaped the biggest yields of all.

With the insight Kabaal felt empowered. He smiled paternally at Sabri. "Listen, Abdul, the world will one day know who you are, but not yet. It is too early. And it would jeopardize the operation."

Sabri nodded distantly.

Kabaal pointed at Sabri. "Soon though it will be safe to tell. And tell we will. Mark my words, Abdul. They will come to deeply regret not making you a general or even their commander-in-chief."

"I will wait for now," Sabri said coolly. "But one day soon . . ."

CHAPTER
23

Savard and Haldane caught the first direct flight to Vancouver out of Heathrow while McLeod stayed behind in London, promising to "clean up the bloody mess."

Recognizing that it would be his last chance at sleep for some time, Haldane dozed on and off in his window seat. It was a restless sleep punctuated by unsettled dreams and one memorable nightmare. In the dream, corpses lay piled on the streets, the same way they had in that village he had seen in Zaire during the Ebola rampage. Except these were not the dirt roads of Zaire, but the familiar streets of his own Glen Echo Heights neighborhood. And the bodies littering the sidewalks were those of his friends and neighbors. The only person left standing, Haldane dashed from corpse to corpse, gaping into the familiar faces of the dead, looking not for any index case but for his own family members.

Haldane woke with a start. He looked over to see Gwen

speaking in hurried, hushed tones on the in-flight "air phone."

She hung up and glanced at him with a distracted grin. "Back from the dead, are we?"

Haldane pulled himself up in his seat and brought it forward. "Just a catnap."

Her brow creased. "You okay? You look like you just saw a ghost."

"Indian food for dinner." With his palms, he wiped the sleep from his eyes. "I always have vivid dreams when I eat spicy stuff." He pointed from the phone to the laptop. "Are you rounding up the troops in D.C.?"

"With something like this there are a lot of people and agencies to coordinate. It's a massive logistics headache."

"Hmmm," he said. "Are there any skeptics left?"

Savard shook her head slightly. "The bullet in the Vancouver index case buried the last of the doubt." She eyed him steadily. "Besides, Noah, the first cases have shown up stateside."

Though the news wasn't unexpected, he felt violated, as if his home had just been broken into. "Where?" he asked.

"Chicago."

"How many?"

"Four so far," she said.

"The link?"

"Football."

"Football?"

She sighed. "All the victims were at the Bears' game at Soldier Field three days ago."

"A football game," he snorted. "I know several of Chicago's ID guys," he said in reference to the infectious disease specialists. "They're world class. I have no doubt they'll handle this well."

"Can it be handled well?"

Haldane didn't answer. The soft hum of the aircraft

filled the lull in their conversation. Finally, Haldane asked, "Gwen, do you have kids?"

"No. My husband . . . ex-husband . . . estranged husband . . ." She laughed uncomfortably. "We're separated, and I can never keep the terminology straight. We tried for a while, but it wasn't to be." She paused. "Truth is, we always seemed to put career in front of family. Shocking that we ended up apart, huh?" She uttered another laugh. "And you?"

"I've got a little girl, Chloe." His smile came out of nowhere.

She pointed at his jeans. "Can I see the photograph?"

"How do you know I carry one?" he asked as he reached for his wallet.

"Bet you carry more than one."

"Mea culpa," he said and flipped open his wallet to show her the side-by-side snapshots. The first caught Chloe in the midst of an openmouthed giggle, and the other, with a demure eyes-to-the-ground pose for the pre-school photographer. "She'll be four soon," he said.

"Sweet." Savard took the wallet from his hand. She studied both photos and then held them up to compare to Noah's face. "I see a lot of you. Especially in this goofy shot." She tapped on the laughing Chloe.

"Thanks . . . I think." He took the wallet back and slid it into his pocket.

"Noah, can I ask you a personal question?"

"Okay."

"Family means an awful lot to you, right?"

"I was bracing for a tougher question than that." Haldane frowned. "Yes, it does."

Her expression didn't waver. "You must travel a lot with your WHO job?"

"Not always. In the last couple of years with SARS, the Avian Flu, and now the Gansu Flu, I have been gone for long stretches. Though, I know what you're getting at.

Each time it does get harder to be away from my family . . . from Chloe." He hesitated. For a moment, he considered telling her about his own recent estrangement, but decided he didn't know Savard well enough to lay his mess at her feet. "I doubt I can do this for much longer, but one of the few perks of being an emerging pathogens expert is that you get to see the bugs where they live and kill, which thankfully is almost always some faraway exotic place." Then he added, "Or at least it used to be."

She brushed the strands of hair back from her eyes. "You didn't expect one to make its way so close to home."

He wet his dry lips with his tongue. "I never expected anyone to go to such an effort to bring it home."

Her eyes held his. "Does it really surprise you, Noah?"

"Don't know about surprise, but it pisses me off." He paused, and then said quietly, "And it scares the hell out of me."

VANCOUVER, CANADA

Four Royal Canadian Mounted Police officers met them at the Vancouver International Airport. Haldane had the naive expectation that all Mounties routinely wore the red and black uniforms with jodhpurs and wide brim hats of the famous musical ride, but these RCMP wore standard gray-green police uniforms. The senior officer introduced herself as Sergeant Monique Tremblay, a homicide detective. Tremblay was tall, thin, and looked to be in her late forties. She spoke with a trace of a French-Canadian accent and with short hair brushed forward in gelled spears and her funky stained-glass earrings, she managed to infuse her nondescript uniform with a flare of élan.

"*Parlez-vous français?*" Tremblay asked Savard when she heard the surname.

"*Un peu, mais il y a personne ici avec qui je peut parler en français,*" Gwen said, and then switched to English. "My dad was born in the States. He didn't speak any

French. I took a few courses in college out of ancestral guilt."

"*D'accord.* I'm from Montreal, but no one speaks French in Vancouver, either." Tremblay smiled and led them to her unmarked police sedan waiting out front. Haldane climbed into the back, leaving the front seat for Savard. As they drove, Tremblay explained, "The body surfaced on the south bank of the Fraser River."

"Which is where?" Savard asked.

Tremblay pointed ahead to an approaching bridge. "We're just about to drive over the Fraser on the Arthur Laing Bridge. The river marks the southern border of Vancouver proper, dividing her from the suburbs like Richmond where we are now. Had she washed up on the Vancouver side, the RCMP wouldn't be involved. It would be a Vancouver Police Department matter," she said.

"Lucky you," Haldane said.

"You think?" Tremblay laughed. Once on the bridge she pointed to her right. "The body was found about four miles east of here by a man walking his dog along the river at dawn."

"And she had been shot?" Savard asked.

Tremblay nodded. "Small caliber bullet in the forehead. Exit wound in the back of her skull. No sign of the bullet."

"Any chance of suicide?" Savard asked.

"Doubtful," Tremblay said. "The Forensic Ident guys say that the gunshot wound is incompatible with self-induced injury, but more compelling are the deep gouges around her ankles."

Savard nodded. "Ligatures?"

"Yes," Tremblay said. "We believe she was weighted down by something, but her legs must have slipped free of the cord anchoring her."

Gwen looked over at the detective. "Can you describe her?"

"She was darker skinned—central Asian, Persian, or

more likely of Arab origins. Probably mid-twenties. Five feet one inch with long curly black hair. No ID on her. Dressed in jeans and blouse. Her entire outfit came from the Gap, so it's not going to help us narrow down her origins much." Tremblay sighed. "Her description fits the one from the witnesses at the Vancouver Aquarium. Allegedly, she walked around the Aquarium going from show to show coughing on people." She smacked her steering wheel once with a clenched fist. "She has already killed a nineteen-year-old Aquarium employee. Who knows who is next? She might as well have emptied a loaded magazine into the crowd!"

"No leads?" Savard asked.

"Nothing so far. We don't know where she died, or even where the body was dumped. It's possible it was farther east toward New Westminster and then floated down. And there are no missing persons who fit her description." She sighed. "We need a big break on this one."

Haldane leaned forward and rested his elbows on the front seats' headrests. "I think her body surfacing *is* the break," he said. "Now we had better capitalize on it."

The conversation lapsed. Haldane stared out the window at the snowcapped mountains and the lush greenery of the strikingly pretty city around them. He had a soft spot for Vancouver. The world-class outdoors activities in the city where "the mountains kissed the sea" had so enticed him that he once considered relocating there to work in HIV research, but Anna hadn't wanted to move so far from her family.

Arriving at the Vancouver Hospital, Monique Tremblay led them down to the morgue in the basement. Weaving through the hallways, she guided them to Dr. Jake Maguchi's office. Maguchi jumped out of his chair to greet them. The squat Japanese-Canadian pathologist struck Haldane as a study in cultural contradiction. Wearing a ponytail and a diamond stud in his ear, he bowed by way of introduction. Then he smiled broadly. "I've never had such international bigwigs come to visit before." Haldane found Maguchi's laid-back, West Coast dialect spoken with a Japanese accent as jarring as his appearance.

"Thanks for seeing us, Dr. Maguchi," Gwen said as she settled into her seat. "We are impressed by how quickly you diagnosed the Gansu Flu."

Maguchi mopped at his sweating brow with the sleeve of his lab coat. "No thanks to me. The ER team already suspected the diagnosis in the first victim. And as soon as I cracked the chest on the second—"

"Excuse me," Gwen cut in. "Can you back up?"

"No worries." Maguchi nodded with a smile. "The first cadaver came from our own emergency room. A nineteen-year-old university student. Nicole Cadullo. She was found near dead by one of her roommates, after she had coughed up buckets of bloody sputum. The ER boys recognized how unusual her sudden presentation was. With all the news . . ." He circled a finger in the air. "They put two and two together. Stuck the patient in full isolation and sent off the lab work. Couldn't save the poor girl, though. Nineteen! The bug ate her alive." He reached for a glass of water on his desk and took a long swallow. "By the time I finished the autopsy we had heard a preliminary report from the virology lab that it was the Gansu strain of influenza."

Gwen nodded. "And the second case?"

"Get this!" Maguchi snapped his fingers. "I've just slipped out of my spacesuit," he said, in reference to the biohazard suit, "and who should be my very next autopsy? The Jane Doe from the river." He mopped his sweaty brow again. "Whew, they got the heat cranked up today." He took another sip of water. "No mystery about cause of death with that hole in her forehead. I was just painting by the numbers, really. But when I cracked open her chest, I couldn't believe what I saw inside. Her lungs were chock-a-block full!"

"Wouldn't you expect that in a drowning?" Savard asked.

Maguchi shook his head. "Two types of drowning, wet and dry. Wet drowning occurs when people aspirate the water and fill their lungs. Dry drowning, which is more common, is when the larynx goes into spasm and chokes off the passage to the lungs before much water gets in. It's protective for about five minutes and then you die from lack of oxygen anyway. Either way, it's irrelevant because our Jane Doe didn't drown. She was dead when she hit the water, so she wouldn't have inhaled anything. Besides, it wasn't water we found in her lungs."

"Pus?" Haldane guessed.

"More than that, it was a hemorrhagic, purulent exudate. The same blood-streaked junk I saw in the lungs of the Cadullo girl. I was flabbergasted. Their lungs were interchangeable." Maguchi rose to his feet. "Come on. You got to see this."

Tremblay blocked his path. "Jake, what about my photo?"

"Oh, yeah, yeah. I got it." Maguchi spun around and combed through the piles of paper on his desk.

Haldane and Savard both looked to Tremblay for an explanation. "Dr. Jake is a wizard at bringing corpses—especially unidentified persons—back to life with computer-enhanced photography," she said.

Maguchi reddened. "Guy's got to have a hobby." He grabbed a manila envelope and pulled out the stack of eleven-by-eight photos. "This one couldn't have been simpler. No fancy software required." He passed Tremblay the first snapshot.

Haldane and Savard leaned over either shoulder to view the photo. Despite her open eyes, the woman with the cherubic face and springy black hair still looked very dead to Haldane, even if he could ignore the dime-shaped hole less than an inch above the inner edge of her left eyebrow.

But in the next photo Maguchi passed them, Jane Doe sprang back to life.

"I just did some very minor touch-ups with my photo editor," Maguchi said modestly.

Not only was her forehead unblemished but now her cheeks and lips had filled with natural color. Maguchi had imbued the photo with another quality that Haldane couldn't put his finger on, which invigorated the woman's face to the point where it looked as if she had actually posed for the camera. She was not pretty, but she had a pleasant young face. It was full of hope and promise, not the face of the indiscriminate killer she turned out to be.

"You're a genius, Jake!" Tremblay said and then took the photo and tucked it back in the envelope with the others.

Maguchi grabbed a CD off his desk and passed it to Tremblay. "The electronic copies are on this."

"What are you going to do with them?" Gwen pointed at the envelope.

"Circulate them." Tremblay shrugged. "TV, newspapers, Internet . . . everywhere I can."

"Then everyone will know that somebody is intentionally spreading this thing," Savard said.

"Don't they deserve to?" Tremblay stiffened. "Besides, how else will we track down her identity and find her killer." She shook the envelope in her hand. "This photo is the key."

Haldane nodded. "Sergeant Tremblay is right, Gwen. The wider the circulation the better. This is what they didn't count on. It could lead us to the source."

Savard nodded.

Tremblay passed Savard and Haldane each a card. "I will catch up with you later, but if you have any questions or concerns, I am always reachable by cell phone."

Maguchi reached for his glass of water. He took another big swallow and choked on it, which sent him into a long coughing fit. "Sorry, I have a bit of a drinking problem."

He gasped a laugh at his own tired joke once he finally had caught his breath.

Maguchi led Savard and Haldane to the dissecting suites. They stopped in front of a series of doors. One door had a large plastic biohazard sign hanging from the double doors. Maguchi pointed at it and then indicated the table beside it with gowns, masks, plastic face shields, and gloves. "No doubt the virus is long dead, but we can't afford to take chances," he said as he slipped on his gown and adjusted his face mask.

Once garbed, Maguchi thrust open the double doors and walked into the room with the others in tow. Aside from a sink, garbage can, and dissecting tray the only other furnishing in the white tiled room was the heavy metal gurney in the center.

Naked, the woman from the photos lay on her back with eyes fixed on the ceiling. Short and slightly over-weight, she had olive colored skin and thick pubic hair consistent with her presumed Semitic origins. Her long hair fell back on the gurney, exposing the edges of the cut at the base of her hairline made by the skull saw in order to extract her brain. She had a deep Y-shaped incision that started above her breasts and then ran down between them and along the midline past her belly button. The skin folded together at the edges of the incision, threatening to peel back any moment like an unzipped jacket in the wind.

More than the surgically induced mutilation, her tender age disturbed Haldane. He doubted she was far past her teens or old enough to appreciate the repercussions of her ruinous and self-destructive killing spree. What a god-damn waste! he thought.

Standing at the head of the table, Maguchi grabbed a blunt metal probe from the dissecting tray. He brought it up to the bullet hole above the cadaver's left eyebrow. "If you look close, you can see the black stippling around the entry wound."

Haldane leaned forward and saw the speckles, which looked like fleas caught scurrying from the wound.

"Powder residue," Maguchi said. "Means the gun was fired from no more than two feet away from the girl's head." He put his gloved hand behind her head and lifted it off the table. Then he stuck the probe through the hole in her forehead and directed it toward the exit wound so that the probe was sticking out at a forty-five-degree angle from the skin. "See the angle of the bullet entry?"

"Somebody was standing above her?" Savard suggested.

"Exactly." Maguchi nodded. "Unless the killer was standing on a chair, she was kneeling when she was shot."

"Praying?"

Maguchi chuckled. "Can't tell that from an autopsy, but I do know that she must have known what was coming."

Maguchi pulled out the probe and dropped it back on the tray. "Now, let's have a look at her chest." He pivoted and tripped, falling against the side of the gurney.

Haldane reached over and steadied his arm. "You okay?"

"Just a little clumsy." Maguchi chuckled. "It's why I got kicked out of the neurosurgery program." He pushed himself upright. He stepped over to the corpse's midsection. With both hands, he folded back the skin of the incision, opening it like a tent. Her intestines had been removed, and her chest cavity was so empty it displayed the ridges of her vertebrae poking through from the back. He pointed to a smooth shiny surface, separating the chest from the abdomen. "Look at her diaphragm and chest wall." Gobs of blood and yellow-green pus still clung to the diaphragm and along the inside of the chest, more so on the left than the right side, looking like the skin on top of a left-open paint can.

"She had a big empyema, meaning the pus was trapped between her drenched lungs and the chest wall," Maguchi said. "When I made the first cut into the chest, the stuff sprayed out and hit me in the gown like a garden hose. There must have been four or five liters' worth in her chest, which trust me is a huge amount."

Haldane could picture it in his mind. He had experienced the same phenomenon putting chest tubes in live patients, but he viewed Maguchi questioningly. "Empyema? That's unusual for a viral pneumonia."

"I know," Maguchi said. "But the previous cadaver had the same."

"Dr. Maguchi," Gwen said, "can you tell how long she had been submersed?"

"Not long," Maguchi answered. He ran a finger over the arms and legs. "See her limbs? No skin sloughing at all, which at these temperatures would occur after twelve to twenty-four hours. And she's got none of the log scrapes or nibbles that we tend to see after twenty-four hours."

"Nibbles?" Gwen shrugged.

"Fish bites," Maguchi said nonchalantly.

Savard showed no sign of reaction. "So she was found at dawn yesterday," she said. "Means it was likely that she was shot and dumped in the river either early that morning or late in the previous evening."

"Yup. I've put time of death between midnight and 2:00 A.M." He turned away from the cadaver and started for the door. "Come on. I want to show you her lungs. I have them in the room next door."

Maguchi stumbled as he headed for the door. He made it within a few feet of the wall when his legs buckled. He dropped to his knees. He grabbed for the sink on the wall in front of him, but his arm span wasn't long enough to reach. He flopped forward and hit his head on the floor with a loud thud.

Noah lunged forward but reached Maguchi a moment too late to stop his head from making contact with the floor. Haldane rolled Maguchi from facedown onto his side. A cut had opened above the pathologist's left eye and blood started to leak out from under his face shield and drip on to the floor.

When Haldane put a hand to Maguchi's forehead, the skin was burning hot. "Jake, are you okay?"

Maguchi stared back at him, bleary-eyed. "It couldn't be. I took precautions."

"What's wrong?" Savard said, crouching on the other side from Haldane and leaning over Maguchi.

"Hot and cold," Maguchi said. "And the aching. So stupid! I never put it together. I have the bug, don't I?"

"Do you know where you are?" Haldane asked.

"In big trouble is where," Maguchi said with a weak laugh.

"Your breathing okay?" Haldane asked.

"No problem. A tickle in my throat." He gawked at Haldane, fear creeping into his eyes. "I took all the precautions."

Haldane shook his head slowly. "When you started the autopsy on the Jane Doe, what were you wearing?"

"Gown, mask, gloves, and all that," Maguchi said.

"But no eye shield, right?" Haldane said. "You didn't know she had the Gansu Flu."

"Yeah, but still—"

"The empyema, Jake. Remember?" Haldane said. "You told us it sprayed into your chest. The splash probably got up by your eyes and face. Droplets could have snuck under your mask. Or maybe you rubbed your eyes later with the virus still on them?"

Maguchi nodded. Then he glanced urgently from Haldane to Savard. "Get away from me! I could spread it to you two."

"It's okay, Jake," Haldane said calmly. "We're wearing universal precautions."

"But back in my office you weren't!" Maguchi pointed out anxiously.

"You weren't coughing then," Haldane said with a confident nod.

But when Noah looked up and caught Gwen's concerned eyes, a cold rush ripped through him as he remembered Maguchi's drinking water-induced coughing spasm.

CHAPTER

24

The meek face stared harmlessly up at Sergeant Achmed Eleish from his computer monitor, but he knew that in the last few hours of her life the woman had been anything but harmless. He reread the cautiously worded description on the Interpol Web site. It characterized the woman as a "person of interest" in connection with the outbreak of the Gansu Flu virus, which had infected thirty-two people so far in Vancouver. Eleish had seen enough Interpol bulletins to know that "person of interest" always meant the prime suspect. And though the caption implied otherwise, he suspected she was already dead.

He studied the woman's features. No doubt she was an Arab, quite possibly Egyptian. And as always, young; as young as his two daughters who, thankfully for their proud father, had opted for careers in education rather than the Islamist lifestyle that had enjoyed such a dramatic surge in popularity among Egyptian youth of all classes.

Eleish patted around his desk until he found the pack of cigarettes. He lit one and took a deep soothing drag, trying to quell the indignation. Every time a plane crashed, a bridge collapsed, or a building detonated unexpectedly, Islam was suspect. Enough prejudice and ignorance existed to wrongfully incriminate his beloved religion for every wanton act of violence without help from the extremists. Now the lunatics wanted to forever associate Islam's holy name with the taint of bioterrorism. "Damn them," he grumbled to himself.

Hazzir Kabaal. Eleish couldn't shake the suspicion.

Was this why Kabaal had suddenly disappeared—to spread his viral menace across the globe? Eleish knew of only one way to find out.

Later in the morning, when the captain left for a meeting, Eleish broke the old man's dictum and slipped into his office because it boasted the only decent color printer in the building. He printed off two copies of the picture and tucked them into his jacket pocket. Then he headed out to his car.

Eleish abandoned his search for a shaded parking spot on the dusty street and settled for the partial shade of one of the many identical concrete apartment blocks lining the opposite side of the street, because it provided a discreet view of the Al-Futuh Mosque's entrance. It was a scorching hot day even by Cairo standards, and Eleish thought he might melt to the front seat of his rusted brown Mercedes if he had to wait long.

Fortunately for him, the Dhuhr, or noon prayer, ended on time. As soon as he saw people stream out of the mosque, he stepped out of his car and walked into the grocery a block down the street. He pretended to browse the newspaper rack while he kept an eye on the robed men who passed by the window of the store.

Eleish wasn't interested in the men. If the woman

whose photo he carried in his pocket was a member of the mosque, theoretically, only two men—her father and her husband—could recognize her. No other men should have seen her without her *hijab*, or veil, which cloaks an orthodox Muslim woman's face from all other men's view.

When the last of the men had passed, Eleish sauntered out of the store and turned back toward the car. A group of three female stragglers, dressed identically in black floor-length robes and hijabs, approached walking away from the mosque.

As per custom, they stopped talking and lowered their gaze to the street as Eleish neared. But when they were within arm's length, he stopped. "Dear ladies." He addressed them with a slight bow.

Alarm registered in the three pairs of eyes as they glanced from one to another at Eleish's shocking breach of etiquette.

"Please, do not be alarmed." He showed them his official badge in his wallet, but that had little effect on their distress. "I am an officer with the Cairo Police."

The tallest woman in the middle spoke up without making eye contact. "Our husbands are only a little ahead of us. Please, you should speak with them."

"No, dear ladies, I need the help of a woman."

His comment only seemed to agitate them more. They took a step back in unison and huddled closer together. He pulled the photo out of his jacket pocket and held it in front of the women. "Do any of you know this girl?" he asked.

He had to hold the picture up to eye level, before any of the women would even glimpse it. Eleish thought he saw a glimmer of recognition in the eyes of the shortest one on his right, but she said nothing as she lowered her gaze back to the sidewalk.

"Please. It is most important."

None replied.

"Look. Her parents contacted us," he lied. "She disappeared almost two weeks ago. No one has seen her since.
Her parents are desperately worried."

The shorter one mumbled something that Eleish could
not make out. The tall woman shot an icy glance at her
friend and then turned back to Eleish. "Please, Officer, I
beseech you to raise this matter with the men of the
mosque."

Eleish ignored her, and focused his eyes on the shorter
woman. "If you know anything, tell me now." He tapped a
finger on the photo. "She is in trouble. I might be able to
help."

"What kind of trouble is Sharifa in?" she asked, her
voice barely above a whisper.

The tall woman reached out and laid a hand on her
friend's shoulder as if to lead her away from Eleish, but he
raised a palm to stop her. "You do know Sharifa then?" he
said. "Listen, we are concerned that she might have been
abducted."

This caught the attention of even the tall woman. She
let go of her friend's shoulder.

"There have been some attacks by a man not too far
from the mosque." Eleish shook his head gravely. "The
monster is targeting pious women. Women who wear the
hijab. And Sharifa . . ." He snapped his fingers as if
searching his memory for the surname.

"Sha'rawi," the short woman supplied it for him.

"Yes, of course," he said. "We have one body. Excuse
me, ladies, for my frank description, but it is in such a
condition that we cannot identify it. We have no reason to
believe that Sharifa Sha'rawi is this woman, but we know
that she has been missing since before we found the
body . . ." He let the implication hang in the hot air.

The third woman who hadn't spoken a single word in
Eleish's presence uttered a gasp and swayed on her feet.
The tall woman shot out a hand to steady her.

Eleish heard the sound of shouts. He looked over the women's heads to see two robed men advancing quickly toward them and yelling to him.

"You have been most helpful." Eleish swiveled and began to walk away. "I will be in touch soon with hopefully good news of Sharifa's safe discovery."

He strode quickly for his car, resisting the urge to run. He hopped into the driver's seat and started the ignition before glancing in the rearview mirror. The two men had stopped to question the women, but he could see their irate faces fixed on him as he pulled out and drove away.

Driving back into Cairo's smoggy congestion, Eleish was sweating; more than just from heat. Now that he had traced the terrorist in Vancouver back to Kabaal's own mosque, he was convinced beyond a doubt that he had linked the man to the bioterrorist conspiracy. He felt deeply satisfied to finally validate years of suspicion, but by doing so, he realized he had just endangered his life along with those of his wife and daughters.

CHAPTER

25

Gwen Savard sat at the desk in her spacious "executive suite" on the thirty-second-floor of the Harbourview Hotel, gloomily staring out the window at world-famous Stanley Park, Coal Harbour, and the snow-dusted North Shore Mountains beyond. Gwen was as close as she was going to get—for the next four days, at least—to the glorious December sunshine outside.

Jake Maguchi's coughing fit sentenced Gwen and Noah to a minimum of five days in quarantine. Noah had had to fight to convince the authorities that while symptom-free Gwen and he presented no risk to the general public and required only isolation. When the staff at the American Consulate finally came around, they insisted on quarantining the two doctors in style at the five-star Vancouver hotel.

The staff set up a functional office for Gwen, including fax, two phone lines, high-speed Internet, and computer with video-conferencing capability. Though fully connected to the outside world, she couldn't shake her sense of solitude.

Haldane had made light of the situation, comparing his predicament to a bomb squad technician who had stepped on a land mine he was supposed to diffuse. Gwen suspected that behind his relaxed exterior, he shared her fear of the unknown, but his professionalism never wavered. From the moment Maguchi collapsed, Haldane—in spite of potential exposure to the deadly virus—stuck by the pathologist's side, refusing to relinquish his care until convinced Jake was in safe hands. A scientist, not a physician, Gwen had little to do but stand back and admire Noah's cool competence and gentle bedside manner.

Noah's selfless efforts seemed to have been in vain. Gwen had spoken earlier to one of the doctors at the ICU who told her: "Dr. Maguchi is fighting an uphill battle." When pressed, the weary doctor added, "It will require a miracle of biblical proportions for him to survive another twenty-four hours."

Though Savard had only known Maguchi for minutes, she had warmed to him right away. Not only did his dismal prognosis sadden her, it heightened her own sense of vulnerable captivity.

Gwen's reflex response to a challenge had always been to step beyond her comfort zone and into the eye of adversity, but now adversity had entrapped her. She had no choice but to wait and see if the virus, from which she was supposed to protect her country, infected her. The specter of failure loomed all around. She tried to quell the memories of being the little girl who always managed to disappoint her mother, but she couldn't shake the feeling that the child had grown up to fail her entire nation.

Despondent, she reached for the remote and turned the TV on to CNN. Ominously, the network had gone to twenty-four-hour coverage of the story. A subtitle in red ran along the bottom of the screen, screaming the alternating headlines: "Department of Homeland Security upgrades terrorist threat advisory from code orange to code red" and "22 dead, at least 100 infected in Illinois." Gwen already knew about the spiraling human toll, but the TV clips of hearses pulling away from hospitals and interviews with distraught families brought the bioterrorist attack on her country home in a visceral way that the sterile government statistics hadn't. Gwen was further dismayed by the coverage of the rest of the country's reaction. Though no cases had been reported outside of Illinois, in cities as remote as Houston and Los Angeles people had begun to stockpile gas masks and nonperishable supplies.

A musical tone from her computer indicated someone was requesting a videoconference. She muted the TV with the remote and then clicked on the computer's messenger icon. A video window popped open framing Alex Clayton inside. He was dressed as suavely as ever in a dark-on-dark shirt and jacket ensemble, but his hair was uncharacteristically out of place and deep bags had formed under his eyes. Suddenly he looked all forty of his years to Gwen.

"Gwen!" Clayton held out his hand to the camera. "How are you?"

She smiled halfheartedly. "Stuck indoors on a beautiful day, but otherwise okay."

"We cannot afford for you to get sick, do you hear?" he said, stone-faced.

"Your concern is touching, Alex, but I have no intention of getting sick."

His expression softened. "What are the chances?"

"Hard to know, but Noah figures they're slim. Probably less than ten percent."

Clayton squinted. "Noah?"

"Dr. Noah Haldane, the WHO expert on emerging

pathogens. He might be the world authority on the Gansu Flu." She sighed. "And he's quarantined one room over from me."

Clayton's face broke into its first flicker of a smile. "For what it's worth, my mom always forces cod liver oil and vitamin C down my throat at the first sign of cold or flu."

"I'll keep it in mind." She laughed. "Your mom got any homespun remedies for level-four lethal viruses?"

The levity vanished from his expression. He ran a hand through his disheveled hair. "All hell is breaking loose in Washington, Gwen. This could be worse than 9/11. The President wants answers."

Gwen nodded calmly. "What do you know so far?" She knew their secure socket Internet connection meant they could talk freely.

"Not enough," Clayton sighed. "We've got our bureaus in the Middle East working twenty-four/seven to identify the woman but so far *nada*. And the RCMP haven't figured out how she got into Canada." He shrugged. "One small break. We think we know how the terrorists got their hands on the virus in the first place."

"How?"

"Carnivore picked up an e-mail a couple of weeks ago sent by a deputy director of a hospital in Gansu to his supervisor. In it, he confesses to helping two Malaysians steal blood from an infected patient. We checked it out with the Chinese. Apparently, the guy killed himself after he sent the e-mail, and his supervisor hid the message out of fear of reprisal." Clayton interlocked his fingers in front of him and cracked the knuckles aggressively. "That weasel is going to learn the meaning of fear, but in the meantime the trail has gone stone cold."

"What about the Malaysians?"

"Could be from the militant group, Jemaah Islamiah. The same ones who masterminded the Bali bombing." He paused. "But our analysis tells us this is too sophisticated for them. And when you throw in the dead Arab woman in Vancouver and the other in London . . ." He shook his head. "It's likely the Malaysian role was limited to getting the virus out of China."

Gwen studied her desktop, assimilating the details. "And from China to Africa?"

"It looks that way," Clayton said. "Especially when you add the executed terrorist to those missing African lab supplies."

"Al Qaeda?" Gwen asked.

"Always possible."

"What's next, Alex?"

He shook his head and his shoulders slumped. Even in the small video box, Savard saw the change in Clayton. He had lost much of his cavalier edge. She decided Clayton embodied the mood of his country: once cocky and invincible, the attack on Chicago had exposed vulnerability and shaken his confidence to the core.

"We've doubled the staff at Carnivore," Clayton said. "Our satellites are trained on all global hotspots. We're working with the RCMP to track the Vancouver terrorist's trail and find her accomplices. We're sending scores of agents and special ops people to the Middle East and East Africa."

"Are those governments cooperating?" Gwen asked.

He held up his palms and shrugged. "They always swear that we have their full and utter cooperation, but you know how it works. Half the time they're secretly funding the bastards."

Gwen's mind raced. She nodded at Clayton. "Okay, Alex. We need to organize a crisis conference call for the Bioterrorism Preparedness Council. Today," she said. "We better brace for a possible massive invasion of the Gansu Flu in the next few days. Worst-case scenario, we're talking about hundreds of thousands of potential victims. So we need to initiate the emergency response plan ASAP. Agreed?"

Clayton nodded. "Let's say 3:00 P.M., Washington time."

"Good. Thanks."

Gwen watched as Clayton patted around his desk before finding a pair of chopsticks to hold up to the camera. A glimmer of his old self resurfaced. "All things considered, I think you should have gone with me for sushi instead of flying off to play hero."

Savard laughed. "Have to admit, I would've even pre-ferred *that* over quarantine."

"Stay well," Clayton said and then the video frame went black.

Gwen picked up her secure phone line and dialed the number from memory. The executive assistant to the Sec-retary of Homeland Security patched her call straight through. "Mr. Secretary?" Gwen asked.

"Hello, Gwen," the Secretary, Theodore "Ted" Hart, said in his gravelly, New England drawl. "You are still healthy, I trust?"

"Fine, Ted."

"Gwen, our office has been fielding a lot of questions," Hart said. "The press is looking for you."

"Of course," Gwen sighed. "They want answers from the 'Bug Czar.' What are you telling them?"

"The usual runaround. We can stall them for a few days." He paused a moment. "But when you're out of quarantine . . ."

"I'll face the music, Ted. I promise."

"Fine. Are you up-to-date on the *situation*?" Hart asked.

"I just spoke to Alex Clayton."

"The CIA dropped the ball on this one," Hart said in response to the name. "We should have had more—hell, some—warning about this virus!" Savard wondered if the comment was for her benefit, or if Hart, ever the political animal, was already lining up scapegoats. "Listen, Gwen, it's up to us to minimize the impact of this attack. The President expects it. As do the American people."

Gwen was tempted to remind him that he was speaking to her, not the cameras, but she held her tongue. "Ted, we're not totally unprepared," she said. "But we have to enact our ERPBA for every urban center."

"The *what?*" he asked.

"The Emergency Response Plan to Biological Attack. It puts the emergency health-care command structure in place for responding to this kind of attack. We've already run at least one mock disaster in most cities with a simulated smallpox outbreak."

"How did we do in the dry run?" Hart asked.

"So-so," Gwen admitted. "But our big advantage with the Gansu Flu is that it is nowhere near as contagious as smallpox." She paused, before adding, "Of course, it is just as lethal if not more so than smallpox."

"Hmmm," Hart snorted, sounding unimpressed. "All right, consider the plan green-lighted. What else?"

"We need to coordinate with CDC and Department of Health to implement wide-scale screening facilities," she said.

"Fine," he said. "Next."

"We should issue a nation-wide alert," Gwen said. "People across the country should be instructed to go to a screening clinic at the first sign of fever or cough. And, Ted, I think it should come from the President himself."

Hart unleashed a wet smoker's cough into the receiver. Gwen imagined that her boss, a pack-a-day smoker at the best of times, would have doubled his consumption during this crisis. "Gwen, the American public is jittery enough as is. Did you see the papers this morning? Some poor Pakistani boy was beaten to within an inch of his life at a convenience store in Missouri because he was coughing. With the cold and flu season upon us, is it a good idea to send people into a panic at the first sniffle?"

"It has to be done, Ted," Gwen said firmly.

Gwen could hear Hart wheeze slightly as he mulled it over. Finally he said, "I will speak to the President. Anything else?"

She hesitated, vacillating on whether to mention her mentor's work.

"What is it, Gwen?" he demanded.

"My old professor, Dr. Isaac Moskor, has been developing a new treatment for influenza. The early results are encouraging."

"For the Gansu Flu?" Hart breathed excitedly.

"No, for the common flu, but the Gansu strain is related," Savard said. "I've set him up in a secure level-four lab at the CDC to run tests on infected monkeys."

"Good," Hart said. "You make sure whatever he needs is top priority there. Am I clear?"

"Will do. Believe me, Isaac will do everything possible to make this work." Savard couldn't keep the pride out of her voice. She cleared her throat. "One last thing," she said, bracing for Hart's response, "we should consider the borders."

Another heavy cough. "What about the borders?"

"I think it would be wise to suspend travel into and out of the U.S. for everyone except those with special clearance."

"Christ, Gwen!" Hart growled. "We've already gone to the highest level of alert. We've canceled half the international flights and delayed the others for hours. The airport, harbor, and border screening couldn't be more rigorous."

"Mr. Secretary, with all due respect, that is not enough."

"Do you realize the implications of this?" Hart asked quietly.

"So far, only one U.S. city is affected," Gwen said evenly. "Until we know where it's coming from, this 'Killer Flu' could spread to a new city with every flight or ship we allow into the country."

Gwen thought she heard a cigarette lighter clicking in the background. "I have heard that this virus is relatively easy to incubate," Hart said. "How do you know they aren't already established somewhere inside our borders, infecting more suicide carriers to dispatch throughout the country?"

"I don't," Gwen conceded. "But odds are that their infrastructure is still based abroad."

There was a long moment of silence, broken by a hacking cough. Then Hart said, "No. No. No. Listen, Gwen, as it stands our economy is paralyzed. The Dow has already dropped twenty percent in two days." She could picture her tall boss with his graying temples and distinguished features, his face creased into that disappointed father-knows-best look he had mastered. "We cannot fence America off from the rest of the world," he said.

"Why not?" Gwen asked.

"Because it would be tantamount to admitting that the sons of bitches have won!"

"Mr. Secretary, let's be honest. Right now they are winning the battle," she said authoritatively. "If we don't act decisively, they might win the war."

"Then goddamn it, let's act decisively!" Hart said. "We will protect our citizens. And we will hunt down the monsters behind this and wipe them off the face of the earth. But in the meantime, we will not cower behind barricades."

Gwen knew Ted Hart well enough to realize there was no point in arguing further. "Okay, Ted, but you ought to keep it in mind."

"We'll see," he said. "I'm off to meet the National Security Council. And then to see the President. I'll call you after."

She dropped the receiver into the cradle and slumped back into the chair at her desk. There were so many people to coordinate, but she couldn't escape the growing sense of futility. Until they got to the source of the deliberate spread, they were just a bunch of rats running on wheels.

Her phone rang. She picked it up and said, "Gwen Savard."

"I got a bit of a hole in my social calendar," Haldane said. "Okay if I drop by?"

She let out a tired laugh. "I might be able to squeeze you in."

Gwen had barely secured her mask when she heard the rap at her door. Haldane stood on the other side in a T-shirt and jeans. Aside from his face mask, he looked as if he were on his way out for a coffee and a newspaper on a lazy Sunday morning.

As soon as he stepped into the room, he tore off his mask. He wadded it into a ball in his hand. "I hate these things."

"Odd for a doctor who specializes in communicable diseases," Gwen said, instinctively taking a step back from him.

Haldane flashed a mischievous smile. "Yeah, well, I now realize I might have made a fundamental mistake in career planning."

"You too?" She laughed. "Aren't you gambling with us by removing the mask?"

"I don't have a fever or cough; besides, I haven't touched a Caesar salad in days, so chances are my breath won't kill you."

Gwen pulled off her mask and folded it on her desk. "How are you holding up?" she asked.

"Going stir crazy. I'm already sick of the room-service food, not to mention the way we have to exchange trays with them like we're radioactive. Otherwise, I'm terrific. You?"

"Same." She nodded. "I've got so much to do. Hard to know where to begin."

Haldane sat down on the couch across from her chair

and leaned back with his hands folded behind his head. "Let's start by comparing notes."

Gwen admired his calm. And she found it difficult not to notice his blue-gray eyes. When he had turned to sit down, she caught herself noticing the way his jeans clung to his muscular rear end. Snap out of it, Gwen! she told herself, but she wrote the inappropriate thoughts off as a symptom of her isolation. Forcing them from her mind, she focused on summarizing for Noah her discussions with Clayton and Hart.

When she finished, Haldane said, "The Secretary might be right. No guarantees we could stem the flow of the virus even if we could shut down the borders."

Gwen didn't feel like arguing the point again. "And you? What have you learned?"

"Mixed news on the global front." Haldane shrugged. "Hong Kong, maybe because of their SARS experience, has been the most successful in limiting the virus's spread. Less than one hundred total cases and no new ones reported in forty-eight hours. The story is not so rosy in London." He shook his head and sighed. "Over 700 infected with 145 dead so far. Sporadic clusters of infections have spread to mainland Europe—six in Amsterdam, two in Brussels, three in Hamburg—all traceable back to that first woman in the elevator. You heard about Chicago. And here in Vancouver, there are at least fifty-five infected and thirteen dead."

Gwen sighed. "Which could rise to fourteen very soon."

Haldane looked down at his feet. "Yeah, Jake is not doing well," he said softly.

"It's so damn unnecessary!" She studied him for a moment without speaking. Then she bit her lower lip. "Noah, are you scared?"

"Of coming down with this virus?"

"Yeah."

"Very. But the odds are stacked in our favor." He tapped his fist on the sofa beside him. "It pisses me off, though."

"What does?"

"Being imprisoned here"—he circled a finger around the suite—"while that virus is loose out there. I should be in Chicago now, not stuck in quarantine."

"Me, too."

He looked up at her with a frown. "Actually, where I should be is home in Maryland. It's my daughter's birthday in three days . . . I promised her I'd be there with balloons."

Recognizing the pain in his eyes, Gwen felt a pang of sorrow. "It's not fair, Noah."

Haldane shrugged. "Fairness seems to be in pretty short supply these days."

The phone rang. "Gwen Savard," she said into the receiver. She listened to the woman on the other end of the line and then closed her eyes for a moment. "I am so sorry," she said, before hanging up the phone.

"Jake Maguchi?" Noah asked.

"Yes."

"Damn it!" Haldane punched the sofa beside him. "Why would anyone—" He stopped in midsentence. He snapped his fingers at Gwen and pointed to the TV. "Turn the volume up!"

Gwen followed his eyes to the TV screen where the words "Breaking News" flashed above the head of a concerned-looking anchorman. She hit the volume button just in time to hear the anchorman say somberly: "If American troops do not withdraw in the next four days, the group, calling itself The Brotherhood of One Nation, has vowed to 'unleash an army of martyrs' to spread the virus across the country."

CHAPTER

26

The Brotherhood of One Nation. Their name dominated the Internet. Sitting alone in his plush office, Hazzir Kabaal shook his head in disbelief. Sabri and he had only hit upon the name the day before issuing their taped ultimatum. Now it was on the tongues of people around the planet.

Kabaal surfed all the major news outlets from his own newspapers' Web sites to the other major Arabic, European, and even the U.S. network sites. The only news item competing for any global attention was the photo of the operation's latest martyr, Sharifa Sha'rawi. Her restored face ran side by side to most of the stories concerning The Brotherhood's claim of responsibility. When he first saw the photo from Vancouver, it was so lifelike that for a disoriented moment Kabaal worried she might have been captured alive.

Poor Sharifa, Kabaal thought. Orphaned as a young

child, she had grown up without a chance of finding a husband. At the pivotal moment of her mission, she had been turned away at the U.S.-Canadian border without ever reaching her target of Seattle. Nothing in life had gone well for the unfortunate girl. Now even in death she had found mishap when her body had broken free of the bindings and surfaced on a riverbank, jeopardizing the entire operation.

That mistake would have been less problematic were it not combined with Kabaal's self-confessed misjudgment in stopping Abdul Sabri from killing Sergeant Achmed Eleish earlier. As soon as Kabaal heard a policeman had been nosing around the Al-Futuh Mosque and asking about Sharifa, he knew it could be no one but Achmed Eleish. Now the relentless detective had uncovered Sharifa's name.

But Kabaal noted with guarded optimism that Sharifa was still described as an "anonymous terrorist" by the media. Perhaps Eleish had not shared his detective work with anyone. Maybe, as Abdul Sabri had suggested before leaving to find Eleish, the policeman was determined to single-handedly dismantle their operation. Kabaal dearly hoped so. As a force of one, Eleish was no more than a flea on a camel, but if he turned to the Egyptian authorities or worse the Americans . . .

Hazzir Kabaal refused to obsess over Eleish's intentions. Kabaal knew he was as always in Allah's hands. Still, His ways were mysterious. Mistakes had crept into the operation where none had been before, but those blunders and their inherent dangers were not what kept Hazzir Kabaal awake night after night.

No. It was the resurgence of his doubt.

Their plan had thus far had an even greater impact than Kabaal anticipated. Perhaps, too successful. What if the virus they had freed was already unstoppable? Or what if the American President didn't bow to their demands? They would have no recourse but to follow through with their threat to unleash the promised army of martyrs.

CAIRO, EGYPT

Sergeant Achmed Eleish had spent a busy twenty-four hours since solving the mystery of the Vancouver terrorist's identity. Most of his time had been dedicated to convincing Samira and his two daughters that they would have to leave Cairo. The girls were appalled at the thought of abandoning their teaching responsibilities in the middle of the school year. It took all Eleish's powers of persuasion to finally convince his family to temporarily relocate to his cousin's house in Alexandria.

After his two daughters had already boarded the train for Alexandria, Eleish stood alone on the platform holding his wife's hand. Samira's eyes were dry and her poise as unfaltering as ever, but earlier in the morning he had heard her sobbing softly in the bedroom, unaware that he was still at home.

Staring into his wife's stoic face, Eleish had trouble keeping the tears from his own eyes. He squeezed her hand tenderly. "It will just be a short while, Miri."

"I know," she said softly.

"I need a break," Eleish continued rationalizing aloud. "Maybe in a few days I could come up and join you in Alexandria. It would be like the old days. A family vacation with the girls."

Samira smiled poignantly. "That would be nice." Then she added distantly, "Like the old days."

The loudspeaker called out the final boarding call for the Alexandria-bound train.

Samira leaned forward, touched her fingers to his lips, and then turned to walk up the train's steps. She stopped on the last step. "I won't tell you it's not worth it," Samira said. "I know you have no other choice, but please, Achmed, be careful. Don't trust anyone. His influence reaches far and wide."

"I promise." Eleish's voice cracked. "I will come for you soon."

She smiled and waved once, then disappeared into the train.

After the train pulled out, Eleish found a public rest room in the station and changed into a galabiya that he hadn't donned in almost ten years. He had once swum in the garment, but now it fit too snugly. He studied his profile in the mirror, surprised at how his belly had grown in the interim. He lifted the bottom of his robe and tucked his automatic handgun into the leg holster beside the handcuffs.

From the train station, Eleish went directly to the Al-Futuh Mosque. He parked a few blocks away and walked a circuitous route to the mosque, pleased that the pedestrian traffic had thinned in the late afternoon. The fewer people he saw, the better.

He timed his arrival to coincide with Maghrib, the evening prayer, knowing that most of the congregation would leave for dinner afterward. As Eleish walked down the dusty, smoggy Cairo street, he paused when he heard the beautiful adhan, or call to prayer, echo out from the loudspeaker of the mosque's prayer tower. Though headed for inhospitable territory, he felt no apprehension, knowing that he approached the house of God.

He joined the traditionally dressed congregation—men in white galabiyas and women wearing *jihabs* and floor-length black coverings—as they shuffled into the majestic gold-domed mosque. Eleish had little concern of raising suspicion among the regular congregation. He doubted his own brother would recognize him in his galabiya.

Inside, the women and men separated into their

respective sections in the large prayer hall. Facing the *qibla* (the wall directed toward Mecca), Eleish recited his prayers with genuine vehemence, but he kept a watchful eye on the old man standing on the pulpit by the *qibla*. He had never before seen Sheikh Hassan at prayers.

The Sheikh wore a traditional clerical robe along with a white Islamic turbar and a long gray beard. Stooped forward and with a rough tremor in both hands, the emaciated cleric epitomized the frailty of old age. But when Hassan spoke in his low-pitched staccato, his voice resonated with a ferocious power that erased the ravages time inflicted on his body. Eleish had no doubt that the Sheikh was a man born to lead.

After prayers ended, Eleish didn't exit through the same doors as most of the others. Instead, he wandered out into the courtyard under the arcaded portico. With his arms folded across his chest he pretended to admire the wells and fountains in the courtyard while he passed the time.

After a few minutes a tall, robed, bearded man with a thick neck and opaque brown eyes approached him. "My brother, is it not time to leave for dinner?" the young man said with a hint of warning.

"Of course, of course," Eleish said, recognizing the man for some sort of guard despite his plain robe. "I was simply admiring your beautiful mosque. I am from the north, but I have long heard of the splendor of the Al-Futuh Mosque. Words are cheap, though. It is such a joy to behold in person."

The man nodded, unmoved. "Let me walk you out, brother."

Eleish uncrossed his arms and flashed the gun that he had concealed under his sleeve since extracting it from the leg holster in the courtyard. "I would prefer that you walk me into the madrasa," Eleish said, in reference to the school and residence behind the mosque.

The man's eyes blackened. "Pointing a gun in the house of God?" he snapped without a trace of fear.

"Now," Eleish growled and waved the gun at him. "Either you start walking, or you die here . . . in the house of God."

The tall man glared at Eleish; hatred crystallized in his eyes.

Eleish recognized the look. He had seen it in the faces of other extremists, right before rash reactions had led them to a quick martyrdom. Eleish steadied his gun, aiming at the man's face. But rather than rush at Eleish, the man casually turned and began to walk across the courtyard. Never lowering his weapon, Eleish followed him across the courtyard and into the building behind.

They walked down a dark narrow corridor, whose faded gray walls were devoid of any decoration. "I want to speak to the Sheikh," Eleish said.

"You mean, to kill him," the young man said flatly while keeping his head fixed straight in front of him.

Eleish shook his head at the man's back before realizing the futility of the gesture. "I mean to speak with him," he said.

"Then follow me."

Their footsteps echoed in the otherwise still hallway. They walked past a series of doors toward an L-turn at the end of the corridor. Just as they reached it, the creaky sound of a door opening behind them caught Eleish's attention.

"Son, is that you?" a deep voice asked.

Even before glancing over his shoulder, Eleish recognized the Sheikh's voice.

"Go back to your room, Father!" the tall man screamed. In one motion, he pivoted and lunged at Eleish.

Eleish jumped back. Stumbling, he had to steady himself against the wall behind him, just as the young man landed hard at his feet and grabbed wildly for his ankle. Eleish jerked his foot free of the man's grip. Once he had regained his balance, he knelt forward and rested the gun's muzzle against the fallen man's forehead.

"No!" Sheikh Hassan screamed. "Leave Fadi be! Save your bullets for me."

Without budging his gaze or the barrel of his gun, Eleish spoke to the Sheikh in a calm but commanding tone. "I have not come to kill anyone. But so help me Allah, I will kill both of you if need be."

Lying on his belly, the young man stared up hatefully at Eleish, his eyes challenging him to pull the trigger.

The Sheikh must have recognized the expression because he shuffled closer and spoke to the young man. "Fadi, leave it be. The man has come to talk. So we will talk. All are welcome here."

Eleish rested a foot on Fadi's back. "Put your hands behind your back!" he barked.

Fadi glanced over to the Sheikh before complying.

With his free hand, Eleish reached down and pulled a pair of handcuffs from under his robe and then cuffed the young man's hands behind his back. Once Fadi was secured, Eleish turned to the Sheikh. "Where is a private place for us to speak?"

Hassan pointed a shaky hand back to the door from where the light emerged. "In my room."

Eleish pulled Fadi to his feet. He pushed him forward as they followed the shuffling cleric back to his room. The last one to step inside, Eleish closed the door behind them. Smelling musty from stale air, the room looked more like a dusty old library than someone's living quarters. Aside from a metal cot in the corner, the room was littered with old books and parchments. The bookshelves overflowed. And stacks of books rose from the floor. A large leather-bound volume was open on the reading stand with a magnifying glass resting atop.

With a wave of his gun, Eleish directed Fadi and the Sheikh to move to the far wall.

Standing against the wall, the Sheikh opened his mouth in a forlorn smile, which exposed two decaying front teeth flanked by spaces where other teeth should have been. "How can we share any kind of discourse at gunpoint, my son?"

Like a tail wagging on a wolf, the grin struck Eleish as out of place on the feisty old cleric. "We will manage," Eleish said.

Wide-eyed, Fadi glanced at Hassan, but the Sheikh shook his head ever so slightly and then turned back to Eleish. "It is God's way." He shrugged calmly. "Are you a believer, my friend?"

"In what you preach?" Eleish asked.

"In Allah," Hassan barked, but then resumed his pleasanter tone. "And the life he commanded us to live as told to the Prophet."

"I am a Muslim," Eleish said.

"Then we are brothers," the Sheikh said confidently. "And we have nothing to fear of each other."

"I wish that were so," Eleish said. "I am just not sure which of us has more to fear."

"Clearly it is you." Hassan raised a defiant, tremulous finger. "I fear nothing but the judgment of God."

Impatient, Eleish shifted from one foot to the other. He waved the gun at the Sheikh. "Hazzir Kabaal. You know him, don't you?"

Hassan folded his skinny arms across his chest. "Why do you ask after him?"

"Do you know him?" Eleish said, raising his voice along with the barrel of the gun.

"Abu Lahab is a student of mine," Hassan said.

"Where can I find him?" Eleish asked.

"Not here."

"Where is he?" Eleish spat.

The Sheikh shrugged. "I am not his keeper."

Eleish's irritation got the better of him. "Do you have any idea what sort of crimes Kabaal is responsible for?"

Hassan grunted a bitter laugh. "Abu Lahab acts in the service of God."

"The service of God?" Eleish snorted. "The man has spread a deadly virus among innocent people. He murders women and children in the name of Islam. Do you call that the service of God?"

"Innocent?" Hassan grimaced as if pained. "There is nothing innocent about the enemies of the faithful. Open your eyes!"

"To what?" Eleish shot back. "The bilious hatred that you preach."

"I do not hate anyone," Hassan said calmly. "What I preach is the preservation of our way of life."

Eleish shook his head vehemently. "The Koran extols peace and tolerance. You and your kind . . . You twist the beautiful words until nothing is left but bigotry and loathing." He sighed heavily. "There are so few of you hate-mongering extremists. And so many of us peaceful Muslims. Yet your kind defines the face of Islam to the rest of the world. And what an ugly face it is."

"Mohammed said that those who are not for Islam are against it." The Sheikh shrugged unapologetically.

"So death to all the nonbelievers?" Eleish scoffed.

"I wish I could make you understand." Hassan's face assumed another sad, missing-toothed smile. "Are you too blind to see the threat?"

Eleish threw up his free hand. "What threat?"

"Ever since the Turks dispensed with the Caliphate . . ." Hassan said obliquely and then sighed. "In many ways, Islam is like me. Old and weak. Incapable of protecting itself." He pointed a finger at his own chest. "But inside, it is strong and pure. Do you understand, my brother? The heart and soul of Islam is good but the body ails. And the

infidels . . . those Western heathens, the Americans . . .
are the opposite. Their body is fierce and mighty, but their
soul is crippled and the heart very weak."

Eleish listened to the crafty old cleric, aware of his
manipulative sermonizing but engrossed by the delivery.

"And the strongest of hearts might not be enough to
save us. The Americans are camped at the gates of the
Tigris and within a stone's throw of Mecca." He pointed at
the wall as if Mecca were just on the other side. "The
lands that practice the laws of the Shari'ah have fallen,
one after the other, under the weight of the American
bombs. If we do nothing to stop them, they will eradicate
Islam in their lust for oil. Very soon, we will be powerless
to stop them." He exhaled slowly. "Hazzir Kabaal is fighting to save Islam. He is fighting the holiest of Jihads with
the only weapons available to him." His voice warbled.
"And you should drop to your knees and pray to God for
his success."

Eleish shook his head. "You are a deluded old man."

Fadi, who had silently watched the discussion, took an
aggressive step forward, but the Sheikh stopped him with
a bony hand laid on his chest. Hassan turned back to
Eleish. "Listen to me, brother—"

"No." Eleish walked forward until he was three feet
away from the Sheikh. "I have no more time to listen to
you." He leveled the gun at the Sheikh's head. "Where is
Hazzir Kabaal?"

Hassan laughed softly. "Do you honestly believe I am
afraid of death?"

Eleish shook his head slowly. "No, I don't." He swung
his gun over until it pointed at Fadi's head.

"What are you doing?" the Sheikh demanded shrilly.

"I will give you one last chance, and then I'm going to
kill your son."

Hassan's expression creased into a fleeting cringe, long

enough for Eleish to know he was right. "Fadi is not—" Hassan started to say calmly.

Eleish cut him off with a snap of his fingers. "I will kill your son on the count of three, if you do not tell me where I can find Hazzir Kabaal." Eleish shoved the muzzle against Fadi's forehead. "One . . . two . . ."

Hassan's eyes widened and his hands shook wildly.

"Don't tell him anything, Father!" Fadi implored. "Let me be martyred!"

Eleish shrugged. "So be it. Three." He slowly began to squeeze the trigger.

"No!" Hassan squeaked. "Somalia. He is in Somalia."

Fadi's head stayed immobile but his eyes shot over to the direction of the Sheikh. "No, Father!"

"Where in Somalia?" Eleish demanded, not releasing his finger from the trigger.

"I do not know," the Sheikh cried. "He has a camp there—a base—but I am too old to travel there."

Eleish's gaze skipped from father to son. "But you know, don't you?" Eleish said.

Fadi sneered in response.

"Do you want to see your father die?" Eleish asked.

Fadi grinned malevolently. "If it means protecting the Jihad, I would see my whole family die." He glanced at his father with an expression of sheer contempt.

The old man's face flushed with shame and his chin dropped to his chest.

Eleish knew there was nothing more he would learn from either of them.

After leaving the mosque, Achmed Eleish sat in his car and smoked five cigarettes in a row, trying to quell the tremor in his hands. For a moment, he considered continuing his solo pursuit of Kabaal all the way to Somalia, but he dismissed the idea as foolhardy.

In a cloud of smoke, Eleish weighed his next step carefully. In the end, he knew to whom he had to turn. Even though the captain of the Cairo Police detectives was only in his early sixties, the little man had seemed old to Eleish for all twenty years he had known him. Captain Riyad Wazir was a throwback. Never seen in anything but a neatly pressed uniform with spit-polished shoes, Wazir always toed the official line and his preoccupation with procedure and bureaucracy bordered on obsessive. But Eleish would have gladly trusted his life in Wazir's hands, because the captain's ethics were as meticulous as his paperwork.

Once the thump in his chest had settled, Eleish reached for his cell phone. He dialed the direct line to the captain's office, but after five rings he was transferred back to the main switchboard. Eleish glanced at his watch, which read 7:00 P.M., meaning that Wazir must have left for the day. He asked the operator to transfer him to the detectives' desk, knowing there would be at least one detective on duty.

"Cairo Police," the disinterested voice said on the other end of the line.

Eleish was dismayed to hear the voice of his least favorite colleague, Constable Qasim Ramsi. For a moment, he considered hanging up on the crooked officer. "Listen, Qasim, it's me, Eleish," he said. "Do you know the Al-Futuh Mosque?"

"Of course."

"If you send officers there you will find Sheikh Hassan and his son Fadi handcuffed to a toilet in the bathroom of the madrasa behind the mosque," Eleish said.

Ramsi whistled into Eleish's earpiece. "Holy Mohammed! Have you lost your mind? You handcuffed the Sheikh to a toilet?" His voice squeaked at the end. "You will be destroyed," he said almost jovially.

"I cannot explain over the phone," Eleish said. "The Sheikh and his son are involved in a terrorist conspiracy to destabilize the government. And more. Just make sure they are picked up!"

Eleish hung up before Ramsi had a chance to reply. Satisfied that his hands were still enough to drive, he started his car and pulled out of the spot.

He had intended to drive directly to the office, but as his home was on the way he decided to stop in to shower and change before going into headquarters to file his report. He tuned the radio to an Egyptian pop station. He tapped his steering wheel to the beat of the music as his hyper-vigilance gave way to a pleasantly contented mood.

Eleish parked in front of his twenty-seven-story apartment building. Alone, he rode the elevator to the nineteenth floor. He unlocked both deadbolts—knowing how bad property crime was in Egypt, he had insisted on the second deadbolt—and walked into his living room. He dropped his keys, phone, and gun on the kitchen countertop.

The apartment felt empty without the women, but after his visit to the Al-Futuh Mosque, he was confident that they would only be parted for a matter of days or weeks. However long it took to find Kabaal.

Abiding by his wife's strict edict not to smoke in the apartment, he slid open the sliding door and stepped outside onto his balcony in the warm Cairo dusk before lighting up another cigarette. This time he only allowed himself one smoke as he stared out on his beloved city of a thousand minarets, which was never more beautiful than at dusk.

Returning to the living room, he left the door open to circulate the air through his apartment. He walked out of the living room and into his bedroom where he sat down at the desk across from the bed. He booted up the desktop computer (an unexpectedly generous present from his daughters on his fiftieth birthday last year) and waited. Once the main screen appeared, he clicked on the icon to initiate his e-mail program. He knew how long it would take the

modem to establish a connection on the overburdened
server, so he rose from the desk and headed for the shower.

He enjoyed a long hot shower, trying to scrub away the
memories of the conversation in the mosque and the
Sheikh's assertions that Islam was at imminent risk. Such
hateful fear-mongering stoked the growing flames of
Islamism and drove the people who followed the Hazzir
Kabaals of the world, but Eleish couldn't help wonder
whether a kernel of truth existed in the argument.

Turning off the tap, Eleish reached for a towel. He
stopped when he heard a soft thud. His heart skipped a
beat. He listened. Nothing. He grabbed the towel and
dried himself. He stepped out of the shower, put on his
robe, and then stood inside his bathroom, listening. He
waited a full minute without hearing another noise.

He stepped back into his living room. He had just sat
down at his desk when he heard a bang, followed by three
loud thumps.

His palms moistened. His heart smashed against his rib
cage. The noise came from his front door.

His gun! For an agonizing moment, he wavered, but
decided he had a higher priority to address. He reached for
the mouse and clicked on the "new mail" icon and then
frantically one-fingered typed the captain's e-mail address
in the "send to" box.

Thud! Thud! The noises came from the door.

In the "message text" box, he typed wildly in note form.
"Vancouver. Virus carrier = Sharifa Sha'rawi."

Eleish heard a series of sharp cracks, as someone emptied a round of gunfire into the door.

He typed: "Hazzir Kabaal = leader. Major Abdul
Sabri?"

A creaking noise indicated the door hinges were beginning to give way.

He kept typing. "Al-Futuḥ Mosque. Sheikh Hassan."
Crash! More wood splintered.

"Base in Somalia," he typed. He grabbed the mouse, but his shaking hand overshot the "send" key twice before finally making contact. As soon as the musical tone confirmed that the e-mail had been sent, Eleish reached down and yanked the plug out from the back of the computer.

He leaped to his feet and ran for the kitchen.

Eleish made it to the living room just as his door toppled backward into the room. He froze in his tracks five feet from the countertop and his weapon. Someone else's gun pointed at his head.

A hulking man casually stepped over the smashed door and into the apartment. Eleish instantly recognized him as Major Abdul Sabri.

From ten feet away, Sabri cocked his head at Eleish. "Sergeant, I've been looking all over for you," he said softly.

"You could have just called." The joke seemed to Eleish like something one of his literary detective heroes might have said, but it drew no response from Sabri.

"Sergeant, you and I have things to discuss," Sabri said inexpressively.

The sweat dripped down Eleish's neck and onto the collar of his bathrobe. His mind raced in time with his pounding heart. Without looking over at the counter, he tried to calculate how best to lunge for his gun. "Okay, we will talk," Eleish said. "But can I put some clothes on first?"

Sabri shook his head slowly from side to side. "And, Sergeant, there's really no point in going for your gun. You'll be dead before you reach it."

Eleish had a flashback to the photo of his burnt and beaten informer, Bishr Gamal, whose ear had been hacked off. He doubted he could withstand that kind of torture without talking. He swallowed hard. "Wouldn't you prefer me alive?" he asked.

"Prefer, yes," Sabri said. "Required, no."

Suddenly Eleish's path cleared before him. A tranquil

calm enveloped him. An absolute peacefulness he had never before experienced. He smiled widely at Sabri. "Allah is most great," he spoke the words from the call to prayer.

Sabri's eyes narrowed and he raised his weapon to eye level.

Eleish didn't lunge for his gun. Instead, he spun and ran for the open balcony door.

"Stop!" yelled Sabri.

Eleish heard a bang and felt a searing pain in his left shoulder and his arm fell limp at his side. But the bullet wound didn't slow him as he reached the balcony in one stride and hurled himself over the railing.

"Allah is most great!" he repeated as he felt the air rush by his head.

CHAPTER
27

Since Rand Delorme uncovered Dr. Ping Wu's e-mailed confession, his coworkers at Carnivore accused the young agent of having undergone a personality transplant. Once only distinguished for his frosted highlights, black bowling shoes, and rebellious attitude, Delorme was now known for logging the longest hours and clearing the most intercepted e-mails. The day before, his supervisor had written in his monthly evaluation that Rand was "a man on a mission." And he was. To Delorme, each new e-mail Carnivore earmarked for human review was another potential opportunity to foil terrorism.

With the extra bodies covering Carnivore, the agents had caught up entirely on the backlog. Less than half an hour after it was sent, Achmed Eleish's e-mail popped up on Delorme's screen. Carnivore had graded it as "highly suspicious," so Delorme approached it with more circumspection than he otherwise might have.

Delorme reviewed the "To" and "From" rows. Both the sender and the receiver had the same domain, CairoPol.com, which he learned with a quick Internet search belonged to the Cairo Police Department. Delorme looked at the path and was surprised to see that the e-mail never reached its recipient. He wondered if the sender had mistyped the second letter, spelling "RWszir" instead of "RWazir." Whatever the reason, the e-mail had bounced back to "AEleish" as "undeliverable."

Savoring the contents like the last chapter of a favorite mystery, Delorme turned to the body of text. His pulse quickened with the very first word, "Vancouver." By the time he had read the brief series of cryptic notes about a virus carrier and a base in Somalia, he trembled with excitement.

Rand Delorme didn't know exactly what the message meant, but he was convinced beyond a doubt that he had just hit the motherlode of e-mail intercepts.

Smiling, he reached for the phone.

HARBOURVIEW HOTEL, VANCOUVER, CANADA

Four days of quarantine had passed without incident for Savard and Haldane. Noah had checked his temperature after waking, but he knew he hadn't spiked a fever. While he had always considered his chances slim, by day four he was certain he hadn't caught the Gansu Flu from the now-deceased Dr. Jake Maguchi. The realization that he was free of risk brought an unexpected wave of relief.

However, sitting at his laptop computer and staring at the camera clipped on top, butterflies still fluttered in his stomach. Two videoconferences awaited him. The second was with the President and the senior members of the National Security Council, but it was the first call that provoked the most anxious anticipation.

Noah felt sad and guilty about having to miss Chloe's birthday party, but in four introspective days of quarantine he had come to realize that there would likely be many missed milestones in his daughter's life. He had heard from friends, who alternated custody of the kids with ex-spouses on holidays like Christmas and Thanksgiving, that special occasions were the most difficult times to be separated from their children.

Noah had little doubt that many lonely times awaited him, but things had changed in the past days. The anger had drained from his system, replaced by resignation. Realizing how weary he was of fighting for his wife's affection, he felt ready to step away. He had begun to envision a life without Anna. He even considered where to live, realizing that it would have to be in the Glen Echo Heights district, so that school and friends would not be an issue for Chloe as she shuttled back and forth between homes.

A musical tone rang out from his computer. He clicked on the icon and the video window box popped open with his wife's and daughter's images framed inside. The video feed was of the low-resolution, jumpy home Internet-camera variety—a far cry from the high-quality videoconferences he had sat through over the past days—but Haldane didn't care. He was thrilled to see his daughter's face again.

Chloe sat on Anna's lap in a chair in their home office. A sea of multicolored, helium-filled balloons filled the backdrop and Chloe held a bouquet in her hand. Haldane was tickled to see Chloe wearing the Snow White princess dress he had ordered online for her.

"Happy birthday, Chlo!" he said.

"Daddy. Daddy! My balloons!" she said and tugged at the bouquet in her hand.

Haldane beamed. "And your dress. You look so pretty!"

"All my friends are princesses," Chloe said, referring to the theme of her party. Then her forehead furrowed into a concerned frown. "Daddy, what if someone else is Snow White?"

"You'll always be the most special Snow White. The fairest of them all." Haldane winked and then nodded solemnly. "But don't tell the others. It will be our secret, okay?"

"Secret!" Chloe bounced up and down on her mother's lap. "Daddy, are you going to play the hide-and-seek game with me and my friends?"

Haldane felt a little jab in his chest. "Chlo, I am too far away. I can't make the party. You knew that, didn't you?"

Chloe gave a little shrug that squeezed Haldane's heart. The gesture came straight out of her mother's chromosomes. "I guess."

Anna rubbed Chloe's shoulder. "Daddy will be home soon and then you'll have another party, remember?"

Chloe nodded, but the disappointment stuck to her face.

"Why don't you go downstairs and see if Nana needs help with your cake?" Anna suggested to her.

The mention of her cake was enough to wipe the dejection off Chloe's face. She hopped off Anna's lap and started to run out of the frame, but she turned back to Noah with a big wave. "Bye, Daddy!"

"Happy birthday, Chloe. I love you!" Haldane said and then she was gone.

Anna sat alone in the chair facing the camera. In jeans and a white turtleneck, her black hair was tied back in a ponytail. Haldane had almost forgotten how beautiful his wife was. The realization didn't engender the usual yearning in him. Whether spontaneously or by willful suppression—Haldane wasn't sure himself—he had not thought of his wife in a sexual sense for some time.

With Chloe gone from the room, Anna's carefree expression gave way to a grimace. "Noah, you are still okay, right?"

Haldane nodded. He forced a smile. "I'm not going to catch this virus."

Her expression didn't budge. "But you're still in quarantine?"

"A formality. I've got less than twenty-four hours to go." Haldane nodded reassuringly to her. "Anna, I would have known by now."

"That's wonderful." Anna exhaled heavily and for a moment it looked as if she might burst into tears, but she held her composure. "Noah, people are so scared here. Chloe's preschool is two-thirds empty. Half the kids canceled for the party. A lot of people won't leave their house."

"I've seen it before." Haldane nodded. "It's only natural, Anna."

She shook her head. "There's nothing natural about any of this! What if the virus comes here? Washington would be the obvious choice for them."

"If it comes, we'll deal with it. It will be okay," Noah promised. "Anna, believe me, they can't win. All viruses are stoppable. This bug is no exception," he said, sounding more definite than he felt.

"Will you come home tomorrow, once your quarantine is over?" Her brown eyes implored.

"It depends."

She held her hands out in front of her. "Look if it's about me . . . us . . . I've been doing a lot of soul searching, lately. Julie knows how confused I am. Nothing is written in stone. Maybe—"

"Anna," Haldane cut her off. "It has nothing to do with us. I hate being away from Chloe a second longer than I have to."

He realized from her fleeting wince that the comment might have come across as cold, which he hadn't intended, but nor did he want to rip the scab off the wound again, so he let it stand. "I've already lost four precious days stuck here. I have to go where I am needed now. We're running out of time."

She nodded distantly. "Only two more days until the terrorists' ultimatum expires."

"A lot can happen in two days."

Anna nodded grimly. "I better get downstairs to Chloe and Mom. The kids will be here any second," she said.

Noah noticed with newfound ambivalence how Anna had withdrawn again. He was so tired of their constant emotional tug-of-war. "I wish I could be there. Good luck with the big party." He forced a reassuring smile. "Anna, everything is going to work out."

Haldane clicked the video box closed and stared at the blank screen.

Three hard raps at the door interrupted his thoughts. Haldane didn't even remember ordering room service, but he hadn't eaten today and his stomach had begun to growl. "Leave the tray at the door, thanks!" Haldane called out.

"Yeah, right!" a Scottish accent bellowed from the other side. "I've just flown four thousand goddamn miles so I can bring you your lousy lunch."

Haldane hopped out of his chair pleased to hear his friend's voice. He slipped on his N95 mask and walked to the door. "You wearing precautions, Duncan?" Haldane asked at the door.

"Again, Haldane, I want to reiterate that we don't have *that* kind of a relationship." McLeod unleashed a roar of laughter. "But I do have my clown mask and hat on if that helps."

Haldane opened the door. Duncan McLeod stood on the other side with a surgical mask covering his scraggly beard. He wasn't gowned. And a baseball cap stood in for the shower cap he was supposed to wear. His asymmetric eyes twinkled with the obvious humor he found in their situation. "Haldane! I'd give you a big hug, but I don't particularly want to die."

Haldane laughed. "Finally, there's an upside to my quarantine."

McLeod bellowed another laugh. "Ah, Haldane, I might actually have missed you if this fucking virus had killed you." He sauntered into the room and flopped into the loveseat behind the desk. Pointing at the mountains outside the windows across from him, he said, "When I was quarantined with TB, I was stuck in a mud hut in Borneo. You've got a slightly better deal here."

Haldane followed after the Scotsman. "Not that I am unhappy to see you, Duncan, but what are you doing here?"

"The great Jean Nantal sent me. He spewed some crap about me being the new authority on the Gansu Flu PCR probe test. Set up a bunch of meetings for me with the Vancouver infectious disease boys." McLeod shrugged. "But let's face it, he sent old expendable McLeod to keep an eye on his golden boy." McLeod clutched his chest. " '*Tis a far far better thing I do than I have ever done*' and all that shite."

Haldane rolled his eyes as he sat down in a chair across from McLeod. "How is London?" he asked, but judging by his colleague's jovial mood he knew the reports about the stabilizing situation in England must have been true.

"It's a buyer's market, if you're looking for real estate." McLeod shrugged. "Hardly a soul on the street. But I have to hand it to Nancy Levine—delightful chatterbox that she is—her team has done a good job under trying circumstances. The new case rate has steadily declined for the past three days. And no deaths in almost forty-eight hours."

"What are the latest totals?" Haldane asked.

"A thousand give or take infected. Two hundred dead." McLeod pulled off his mask. "Christ! I'm tired of these things. I know you're no risk to me." He paused, before his lips broke into a crooked smile. "But do me a favor and leave yours on, all right?"

Haldane sighed a laugh. "What about the clusters in Europe, Duncan?"

"Far as I know they're all contained." McLeod scratched his beard. "But, Haldane, the entire damn outbreak was all caused by one lousy terrorist. Imagine what an army of the buggers could accomplish."

Noah nodded. "We are more prepared now. It would be—will be—harder for them to spread the virus."

"Harder. By no means impossible," McLeod pointed out, stretching in his seat. "What's the local news?"

"Latest report is that the virus is contained in Vancouver, too. The death toll stands stable at 45, with 240 infections. No new cases in the last day." Noah nodded. "The photo of the dead terrorist has paid dividends, though. She was spotted several places, including the U.S.-Canada border. She and a young male Arab were turned back when their papers didn't clear. And several people recognized her—traveling alone—on a flight in from Paris."

McLeod sat forward in his seat. "And from Paris?"

Haldane shook his head. "She was traveling under a bogus alias with a stolen passport. So far the trail dries up in France."

"Shite! The damn French!" McLeod said.

Haldane frowned. "Including Jean Nantal?"

"You mean the bugger who keeps dumping us in the middle of these plagues?" McLeod screeched. "He's the worst of the bloody lot."

They shared a long laugh. McLeod was the exact tonic Haldane needed for his state of mind.

Another knock came at the door. "I hope you ordered enough for two," McLeod said. "I'm famished."

Gwen Savard's voice drifted through the door. "Noah, it's me. I've got big news!"

Haldane was surprised by how much the sound of her voice pleased him, regardless of her news. He opened the door and Gwen flew in. She glanced over at McLeod with a look of surprise. "Oh, hello, Duncan." She offered a quick smile. "Good to see you."

"Lovely to see you upright, Gwen." McLeod grinned mischievously. "I was expecting to have to identify both of your sorry corpses in some drab Canadian morgue."

Gwen chuckled distractedly. "I just heard from Washington," she said with her back to the window. "We might have had a huge breakthrough."

Haldane followed her back to the couches and stood between McLeod and her. "What's up?"

She smiled widely. "We think we know who's behind The Brotherhood of One Nation."

"So tell us!" McLeod said.

"The CIA intercepted an e-mail sent by an Egyptian cop. In it he names the dead terrorist from Vancouver along with the leaders of the group." Savard spat out the words rapid-fire. "Says they have a base in Somalia."

"Oh, Christ," McLeod moaned. "They're going to dump us in Africa now."

Haldane ignored him. "Who are 'they'?" he demanded.

Gwen threw up her hands. "Some media mogul from Cairo, Hazzir Kabaal. And an ex-special forces army major. No one knows much about either of them."

"Where in Somalia?" Haldane pressed.

Gwen shook her head. "The e-mail didn't specify."

"Well, why doesn't someone bloody well ask the chap who wrote it?" McLeod piped up.

"Because he's dead," Gwen said. "He was found indented in the sidewalk below his nineteenth-floor apartment with a bullet in his back. Killed minutes after sending the e-mail."

"That's a reasonable excuse, I suppose," McLeod grumbled.

"It's all just happened in the last hour or so," Gwen said. "We don't know much yet."

"Somalia," Haldane said, falling back into his chair.

"If I remember my geography that's a fair-sized country."

"And bloody hot," McLeod added. "Not to mention anarchic, flea-bitten, and exceptionally violent."

Gwen glanced at her watch. "Noah, our videoconference with the President is in ten minutes. Are you ready?"

Haldane nodded.

Gwen turned to McLeod. "Sorry, Duncan, you don't have the security clearance—"

McLeod held up his hand. "I know. I know. You damn Yanks are worse than the Chinese when it comes to this kind of high-level paranoia." He chuckled. "Much as it tears me apart, I'm going to take my leave of this merry little leper colony and find me some lunch."

Haldane sat in front of the camera, as the technical team remotely assumed control of his computer. The split video window that emerged was unlike the ones he had grown used to in past days. He understood that this hookup was more secure than anything he had seen before, but he knew nothing of the technology behind it.

After a few minutes of technical futzing, Gwen appeared in the smaller box on the right side. In the larger box on the left four people sat on one side of a long oval table. Haldane instantly recognized them, but Ted Hart introduced the group as if Haldane had never heard of the nation's leaders.

"Dr. Haldane, I would like to introduce you to the President, the National Security Advisor, Dr. Horne, and the Secretary of Defense, Secretary Whitaker. I'm Ted Hart, the Secretary of Homeland Security," he said equally as unnecessarily, having received more airtime than Larry King and Oprah combined in the past week.

The President leaned back in his leather chair. In his early fifties, he wore a navy suit with an open-collared light blue shirt, and he towered half a head above the others at the table. He had thick salt-and-pepper hair, expressive gray eyes, and a prominent chin. He wasn't classically handsome, but he had a commanding and compassionate countenance. Haldane decided he had a perfectly presidential face for photo-ops.

On the President's right sat his National Security Advisor, Andrea Horne, a handsome African American woman with curly black hair and stylish half-glasses perched halfway down her nose. To the President's left sat his Secretary of Defense, Aaron Whitaker, a scrawny balding man in his mid-sixties with pasty skin and (Haldane knew from his press conferences) a wolverine's disposition. To Whitaker's left sat Ted Hart.

"Hello," Haldane said, feeling unexpectedly bashful in the presence of such executive power.

The President smiled and nodded once into the camera. Horne said, "Welcome, Drs. Haldane and Savard," while Whitaker did not acknowledge either of them.

"Gwen, Dr. Haldane, you are up-to-date on the latest developments from Egypt, I trust?" Hart asked.

"Ted, we know of the intercepted e-mail but the details we've heard are sketchy at best," Savard said.

"Allow me to elaborate." Hart glanced at the President who nodded his approval.

A photo of a smiling handsome man, who looked to Noah like a playboy son of some rich emir posing for the paparazzi, appeared at the bottom of his screen. "Meet Hazzir Kabaal—an Egyptian publishing magnate who owns several papers which pander to the pan-Arabic and Muslim Brotherhood movements. Don't let his dapper wardrobe fool you. Kabaal has financial ties to militant groups from the Hezbollah to the Abu Sayyef."

The photo on Haldane's screen switched from Kabaal's unctuous grin to the expressionless face of an army officer with pale blue eyes. "Major Abdul Sabri. Formerly with the Egyptian Special Forces. He specialized in counter-insurgency, but we assume has since switched sides. Apparently, Kabaal, Sabri, and several known associates left Cairo three weeks ago to whereabouts unknown."

"They're in Somalia," the Secretary of Defense grunted with confidence.

The face of an old Islamic cleric replaced Sabri's on the screen. "Sheikh Hassan. A firebrand Islamist and, we believe, the spiritual leader of the group. The same officer who sent the e-mail arrested Hassan and his son at their Al-Futuh Mosque shortly before he was murdered. The Egyptian authorities are holding both men and several others they've rounded up from the mosque. The CIA has already sent a team to Cairo to begin interrogations."

Haldane cleared his throat. "Mr. Secretary, do you believe the policeman's information is correct about the base in Somalia?"

"We have nothing in the way of proof, Dr. Haldane," Andrea Horne answered for the Secretary in her clipped Ivy League cadence. "However, the rest of the officer's information has thus far panned out."

"Any idea where in Somalia they might be?" Savard asked.

"Somewhere north of Mogadishu," boomed Secretary Whitaker in a surprisingly powerful voice for his shrunken form. "It's the goddamn Wild West up there. Lawless!"

A map of Somalia popped up in the bottom frame of Haldane's screen. Forming a sideways "V" that hugged Ethiopia and ran along the eastern coast of Africa, it stuck out into the Indian Ocean at its vertex.

"The CIA is reviewing the satellite imagery," Hart explained. "But Secretary Whitaker is right, the north would be the easiest place to conceal a base."

Whitaker shook his head. "We ought to go in en masse."

"Do you remember our last Somali experience, Mr. Secretary?" Horne glanced at her colleague with a flicker of annoyance. "The disastrous deployment in the early nineties?"

Whitaker snorted a laugh. "Andrea, we're not talking about a humanitarian mission this time around. We find this terrorist base, and we replace it with a fifty-mile-wide crater."

"Might not be so simple," Gwen said.

"And why not, Dr. Savard?" Whitaker's fierce eyes challenged through the computer screen.

"Because, Mr. Secretary, wiping out their base does not necessarily mean wiping out the virus," Gwen said.

With fingertips touching a few inches from his chin, the President sat forward in his chair. "Please explain, Dr. Savard," he said in his slight southern drawl.

"Initially, when the terrorists were trying to incubate the virus they would have needed a moderately sophisticated virology lab."

"But now?" the President said.

"Mr. President, once they had established enough of a live base—say in eggs, chickens, primates, or even human volunteers," Gwen stressed the last words. "They could take these live incubators anywhere and continue to infect more 'suicide bombers.'"

"So they wouldn't need their base anymore?" the President said.

"Mr. President, they may not need their base for a laboratory," Secretary Whitaker said. "But they still need their base as a *base*. Where are a bunch of terrorists with infected chickens, monkeys, or whatever going to go?"

The NSA nodded. "The Secretary has a point, sir," Horne said. "They need a protected space from which to run their operations."

"But if they know that we know . . ." Ted Hart joined the discussion. "Then it's hardly protected."

The President tapped his fingers together and then nodded. "Seems to me the first priority is to find this base in Somalia." He stared directly into the camera again. Haldane recognized the earnest expression for the one that had made his campaign ads so effective. "Doctors, do either of you have any suggestions?"

Haldane cleared his throat again. "Birds, sir."

"Birds?" The President frowned.

"Birds are the natural carriers of all influenza viruses," Haldane explained. "Without becoming sick themselves, they develop high levels of the virus in their bloodstream. If any of the virus has leaked from their lab, we would best find it among the local bird population."

Whitaker shook his long narrow head angrily. "Let me get this straight, Dr. Haldane. You're suggesting we go on a bird hunt through Somalia?" he scoffed. "Even if we did get lucky, wouldn't it take weeks to check the blood of these animals?"

"Not necessarily," Haldane said. "We have a rapid diagnostic test—what we call a PCR probe—for the virus that could give us a preliminary answer in less than two hours."

"The terrorist's ultimatum expires in forty-eight hours," Horne pointed out.

"Which means we have to act now." Whitaker jabbed the tabletop with a fingertip. "We send the army and marines into Somalia, find this base, and eliminate it."

Ted Hart turned to the Secretary of Defense. "Aaron, what if Gwen is right, and they've already left Somalia with their virus?"

"We know who they are. They are not ghosts anymore," Whitaker boomed. "So wherever they go, we will find them."

"We've known who Bin Laden is for over fifteen years," Hart pointed out.

Whitaker shook his head dismissively.

The President dropped his hands to the table and stared directly into the camera again. "Doctors, you heard the ultimatum. If their 'army of martyrs' reached our cities, what would be the fallout?"

"Mr. President, all U.S. cities are enacting the Emergency Response Plan to Biological Attack as we speak," Gwen said. "But it takes time to roll out such a complex infrastructure. I don't think forty-eight hours is enough time."

The President furrowed his bushy eyebrows. "Dr. Haldane, I understand you are the world authority on this virus. Your thoughts?"

Haldane took a deep breath, and composed his thoughts. "Mr. President, we have the advantage of preexisting panic. People are already isolating themselves, which actually helps in a case like this. Also, while highly lethal, this virus is not as contagious as many, so limiting the spread is possible as demonstrated in China, Hong Kong, and now London." He wet his lips before continuing. "But outside of China, what we've seen so far—eighteen hundred infected and four hundred deaths—has been the result of four infected terrorists. If an army of them arrives . . . Excuse me, Mr. President, but God help us all."

Everyone in the screen lapsed into silence. Finally, the President leaned back in his chair. He looked to his advisors on either side of him. "Ideas?"

Andrea Horne spoke. "The ultimatum said that we had to 'begin withdrawal' by the deadline. Our troops in Kuwait and the few left in Saudi are relatively inactive right now. Maybe we could begin by withdrawing them."

"We can't bow to these parasites!" Whitaker slapped the tabletop angrily.

"I think you misunderstand my point—" Horne began.

Whitaker jabbed a finger at her. "Redeploying one single soldier would be an invitation to any fanatic with a bug or a bomb to hold America hostage. Mark my words. We withdraw from the Arabian Peninsula and it will never end!"

Hart cleared his throat with a cough. "Aaron makes a good point, Mr. President. Our policy with good reason has been to never negotiate with terrorists."

Horne's palms shot up in the air. "I am not proposing negotiations! I am suggesting a stall tactic to make them think we are complying in order to buy us a little more time. Nothing more."

The President stared at the table for several seconds before nodding resignedly. "I'm afraid Andrea is right." He turned to his Defense Secretary. "Start making plans to pull our troops."

Whitaker opened his mouth to rebut, but the President cut him off with a sweep of his hand. "That leaves us forty-eight hours to track down these sons of bitches," the President said. "I authorize you to use any and all means necessary to do just that." He looked around the faces at the table and then stared directly into the camera. "Am I clear?"

CHAPTER

28

Hazzir Kabaal stood outside the complex in the punishing African midday heat, waiting.

His expensive desert boots had crusted with dirt and grime and for the first time in his life he had let his beard grow. Realizing that no one in the complex, or all of Somalia, cared about his attire, he had traded his pressed khakis for the more comfortable native robes. He wondered if he would ever again have cause or opportunity to don his favorite handcrafted Italian suits or leather shoes. Not likely, he realized with a twinge of melancholy.

A cloud of dust streamed down the dirt road and toward him. A block away, the cloud slowed and the dust settled enough to allow the tan-colored truck to emerge from within, allowing Kabaal to see that Abdul Sabri was the sole occupant in the truck.

Sabri brought the car to a stop directly in front of

Kabaal. The driver's door popped open and Sabri stepped out and then stretched at the side of the road.

Kabaal walked over to greet him. "Abdul, you are well?"

"I am," Sabri said, stifling a yawn. "Your friend is not."

"My friend," Kabaal grunted. "What did Sergeant Eleish have to tell you?"

Sabri shrugged and then shook his head.

Kabaal narrowed his gaze. "You were going to talk to him first!"

"Hard to talk to someone who is leaping out of a building," Sabri said unapologetically.

"This is not good, Abdul," Kabaal said. "So you have no idea who he might have spoken to?"

Sabri shrugged again. "It's likely he spoke to someone, though."

"Why do you say that?" Kabaal asked.

"There has been much activity at the mosque."

Kabaal felt his hair stand on end. Each word out of Sabri's mouth raised his level of alarm a notch. "What activity?"

"The police have arrested the Sheikh and his son," Sabri said as nonchalantly as if commenting on the weather. "They are rounding up others from the mosque for questioning."

Annoyed at his lieutenant's indifference, Kabaal shook a finger at him. "And this does not concern you?"

"Not particularly."

"For the love of the Prophet, why not?"

Sabri flashed the widest grin Kabaal had ever seen from him. "It has started, Abu Lahab."

"What has?"

"After the police raided, there was a protest outside the mosque," Sabri said. "It turned into a riot. In Cairo! The people rose up spontaneously in the streets."

"What happened to the rioters?" Kabaal asked.

"The troops came. Several were killed, the rest arrested."

Kabaal frowned at Sabri and shook his head in exasperation. "But this is all good?"

"If the brothers are willing to stand up to the might of the Egyptian army in Cairo, what do you think will happen in Baghdad, Kabul, Riyadh, and Jakarta?" Sabri drifted a finger from Kabaal to himself. "It's because of us, Abu Lahab. The Brotherhood! We have empowered the people. Wait until you see what happens when we bring America to its knees."

Kabaal considered Sabri's argument. "I wonder," he said distantly.

"There's nothing to wonder, Abu Lahab. America is weak. With the help of the virus, she will collapse under her own weight like a rotted tree in a storm. And then we will be able to deal with the treacherous infidels who run our governments." He looked down and nodded, giving Kabaal the impression that he was talking to himself. "And we will start with the worst of the offenders in Egypt. This is what you dreamed of, is it not? Our lands governed by the laws of the Shari'ah. The return of the Caliphate."

For the second time in a week, Sabri surprised Kabaal with his passionate outburst. Kabaal realized that Sabri's normally disinterested exterior was nothing more than a facade. Like the door on a blast furnace, it concealed a raging fire within. And Kabaal was no longer certain that the heat inside could be contained.

"Abdul, if the American President has any sense at all, he will decide to pull his troops out of our occupied lands," Kabaal said. "Then the events can unfold as you have described them without the help of the cursed virus."

Sabri grunted.

"You think not, my friend?" Kabaal demanded.

"They will not—they cannot—negotiate with us," Sabri

said as he walked to the trunk to grab his small knapsack. "We will have to release the infected martyrs upon them." Sabri slung the pack over his shoulder and started walking toward the door of the complex, but he stopped halfway and turned back to Kabaal. "You are prepared for that eventuality, are you not?"

There was no deference in Sabri's tone. Kabaal knew it wasn't even a question. Before he could respond, Dr. Anwar Aziz burst out of the front door of the complex.

"There is news," the fat microbiologist panted, leaning forward to catch his breath.

"What news?" Kabaal asked.

"The Americans," Aziz wheezed. "Come, come. You must see." He took one last gulp of air and then turned and rushed back into the building.

Kabaal and Sabri followed the scientist into his ground-floor office. They crowded around his computer screen. When Aziz tapped the keyboard, a TV news video clip popped up on the screen. Inside the video box, the American President stood at a podium in front of a single microphone. The quality of the image was poor and the action was slightly discordant with the sound, so the President's mouth and gestures lagged a moment behind his words.

"Good evening," he said in a businesslike tone. "No doubt, every one of you is aware of The Brotherhood of One Nation's threat to dispatch terrorists infected with the Gansu Flu across our country if their demands are not met. Their deadline is less than thirty-six hours hence.

"After consultation with members of my cabinet, I am announcing that in the next twenty-four hours the United States will begin to withdraw our troops from bases within the Arabian Peninsula." He cleared his throat. "Once the redeployment from the Gulf States is complete, we will begin a similar process in Afghanistan, to be followed by Iraq and all other sovereign Islamic nations. Such mass troop and equipment transport is a colossal logistic endeavor. However, we will undertake to complete the withdrawals as rapidly as we can in an orderly fashion."

The President's jaw set in a pained expression. "While it is our policy to never negotiate with terrorists, I believe that the extreme circumstances and cataclysmic potential of not cooperating outweigh the principle. While highly regrettable, I believe this option will serve to protect millions of Americans and is the only course of action my conscience allows me to pursue. As your President, I accept full responsibility for this decision."

The President offered the camera a long, determined stare before he added, "Good night and God Bless America." Then he stepped away from the podium.

Kabaal turned to Aziz, wrapped his arms around the scientist's flabby midsection, and gave him a congratulatory hug. "God is great!" Kabaal said happily, before releasing Aziz from his grip.

"Yes, yes, Abu Lahab," Aziz said. He stumbled a step back and then flushed with a mix of joy and embarrassment. "Well done, Abu Lahab. Well done. Allah be praised."

"See, Major, I told you the Americans would see the light!" Kabaal said and turned to Sabri.

Instead of elation, Kabaal saw the opposite on the ex-army officer's face. Sabri's light blue eyes glared at the computer screen and the corner of his lip curled into a snarl. "Can you not see what they are doing?" Sabri asked.

"Acquiescing to our demands?"

Sabri snorted. "They are stalling."

Aziz dabbed his brow and asked Sabri, "How do you know, Major?"

"Because, Doctor, it is exactly what I would do if I were in their shoes," Sabri said. "There is no military consequence of withdrawing troops from Kuwait. None. But it will buy them time to come looking for us."

Kabaal ran a hand through his hair. He studied Sabri,

guardedly. "Abdul, I am beginning to suspect you had hoped the Americans would turn down our ultimatum."

"What I wanted or hoped for is not the point, Hazzir," Sabri said coolly. "There was no chance they were going to comply in good faith with our demands."

"How do you know?" Kabaal's hands shook in front of him.

"For David to fell Goliath, he needed a large stone. All that we have slung at the Americans so far are pebbles."

"So what are you suggesting?" Kabaal smoothed back his hair. "That we proceed with our threat, even though the President just agreed to our demands in front of the world."

Sabri's eyelids lowered to half-mast. "I suggest we flush out their true motives."

"How?"

"We give the Americans a very specific timetable for troop pullouts. Set in terms of hours—at most days—but definitely not weeks."

"Is that realistic, Major?"

Sabri shrugged. "Do you remember Iraq? If they can invade a country in days, then they can withdraw in the same time."

Though Kabaal questioned Sabri's motives, he could think of no reason not to embrace the suggestion. He nodded. "We will send them another message."

"I will make the arrangements," Sabri said. Then he glanced from Aziz to Kabaal, his face blank but his eyes ablaze. "And I will ready the martyrs."

CHAPTER
29

Gwen Savard double-checked her temperature. When both readings confirmed she still had not developed a fever, she swept up the small stack of used N95 masks off the desk in front of her and dumped them, with profound satisfaction, into the room's trashcan.

The quarantine was officially over.

Gwen only allowed herself a moment of celebration. The clock was ticking ever louder now. The terrorist's ultimatum was set to expire in less than twenty-four hours. And Gwen, like everyone else in the American Administration, had no idea how they would react to the President's televised promise to pull troops from the Arabian Peninsula. So far their only response had been silence.

Gwen hurried back into the bedroom and tossed the rest of her clothes into her suitcase. Once packed, she sat in front of her computer and scanned through her most recent e-mail, paying attention only to the messages that pertained to the immediate crisis. And only those few she deemed urgent.

She was about to power off her computer when the musical tone rang, indicating a request for a videoconference. She would have ignored it but for the name of the requestor, which appeared in the corner of the screen.

With a mouse click, a video window popped open framing most of Isaac Moskor's head and shoulders inside. He wore a rumpled white lab coat and his white hair stuck out in spears from his head. "Hey, kid, how you doing?" Moskor drawled in his deep Jersey tone.

She was comforted by the image of her mentor, the same way the sight of her favorite uncle used to buoy her spirits as a child. "Fine, Isaac." She smiled broadly and swept a hand down her body by way of proof. "Survived my quarantine intact. But you caught me just as I'm about to head back to Washington."

Moskor nodded.

"You all settled in at the CDC?" Gwen asked.

"Hmmm." He shrugged his huge shoulders. "I miss cold, dumpy little New Haven. Atlanta is too big for me." His expression broke into a crooked grin. "Guess I'm just a hick at heart."

Gwen offered a quick grin, but she felt too pressed for time not to get down to business. "And your lab?"

"Amazing what can happen if the government takes an interest in your work." He shook his head. "I spent most of my academic life begging, borrowing, and stealing enough to set up a bare-bones lab. But I come down here and in twenty-four hours I got the Taj Mahal at my disposal."

"Nothing you don't deserve, Isaac," she said. "Have you begun to run experiments?"

Moskor nodded. "Yeah, we started with a group of fifty African green monkeys six days ago. Infected all of them with viral-loaded serum, then divided the monkeys in two groups. Twenty-five got twice-a-day doses of A36112. And the control just got standard antiviral drugs."

"And?" Gwen leaned forward in her chair.

But Moskor was immune to the urgency in her tone. "Can't get used to these videoconferences." He reached forward and adjusted his camera, making his image shake on Gwen's screen. "Always feel like I'm on the set of *Star Trek*. I half expect to see you disappear and Mr. Sulu and Scotty to pop up on the monitor." He adjusted his camera one more time. "You sure it's safe to discuss things over this line?"

"Totally." Gwen nodded impatiently. "Tell me."

"You weren't exaggerating about this Gansu Flu. Scary bug. Reminds me of what I saw when I toured that lab in Washington running the Ebola experiments."

"About the two groups?" Gwen tried to force him back on topic.

He offered a hint of a smile. "So far, the virus has killed nine of the twenty-five monkeys in the control group."

Gwen felt her heart speed up. She knew he was holding back promising news. "And the treated monkeys?"

He bit his lip, but his smile grew a touch wider. "So far—and I can't stress enough how early we're talking here—in the monkeys treated with A36112, only one has died."

Savard leaped out of her chair.

"Whoa! Where did you go?" Moskor said. "I'm talking to your belt now."

Savard sat back down. She felt giddy from the news. She had to clear her throat and fight back the tears. "Isaac, you've done it!"

Moskor blushed slightly and shook his large head. "We—don't forget Clara and the rest of the team—haven't done anything yet."

Gwen started to speak, but Moskor cut her off with a wave of his big hand. "Kid, I know how promising this looks, but let's not get way ahead of ourselves. We're talk-ing about four days of treatment on twenty-five lab mon-keys."

"But, Isaac, those results are astounding," Gwen squealed. "One-third dead compared to one in twenty-five. That's almost unfathomable."

"Way too early for that." Moskor shook his finger. "Some of the monkeys in the treatment group are still pretty damn sick! We don't know that more won't die today. We need far bigger numbers and more time before we go concluding anything."

Savard shrugged. "Look, Isaac, far as I'm concerned, you can have every African green monkey in the world. But what we don't have is more time. We might be facing a pandemic tomorrow. I mean, literally, tomorrow."

Moskor stared at her for several seconds without remarking. Finally, he said, "So you want to go straight to human trials?"

"No." Savard shook her head adamantly. "No more tri-als at all. We need to put this drug into mass production."

Moskor's face crumpled into a series of wrinkles. "Mass production?" he repeated.

"Today, Isaac," she said with authority. "If need be, we'll borrow every pharmaceutical plant in the country to mass-produce this drug."

Moskor's jaw dropped.

"How hard was it for you to manufacture the pills?" Gwen asked.

Still appearing stunned, he shrugged. "It's a simple organic compound. Easy to make a couple hundred pills. But what you're talking about?" He held his palms up.

"What I'm talking about is millions of doses," she said, already planning the logistics in her mind. "Isaac, have you got an intravenous preparation for this?"

"Yeah." He nodded. "We've had to use it on the sickest monkeys who aren't able to swallow tablets."

"Perfect," Gwen said. "We'll need to produce both."

Moskor cast his eyes down. "I knew this was a possibility when you sent me to Atlanta. And, kid, I know you are doing what you think you have to do," he said softly. "But to me this is still bad medicine. You don't jump from half-baked, half-finished studies to treating live sick people, no matter how tempting the results may seem. It's been done before." He paused. "And the literature is littered with stories of enough premature corpses to tell me that it's a very bad idea."

Gwen wished she could reach out and touch her troubled friend. Instead she just nodded. "Isaac, you have no idea how many premature corpses might be littered if we don't do anything. Of course, people might die. Even directly as a result of being treated with A36112," she acknowledged. "But what you've given me—what you've given the world—is more hope than we had yesterday. I know it's too early to know for sure, but you might have found a cure for the Killer Flu. And we don't have time to confirm that in a lab."

He leaned back in his seat, his expression somewhere between satisfaction and skepticism. "So the real world is going to be our lab, huh?"

"There is no other way," Gwen said.

CHAPTER

30

Free of quarantine, Noah Haldane stepped out of the elevator into the lobby for the first time in five days. He wanted to drop his suitcase and run out into the December sunshine that streamed in through the hotel's huge windows, but Duncan McLeod, bearing a tray holding three coffees, beckoned him from the other side of the lobby.

"Christ!" McLeod bellowed when Noah had made it halfway across the floor. "Now that it's safe to hug you, I got no interest. Funny that."

"I've overcome bigger disappointments," Haldane said with a slight smile as he eased a cup out of the tray. "Thanks. Any sign of Gwen?"

"Not yet," McLeod said. "She's probably getting herself all gussied up for me."

Haldane chuckled as he inhaled the sweet aroma of the coffee. Since childhood he had always preferred the smell to the actual taste, but after an anticipatory night of restless sleep, he needed every drop of the cup in his hand to keep him going.

"You laugh, Haldane, but the McLeod charm is a mysterious and powerful force." He fluttered his eyelids, making his lazy eye even more noticeable. "That my heart has already been claimed only drives the ladies that much madder."

"One can only imagine," Haldane said.

McLeod gestured at Haldane with his chin. "I thought I sensed a little something between the likes of you two up in your room. No?" He raised an eyebrow. "You didn't succumb to a mutual case of quarantine fever, did you?"

Haldane shook his head. As he was about to advise McLeod to let it go, he glimpsed Gwen emerging from an elevator. Rolling her suitcase behind her, she half jogged toward them. And Noah noticed that she still had a slight limp in her step as she approached.

She wore a knee length green suit, which showed off her lithe calves. Her tawny blond hair was clipped back behind her ears. As she neared, Noah saw that her face was flushed and her eyes wide with excitement.

Catching Noah off guard, Gwen threw her arms around him, almost spilling his coffee. The pressure of her firm body against his stirred something inside, but realizing the hug had lasted a moment too long, he let go at the same moment she did. The embrace might have been innocent enough—nothing more than any two friends might share—but it was their first physical contact beyond a handshake, and it left him even more confused.

"You missed a spot," McLeod said to Gwen and pointed to himself with a thumb.

With a laugh, Gwen leaned forward and, avoiding the coffee tray in his hand, pecked McLeod on the cheek. McLeod reached down, pulled a coffee from his tray, and handed it to her.

She smiled her thanks.

"You seem awfully happy to be free of quarantine," Haldane said to her.

"It's not just that." She shook her head enthusiastically. "I've got news." She flashed an openmouthed smile, and Noah noticed how perfect her teeth were. "And for a change it's good news."

"What is it?" Haldane asked.

She raised her coffee cup, as if offering a toast. "My mentor, Dr. Isaac Moskor, had a huge breakthrough with an experimental antiviral he's developed."

"With the Gansu strain?" Haldane said, suddenly swept up in her excitement.

Savard nodded and told them about Moskor's early results with the experiments on the African green monkeys.

When she described the scientist's reticence in proceeding to production of the drug, McLeod nodded in full agreement. "He's got a point. Those are some bloody shaky grounds for exposing millions of people to a completely untested drug."

"Under normal circumstances, no question," Haldane said. "But with what we're potentially facing?" He crumpled the empty cup in his hand. "We're grabbing at straws here, and this one is as good as or better than any we've seen so far."

United Flight 3614

The three doctors spent most of the flight back to Dulles Airport lost in their own work. Savard had her laptop computer propped open on the tray in front of her, but she only seemed to hang up the air phone long enough to place another call. McLeod sat across the aisle from the other two, reading glasses on as he scanned through reams of journal articles. Though he went to great pains to imply otherwise, McLeod was among the brightest and most knowledgeable virologists Haldane had ever met. Aside from the levity he provided, McLeod was the stabilizing force on the WHO's emerging pathogens team.

Haldane focused his attention on Somalia, one of the few African countries where his WHO job had never taken him. Using his laptop's electronic encyclopedia, he scanned the sordid history of the former British and Italian colony while acquiring a rudimentary understanding of its arid climate, plainslike geography, and strife-ridden politics. He studied a detailed map. In a nation ruled by anarchy, it seemed to Noah that there was a vast amount of territory within which to hide a small terrorist base. Pinpointing their lab might prove a daunting task even for the most powerful military and intelligence force on the planet.

While he worked, Haldane couldn't help overhearing snippets of Gwen's conversations from the seat beside. In the course of the flight, it sounded as if she had made strides in securing a pharmaceutical plant to mass-produce Moskor's new antiviral drug. Though he could only hear one side of the conversation, Haldane was impressed by her powers of persuasion, employing equal parts charm and intimidation to achieve her goal.

Catching her between phone calls, Haldane reached over and touched her on the sleeve of her jacket. "Gwen, if everything goes without a hitch, when is the soonest this drug would be ready?"

She shrugged. "They tell me three to four weeks."

"Hmmm," Haldane murmured.

"That's what they tell me," she said with a slight smile. "I've told them it has to be ready in one. Maximum."

Haldane nodded and pulled his hand from her arm.

She kept her eyes fixed on him. "You must be happy to be going home to her." Haldane didn't know whether Gwen meant his daughter or his wife, until she added, "You can finally celebrate her birthday in person."

He grinned. "Yeah, I'm pretty excited."

She cleared her throat and looked down at her notebook computer. "How will the rest of the reunion go?"

Haldane shrugged. "No idea," he said honestly. He had shared little with Gwen about his marital discord; and he never mentioned Anna's confused sexuality or infidelity. Gwen had inferred most of what she knew from how infrequently he spoke of his wife.

Gwen uttered a nervous laugh. "My situation is a bit more straightforward. I only have to settle up with my cat."

"And the media," Noah reminded her.

She closed the case on her laptop computer. "Yeah, them, too. I get the feeling I'm going to be on everyone's dance card once we get to D.C."

"Nervous?" he asked.

"A bit," she said. "It's only fair though. After all, I was supposed to protect the country from this kind of thing."

He shook his head in disbelief. "You don't blame yourself for what's happening?"

Gwen shrugged. When she met his stare, he recognized for the first time vulnerability in her green eyes. He wanted to stroke her cheek and hold her in his arms, but instead he said, "You were one of the few who predicted this scenario. What could you have possibly done differently?"

"I don't know," she said. "All I do know is that I'm the Director of Counter-Bioterrorism and the country is under virtual siege by bioterrorists. In my eyes that doesn't add up to good job performance."

Haldane chuckled sympathetically. "My job involves dealing with emerging pathogens, but I don't beat myself up every time some new virus or parasite pops up."

She smiled warmly, which wiped the fragility from her face but left the melancholy in her eyes. "You're sweet, Noah, but it's not a fair comparison." She touched his hand. "Anyway, don't worry about me. My capacity for self-recrimination is very limited. And I can handle the press . . . I think."

He grabbed her hand and squeezed it in his. She held on to his hand for a few moments, before giving it one long squeeze and then releasing her grip.

WASHINGTON, D.C.

It was late afternoon by the time they touched down at Dulles International Airport. An entourage from the Department of Homeland Security's staff met them at the gates and led them out to waiting limos. Outside, in the brisk Washington afternoon, the light was waning in the gray sky. A wind blew occasional flakes of wet snow into their faces.

Treading carefully, McLeod avoided the slushy snow on the sidewalk. "Christ, Haldane! And I thought Glasgow was dreary in the wintertime," he said.

As they loaded into the waiting limo, one of the DHS staffers said almost apologetically, "Secretary Hart left strict instructions to take you straight to his office for a debriefing."

Gwen shook her head. "We need to make a stop, first."

"Where, ma'am?" the young aide asked.

"Langley," she said.

Haldane vacillated as to whether to join the others at the CIA headquarters or race straight home. In the end, he decided that business matters had to take precedence, but as the cars pulled up in front of the steel and glass buildings on the west side of the sprawling CIA complex he felt anguished knowing that he was less than three miles from Chloe on the other side of the Potomac.

After clearing security, which included metal detectors and a manual pat-down, they were ushered into a wide-open hallway with marble walls and pillars. A man dressed in an expensive-looking navy suit and pale blue shirt, but no tie, strode purposefully toward them. Haldane estimated that the man with the gelled black hair and Mediterranean good looks was, like him, straddling forty.

The man walked straight up to Gwen and gathered her in a tight hug, causing Noah an unexpected pang of jealousy. After he released her, Gwen pointed to her two companions. "Alex, these are my colleagues Noah Haldane and Duncan McLeod."

"It's a pleasure, Doctors. Alex Clayton." He shook their hands and flashed his best Pierce-Brosnan-playing-007 smile.

In spite of Clayton's affability, Haldane resolved not to like the CIA man.

Clayton led them through a maze of corridors and up two separate elevators, before they reached his spacious office with the gold nameplate that read: "A Clayton, Deputy Director of Operations." In front of his mahogany desk, a circular meeting table stood with six chairs around it. Lost in conversation with Gwen, Clayton nodded at the table, indicating to Haldane and McLeod to take a seat.

"Shite, Haldane, my whole department could be run out of this office," McLeod grumbled as he joined Haldane in a seat beside him.

Eventually, Gwen sat down beside Haldane, and Clayton beside her. Once seated, she continued to update Clayton on the developments in Moskor's laboratory. He nodded several times and once even whistled appreciatively. When she finished, he beamed. "Gwen, this could be the break we needed."

"Or it could be absolutely nothing," McLeod grunted with his arms folded on the table and his head perched on them.

Clayton turned from Gwen and appraised McLeod with an amused smile. "You're not exactly 'the glass is half full' kind of a guy are you, Dr. McLeod?"

"Depends what's in the glass," McLeod said without lifting his head. "If it's just a bunch of monkey piss, I don't get too excited even if the glass is flowing over the top."

"Touché." Clayton laughed.

"Alex, I think I've shared all our developments with you," Savard said. "Your turn."

"Fair enough." Clayton nodded. He pointed at a white screen on the far wall as he opened his laptop computer. "I'll need visuals for this."

"Let's begin with the intercepted e-mail from the Cairo police detective, Achmed Eleish." Clayton tapped a few keystrokes and the picture of the murdered Vancouver terrorist popped up on the screen. "The Egyptian government has corroborated most of Eleish's story. This woman is exactly who he said she was, Sharifa Sha'rawi. She used to be a regular at the Al-Futuh Mosque, home to many of Cairo's extremists. So far the Egyptians and our people have got nothing out of the mosque's Sheikh and his followers, but it's still a work in progress."

He tapped away at his keyboard before Hazzir Kabaal's groomed image filled the screen. "Okay, Hazzir Kabaal. Up to now only a financer of terrorism, but when the Egyptians raided his home and office they found all kinds of material—from Islamist literature to books on microbiology and viruses—that fit the bill."

Clayton hit two more keys. Abdul Sabri's photo from his military record popped up on the screen. "Now, this guy is by far the most interesting character of the motley crew. The Egyptians have given us his file, and it's a doozy. As a major with their Special Forces, Sabri developed a talent and appetite for brutal operations. Massacres might be a better word. Some of the stuff he carried out . . ." Clayton shook his head.

"Don't be too jealous," McLeod said. "Your agency carries out more than its share of global atrocities."

Clayton shot him an annoyed glance, which lacked any sign of his earlier amusement. "Even the Egyptian Special

Forces eventually washed their hands of Abdul Sabri, declaring him too violent. But the most bizarre thing? Sabri used to torture and slaughter the same extremists he now works for. Makes little sense."

"Maybe the 'what' is more important than the 'who' for Major Sabri," Haldane said.

"Maybe." Clayton frowned skeptically. "Regardless, Sabri is one dangerous S.O.B. And the Egyptians are convinced that he was behind the murder of the policeman in Cairo. In fact, they believe Eleish jumped over his own railing to avoid Sabri's notorious torture technique."

"Poor man." Gwen shook her head in disgust. "Are we any closer to locating Kabaal, Sabri, or their lab?"

Clayton tapped a key. A map of Somalia, sandwiched between Ethiopia and the Indian Ocean, appeared on screen. Lines and colors divided it into various states and political allegiances. "We're still working under the assumption they're in Somalia." Clayton cracked his neck from side to side. "We have several leads, but . . ." He held up his hands and sighed.

"But nothing concrete?" Gwen asked.

"Problem is, Somalia isn't really a country in any traditional sense. It's just a hodgepodge of gangs, tribes, and secessionists. The northern region regards itself as an independent state called Somaliland. As does the middle region, Puntland. The south is in disarray. Political and ethnic parties compete with the warlords and other opportunists for every square inch."

Gwen leaned forward in her chair. "So it's impossible to get any government cooperation with tracking these terrorists down?"

"To begin with, there's no government to cooperate with," Clayton said. "But a bigger problem is that there are so many people up to no good—smugglers, drug traffickers, and other terrorist networks—that we're finding all kinds of criminals crawling out of the woodwork. They know we watch from the skies with our satellites, so their movements are calculated to confuse." Clayton hit a key and a few points on the map flashed in red. "We have picked up some unusual hot spots of cell phone and Internet activity at a number of sites. One just south of Mogadishu in Marka. Another outside Kismaayo. And one a few miles north of Hargeysa. We're keeping a close eye on all of them."

Clayton tapped a key and the screen went blank. "We've put several more agents on the ground. I think the key to finding Kabaal and his lab will be human intelligence."

"Doesn't sound like there's much of *that* in the region," McLeod deadpanned.

Clayton ignored the remark. "Information is very cheap in Somalia. For twenty U.S. dollars many of the locals would sell out their own mothers. My gut tells me that's how we're going to find him."

Clayton nodded to himself and then, as if in afterthought, he pointed at Haldane. "Oh, yeah." He grinned. "We're bird hunting, too. See if we can find us some infected turkeys or something to lead us to the terrorists."

Just as Haldane was about to reply, Gwen touched him on the wrist and said to Clayton, "Alex, we scientists might surprise you yet with our usefulness."

GLEN ECHO HEIGHTS, BETHESDA, MARYLAND

At just before 8:00 P.M., the limo pulled up to Haldane's colonial-style home in the middle-class Washington suburb.

Haldane had never formed much of an attachment to this house or any other place he had ever lived, but his heart pounded when he stepped out of the car. He took his suitcase from the driver and raced up the path to his front door, desperate to see Chloe though nervous at the prospect of facing Anna again.

The door opened before he reached it, and Chloe,

dressed in her Snow White outfit, raced out to meet him. She jumped into her dad's arms while he swung her around in the air, stopping only to cover her face with kisses while she laughed gleefully.

Leaving his bag on the doorstep, he carried his daughter into the foyer where Anna waited. "Daddy's really home!" Chloe squealed, still wrapped around Noah's chest.

There was an awkward moment when Anna leaned forward to kiss Noah, and it was clear that neither knew where her lips should land. They had once shared such physical synchrony, but now they experienced a clumsy moment as his nose bopped her chin before her lips brushed dryly against his cheek.

"Welcome home, Noah," Anna said with a tentative smile. Then she turned to her daughter with a feigned frown. "Remember what I said? Right to bed once Daddy comes home."

Chloe looked at her dad with pleading, saucer-shaped brown eyes. "You'll put me to bed, right, Daddy?"

"Well . . ." he said. "Only if I get to read all our favorite stories."

"Deal, Daddy-o!" she said, holding up a palm for Noah to slap it in a high five.

He twirled her 360 degrees in his arms. "Let's go!"

As he carried her up the stairs, Anna's voice called after them. "Don't forget her teeth, Noah."

After brushing her teeth and changing her into her new favorite Barbie nightie, Noah curled up with his daughter in her single bed. He read all six stories, which Chloe had carefully selected from her bookshelf, even though she was asleep by the time he started the fourth one. He lay beside her for at least half an hour, savoring her warmth and the sound of her snores, before he wiggled his arm free and rose from her bed.

When he got downstairs, Anna sat in a familiar pose, facing sideways on the couch with her knees pulled up to her chest and a big mug of tea in her hand. His earlier indifference from their videoconference gave way to a wave of nostalgia as he sat down beside her on the couch. For a moment, he thought she might stretch her legs out across his lap as once was her wont, but she kept her feet where they were.

"You must be relieved," Anna said, staring at her cup.

"Yes and no," Haldane said. "Our risk was always pretty low. Besides, the bigger picture isn't any better than it was before my quarantine."

"Still, it's good to be home, isn't it?" she asked quietly.

"Yeah."

Her brown eyes looked up and held his. "Are you going to stay awhile?"

He hesitated. "Probably not." He shook his head slightly. "I might have to go to Chicago to consult on the outbreak there. Or maybe overseas again. Kind of depends what happens next."

She broke off the eye contact and nodded distantly. They fell into an awkward silence. He reached for the remote control and switched the TV on to CNN.

Haldane was surprised to see Gwen's face staring back at him. Still in her green suit with her hair pinned behind her ears, she stood at a podium behind numerous microphones.

"Dr. Savard, when will the Chicago outbreak be contained?" a man asked off-camera.

Gwen stared ahead confidently. "There have been no new cases reported in Illinois today, which fits with the trend of the past three days. It is of course too early to call the outbreak contained, but it's a promising sign." She folded her arms across her chest. "The problem in Chicago was the geographical distribution of the original case clusters following the terrorist attack at Soldier Field. The virus was disseminated farther than in any other place. As you can imagine, the farther the virus is spread, the harder it is to contain."

"But, Dr. Savard," the same reporter persisted, "isn't it partly a reflection of poor planning on the Public Health and your department's behalf?"

She uncrossed her arms. "This is a brand-new form of terrorist threat, involving a flulike virus that has only existed for months," Gwen said calmly. She glared into the audience of reporters, her face devoid of the doubt Haldane had seen on the plane. "To my knowledge, no authority has ever succeeded in preventing the spread of the flu. Medical personnel and others in Chicago have been tireless in their efforts to manage the epidemic. They should be lauded, not questioned. Put the blame where it belongs, with the terrorists. No one else."

"She's very composed," Anna said from the seat beside Haldane.

His eyes glued to the screen, Noah nodded.

"Is she the woman you were quarantined with?" Anna asked.

"Yeah," Haldane said, feeling a twinge of irrational guilt.

"She's very pretty, too," Anna said.

"Sure," Haldane said. "I guess."

Noah could feel Anna's eyes on him. "You must have gotten to know each other in those five days?" she asked.

Haldane turned to his wife. "Look, Anna, we were quarantined in separate rooms," he snapped. "It's not like we were rooming at Club Med together."

"Just asking," Anna said as she took another sip of tea.

"Sorry." Haldane forced a smile. "Must be the jet lag is catching up to me. Yeah, we got to know each other a little. She's a very dedicated woman. And smart, too. I wouldn't want anyone else doing her job—" Haldane stopped abruptly when the TV picture cut from Savard in mid-answer to the CNN anchor desk.

Big letters flashed over the anchorman, which read: "Breaking News!" The anchorman cleared his throat. "We interrupt the DHS news conference to announce CNN has just received word from A1 Jazeera Network," he said somberly. "The Brotherhood of One Nation has sent them another taped ultimatum. Please stand by . . ."

CHAPTER
31

Hazzir Kabaal sat in his office listening to the Egyptian radio station's coverage of The Brotherhood of One Nation's latest ultimatum.

"We have heard the promises from the President, but we know better than to trust his empty words," The Brotherhood's spokesman railed in his throaty tone. "The timetable set out for withdrawal of the infidel troops from our holy lands is unacceptable. The Islamic republics of Afghanistan and Iraq were overrun in days. Not weeks or months." His voice quavered. "The Americans and their so-called allies have three days to withdraw all troops from our Islamic lands. If by Monday midnight there is one foreign soldier left standing in our lands, then our martyrs will sweep over America like a flooding river. And God will have no mercy for those in its path."

Even though Kabaal had written the words, hearing

them spoken back to him over the radio's static made them seem surreal as if part of a play he had penned.

When Kabaal looked up, Abdul Sabri stood silently in the doorway. He had traded his galabiya for military fatigues, and an automatic handgun was holstered prominently at his side. Without waiting for an invitation, as he had always before, Sabri walked into the office. Rather than standing, he sank into the seat across from Kabaal.

"The message is right, Abu Lahab," Sabri said in what amounted to the closest to a compliment Kabaal had ever heard from the man.

"Three days, though . . ." Kabaal said skeptically.

"If they have any intention of complying, it is more than enough," Sabri said.

Kabaal tilted his head from side to side. "We'll see."

"We need to prepare, Hazzir," Sabri said.

Kabaal did not reply.

"Our people are in place, but they need the virus," Sabri stressed.

"Poor Sharifa," Kabaal sighed. The original plan had called for Sharifa to carry the virus to Seattle for further distribution, but it was foiled by her botched attempt to cross the border by car from Canada. And the backup plan fell through when their Chicago courier died before the virus could be harvested from her blood.

"It will be even more difficult to get it into America now," Kabaal pointed out.

"Difficult, but by no means impossible." Sabri shrugged.

"Oh?"

"This time we will send it by more than one route," Sabri said authoritatively. "Maybe one of us will have to carry it there personally. We can afford no more chances."

Kabaal eyed Sabri for several moments. "Major, you fully expect to unleash the virus, don't you?"

"Yes," he said without hesitation.

"Even if the Americans comply with our demands?" he asked.

"They won't," Sabri said without a trace of doubt. "They will come for us here very soon, which is why we have to leave today."

"What makes you so sure?" Kabaal asked.

Sabri shook his head impatiently. His shift in attitude from deference to defiance was no longer the least subtle. "I have been a soldier my whole life. War is in my blood. I understand it far better than you ever will. The Americans assume they can stop us if they can find us in time. And they have capabilities we never dreamed possible. Trust me, Hazzir, they will come. And soon. Now is our window of opportunity."

Kabaal's heart sank. "And where do you suggest we go?" he asked.

Before Sabri had a chance to answer, Anwar Aziz flew into the room. The overweight scientist practically ran up to the desk where Kabaal and Sabri sat. Uncharacteristically, Aziz was grinning from ear to ear.

"Aziz, I take it you have news?" Kabaal said.

"Indeed, Abu Lahab," Aziz chortled. "Indeed."

Kabaal held out his hand. "Please . . ."

Aziz gathered up the seams of his white lab coat and plopped his large bottom in the chair beside Sabri. "Ever since we set up our laboratory, we have done more than just preserve the Gansu virus. We have continued to experiment," he said with a hint of pride. "We have introduced other influenza viruses into laboratory pigs. You see, in microbiological terms, pigs are known as the 'mixing vessel' for certain viruses like influenza."

"Meaning?" Sabri said with a bored sigh.

"Of course, of course." Aziz rolled one hand over the other in a nervous gesture. "The pig's bloodstream is ideal for viruses of various species to interact, to mutate. The organisms trade sections of RNA, their genetic code, between one another."

"And this affects the viruses how?" Kabaal asked.

"Various ways." Aziz dabbed at his brow where beads of sweat had begun to form. "Traits of one virus can be passed on to another. At least, that is what we have been trying to accomplish with our virus," he said as if they had single-handedly created the Gansu Flu.

"Which traits?" Kabaal asked with a raised eyebrow.

"The contagiousness, Abu Lahab," Aziz said. His awkward smile reemerged. "I was never satisfied with the results we attained. The Gansu virus was less contagious than the common cold."

"*Was*?" Sabri sat up straighter and looked at Aziz with renewed interest. "Not anymore?"

Aziz's smile grew wider. "Not anymore, Major. Along with the Gansu strain, we inoculated our pigs with the more contagious but far less lethal forms of the common flu. We tried several recent flu strains without success. But when we introduced the Beijing Flu to the mix . . ." He clasped his hands together in a sign of victory. "Something clicked. It would appear that we have developed a more infective version of the Gansu Flu."

"How much more?" Sabri asked.

Aziz looked down at his hands, and seemed surprised to see how he held them. He unclasped his hands and brushed away at imagined dirt on his pristine lab coat. "In our original human experiments, we had a transmission rate of roughly twenty percent after ten minutes of close contact," he said. "This was comparable to what we found with the monkeys."

"And with this new mutation?" Kabaal asked.

"We have not run the experiment in humans, only monkeys, but the rate is closer to sixty to seventy percent." He nodded proudly. "In other words, it is at least three hundred percent more contagious."

CHAPTER

32

Haldane awoke with a start, but for a moment he was unsure whether he was still dreaming. From the guest-room bed, he stared up at his wife who stood beside him in nothing but a long T-shirt, which only reached her upper thighs. He wondered if Anna had come to join him. That had not been part of the agreement. But the sight of her supple form looming above brought a surge of arousal. Despite his intentions, at that moment he wanted nothing more than for her to shed the T-shirt and climb under the covers with him.

Instead, she raised her hand from her side and offered him the cordless phone. "Sorry to wake you, Noah," she said. The edge in her voice did not strike Noah as apologetic in the least. "But she told me it was important."

Haldane rubbed his eyes in an attempt to regain his bearings. He glanced at the alarm clock on the nightstand, which read: 5:12 A.M. "Thanks," he said, clearing the sleep from his voice. He took the phone from Anna.

Anna hesitated a moment. She stared at Noah with a mix of hurt and concern on her face, before she turned and walked out of the room. Haldane's eyes followed her out of the room as the cold predawn reality sapped every shred of desire from his earlier dreamlike state.

"Hello," he said into the receiver.

"Noah, sorry to call so early," Gwen said.

"No problem." He cleared his throat again and sat up in the bed. "What's going on?"

"The National Security Council has called an emergency meeting for 6:30 A.M. The President wants us both to attend."

Noah hopped up from the bed, fully awake now. "Gwen, what's going on?"

The White House, Washington, D.C.

Haldane had heard of the White House Situation Room, but he never imagined he would see the inside of it let alone be invited to a critical incident meeting there. Haldane followed Gwen and the Secret Service agent through the White House's West Wing. Weaving through the basement floor, Haldane realized that the Situation Room is not one single room but a maze of offices and rooms, the largest of which is a wood-paneled conference room with a long rectangular table in the center and video screens lining the wall.

Haldane wore his most conservative suit, dark gray, with a white shirt and a dark tie. With her hair again pinned back, Gwen wore a businesslike navy jacket and pants, but she complemented her white blouse with a heavy silver chain, giving her outfit a dash of flair. Watching Gwen, Noah realized that he had started to pay attention to the little details about her. He had even begun to anticipate the subtle perfume, which he could smell only from within arm's reach. He had not experienced anything similar for anyone but Anna in so long that the feelings struck him as foreign, and slightly unnerving.

He shook off the thoughts and focused on the reason for his attendance at the White House. His mouth went dry, his palms moistened. A critical incident meeting of the National Security Council meant something had developed in the past hours—good news or bad, he was certain it would be significant.

The Secret Service agent led Gwen and Noah into the conference room where many of the NSC members had already assembled at the table. Savard's boss, Ted Hart, spoke with Aaron Whitaker, the Secretary of Defense, who looked even more hostile now than he had during their earlier videoconference. Andrea Horne, the National Security Advisor, was deep in conversation with a graying, elegantly dressed woman who Noah recognized as the Secretary of State, Katherine Thomason. Other individuals, including the three men in military uniforms, looked familiar to Haldane but he couldn't place their names or titles.

At the far end of the table, Alex Clayton, dressed as suavely as Noah expected in a black suit with a light blue shirt and matching tie, sat chatting to a chubby man with vigilant gray eyes. Haldane assumed that the man was Clayton's boss, CIA Director Jackson Daley. Clayton interrupted his conversation to smile at Gwen and wave her over to one of the empty seats across from his. Clayton's smile vanished when he acknowledged Haldane with a slight nod, leaving no doubt that he reciprocated Noah's opinion of him.

Haldane followed Gwen to the end of the table and claimed the seat beside her. Clayton began to introduce them to Jackson Daley but stopped in midsentence when the President strode into the room. In person, the President appeared even taller than the towering images Haldane had seen on TV. Haldane began to rise out of his seat, assuming it was the proper etiquette, but no one else budged so he inched back into his chair.

The President pulled out his padded leather chair (the seatback of which was a few inches higher than the others), adjusted the water glass in front of him, and then took his seat at the head of the table. He nodded his greeting to several people around the table before turning to Savard and Haldane. "Welcome, Drs. Savard and Haldane, thanks for joining us at this ungodly hour," he said, and most people at the table chuckled politely. "Maybe a quick round of introductions is in order."

Moving clockwise from the President, all nineteen of the attendees introduced themselves by name and full title, but the rapid-fire names of the Secretaries, generals, and senators overwhelmed Haldane. He was too distracted to keep them straight; acutely aware that he sat in the very same room where the Cuban Missile Crisis, Gulf Wars, and other world-shaping events had played out.

After the introductions were complete, the President said, "I have called you together to discuss new developments in our current crisis." He looked over to his National Security Advisor, Andrea Horne. "Dr. Horne can explain further. Andrea . . ."

The attractive African American woman pulled her glasses from her nose and gently laid them on the table in front of her. "Thank you, Mr. President," she said in her crisp cadence. "As you know, we received a second ultimatum from The Brotherhood of One Nation, which has since been verified by the CIA as genuine. They are demanding a complete withdrawal of our military from all countries which they deem 'Islamic lands' in three days—or to be precise, sixty hours from now."

"When pigs fly," Secretary Whitaker grumbled half to himself.

Horne glanced at the Defense Secretary, but continued in her same dry tone. "General Fischer can elaborate, but it is doubtful we could achieve anywhere close to the sort of timetable they have imposed upon us. And even if logistically we could pull our troops back, the potential for destabilization in the regions—especially the Middle East—is difficult to conceive."

Katherine Thomason leaned forward in her chair. "Leaving us where, Dr. Horne?" she asked.

Horne nodded to the Secretary, showing far more patience for her interjection than Whitaker's. "Before we go there, Madam Secretary, we should hear from our colleagues at the CIA. They have other news." She turned and raised a hand toward the end of the table. "Director Daley?"

Jackson Daley leaned forward in his seat. "I think our DDO, Alex Clayton, has prepared something for the members of the NSC."

Clayton rose and buttoned up his suit jacket. "Thank you." He stepped away from his chair and walked to the far end of the table, standing just to Haldane's left and close enough that Noah could smell his expensive cologne.

Clayton pushed a button on the remote in his hand, and the same map of Somalia from his office appeared on the screen beside him. "Late last night, we heard from our field agents in northern Somalia that they think they have located The Brotherhood of One Nation's operations base."

Murmurs erupted around the table. And Andrea Horne tapped the tabletop to quiet the group. "Please go on, Mr. Clayton," she said.

"Our operatives spoke to two men, both local militia members, in the town of Hargeysa. Independently, the two locals confirmed the existence of a base ten miles northwest of the city."

Clayton used a laser pointer to circle Hargeysa on the color map. He moved the red point in a diagonal line up from the city. "Here, at the foot of the Karkaar Mountains, there is an abandoned military complex, including an old hospital. Our informants tell us that starting five or six weeks ago several Arab men began to move supplies into this base. The informants were paid as drivers and guards for these men, but they were never allowed within half a mile of the compound itself. They assumed it was used for drug trafficking."

"Why?" Ted Hart asked him, clicking his pen as if it were a lighter.

"For starters," Clayton said, "there is no other reason to set up a base in this remote region. No legitimate one, anyway. They used similar trucks and followed similar supply routes from Mogadishu as do the smugglers and traffickers, but we believe this was a deliberate ruse to throw off our satellites. Most convincingly, one of the informants peeked under the tarps in one of the trucks. He saw animal cages and lab-type equipment, which he assumed belonged to a drug lab. Several of the other boxes were postmarked for Algeria. And we know a shipment of scientific supplies went missing from Algeria around the same time."

Clayton clicked his remote and the Somali map gave way to topographical photographs that Haldane recognized as satellite images. "We have reviewed the surveillance photos." Clayton continued to click the remote, and scattered dots over the arid savannah gave way to the distinct images of a dirt road and a building. As he clicked, the lens zoomed in on the building until it filled most of the screen. Two trucks and four Jeeps were parked behind it. Two people stood out front. The photo only captured the tops of their covered heads, but both men wore fatigues and had rifles slung over their shoulders. "This base is protected from the north and west by the Karkar Mountains. It is heavily guarded in the other direction." He flashed through a series of photographs, which showed what looked like fields of barbed wire and sentry posts scattered across the terrain. In other shots, armed soldiers stood at their posts with weapons readied.

Ted Hart coughed. "Alex, how do you know this doesn't house some kind of other illegal operation—drug traffickers, smugglers, and so on?"

Clayton nodded respectfully. "Because, Mr. Secretary, according to our informers, the men they met are all ex-Egyptians. And they are all devout Muslims who roll out prayer mats five times a day." Clayton tapped a button in his hand, and the screen filled with the satellite snapshot of a soldier bowing prostrated over a mat. "Not consistent with typical drug smugglers. As well, their sporadic movement suggests that they do not transport anything of significance." He corrected himself. "Aside from infected terrorists."

Clayton hit a button and the screen went blank. "The pieces all fit." He listed the points with his fingers. "Missing lab supplies from Algeria. Egyptian soldiers in Somalia. And a fortified hospital lab at the foot of a mountain range." He nodded confidently. "Ladies and gentlemen, this is The Brotherhood of One Nation's lair."

"Are you certain all the terrorists are still in there, though?" Secretary Thomason asked with a disarming smile.

Clayton's head dropped slightly. "All of them, ma'am?" He shook his head. "We can't know that."

Andrea Horne stood up from her chair. "If we are going to act upon this intelligence, every moment we wait adds to the risk," Horne said, putting her half-frame glasses back on, though she had nothing to read. "I would like to turn the floor to General Fischer who will now share the military options."

Up to this point, Haldane noticed that the white-haired, well-decorated army general, and chairman of the Joint Chiefs, had sat perfectly still for the discussion. He rose unhurriedly to his feet, reaching no higher than five feet eight inches when standing. "Well, folks," General Fischer said in his homespun Texan drawl, "we had about an

hour to come up with an operational plan, so you'll forgive me if the presentation is not as polished as that of our
good friends from the CIA." He turned to one of the other
generals at the table. "General Osborne, would you be so
kind as to get the clicker for me? Thank you, sir."

Clayton passed the remote down the table until it
reached General Osborne. He pressed two buttons and a
map showing East Africa, the Middle East, and the Indian
Ocean between them replaced the satellite imagery.

General Fischer pointed a stubby finger at the screen.
"The most expeditious choice would have been a precision air strike on the compound, but as we understand it
visual confirmation of the site contents is vital." He
chuckled. "Tough to count terrorists and germs after a
bunker buster has dropped in on them.

"So the question becomes: how do we get our special
ops forces to the site in one lightning strike. General
Osborne . . ." On the map two upside down Vs appeared in
the Indian Ocean. "We have two aircraft carriers, the *Lincoln* and the *Eisenhower*, in the region now. The *Eisenhower*, in particular, is in spitting distance of the coast of
Somalia."

Though Haldane maintained a healthy suspicion of military people, he warmed to the soft-spoken general who
was nothing like the humorless robot he had expected. He
found Fischer's presentation strangely reassuring, realizing the nation wasn't quite as impotent as she had earlier
seemed.

"We also have a base in Yemen, just outside Aden at the
tip of the Arabian Peninsula." Fischer accentuated each
vowel in "peninsula." "It's less than three hundred miles
from there to our target. And as luck would have it, our
elite Delta Force is stationed nearby. We can easily fly the
boys across the Gulf of Aden to Hargeysa. With F16s
from the *Lincoln* and *Eisenhower* flying support, we can
transport them over in C-17s along with long-range

assault helicopters. The other chiefs and I agree this is the best option. Really, the only option. General . . ."

A dotted line took off from the tip of Yemen, arced over the Gulf of Aden, and continued inland a few miles over the Karkar Mountains, stopping just short of Hargeysa. The compact, white-haired general again shook his finger at the map. "There's an airfield west of Hargeysa, which we will secure first to bring in supplies and ground forces. However," he emphasized in a slow drawl. "We cannot afford so much as one infected terrorist sneaking off their base. So the original assault has to be carried out with stealth and lightning speed. General . . ."

Fischer waited while the slide changed on the screen to a more detailed map centered on the hospital base. A dotted red line formed around the base. "The air force and navy fighters will establish a kill zone from the air within a three-mile radius of the base." Several Xs appeared south and west of the base. "An advance team of paratroopers will land and secure the perimeter. From the western airstrip, the rest of the ground troops—Army Rangers, Delta Force, and other special ops forces—will join them. Once in position, they will execute a three-pronged assault on the compound from the east, west, and south." The old man's lips cracked into a smile. "We're calling it: *Operation Antiseptic*."

"What size force will we required?" Secretary Whitaker asked gruffly.

"The operation will involve 200 paratroopers, 800 other ground troops, and 150 aircraft, give or take."

"And the time needed to secure the base?" Whitaker demanded.

Fischer nodded. "From the moment we leave Yemen, the plan is to secure the compound within ninety minutes. One-twenty tops."

The President leaned forward in his chair. "When will you be ready, General?"

"We can be ready in twelve hours, sir, which would make it roughly 0200 in Somalia."

A senator, whose name escaped Haldane, spoke up. "And what if one or two of the terrorists sneak out of the compound with the virus?"

"As I said, Senator," Fischer said. "If something so much as twitches in the desert, we're going to know about it. Any unauthorized personnel outside of the compound will be neutralized."

Secretary Thomason touched the base of her pen to her lips. "General Fischer, this is a very well thought out plan." She smiled gracefully. "But it does not address the very likely possibility that some of the terrorists may have already left the base with their virus."

Fischer turned to National Secretary Advisor Horne with a shrug.

"A valid point, Madam Secretary." Horne nodded. "That is why we have invited our counter-bioterrorism experts to the meeting." She looked over at Gwen. "Dr. Savard, can you bring us up to speed on the state of our preparedness in the event of a viral assault."

Savard nodded and rose from her chair. "We have already enacted our Emergency Response Plan to Biological Attack, or ERPBA, in every urban center." With the confident poise Haldane had come to expect from her, Gwen outlined the specifics of the plan for the members of the NSC. She spoke of the country's readiness to face mass casualties, but emphasized the possibility that resources could be overwhelmed, especially if the virus spread to health-care workers. She paused to take a deep breath, and then looked directly at the President. "There is one other potential breakthrough. We have an experimental drug that is showing promise in early testing with the Gansu Flu. As I speak, arrangements are being made to manufacture the drug on a mass scale. We should have a reasonable stockpile in one week."

"Are you certain this drug will work?" Thomason asked.

"No, we are not, Madam Secretary," Gwen said unflinchingly.

Horne looked at Noah with a quizzical frown. "Dr. Haldane, do you have anything to add?"

He swallowed. "I think Dr. Savard's team has done wonders in preparing the country as well as can be expected." He shrugged. "And I think CNN has done a commendable job in scaring the bejesus out of most Americans."

There was a scattering of laughter.

"Fear is an advantage in this situation, as it will keep many people behind closed doors and help diminish spread." Haldane looked down at the table. "But without knowing the size and methods of their 'army of martyrs,' it is impossible to predict the outcome. Despite the best of preparations, the human toll could still be catastrophic."

Gwen spoke up. "Mr. President, there is one other security measure that might be worth considering." She looked to her boss, Ted Hart, who nodded approval. "If the operation goes ahead, I think we should temporarily suspend all flights into and out of the U.S., like we did after 9/11. And the same goes for the ports and borders."

"To all travelers?" the President asked, but he didn't seem too surprised by the suggestion.

"All but official ones," Savard said.

"And I think we need to convince Canada to do the same," Ted Hart weighed in. "As you know, much of our four-thousand mile shared border is unprotected, so we need the Canadians on board, here."

The President nodded. "I will talk to the Prime Minister."

By raising her pen in front of her, Secretary Thomason caught the President's eye. "Sir, this is all good and well, but if one single detail goes wrong with Operation Antiseptic, we will provoke an attack on the country of a scale which we have never before seen."

The President viewed her for a long time before responding. "Katherine, we have not provoked anyone." His eyes fell to the table, and his voice dropped an octave. "I believe with my heart and soul that these terrorists are looking for an excuse to attack us."

Several nods and murmurs rose from around the table.

"I don't disagree," Thomason said. "But it seems to me we have another option."

"Which is?" Whitaker snapped.

"Their ultimatum doesn't expire for two more days. Why not carry out reconnaissance on the base for the next twenty-four hours. We could stop anyone from coming or going. And in the meantime, we would have more time to establish whether this indeed is The Brotherhood's base. And to ensure they are still there. By tomorrow, we would be better prepared to mount the assault."

Haldane found himself nodding along with some of the others.

"Doubtful we'll know any more in twenty-four hours than we do right now," Whitaker grunted and pounded the table once with his fist. "What we might end up doing is forfeiting our only advantage—the element of surprise."

General Fischer smiled benignly at Thomason. "Got to agree with Mr. Whitaker there. Wait till tomorrow, and we might find we're closing the barn door once the horses have already left."

"If they haven't already left now," Thomason said quietly.

The table stilled, as if collectively realizing there was no more point in debating the issue. Only one person could make the decision.

Haldane, along with everyone else at the table, turned his eyes to the President.

CHAPTER

33

Hazzir Kabaal had not checked the Internet since before dinner. Up until then he had checked every five minutes, anticipating some kind of response from the Americans to The Brotherhood's latest ultimatum. But during evening prayers, it came to him in the visceral form of a premonition that he was not going to hear an answer, at least not via the TV or Internet.

Turning away from his computer, Kabaal sat at his desk and read from volume six of the mammoth masterpiece *In the Shadow of the Koran*, written by Sayyid Qutb. Qutb was the father of the modern Islamist movement. His written words, as much as those spoken by Sheikh Hassan, had moved Hazzir Kabaal toward his current course of action. Lately Kabaal found less solace than before in Qutb's text. One quote from the second chapter of the Koran troubled him in particular. It read: "Fight in the cause of God those who fight you, but do not transgress

limits. For God loveth not transgressors." If they had not
yet transgressed the limits, Kabaal thought glumly, then
surely Aziz's supervirus would constitute such a trans-
gression.

After knocking at his open door, the white-coated Dr.
Anwar Aziz walked in followed by Abdul Sabri in military
fatigues. In addition to his handgun, he now carried a rifle
slung over his shoulder.

Kabaal slipped the Qutb book into his desk and nodded
to the two men. "Anwar, Abdul, welcome."

They walked up to his desk, but neither sat in the chairs
in front. With eyes darting about, Aziz appeared more
skittish than usual. Sabri's face was as inexpressive as
ever, though he seemed somehow frostier in disposition.

"Your new virus, Dr. Aziz," Kabaal said to the scientist,
"it is ready for transport?"

Aziz glanced nervously at Sabri before answering. "I
believe so. We have inoculated eggs and several primate
blood samples in which to carry it. Of course, I would
have preferred more time and to have human serum samples but . . ." His voice trailed off.

"They're here, Hazzir," Sabri said almost casually as he
unshouldered his rifle and rested it against Kabaal's
antique oak desk.

Kabaal squinted at Sabri. "Who is where?"

"The Americans are in Hargeysa." Sabri shrugged.
"CIA, I imagine."

Kabaal sat up straighter. "How do you know this?"

"Two strangers were asking questions of the men in
the bars in town," Sabri said. "They were trading drinks
for information about us and our base. Who else would
they be?"

Kabaal nodded. "And you think they know where we
are?"

Sabri frowned as if the question struck him as idiotic.
"Of course, they know."

Rather than alarm, the news brought a sense of calm to Kabaal like a feared prophecy whose realization could not match the terror of its anticipation. "But there were only two of them in Hargeysa?" Kabaal asked.

Sabri shook his head and rolled his eyes contemptuously. "It starts with two spies, and ends with the entire might of the American army falling upon us."

Kabaal folded his arms across his chest. "What are you proposing we do, Major?"

"I am not *proposing* anything, Hazzir," he said unemotionally, but his pale blue eyes were ice. "I am telling you that we are leaving. Now."

"Going where?"

"First, out of Somalia," Sabri said with a disinterested shrug. "Then to America."

"America?" Kabaal grimaced. "You would really go?"

Sabri sighed. "How else will we get Dr. Aziz's virus there?"

"So we are not waiting for our ultimatum to expire?"

Sabri stared at Kabaal coolly. "Do you believe for one moment that they would come to Hargeysa looking for us if they had any intention of complying with our demands?"

"No." Kabaal shook his head slightly and, for no reason, shuffled pieces of paper on his desk. "But I do believe in the honor of a man's word."

Sabri's thick lips broke into a spiteful smile. "With the first infected carrier you dispatched, I think you conceded some of your precious honor."

Kabaal looked up at Sabri, wondering how he had so underestimated the man behind those unreadable eyes. He nodded slowly. "Regardless, I am not going with you."

Sabri scowled in response. "What made you think that you were ever invited?"

Anwar Aziz's eyes went wide and he looked frantically over at Sabri. "But, Major . . ."

Sabri shot out a hand to silence the scientist, but he never took his eyes off Kabaal.

Kabaal nodded calmly. He smiled at Sabri. "So, Major Abdul Sabri now leads The Brotherhood of One Nation?"

"Not just now," Sabri said evenly. "I have done so for a long time. Your role was to finance us. We do not need your money anymore."

Kabaal grunted a laugh. "And you, as our leader, will personally carry the Jihad to the infidel's soil?"

Sabri picked up his rifle and threw it over his shoulder. "I will do what has to be done."

"Do you even remember what the purpose of all of this was?" Kabaal asked.

Sabri stared back in stony silence.

"Islam!" Kabaal barked. "To preserve and protect our faith. We were going to use the one weapon at our disposal that the West did not have a superior answer for."

"So what has changed?" Sabri asked, beginning to pace the floor like a bored sentry.

"Everything has changed! Kabaal snapped. "Once the West saw what the virus was capable of, they were supposed to abide our request. To leave our lands. To allow us to restore leadership to the Caliphate, so the laws of Shari'ah could again prevail." He exhaled heavily. "It is clear though that the Americans will not withdraw. And if we release Anwar's new supervirus, who knows where it will end? Or if it ever will." He looked down at his desk, his fervor waning. "We—I—always understood people would have to die. But this?" He held up his palms. "The virus was supposed to make the world better for us, not to destroy it."

Sabri stopped pacing and shook his head slowly. "Hazzir Kabaal, you are a fool," he said coolly.

Kabaal swallowed the insult without replying.

"You remind me of those armchair generals I used to work for," Sabri hissed. "Sitting in your extravagant homes and offices. Drunk on too much food and power, and soft from pampering and wealth." He flicked a finger at the desk and the rugs decorating the walls. "From the safety and comfort of your palaces, you send true warriors like me out to fight your battles. And then you expect us to win on your weak-hearted terms. I have news for you, *Abu Lahab*, there is no such thing as a bloodless Jihad."

Kabaal digested Sabri's sermon with little emotion. Curious but not fearful, he asked, "What do you hope to accomplish by killing possibly millions of women and children?"

"You never have understood, have you?" Sabri said with a look that bordered on pity. "We could never achieve our cause by holding America ransom like a bunch of cowardly kidnappers. The only way we will save Islam is to empower the people to rise up and fight."

"And slaughtering leagues of women and children will accomplish that?" Kabaal asked.

Sabri nodded. "Exposing the oppressor's weakness. That is how to inspire an uprising."

Kabaal chuckled softly. "And Major Abdul Sabri will be known as the prophet who inspired the people?"

Sabri's eyes narrowed. "I will be remembered long after you are forgotten," he said in a near whisper.

The two men stared at each other while Anwar Aziz shifted nervously from foot to foot and mopped at his sweaty brow.

Finally, Sabri's face broke into a gentler smile. "But you can serve The Brotherhood for one more important purpose, Hazzir."

"Oh?" Kabaal said. "How is that?"

Sabri patted the rifle across his chest. "M16-2A. It is the U.S. Army's standard assault rifle." He lifted it off his shoulder. "A beautiful piece of machinery actually. Fires 5.56-mm bullets. Again, standard U.S. Army issue."

"So it will look like I died at American hands. Clever." Kabaal nodded. "What will you tell the others?"

"The truth." Sabri shrugged. "That you shrank in the face of battle. That you were prepared to betray us at the moment of need."

Kabaal looked over to Aziz. "Will the men believe that?"

"I . . . I . . . don't know, Abu . . ." the fat microbiologist stuttered in a fit of nervous twitches.

"Don't concern yourself, Hazzir," Sabri said soothingly. "It won't matter for much longer."

"To me or them?" Kabaal asked.

"Either."

Kabaal felt overcome with a vague unsettled emotion that verged on regret. He was not afraid to face divine judgment, but he no longer assumed that Paradise awaited him.

"Stand, Hazzir," Sabri instructed. "And walk away from the desk."

Kabaal rose from the chair and took three steps from his desk to the wall, standing in front of his favorite Turkish rug. He stopped and looked from the terror-struck face of Aziz to the placid face of Sabri. "God is great," Kabaal said.

Sabri pointed the rifle at him.

At the same moment as Kabaal heard three muffled pops, he fell painlessly back against the rug behind him as if a gust of wind had blown him. Sabri's face faded away, replaced by that of his own father as a young man. His father was speaking to him, but the words were muffled as if spoken underwater.

The sound grew quiet. The room darkened.

It looked nothing like Paradise.

CHAPTER
34

A Northeaster had swept through D.C., bringing with it a record pre-Christmas cold snap. Bundled up in jackets, gloves, and hats, Haldane and Savard ran the two blocks from her office to the Starbucks, partly out of hurry, but mainly to get out of the bitter chill.

They stepped into the coffee shop just after 8:00 A.M. Huddling at a table inside, Duncan McLeod still wore his hat and gloves. "Shite, for the first time in my life, I miss balmy old Scotland in December!" he said as they approached.

Haldane mustered a smile, but he was still preoccupied. The memories of the NSC critical incident meeting of an hour earlier reverberated in his mind, and he couldn't shake the video images of the looming Operation Antiseptic.

Noah and Gwen made space on the table for all their winter gear before pulling up two chairs. As was their recent custom, McLeod had already bought coffees. He handed them the extra-large-sized cups.

Gwen hoisted her cup off the table and held it up. "Who can drink one of these?"

"I wanted to give you the option of soaking your feet in them, if need be." McLeod shrugged. He looked from Savard to Haldane. "So? What's the big news?"

Noah glanced at Gwen, wondering how McLeod knew anything since they were both sworn to secrecy. "What news, Duncan?"

McLeod squinted at Haldane. "The meeting this morning! When I rang you at home, Anna told me you were called out to some urgent predawn get-together."

Haldane put his coffee cup down. "Listen, Duncan . . ." he began awkwardly.

McLeod slammed down his cup. "Oh, no, Haldane! After all this, you're not going to leave me out of the loop now?"

"This comes from on high. National security issues and all that." Gwen held up her palms helplessly. "We have no choice in the matter."

"Oh, that's right," McLeod grumbled. "I keep forgetting what a major threat to American national security one batty Scotsman could be."

Gwen reached down and stuck a hand in her pants pocket. She pulled out her miniature cell phone, which Noah realized she must have kept on vibrate mode, because he had never heard it ring. "Gwen Savard," she said and listened a moment. "Okay, we're on our way." She put the phone back in her pocket as she stood up from the table. "Noah, we have to go. Now."

Haldane grabbed his hat and gloves and then reached over and patted McLeod on the shoulder. "Think of it this way, Duncan," he said with a wink. "It's one less of those *godforsaken* places you have to visit."

McLeod waved them away with a swing of his arm.

"Get the hell out of here. Go!" He flashed a half grin. "And for the love of Christ, stay safe!"

Haldane and Savard were led directly into the Secretary of Homeland Security's roomy office in the Nebraska Avenue Center. "Doctors," Ted Hart said in his hoarse tone and rose to greet them.

They stood by his desk, but he didn't offer them seats. "Dr. Haldane, after our meeting this morning, a few members of the NSC, including the President, stayed behind to discuss the situation. We decided it would be a good idea for you to go to Somalia."

Haldane nodded without comment.

"Once the terrorist camp is secure, of course." Hart stopped to hack a harsh cough. "We were hoping you would join the site survey team. Your expertise would be invaluable in assessing the state of their lab and so on."

Haldane felt a rush of adrenaline. "Of course, Mr. Secretary."

"Absolutely!" Gwen pointed to her chest. "We'll both go."

"Both?" Hart turned to Gwen with surprise. "No. No. Just Dr. Haldane."

"Ted—" Gwen started.

Hart waved his open palms at her. "No, Gwen! You have a crucial job to perform. The country is relying on you to stay here at home and do it."

Gwen shook her head defiantly. "Everything is unfolding here as we planned. There's little more I can do right now except wait like everyone else."

Hart frowned. "And what can you do over there?" he asked pointedly.

"I am a scientist, too, Ted. I know as much or more about microbiology labs than Noah does." She stared back at Hart, her face fixed in fierce determination. "I know what we're looking for. I feel it in my bones."

"Gwen is right," Haldane said. "She would be a help."

Hart shook his head but with less authority.

Gwen looked down and spoke to the floor. "Ted, they attacked us with the unthinkable. I need to be over there to see this through. You can understand that, can't you?"

Hart stared at her for several seconds before he sighed heavily. "Lucky for you I've run out of time to argue. We need to get you to Andrews Air Force Base ASAP. Your flight leaves in a half an hour."

Gwen offered her boss a grateful smile. "We're gone, Ted."

Haldane had never experienced such a smooth transfer. Their limo pulled up onto the tarmac of the Andrews Air Force Base. They stepped out of the car and walked up the steps into the cabin of the C37A twin-engine jet. Two prepacked generic overnight bags awaited them. And within moments of boarding, they were airborne.

Aside from the flight crew, consisting of a pilot, a copilot, and a junior officer who functioned as a flight attendant, there were no other passengers in the spacious cabin, which wasn't much smaller than a commercial airliner. Once at cruising altitude, the pilot's friendly voice came over the loudspeaker. "Hi, Doctors, we'll be cruising at close to the speed of sound, which should get us to Yemen in just over eight hours," he said. Noah consulted his watch and did the calculation, realizing they should touch down around 12:30 A.M. local time, less than two hours before Operation Antiseptic was set to commence.

Though comfortable in the cabin, Haldane was too keyed up to sleep. Gwen sat beside him, lost in the laptop computer in front of her. He touched her shoulder. "How are you doing?" he asked.

"Good." She smiled distractedly. "Glad to be along for the ride."

"Nervous?"

She turned away from the computer and studied Haldane with a quizzical frown. "They won't let us near the action."

Haldane let his hand linger a second longer on her shoulder before pulling back. "I didn't mean that. It's just that it's all coming to a head."

"Finally," she sighed. "I'm actually relieved. I was beginning to wonder if this would ever end."

Haldane smiled. "As long as it ends well."

"Yeah, that's kind of key. Truth be told, I am nervous." She bit her lip. "But a good nervous, you know?"

Haldane smiled, appreciating how pretty she looked at moments like these when she let her professional guard down.

"Hey!" She leaned forward and rummaged through her handbag at her foot. She brought her closed hand up to him and then turned it over, exposing a brown pill bottle. She popped the lid off to show the small yellow tablets inside.

Haldane studied the unmarked pills for a moment, before it dawned on him. "Dr. Moskor's wonder drug?"

"Well, the wonder part is yet to be proven, but, yeah, this is a bottle of his drug, A36112. It was waiting for me on my desk in a little box with a note that said, 'Go save the world, kid.'" She chuckled. "Typical Isaac!"

Haldane pointed at the bottle. "Have to be a pretty small world to save it with those."

"True." Savard smiled and bit her lip again. "Let's hope we never need a single pill."

Shortly after midnight Yemeni time, Haldane stared out the window as the C37A began to descend into blackness. As he felt his ears pop, he wondered with slight apprehension where exactly in the darkness the pilot intended to land. Suddenly lights broke through the pitch-black, and he could see they were no more than a few hundred feet from a runway.

The plane landed without so much as a bump. As their plane taxied toward the hangar, Haldane noticed how active the airstrip was. To either side, they passed airplanes ranging from fighter jets to the huge Hercules-style transport planes. A long line of planes waiting for takeoff had formed in the opposite direction.

The C37A slowed to a halt beside the massive hangar. Gwen and Noah grabbed their bags and disembarked following the crew.

Standing in the humid Yemeni air—where at midnight it was easily fifty degrees warmer than Washington had been at midday—Haldane began to feel sticky. Glancing around, he could better appreciate the frantic buzz of activity. While the soldiers worked with silent determination, the noise was earsplitting. Cargo doors slammed open and shut. Jet engines fired up. Cars, trucks, and armored vehicles moved in all directions; some carried supplies while others drove into the hulls of the huge transport planes.

Haldane had never before been to an air force base, let alone one that was set to launch a critical military operation, but the sense of purpose was palpable in the air. He welled with patriotism, a rare emotion for him. When he glanced at Gwen, she appeared equally mesmerized by the sight of the mechanized bees' nest.

An officer dressed in fatigues and matching hat drew their attention with arms waving above his head. "Drs. Savard and Haldane?" he yelled out over the noise.

Gwen gave him the thumbs-up sign.

The man waved for them to follow him. Once inside the open hangar, Haldane noticed that the level of noise dropped several decibels to simply loud.

Haldane half expected a salute, but the muscular man with square jaw, cropped hair, and deep acne scars held out a hand for them to shake. "Evening, Doctors, I'm Major Patrick O'Toole with the Seventy-fifth Rangers

Airborne, but everyone 'round here knows me as Paddy," he said with a friendly grin. "I'm to be your liaison officer."

"Gwen Savard," she said, and shook his hand.

"Noah Haldane," he said, meeting the crushing handshake. "But everyone around here will know me as 'Chicken.'"

The major laughed heartily. "Glad to meet you, Chicken. You'll fit right in." He wheeled around and pointed to the other side of the hangar as if directing a car.

Paddy led them to a quieter corner of the hangar, where a makeshift canteen offered self-serve coffee, tea, cookies, and other snacks. "Coffee?" Paddy asked as he poured a cup from the dispenser. Nauseated from the bumpy flight and the engine fumes in the hangar, Haldane declined with a shake of his head. So did Gwen. Paddy shrugged and kept the cup for himself.

They sat down at one of several empty picnic-style tables topped with a few scattered condiments. "Are you aware of the mission details?" Paddy asked.

Gwen nodded. "We attended General Fischer's briefing at the White House this morning."

Paddy's jaw dropped, impressed.

"He only gave an overview of the operation," she hurried to add.

"Okay," Paddy said. His expression stiffened and his tone deepened. "As you are aware, this is a modified lightning strike on the terrorist compound." He put down his cup, and drew a circle around it with his finger. He looked from Gwen to Noah. "Modified, because not only do we need to secure the target, but we can afford zero leakage." He ran two fingers through the air. "By that, I mean, the operation's success is dependent on ensuring that not one single terrorist escapes the compound alive."

Gwen shrugged at Paddy. "So how does that change the tactics of the strike?"

"Good question, ma'am." Paddy nodded. "It slows everything down a little. We have to establish full 360-degree vision from the sky and secure the perimeter to an even tighter degree than usual."

"So they will have more warning when the assault team does arrive?" Gwen asked.

"Exactly!" Paddy said. "But not a lot. We have no enemy air power to overcome. Just a matter of getting our planes and choppers in position, and getting our boys positioned on the ground. We can do that very quickly."

"So where do we fit into the equation?" Haldane asked.

"Well, I don't see a gun in your hand or a parachute on your back, so it means we're pretty much at the back of the pack," Paddy said. "Coming from the White House, you have an important job to do, but we'll have to wait until we get the word from the lead troops."

Paddy pointed toward the end of the hangar at one of the large transport planes that faced them. With its massive front cargo door open and a vehicle parked on the ramp, it looked like a monster with an appetite for metal. "We'll fly in on one of those C17s to the airstrip west of Hargeysa." He shrugged. "Then we'll wait and, with any luck, watch the battle at the mobile command center."

"And then?" Gwen prodded.

Paddy's face shed its expression of affable amusement. His eyes hardened. "My orders are to take you and the rest of the site survey team to the terrorist base once it is secure—and I cannot stress enough—that we are not going *anywhere* until we hear that the site is safe and secure."

CHAPTER
35

An hour after landing in Yemen, Haldane and Gwen sat in the belly of a C17 Globemaster III waiting for takeoff. Unlike their previous flight, they were not the only passengers. They shared the cabin of the C17 with jeeplike HMMWVs (high mobility multipurpose wheeled vehicles), trucks, tanks, and several soldiers, including the other members of the site survey team. Everyone on board wore specially designed camouflage HAZMAT suits with Kevlar vests. Noah, whose nausea rebounded the moment after takeoff, was relieved to learn that they would not have to wear their face masks, which resembled pilot's oxygen masks, until on the ground and closer to the site.

Glancing around the cabin, Haldane felt a sense of protective concern for the soldiers. In the Yemeni evening they had struck him as self-assured professionals, but now in the proximity of the lit cabin he realized how young they were. They had the same hopeful faces as the students in his classes at Georgetown. He had a tough time imagining some of his students coping with life away from mom and dad, let alone poised to storm a terrorist stronghold.

Over the whirr of the C17's multiple engines, Paddy described the plane to them like he was trying to sell it. "Yes, sir! It's the most advanced, versatile, and agile transport plane in the business. Could carry a load of 110 African elephants." He laughed. "Of course, that would be one odd sortie, but you get the idea. As you can see the C17 can fly troops and tanks, but it can also drop two hundred paratroopers behind enemy lines if need be . . ."

While Paddy talked nonstop, Noah and Gwen hardly spoke a word during the flight. Haldane spent much of his time staring out the window, and watching the lights of the F16 escorts as they shaped into eerily beautiful formations off either wing. Fifty minutes and 250 miles after takeoff, the lights in the cabin dimmed and all conversation abruptly ceased. "We just crossed into Somali territory," Paddy whispered.

Six minutes later, a voice on the loudspeaker confirmed Paddy's assertion and added, "The U.S. Airborne Eighty-second Division has secured the western landing strip. We'll be landing in fifteen minutes."

A celebratory cry went up from the soldiers but quickly died back down to the solitary hum of the engines.

Sixty-four minutes after leaving Yemen, the C17 effortlessly touched down on the flare-lit runway in northern Somalia west of Hargeysa. Haldane noticed everyone aboard was strapping on masks and helmets, so he reluctantly followed suit and then he and Gwen joined the soldiers as they streamed out of the plane in two organized lines.

As in Yemen, planes lined either side of the runway, but tanks, HMMWVs, and other vehicles formed armored columns at the side of the road. Masked guards took up positions along the runway. A row of tanks protected the far end. Helicopters hovered above. Haldane thought he saw the glimpse of a sniper's gun barrel peeking out of one of the choppers, but he wasn't sure if he was imagining it.

Even though he felt no immediate danger, the urgency around him kept the adrenaline pumping. And in the equatorial desert night, he baked inside his HAZMAT suit. Jogging after Paddy, he could feel the clingy wetness of his sweat-soaked shirt.

Major Patrick O'Toole strode purposefully to the row of basic wooden huts at the far end of the runway. Two vans, resembling huge mobile homes, were parked near the huts. Painted black, satellite dishes lined their roofs. Haldane assumed they were the mobile command units Paddy had earlier mentioned. Paddy walked to the second van and climbed inside. Gwen and Noah followed him in.

The interior looked to Noah like a scaled-down version of mission control at NASA. Flat TV screens lined the walls. An electronic map of the region spanned the front wall. Complex consoles with multiple digital readouts and buttons stood below the TV screens. Two communications officers sat at the consoles and faced away from the door. Wearing bulky headsets, they worked feverishly at keyboards in front of them, their heads in constant motion as they glanced from the computer screens to the consoles and video screens above.

The officers gave no indication of noticing that Paddy and the two doctors had joined them. When Paddy tapped one of them on the shoulder, he turned his head and gave the three of them a single nod before turning his attention back to his computer.

Paddy removed his helmet and mask. "You can take these off in here," he said to the others. He rolled three chairs over, so that they could sit behind the soldiers and watch the video screens above.

Haldane had watched his share of war movies, but seeing the battle unfold on these close circuit TVs was nothing like what he had imagined. It took his eyes and stomach several minutes to adjust to the shaky, erratic video feed with their flickering imagery. A couple of the screens showed only blackness, as if switched off, but every once in a while the sudden bright flash of an explosion punctuated the darkness.

One of the screens showed a sky view of two attached buildings, taken from what Haldane assumed was a helicopter. The complex, which looked from above like a rundown tenement, was lit up in an incandescent greenish glow. Several objects, likely vehicles, sat immobile in the dirt behind the building. A number of ill-defined objects scattered the ground in front of the building. Haldane wondered if they were people, but they never seemed to move. The only time anything in the frame moved was when, after a series of explosions lit up the screen, the entire complex shook from the percussive force.

But the images that gripped Haldane most were the bank of three screens in the bottom row, which resembled something from a newsroom. Shot through night-vision lenses, the images were in constant motion. It took Haldane a few moments to realize that the soldiers somehow carried these cameras. He glanced at Paddy and pointed to the screens for an explanation.

"Helmet-cameras." Paddy tapped his own head in explanation. "Part of the advanced assault unit."

Transfixed, almost forgetting to breathe, Haldane watched the soldiers study their target as their helmet-cameras panned over the compound.

After two more minutes of surveillance, the three screens abruptly changed in unison when the soldiers wearing the helmet-cameras turned their heads away from the target. The cameras focused on several soldiers lying prone in the dirt with assault rifles held out in front of them. They remained completely still for several long seconds. Then one of the soldiers popped up to his knees. He frantically punched the sky with a finger extended in a "Go! Go!" sign.

"Godspeed, guys!" Paddy muttered.

Suddenly the screens burst into action.

His heart pounding in his throat, Haldane couldn't keep track of the various viewpoints. The feeds from the helmet-cameras became so jerky that it looked as if the whole complex was seesawing in front of them.

Haldane's eyes darted to the previously static sky view, which erupted with activity. The camera zoomed in on the action so that Haldane could now make out the small shapes of soldiers. With explosion after explosion rocking the compound and lighting up the screen, the commandos streamed in from three sides of the complex, advancing in what looked like a full run.

Aside from the tapping of the keyboards and the occasional comment spoken by the communications officers into their radios, the van was silent, but Noah could almost hear the deafening roar and feel the ground shake with each detonation as the commandos approached the complex.

"Shit!" Paddy muttered.

For a moment, Noah was confused by the outburst. Then he saw it. One of the helmet-cameras had darkened. When Haldane looked closer, he recognized stars through the blankness. The cameraman had gone down.

A lump in his throat, Haldane focused back on the sky view. Three or four other commandos lay on the ground, some still and others writhing, while their comrades stormed around them. Haldane watched with relief as the rest of the commandos made it to the edge of the complex without suffering further casualties.

Noah watched the two remaining helmet-cameras as they swept over the peeling paint of the sides of the complex. Their images had stabilized, so Haldane knew they were moving slower now. The cameras panned over the ground at their feet. Numerous bodies of men in dark robes, some with traditional headwear and others with bandanas or bare heads, sprawled on the ground with weapons lying on their chests or fallen beside them. Until he saw the bodies, Haldane had not realized so many enemy fighters had been guarding the building from the outside.

The helmet-cameras didn't linger long on the corpses; instead, they focused in on the other commandos standing in front of a door to the complex. Two of them leveled their rifles at it. The muzzles spat out red fire as they emptied their cartridges into the door. Then another soldier kicked it with the sole of his foot and it fell inward.

Haldane's pulse quickened as the screen darkened and the soldiers stepped into a hallway. The picture tinted even greener from the cameras' night-vision lenses. The commandos moved cautiously. At each doorway and bend in the hallway they formed the same assault pose with men poised on either side, rifles held low. Each time, Haldane held his breath.

Rounding the third corner, Haldane almost jumped from his seat when the screen flashed with fire and smoke. The cameras jerked in every direction before settling again. Then the image focused on a fallen commando, lying with arms twisted over his head. "Damn it!" Paddy said and rubbed at his eyes.

Another soldier knelt forward and struggled to drag his fallen comrade back toward the entrance. The camera swept from the soldier to the far end of the corridor where four robed men had collapsed. Three of them lay awkwardly on the ground, while the fourth sat propped against a wall, gun in his lap and head tilted off to the side like he had fallen asleep at his post but the gaping wound in his face suggested otherwise.

The cameras inched toward the fallen terrorists. Haldane felt his chest tighten with each step as if he were crawling along with the soldiers down the lethal hallway, but they made it past the bodies without further incident.

One of the helmet-cameras focused on a doorway. Two soldiers kicked at the door until it swung open. No one budged for several seconds. Haldane felt the sweat forming on his brow, but he stayed as motionless as the men on the screen.

One of the commandos in front waved his hand indicating to the others to follow. The camera moved into the large open room, which resembled a big classroom except it was scattered with rugs instead of desks. Haldane wiped his brow, relieved that the men were in a more open, safer-looking space than the dangerous hallway. But the soldiers moved with the same cautious urgency. They scrambled across the floor, assuming assault positions by another doorway on the far side of the room.

Just as the cameras caught up to the soldiers, the screen flashed a single brilliant white light and went totally black like someone had switched it off.

The communications officer sitting in front of Noah ripped off his headset, as if in pain, and threw it down on the console.

Stunned, Haldane did not at first understand what he had just witnessed. Then he heard the voice of Gwen beside him. "Oh, no, please, no . . ."

He glanced back to the sky view of the complex, which was now swallowed in flames. Smoke wafted up so high that soon the building was shrouded and Haldane could see nothing but ominous gray.

All eyes in the van watched the dead stillness.

Minutes later, when the smoke finally cleared enough to see, three-quarters of the complex had disappeared. Haldane felt his chest sink. Tears welled in his eyes.

"Damn it!" Paddy spat and dropped his face into his hands.

The longest half hour of Noah's life passed before the call came through on Paddy's radio. Paddy spoke into the radio for a moment, clipped it back on his belt, and then turned to Haldane and Savard. "Okay, the complex—" He paused to get his voice to cooperate. "At least what's left of it is secure."

Haldane didn't ask Paddy about the soldiers trapped inside the collapsed building, because he didn't want to have the last glimmer of hope snuffed out. He forced the bleak thoughts out of his mind, pulled on his helmet and mask, and then followed Paddy and Gwen out of the van.

Haldane noted with admiration that there was no trace of emotion in Paddy's demeanor as he assembled the site survey team in front of the two waiting HMMWVs. Aside from Gwen and Noah, there were four technologists, all members of the U.S. Army Corps of Engineers. They grabbed their equipment bags—loaded with test tubes, specimen containers, and swabs—and then climbed in the backs of the all-terrain vehicles, which took off into the dark smoky night.

It was a bumpy sixteen minutes later before the vehicles turned onto a dirt road. They passed soldiers and trucks, some heading in the opposite direction and others stationary at the side of the road. In the light of the trucks and spotlights ahead, Haldane caught his first glimpse of the still-smoking complex. Most of the structure had collapsed in on itself, but the formerly attached single-story building still stood at the far end of the complex.

They exited the HMMWV about thirty yards from the building. Haldane watched as numerous medics and other soldiers frantically rummaged through the pile of rubble that represented the central part of the complex. Several of the soldiers scrambled over the stacks, trying hopelessly to budge the blocks of cement while yelling to their comrades trapped inside. Haldane was overwhelmed with a familiar helplessness. He wanted to climb on top of the rubble and dig until his hands were raw, but he knew the gesture would be as useless as the shouts and cries of the soldiers standing on the pile.

Paddy waved him over to where he stood by the entrance of the lone building left standing. "Look!" he said, his voice muffled by the face mask. He pointed down. Two soldiers flashed a bright beam on the dead enemy fighter lying by the entrance.

Haldane knelt down to get a closer view of the robed man who lay on his back. Several bullet holes riddled his chest and abdomen. His hand still clutched a rifle. His face was covered in the dust and dirt from the building's collapse, but Haldane still easily recognized Hazzir Kabaal from the photographs CNN had run nearly twenty-four hours a day.

Paddy nodded somberly. "Good," he said, but there was no celebration in his voice. Paddy pointed to what was left of the building. "They didn't have time to detonate this part of the complex," he yelled over the noise of machinery and other people. "The engineers say we can have a quick look. We have to be careful. The explosion weakened its walls. Could go at any moment."

Two soldiers led the site survey team in through the building's back door and down a short hallway, which opened into a large lab. Stepping inside, Haldane was surprised at how big it was. But the place was a mess. Centrifuges, fridges, incubators, and electronic analyzers lay upturned or smashed on the floor. Lab hoods had toppled onto the floor, joining the broken glass and papers strewn all about. Haldane knew that humans, not explosives, were responsible for the room's upheaval. Why? he wondered, but he didn't have time to stop and consider.

A thick door at the far end of the room caught his attention. Grabbing his specimen collection bag, he tapped Gwen on the shoulder and pointed to the door. They hurried over to it. Haldane had to put his full muscle power into yanking open the heavy steel door that was wedged stuck. When the door finally gave way and flung open, it slammed into the wall beside. The memory of Paddy's warning flashed ominously to Noah's mind.

About five feet in front of the first door was another door of the same type, but a block of wood for a doorstop held it open. They passed through the door into a smaller room. A row of cages lined the back wall. Haldane was amazed to see several of the cages rattling and to hear hoots and cries coming from within. When he looked closer, he saw that in a number of cages black-faced and white-chested African green monkeys glared at him in obvious agitation. Haldane felt sorry for the confused animals, but he knew there was nothing he could do for the potentially infectious primates.

"Noah!" Gwen called to him.

He strode over to where Gwen stood in front of a smaller stack of cages. None of these cages shook. When he arrived, Haldane immediately understood why. The monkeys inside were dead. But not from natural causes. The Plexiglas windows covering their cages had been shredded by gunfire.

Haldane turned to Gwen. "Why would they execute a bunch of monkeys?" he asked.

She just shook her head.

Haldane stooped down to pick up his bag. "Gwen, let's get some tissue and blood samples from these animals."

"The live ones?" She pointed at the rattling cages.

"Both!" He thumbed at the murdered monkeys.

As they were removing tourniquets, butterfly needles, and test tubes, a rumbling noise stopped both of them in mid-preparation. Dust sprayed down from the roof.

"Noah . . ." Savard said, her voice rising in alarm.

"I know. I know," he said. "We just need a couple of blood samples."

The walls creaked.

"We don't have time!" Gwen snapped. "The roof is going to collapse!"

"Go, Gwen!" Haldane waved at the door. "I'll just be another moment."

Gwen shook her head. "Not without you. Come on!" She grabbed for his arm and started to yank him away from the cage.

Haldane wriggled free, just as another pile of dust fell from the ceiling.

Paddy's voice yelled from outside. "Gwen, Noah, get the hell out of there!"

Haldane turned and ran to the bullet-riddled cages.

"Now, Noah!" Gwen screamed and waved her arms wildly at him.

"I'm coming," Haldane yelled. "Go."

She dashed for the doorway, but Haldane didn't follow. Instead, he fumbled with the door of one of the cages. But it was locked. With his elbow, he smashed a larger hole through the Plexiglas window.

"Come on, Noah!" Gwen yelled from where she stood at the doorway.

Hands trembling, he pulled away the rest of the plastic. He plunged both hands inside and grabbed hold of the dead monkey. He pulled it out and tucked it under his arm. "Go, go! I'm right behind," he shouted at Gwen.

Gwen sprinted through both doors into the main lab. Haldane ran ten paces behind. Large chunks of plaster fell from the ceiling in the main lab area. The whole building creaked and moaned.

Halfway across the floor Haldane caught up with Savard. She no longer ran, but hobbled on her bad ankle. Haldane slowed to take hold of her arm. "I'm fine! Go ahead and lead the way out!" she shouted at him and wriggled free of his grip.

Haldane jogged beside her.

"Go!" she screamed. "Lead the way for me!"

He ran through the doors and out of the lab. Sprinting down the final ten yards of hallway, he felt the ground rocking and heard a rumbling sound. He lunged out of the open door, landing on top of the dead monkey and rolling over several times, catching his leg painfully on a sharp chunk of wood.

Just as he was pushing himself to stand, he heard and felt a thunderous crash and bits of rock and cement pelted his back. He climbed up to his knees. He looked from side to side, searching frantically, but there was no sign of Gwen.

And the building he had just emerged from was gone.

CHAPTER

36

Gwen couldn't see anything but smoke, dust, and white light. She didn't think she was dead, but she had no idea where she was or what had happened. She remembered seeing Noah dive out the door. Then, just as her own foot reached the doorway, she heard a deafening boom and everything went black.

She felt a weight pressing into her chest, which made breathing next to impossible. She tried to call out, but she choked on the plaster dust in her mouth. The collapse had knocked her mask off, but she still wore her helmet. Her left arm was pinned under the same weight that ran across her chest, but her right arm and her legs were free. With her loose hand, she reached up and grabbed hold of the sharp metallic edge of the object crushing her. It felt like a piece of sheet metal. She tried to pull it off her with one hand but couldn't budge it. Patting along the top, she felt the chunks of plaster and wood that pinned the metal down on top of her.

She flailed her legs, attempting to rock herself free of the grip. No use. She noticed with growing panic that even shallow breaths were becoming impossible. She panted through an open mouth, but it didn't lessen her air hunger. Scared and frustrated, she spat out the contents of her mouth and called out hoarsely, but her lungs were too empty to produce much more than a whisper.

Just as she reached up to grab frantically for the metal edge again, something seized her gloved hand. It took her a moment to realize it was another hand.

"Gwen!" Noah yelled and she squeezed his hand. "Help me! Over here! She's alive!" he yelled out. He released her hand, which caused her a shudder of fear. She wondered if she would suffocate before they could clear the debris trapping her.

Gwen stopped moving in an attempt to conserve her oxygen. She continued to pant without relief. Just as she began to feel drowsy, but still awake enough to know what a bad sign the drowsiness was, she heard a loud scratching noise. Then she felt the object move.

"It's okay, Gwen. We've got you." Noah reassured with a yell. "Hang on. A few seconds, tops."

Suddenly the object lifted off her chest. The moment she was freed she took a long desperate gasp followed by several more, before she spat the dirt from her mouth. The glare from a searchlight blinded her. She instinctively brought her left hand up to shield her eyes without even realizing that she could move it again.

Another weight pressed into her chest, but then she realized it was Noah. He wrapped his arm around her, hugging her and lifting her at the same time. "Gwen!"

"It's okay, Noah," she reassured, and then sputtered a cough. "I'm all right, I think."

He held her in his arms, carrying her away from the pile of rubble that had imprisoned her. "Are you sure?"

"Yeah." She wiped the sand and dirt away from her mouth. "You can put me down now, Noah."

He bent forward and gently placed her feet on the ground. Then he pulled off his own mask, revealing bloodshot eyes and a relieved smile. "I thought you were gone," he said with a shake of his head.

She held on to his shoulder as she tested her legs, not entirely trusting them. She was relieved to find that they supported her. She felt the pain of widespread cuts and scrapes along with a residual aching in her chest, especially with deeper breaths, but she was happy to realize that the worst pain came from the throb in her bum ankle. She laughed out of relief.

Noah joined in the laughter. He leaned forward, threw his arms around her, and gave her another hug. "I really thought you were gone," he said.

"Ouch," she said in response to the squeeze.

He broke off the embrace. "Oh, sorry, I didn't—"

She smiled at him and then reached up and touched his cheek. "I think I'm just bruised." She looked back at the pile of debris under which she had been pinned. She realized she must have been trapped under the tin roof's overhang that used to sit above the entrance, which meant technically she had made it out of the building before it collapsed but was caught by a piece of the falling roof. She turned to Noah. "A millisecond earlier . . ."

"And there would have been a job opening for a qualified Bug Czar," Haldane said.

She laughed again, still giddy with relief.

Another soldier joined the group around her. Paddy reached out and rested a hand on Gwen's shoulder. "Gwen, you okay?"

She nodded.

"Sure?"

"Just scrapes and bruises."

Paddy looked from Gwen to Noah, "Where are your masks?" he demanded.

"Trust me, it's okay now," Haldane said.

"Trust you after *that* stunt?" Paddy thumbed at the building. "Just put it on, okay, Chicken?" he sighed. He pointed several feet away to where two soldiers were bagging the dead monkey in a yellow bag emblazoned with a bright red biohazard insignia. "I sure hope that monkey was worth risking both your lives for."

Lying on a medic's stretcher, Gwen spent the flight back to Yemen in somber silence like everyone else aboard. Once they touched down, Paddy insisted on pushing Gwen's stretcher to the base's hospital himself. She ended up requiring fourteen stitches, an aircast for her ankle, and multiple bandages. When two hours later the X-rays came back as negative, she borrowed a new set of fatigues and signed herself out against medical advice.

A soldier dropped Gwen off at the main hangar. She found Noah and Paddy in the same canteen where she had originally met Paddy. The two men sat at a table lost in their own thoughts with untouched coffees in front of them.

Paddy summoned a smile for her. "You look all right, all things considered."

"All things considered, I feel amazingly all right," she said. She sat down beside Haldane. "What's the news?"

"Operation Antiseptic is over," Paddy said sadly. "Their leader is dead along with at least a hundred other terrorists. No one escaped. Mission accomplished."

"At what cost?" she asked.

"We lost one chopper. Five soldiers died storming the building. And . . ."

Gwen swallowed away the lump in her throat. "And inside?"

Paddy shrugged. His eyes dropped to the table. "Fifty-five American soldiers were inside that complex when it caved in."

Gwen looked over to Haldane. Before she could ask whether any of the soldiers survived, he closed his eyes and shook his head.

Paddy nodded to her. "At least we robbed the rubble of one victim," he said, but he choked on the words and his eyes brimmed over. He wiped away the tears with his sleeve.

Gwen reached over and touched his other hand gently. "Your unit?"

"Yeah." He nodded, and then cleared his throat. "I knew every one of those Rangers in there. Great kids. Great Americans." Tears running down his cheeks, he stared hard into her eyes. "I hope you'll tell the President."

She met his gaze. "I will, Paddy."

WASHINGTON, D.C.

Gwen fell asleep the moment her C37A took off from the base, and she didn't wake up until they reached Andrews Air Force Base. With the change in time zone, they landed in Washington at 9:50 A.M., ten minutes before they had technically left Yemen. As the plane came to a halt on the ground, she stretched in her seat, sending a cascade of pain through her that started in her scalp and didn't stop until it reached her toes. She knew how lucky she was not to be coming home in a box or worse, like the fifty-five young men and women buried under the rubble, so she swallowed three of the painkillers the doctors had given her, brushed her hair, and gritted her teeth.

When she turned to Noah, he was wide-awake and watching her, but he looked exhausted. She wondered how much of the flight, if any, he had slept, but she didn't ask. Instead, spontaneously, she leaned forward and kissed him on the cheek, nuzzling against him for a few seconds and enjoying the rough feel of his warm stubble against her lips.

"Oh." He grinned and eyed her in bewilderment. "What's that for?"

"To thank you for saving my life in that rubble," she said, and then blushed slightly.

"Thank me?" He looked away. "I almost got you killed back there with my stubbornness. You should kick me in the groin, not kiss me."

She feigned a scowl. "Wait to see what happens when the pilot turns off the fasten seat-belt sign." They both laughed.

Noah didn't offer her his arm when she hobbled down the steps of the plane, but he walked slowly beside her as she limped into the terminal building. Gwen suspected he was prepared to catch her at a moment's notice.

"You ought to go home and get some rest," Haldane advised.

"You need rest more than I do," she said, surprised at how defensive she sounded to herself. "I had a great sleep on the flight. I'm good."

The limo waited for them out front of the terminal. Staring out the windows, neither Noah nor Gwen spoke a word during their ride into the city. The driver dropped them off at Gwen's office in front of the Nebraska Avenue Center. The security officer at the front door greeted Gwen with a warm smile, and she felt embarrassed that his first name slipped her mind.

In a duffle coat and a fur hat, McLeod met them in the lobby. He threw his arms around both of them, wrapping them in a warm embrace. When he finally released them, he wagged a finger reproachfully. "Shite! Why is it that I can't leave you two alone for five minutes without a building falling on you?"

"Guess we're lost without you, Duncan," Gwen said, genuinely pleased to see him. "Anyway, how did you know about that?"

McLeod pointed at Haldane and grunted. "Him!" He shook his head. "Called me from the airport. The man can't keep a secret." He winked playfully at Gwen. "You know he kisses and tells, too."

Gwen reddened slightly and cursed herself for reacting like a schoolgirl. She turned away from the others and limped over to the elevator.

Another security guard escorted them from the elevator into the Department of Homeland Security. Despite being a Sunday morning, Gwen was pleased to see that the department was half full. She led Haldane and McLeod down a corridor, past several empty cubicles, and into her private office. Once seated around her desk, Gwen and Noah took turns updating McLeod on the raid in Somalia and the result. With his coat on and hat in his lap, McLeod's face contorted in rapt attention as he sat and listened.

After they were finished, McLeod said, "Kabaal is dead. Good riddance to him. But what about this Sabri fellow?"

"Hopefully, he was inside the building when it collapsed," Gwen said.

"Hopefully," McLeod echoed distantly.

Haldane nodded. "They're collecting DNA from the scene, but we may never know if he was there or not."

McLeod lifted his hat and put it back on top of his tousled red hair. "Or we might know soon."

"Meaning?" Gwen demanded.

"Well, I think it's safe to assume that, technically, you haven't met the terms of the ultimatum from the Brotherhood of One Mean Bugger—or whatever the hell they call themselves," McLeod said. "And if this Sabri bastard is still alive . . ."

Gwen's jet lag was catching up to her. "I haven't heard of any new viral outbreaks, yet," she snapped.

"Me neither," McLeod agreed. He adjusted his hat. "But you Americans are so damn secretive, you'd probably keep denying it until you were the last two left standing on this frozen continent."

Haldane showed a tired grin, while Gwen looked as if she fought off a grimace. "What is the situation with the rest of the world?" Haldane asked.

"Surprisingly, not bad when it comes to the Gansu Flu," McLeod said. "It's quelled in the Far East. Neither London nor Vancouver has reported a new case in three days. The scattered outbreaks in Europe are contained. Even in Illinois, the news is better. I think there were only a handful of new cases yesterday."

Haldane leaned forward and rapped his knuckles on Gwen's oak desk. "Maybe, we're winning for a change," he said.

McLeod held up two sets of crossed fingers. "Providing the U.S. Army didn't drive past an 'army of martyrs' heading the other way, Haldane, you could be right."

With the same lights-flashing police escort as on their last trip, a limo picked up Haldane and Savard and rushed them over to the White House.

Two somber Secret Service men ushered them through the West Wing down to the same Situation Room where they had sat less than thirty-six hours earlier, but a much smaller group attended now. Aside from General Fischer and Andrea Horne, only the Secretaries of State, Defense, and Homeland Security plus the Directors of the CIA and FBI were present.

Ted Hart frowned at Gwen as she walked into the room. "Gwen, I hear you came very close to getting yourself killed over there. That is the last time—"

Gwen raised a hand to cut him off. She brought the other to her chest. "I swear, Ted, never again."

Appearing less than satisfied, he shook his head angrily. He opened his mouth to say something, but closed it again when the President strode into the room.

Without acknowledging any of the others, he sat down at the head of the table. "Thank you for coming," he said, staring ahead at the far wall. "Before we begin I would like to request a moment of silence to recognize those brave young Americans who gave their lives this morning to protect the safety of all our citizens." He bowed his head and closed his eyes, but he didn't speak another word. Gwen knew that the quietly religious man was deep in prayer.

After a full minute of silence, he said, "Okay, thank you. Dr. Horne will lead the discussion from here . . ."

"Mr. President," Gwen spoke up from halfway down the table and all heads turned to her.

"Yes, Dr. Savard?" he asked with a mildly perplexed expression.

"I promised one of their comrades that I would tell you that the U.S. Rangers who died in Somalia were great Americans. Each and every one of them."

He stared at her for several moments before his face broke into a paternal smile. "And you have my promise that I will recognize them as such. Each and every one of them."

"Thank you, Mr. President," Andrea Horne began. "Most of us watched in this very room the video feed from Operation Antiseptic. Drs. Haldane and Savard were even on-site," she said, and Gwen thought she caught a fleeting disapproving glance from the NSA. "I've asked General Fischer just to give us a short debriefing on the operation."

Fischer climbed to his feet. "Don't know if 'short debriefing' is in my vocabulary, but I'll try," he said with a pained smile. He went on to give a concise review of the logistics of the operation and how it played out up until the point of storming the building.

"Once we had secured the immediate perimeter of the building, we had no choice but to go in," Fischer drawled. "Our boys and girls would have been sitting ducks waiting outside the building any longer, taking on fire. Besides, you—" he said with slight implication in his tone, but looking at no one in particular—"wanted visual confirmation of their nest and laboratory." He hung his head low. "As you know, the building was booby-trapped with high-potency explosives. Our people didn't stand a chance once inside." He looked up, his eyes burning with wounded pride. "But the Seventy-fifth Rangers Airborne Regiment and the rest of our military achieved the objective over there. We got their leader, and not one terrorist escaped the operation."

"Thank you, General," Horne said earnestly. She turned to Ted Hart. "Mr. Secretary, can you enlighten us as to the state of Homeland Security?"

Hart cleared his throat with a harsh cough. "It goes without saying that the alert level is still on 'code red.' Our borders are closed to all commercial travel. We have extra law enforcement and emergency services standing by in every region of the nation."

"Mr. President," the nondescript, bespectacled Director of the FBI chimed in. "We have every available field agent on the street working with the local law authorities."

Ted Hart nodded. He looked over in Gwen's direction with a raised eyebrow. "Dr. Savard, can you update the status of the new drug treatment?"

"Potential treatment," Gwen emphasized. "The manufacturing plant is up and running. We'll continue at it twenty-four/seven, but we're at least six days away from production."

Aaron Whitaker spoke up. "No question. Our military did us proud over in Africa." He saluted General Fischer with a tap over his bushy eyebrow. "Although we got Kabaal, we haven't confirmed we nailed Abdul Sabri. So I think we had better operate under the assumption that we have not eliminated this particular terrorist threat. And even accept the possibility that their army of terrorists is already on our soil."

Though Gwen did not like the belligerent Secretary of Defense, she nodded fervently in agreement with his point.

"Mr. Secretary, that is exactly what we are assuming," Ted Hart said, crossing his arms over his chest.

Katherine Thomason raised a hand.

"Yes, Madam Secretary?" Horne said.

"I understand. And I agree with the others." Thomason closed her eyes and nodded solemnly. "But we may never know exactly who among the terrorists died in that Somali lab."

"Your point, Madam Secretary?" Horne asked.

"Say, by the grace of God, days pass . . . weeks pass . . . and we see no signs of the virus. Just how long do you propose that we run the country as a fortress?"

The President leaned forward and tapped his touching fingers against his chin, which he often did right before intervening in a conversation. "Katherine, America will be a fortress until the moment we believe it safe to be otherwise." His eyes narrowed. "And not one second sooner."

CHAPTER
37

When Noah awoke in his guest bedroom, he realized he had slept past The Brotherhood's midnight deadline for troop withdrawal and right through until late Tuesday morning. Though he knew the ultimatum was moot after the raid on the Somali base, like most other Americans, he still anxiously anticipated the deadline's passing.

When he saw that it was already 10:21 A.M., he reached for the portable phone and dialed Gwen's cell number.

"You just waking up?" Gwen asked in amazement.

He recognized from her light tone that nothing ominous had happened during his sleep. "Weird, huh?" he said. "I find a one-day round-trip to an African war takes a toll on my body. Maybe I'm low on melatonin." He chuckled. "No word?"

"Nothing," she said. "But no news is definitely good news in this case. How are you?"

"Fine," he said, standing from the bed and walking to

the mirror over the dresser. "More to the point, how are you?"

"A little sore, but it's mainly my ankle. Otherwise, okay."

Haldane paused. Up until this moment their days had been so preprogrammed through this crisis. "So, um, what's next?" he asked, studying his face's dense stubble in the mirror and noting how much more hollow his cheeks had become since the appearance of the Gansu Flu.

"We prepare for the worst. And we hope to hell it doesn't happen." She paused. "I don't know, Noah, but something feels incomplete, you know?"

It wasn't until she spoke the words that he realized they encapsulated his feelings, too. "Exactly," he said.

"Let's meet in my office in a this afternoon to review where we stand, okay?"

"Done."

Haldane hung up the phone and headed for the shower.

Stepping out of the bathroom with a towel wrapped around his waist, Noah met Anna in the hallway. "Morning." She offered him a cup of tea along with a coy smile.

"Hi." Noah accepted the cup, feeling an unexpected level of discomfort at what had once been a morning ritual for them. "Chloe at preschool?"

"Yeah." Anna smiled. "It was all I could do to stop her from waking you this morning."

"Thanks." He forced a smile, but his unease didn't let up.

She pointed at the deep abrasion that ran along the inside of his left thigh and down to his ankle. "I thought you said nothing happened to you on your African trip."

Haldane shrugged.

She folded her arms across her chest and frowned slightly. "Chloe is going to need her dad for a lot longer, you know?" she said with a trace of bitterness.

"I didn't choose any of this," Haldane snapped.

Anna shrugged and then said in a smaller voice, "You didn't choose a nine-to-five stay-at-home job either."

Haldane held up his palms. "But if I had, everything would be perfect between us, right?"

"I . . . I didn't mean that," she stammered. Her face flushed with anger. "I just want things to be right again for Chloe. For us! And you don't seem to want to help me much with that."

She turned to leave, but Noah stopped her by gently catching her wrist. "Anna, I know how hard you're trying to do what's right," he said. "But I don't believe you even know what you want."

She started to say something, but Noah cut her off. "And, Anna, truth is I don't know what I want anymore either," he said softly.

After spending much of the day in a teleconference with Jean Nantal at the WHO, Haldane and McLeod arrived at Gwen's office in the midafternoon. Noah couldn't deny his disappointment to see that Alex Clayton already sat in the chair across from her, looking very much at home with his Armani sports jacket unbuttoned and hands folded behind his head.

In jeans and a sweater, Gwen sat behind her desk, her face creased with a look of concern. "Hi," she greeted them distractedly.

After they took their seats around the small conference table, McLeod nodded to her. "Gwen, what's the matter? You look like you're still carrying part of a building on your back." But Haldane noticed the genuine concern behind the Scotsman's quip.

"A couple of developments," Gwen said gloomily. "Alex, why don't you start?"

He pulled his hands off his head and shrugged. "We just got the preliminary report from the army pathologist who did the autopsy on Hazzir Kabaal."

"Let me guess," McLeod said. "He's not dead, after all?"

Clayton shook his head. "Oh, he's very dead. In fact, the pathologist thinks he was killed twice."

Haldane leaned forward in his chair. "What are you talking about?"

"The guy was riddled with bullets. All the same 5.56-mm caliber." Clayton shrugged. "But because of something about the lack of capillary leakage or whatever . . ." Clayton threw up his hands. "The pathologist could tell that several of the wounds happened posthumously."

"So what? Kabaal was lying out front in a firefight," Haldane argued. "Surely, he could have been shot in the crossfire after he had already died."

Clayton shook his head. "The pathologist says no. He thinks there were at least a couple hours between the two sets of wounds."

Noah leaned forward in his chair. "Is he sure?" he asked.

"No," Clayton said. "Not positive."

"But if he is right . . ."

"Maybe one of his own people took care of Hazzir Kabaal," Clayton said.

"Ach," McLeod harrumphed. "Then why would they leave him out front of the complex?"

"To make us think he died in the firefight," Clayton said.

"Listen to me." McLeod tapped the table in front of him. "Why would it matter where he died?"

"What if someone was covering their tracks?" Haldane hypothesized aloud. "They dump Kabaal's body outside and then take off. Then later, after whoever is left inside detonates the complex, we have no way of doing a body count."

Clayton nodded slowly, picking up on Haldane's thought. "But we assume they're all in there because their leader is there!"

At the suggestion, the room lapsed into grim silence.

"There's something else," Gwen said, stone-faced. "I just heard from the CDC a half an hour ago."

Haldane felt the blood drain from him. His heart pounded in his ears. He rose from his chair. "Gwen, please don't tell me . . ."

She shook her head. "No. There are no new cases of the virus."

Haldane exhaled heavily. The pounding lessened. "But?"

"The monkey you dragged out of the lab," she said.

"What about him?" Haldane asked, still hovering above his seat.

"CDC ran tests on his serum." She brought her fingers to her temples, and began to rub.

"And?"

"He wasn't suffering from the same strain of Gansu Flu as the others."

"What fucking others?" McLeod jumped in.

Gwen stopped rubbing. She leaned forward in her chair. "The victims from Chicago, London, Vancouver, or China."

Haldane shook his head in confusion. "So it's not the Gansu Flu?"

"No, it is," Gwen said. "But it is a mutation. It's not H2N2. It's H3N2."

Clayton held up a hand. "Okay, stop the hocus-pocus. Tell me in plain English what the hell you are talking about!"

"The Gansu Flu virus is a mutation of influenza, right?" Gwen hurried to explain. "All flus, including the Gansu Flu, are sub-typed by two proteins on its shell—H for hemagglutinin and N for neuraminidase. Until now, we have only seen the Gansu Flu H2N2. But the new virus found in the monkey is a Gansu Flu H3N2."

"I get it." Clayton nodded. "But what does it mean?"

"It means," Haldane said slowly, "that the terrorists have created a new virus."

"But how could it be any worse than what they've already thrown at us?" Clayton asked.

"Well, Mr. Bond," McLeod said. "The bug could be worse if it was more lethal—but it's hard to imagine a flu virus much more deadly than Gansu H2N2—or if it were more contagious. And sadly, there is a lot of room for improvement on that front with H2N2."

Haldane felt a chill as if he had just stepped into the Washington air. He intuitively knew McLeod was right. "Son of a bitch!" he said. "They've come up with a more contagious form of the bug."

"Shite, can you imagine?" McLeod said, shaking his head and sighing.

"No," Clayton said. "I don't have a PhD or MD so explain exactly to me what that would mean."

"It's an exponential thing, Alex," Gwen said quietly, her slim fingers still resting on her temples. "If you make a virus twice as contagious, then twice as many people are likely to become infected. And now double the number of people are infected to pass it on to twice as many people. So by the second 'generation' alone there are four times as many people infected. And so on . . ."

McLeod pointed to Clayton. "You can see how it wouldn't take long to cause a wee problem."

"I understand that, but"—he held up two fingers—"A, we don't know that this new virus is any more contagious than the last, and more importantly, B, we still don't know that an army of terrorists is left alive to spread it."

Gwen nodded. "The first part is easy. CDC can give us an answer in days as to how contagious it is. The second part . . ." She shrugged. "Especially after those autopsy findings on Kabaal."

"Besides, you wouldn't need an army to spread it," Haldane said wearily, as much to himself as the other members of the group.

"How come?" Clayton asked.

Haldane sighed. "With the previous strain, four terrorists caused vicious, but subsequently controlled, outbreaks in four cities. But with a superbug that was much more contagious . . ."

Clayton squinted hard, struggling to put it together.

McLeod threw up his hands. "Once this cat gets out of the bag, there's no stuffing her back in."

Clayton's mouth opened in realization. "So you're saying that if the bug is infectious enough, only a few terrorists would be needed to start a pandemic?"

Haldane nodded slowly. "Or maybe only one."

CHAPTER
38

Since he ran away from his Jericho home at age thirteen, Dabir Fahim had spent most of the past ten years on cruise ships. A tireless worker, the young Palestinian had struggled his way up the ladder from cabin boy to waiter and from small ship to transoceanic liner. Dabir, who went by David, had worked aboard the *Atlantic Princess II* since her maiden voyage two years earlier. He took a proprietary sense of pride in the vessel that he'd never felt for his war-ravaged homeland.

Aside from his outgoing personality and gift for languages, Dabir excelled at his job because he understood people. He never forgot a name or a face. And he had a gift for predicting what people wanted sometimes before they even knew themselves. But the tall muscular man Dabir served on the sixth and final night of their journey perplexed the young waiter with his distinct but unreadable face. In spite of the man's piercing blue eyes, smooth face, and designer French clothes, Dabir had no doubt that he was a fellow Arab. He also suspected they shared the same sexual orientation, but Dabir was far too professional to ever flirt with a client, no matter how attractive.

Dabir had seen him only one other time in the seven-day passage. He wondered if he traveled with the silent, little bearded Arab man Dabir had once served lunch to, but they seemed a very unlikely and mismatched couple.

Bringing the enigmatic man an espresso after dinner, Dabir decided to satisfy his curiosity. "A good meal, yes?" Dabir asked in Arabic.

Though the man neither moved the cup from his lips nor changed a muscle in his face, his eyes burned into Dabir, sending a chill up the young waiter's spine. "Excuse me," the man said in English, "I do not understand what you have said."

"Oh, excuse me . . ." Dabir stuttered. "I thought you might speak Arabic, er, like me."

The man put his cup down slowly. "My father did," he said coolly. "But he left my mother and me when I was only two. After that, there was never much reason to learn Arabic in Marseille."

"Oh, I see," Dabir said, knowing there was nothing French about the man's accented English.

The man smiled slightly, which only intimidated the young waiter more. Dabir stood frozen on the spot until the man directed his pale eyes to the tables to his left. "I believe other guests need your service," he said.

Relieved, Dabir hurried away from the table.

WASHINGTON, D.C.

Only eight days had passed since the raid in Somalia, but Haldane felt as if months had gone by since Gwen and he escaped the crumbling wreckage.

The city—the entire country—had changed in the past week, as if the nation were holding its collective breath and bracing for the worst. Work shut down to essential services level. Most people avoided going out. And no one seemed to pay any attention to the fact that Christmas was only six days away.

But for all the collective angst, so far nothing had happened.

As he drove downtown, Haldane was struck by how few cars drove on the Beltway, which usually was clogged with traffic at all times of day, especially during the morning rush.

Like every day since their return from Somalia, Haldane, McLeod, and Clayton met at Savard's DHS office. As soon as Gwen's secretary dropped off the coffees and closed the door behind her, Gwen leaned back in her chair and ran a hand through her pulled-back blond hair. "We have the results from the CDC tests on the Gansu H3N2 strain found in the dead monkey."

"It's not good news, is it?" Haldane asked.

She shook her head. "No."

"Just how bloody bad?" McLeod asked, scratching at the beard that had grown even scragglier over the past week.

"One of the terrorists must have had significant microbiological expertise," Gwen said with a mix of awe and revulsion. "He or she managed to introduce sections of the Beijing Flu's genetic code into the Gansu Flu. The end result is the much more contagious H3N2 strain of Gansu Flu."

"Oh, for Christ's sake, Gwen!" McLeod said. "How much more contagious?"

"The results are preliminary . . ." She looked down and shook her head. "But so far, it's measuring out to be about as contagious as the common cold."

Haldane felt as if he had been punched. He looked over to McLeod, whose face had blanched. Even Clayton's eyes were wide with worry.

McLeod turned to Haldane. "It's the return of the Spanish Flu," he said hoarsely.

"How bad was the Spanish Flu?" Clayton asked.

"It killed twenty million people in less than four months, at a time when the world had a third of its current population and had no air travel," McLeod said. "Overall, you might say it was fairly bad."

Clayton's brow furrowed. "And this terrorist virus could be the new Spanish Flu?"

"We're overdue." Haldane shrugged. "We always knew the next pandemic would come. It's just that no one suspected that anyone would deliberately initiate it."

Gwen leaned forward in her chair and placed both hands flat on her desktop. "No one has initiated anything, yet!" she said fiercely. "And I'm not about to sit back and let them."

The others, even McLeod, nodded.

Haldane looked over and noticed the way Clayton eyed Gwen. Noah recognized the admiration in his eyes. But somehow, the CIA man's feelings were less threatening to Noah now. It was as if their shared sentiment bonded them in common interest, like two people who shared a passion for the same music.

Haldane asked Clayton, "No word on Sabri or anyone else from the terrorist base?"

"All of the Agency's resources are directed to finding him, but so far nothing." Clayton sighed. "If he got out of that complex alive, then he's doing a damn good job of keeping a low profile."

McLeod looked at Gwen. "What about your friend's drug? Where does that stand?"

She pulled her hands from the desk and brought them to her temples. "The news isn't good there, either."

"Why? What's wrong?" Haldane asked. "The drug doesn't work against this new strain of the virus?"

"No, that's not the problem. It seems to work just as

well." She started to work her temples again. "As you know, the early results with the Gansu Flu virus were very promising. Mortality was reduced from twenty-plus percent down to three percent in test monkeys."

"Bloody impressive!" McLeod said.

Gwen shrugged. "But then two of the monkeys who recovered from the virus went on to die from overwhelming hepatitis."

"Medication-related hepatitis?" Haldane asked.

Gwen shrugged. "Too early to know."

"And none of the untreated monkeys developed hepatitis?" McLeod asked.

She shook her head.

"But, Gwen," Haldane said. "You told me earlier that there were no serious complications when the drug was tested in healthy animals and people."

"True." Gwen sighed. "This was exactly what Isaac feared. That if we jumped the gun, we would learn about the complications and side effects of his drug the hard way."

McLeod brushed the concern away with a sweep of his hand. "The same damn monkeys who died of hepatitis might well have died from the virus without treatment."

"Duncan's right." Haldane nodded. "If this drug reduces viral-related mortality tenfold but causes a small percentage of serious complications, then it's still a huge overall win for the average patient."

"But the FDA wouldn't see it that way." Gwen held up her palms. "And neither does the President. Apparently, he remembers Gerald Ford's Swine Flu vaccine catastrophe of 1976. He has asked us not to proceed with production of the drug until we establish the scale of the hepatitis problem."

"That's crap!" McLeod snorted. "That could take months. And we might not have months."

Haldane stared at her for a long time. "Gwen, wouldn't

you take your chances with this pill if you had the Gansu Flu?"

"In a heartbeat," McLeod answered for her.

Gwen considered the question for several moments and then nodded slowly. "I will talk to the President again."

CHAPTER

39

Haldane stopped packing his suitcase to watch his daughter play on the floor at the foot of the bed. Three days after Christmas, Chloe was still too distracted by the sheer volume of her toys to play with any single one of them.

Though it had been a tense apprehensive Christmas for her parents, Chloe was joyfully oblivious to the personal and global drama unfolding around her. Her parents worked hard to ensure that Chloe stayed unaware. They never discussed their impending separation in front of her. And they never watched the TV's twenty-four-hour coverage of the crisis while Chloe was around. Haldane hardly ever watched the news, because he had an inside track. He knew that no sign of the virus or terrorists had emerged in the two plus weeks since Operation Antiseptic.

Chloe jumped from toy to toy and changed her costume every few minutes. Finally, when the toys covered half of the floor in the bedroom, she abandoned them altogether

and hopped onto the queen-size bed beside Noah's suitcase.

"Daddy, you just went away," Chloe said, bouncing on
the bed. "Why do you have to go again?"

"This is a different trip, Chlo." Haldane smiled. "It's
way better. You're going to get to see me all the time."

"How can I?" she asked.

"Because I'm only going a few blocks away," Haldane
said. "You're going to come over lots. Some nights you'll
have sleepovers with me. And other nights you'll stay here
with Mommy."

She stopped bouncing. "Why don't you stay here,
Daddy? Then I can spend every night with both of you."

Haldane felt his heart squeeze. He reached for his
daughter and wrapped her in a big hug. "Ah, Chlo, it's a
bit more complicated than that. But it will be okay. You'll
see."

In what would have constituted a miracle three weeks earlier, Noah found a parking spot right in front of the trendy
downtown Italian restaurant. Like many in the area, it had
reopened its doors after Christmas for the first time in
almost two weeks, indicating to Noah that people were
starting to venture out again. While a small degree of nor-
malcy was returning to life in Washington, the popular
Washington nightspot was still no more than a third full.

Haldane was the first to arrive. He chose a table in the
corner by the window. As soon as he reached his seat, he
ordered a Heineken to help quell the butterflies that sprang
to life in his stomach. His drink arrived at the same time
Gwen did. Haldane flagged her over with a wave, but she
had already spotted him.

She wore a silky white blouse with a dipping neckline,
and black pants with a high waist that hugged her hips and
accentuated her long, slim legs. She had let her unpinned
blond hair fall down to her shoulders. While Noah had

grown accustomed to seeing her dressed in business suits for the TV cameras she faced on a daily basis, he had never seen her in chic evening wear. He admired her feminine grace as she strode across the floor, but he suddenly felt awkward too, as if he had forgotten a step in the middle of a dance.

He rose to greet her with a kiss on the cheek, stealing a moment to inhale her fragrance.

After the waiter had brought her wine, Haldane shook his head and exhaled. "You look . . . wow . . . lovely." He smiled. "Too bad Duncan couldn't see you like this. He's an admirer, too."

"Thanks . . . I think," she said. "Why couldn't Duncan join us tonight?"

"Primarily because he wasn't invited."

"I wasn't entirely sure why I was invited, either," she said with a playful smile. "Didn't you call it a working dinner?"

Haldane felt the butterflies flutter faster. "Oh, I just thought you might like to have dinner . . . you know . . . just the two of us," he faltered.

She reached over and rested a hand on his. "I didn't know if this was business or . . ." She let the sentence hang unfinished.

Haldane enjoyed the warmth of her hand's caress. "It's mainly the 'or' part, but since you mentioned it, any news this afternoon?"

She let go of his hand, and Noah kicked himself for asking. "Hmmm," she said. "More problems in Atlanta with Isaac's drug."

"You mean about the media leak?" he said and then went on to explain: "I heard something on the radio on the way in."

"It makes me so mad! I guess they were bound to find out eventually, but it's way too early. Especially with the problems we're having." She looked down at her wineglass and twisted it by the stem. "The press doesn't seem to know too much, but it's only a matter of time."

Haldane nodded. "What's going on with the drug?"

"Not much change." She stilled her wineglass and looked up at Noah. "The risk of hepatitis runs at about two and a half percent, but that's overshadowed by how well it works in treating both strains of the Gansu Flu."

"How well does it work?" he asked.

"The death rates drop from twenty-five percent down to five percent in the treated group."

"Even factoring in the risk of hepatitis?" Haldane asked.

Gwen nodded. "So the pharmaceutical plant is up and running again. We should have some of the drug ready for distribution by week's end."

Haldane raised his half-empty beer glass. "Here's hoping it all goes to waste."

Her face softened and broke into a warm smile. "I'll drink to that," she said, and she tapped her glass against his.

"Two weeks and we haven't seen hide nor hair of The Brotherhood," Haldane said. "That has to bode well, right?"

"Let's hope," she said. "I think the country is collectively exhausted from living under the constant threat."

Haldane pointed around the room with his glass. "People are starting to get back to their normal lives."

Gwen shrugged. "I wouldn't call it normal."

"At least people are getting out of their houses," Haldane said. "Many have gone back to work. The borders have opened to some travel."

"Not much. The airports are zoos. Few international flights are getting in. And according to Ted, the DHS will maintain the level of alert at code red for the foreseeable future."

Haldane waved his hand. "Okay. No more talk of this. It's ruining my appetite."

"Fine by me." She picked up the menu in front of her. "Speaking of appetites . . ."

They stuck to their agreement and didn't broach any work-related topics for the rest of the dinner, filling the time with happier small talk. When the meal came, Noah was impressed by Gwen's appetite. Most women he had dated never ate on a first date, but Gwen ate through four courses, including dessert. "How do you stay so thin?" he asked her, dropping his jaw in exaggerated amazement.

"I inherited my mom's metabolism. That and her blinding perfectionism." She sighed. "I know I'm lucky, but you have no idea how unpopular the combination of my hefty appetite and relatively lean weight made me with some of the girls at school." She laughed. "Of course, the perfectionism didn't help either."

Haldane reached over and took her hand in his, intertwining their fingers. "You seem pretty popular in our social circle."

She squeezed his hand, but her forehead creased in confusion. "We have a social circle?"

"A tiny little one when you throw in Duncan and Alex." She laughed. "More like a square."

"Speaking of Alex . . ." Haldane said.

She raised an eyebrow. "What about him?"

Haldane shrugged, feeling a touch embarrassed. "You two seem pretty close, is all."

Gwen viewed Noah for a moment, before speaking. "You're getting jealous on a first date? I knew you seemed a bit too perfect. Now the red flags are going up," she said but held onto his hand.

"That's not what I meant." Haldane laughed. "It's just that I don't want to get in the way of you two, you know?"

She pointed around the romantic restaurant and then to the two glasses still in front of them. "Aren't you kind of in his way now?"

"I guess." He chuckled. "Look, I've tried my hardest to

despise the guy, but for whatever reason, he's grown on me." He tried to muster his most valiant face. "If there is something between the two of you, I am happy to take a step back."

She smiled, but Noah suspected that she wasn't buying his routine. She pulled his hand up to her lips and kissed it. "Don't worry about Alex and me."

He realized she had evaded his question, but he didn't care. He enjoyed the feel of her warm breath and soft lips against his knuckles. He had already forgotten about Clayton.

After Haldane paid the bill, they walked hand-in-hand the half block to her Lexus. Standing by her driver's door, he said, "I wasn't sure you knew how to drive. I thought you just took stretch limos everywhere."

"Only to the White House," Gwen said, and stepped in closer to him so that her legs touched his.

He put an arm around her and pulled her nearer. He leaned his head in until his lips touched hers. Their first kiss was tentative. But when Gwen pressed forward again, her lips were wetter and parted. Pulling her tightly against him, Noah kissed her harder. When her lips parted further and her tongue brushed against the inside of his lips, arousal tore through him like a dam breaking.

He wanted nothing more than to tear off their clothes, to kiss every inch of her body, and to take her on the spot. Inside the car, outside in the freezing air, he didn't care. His desire for her swallowed him.

He knew he had to wait, but didn't know if he could so he kissed even deeper, releasing months of pent-up desire through his mouth, lips, and tongue.

Gwen felt giddy as she pulled away from the restaurant. It wasn't so much Noah's company—though between his charm and their desperately sensual kiss she would have gone home with him if he had asked—as having the opportunity to finally relax. She had been so wired up for what seemed like forever with the miserable Gansu virus that she had forgotten what it felt like to unwind and enjoy a night out without carrying the weight of the world.

Driving home through the sparse traffic, she barely listened to the news anchorman recite the same recycled stories of the past week. She only focused in when she heard her name mentioned. "But Dr. Gwen Savard, the country's Director of Counter-Bioterrorism, again refused to comment on rumors that the DHS is mass-producing a new drug to treat the Gansu Flu," the anchor said in a baritone rich with accusation. "In other news the reigning monarch of the oceans, the *Atlantic Princess II,* suffered her first blemish in two years at sea when a crewman was found murdered a day after the ship arrived in Miami. The twenty-three-year-old's body was found in the laundry, stabbed twice in the chest. His male partner, a fellow waiter, is being held for questioning—"

Not wanting to have her perfect mood deflated, she cut the anchorman off in midsentence and popped Joni Mitchell's *Greatest Hits* into the CD player. She belted out the words to "Big Yellow Taxi," happily burying the thoughts of hepatitis, viruses, and terrorists.

She was still singing when she pulled into the underground garage of her condominium complex. She opened the security gate with the remote and circled down the three levels to her parking spot. She pulled into her spot and cut off the ignition to her car.

She picked up her purse and began to climb out but then remembered her cell phone. She reached into the glove compartment and pulled it out. Deciding to check her voice mails on the way up, she closed it in her palm and climbed out of the car.

The fluorescent light still flickered a light glow above her parking stall as always, but now two more fluorescent lights had burned out so the lower level was cast in near darkness, lit by a solitary lightbulb over the elevator and stairwell.

She stepped carefully in her heeled boots, realizing that she was gambling with her ankle in the dimness of the parking lot. Halfway from her car to the stairwell, she thought she heard a noise behind her and assumed one of her neighbors had pulled in to the level above. She stopped and listened, but heard nothing. She turned and walked faster to the elevator.

When she got to the elevator, she pressed the call button but it didn't light up. She tried it with two harder pushes but was rewarded with nothing. Annoyed, she turned for the door to the stairwell. Gazing through the small glass cut in the steel door, she noticed that the stairwell's light had burned out, too.

She glanced around the garage again, listening for the earlier noise, as the mounting coincidences grew more difficult to explain. Her palms dampened. She dug around in her purse before realizing that she had left the small can of bear spray in her "day" handbag.

She stood outside the door, vacillating. She considered climbing back in her car and driving out front of the building, but the thought struck her as paranoid. She took a big breath and yanked the door open to the dark stairwell.

When the door closed behind her, she had to grab on to the handrail to lead her up the stairs. She climbed the first five steps tentatively, more concerned about twisting her ankle than out of alarm. She reached the first landing, stopped, and listened for a moment.

Nothing.

Just as she rounded the corner to take the next step, she felt sudden pain in her teeth. Her mouth filled with the taste of leather. At the same moment, an arm wrapped around her chest and pulled her backward until she almost fell. Something hard pressed through her coat into the small of the back. She knew it was a gun.

"Do not speak, Dr. Savard," a voice whispered in her ear. "Or you die here."

She stood motionless, her mind racing.

"Take me to your car," the whisperer said. "Now!"

Suddenly he spun her in the opposite direction. He released her from his grip but only to shove her forward. She almost stumbled down the stairs before regaining her footing. With the gun jammed into her back, she walked slowly and deliberately. With each step, she brought her hand closer to her waist.

"Faster!" the whisperer urged.

She reached the last step of the stairs. Realizing it would be brighter as soon as she stepped out of the stairwell, she feared she might miss her opportunity. With her next stride, she pulled her thick belt back with her thumb and tucked her tiny cell phone down the front of her pants behind the belt and inside of her underwear's waistband.

"Open the door!"

She reached her now-empty hand forward and opened the stairwell's metal door. He shoved her through it and out into the garage. In the dim light, prodded with the push of the gun barrel, she walked faster toward her car. When she reached the car, she felt a tug on her shoulder as her purse was yanked from her.

She heard him rummaging through the purse and then heard her keys jingle. The car's lights flashed twice as her abductor unlocked the door with the remote. "Open the back door!"

She pulled open the door to the rear seat. Rather than climb in, she wheeled to face her abductor and was met by the sight of his implacable face and intense, light eyes. Her eyes skipped from the gun in his left hand to the object in his right. Seeing only the needle, it took her a moment to realize that it was attached to a syringe.

Instinctively, she pulled back, but it was too late. His hand flew at her, and she felt a sharp sting in her left shoulder. With a huge shove from his other hand, she flew backward through the open door into the backseat, slamming her head against the seat-belt buckle.

Lying on the cold leather, she was overcome by nausea. The car's interior whirled. She swam on the seat. Her eyelids felt heavy. A faint taste of vanilla replaced the leather. She fought to stay conscious, willing her body to resist whatever she had been injected with, but the taste grew stronger.

No matter how hard she tried, she couldn't stave off the encroaching blackness.

CHAPTER

40

DEPARTMENT OF HOMELAND SECURITY, NEBRASKA AVENUE CENTER, WASHINGTON D.C.
Haldane was the first to arrive at the DHS building. Gwen's
secretary, Arlene, led him into Savard's office and brought
him a fresh coffee. She passed it to him with a warm smile,
and Noah wondered for a fleeting irrational moment if
Arlene had heard about his date with her beloved boss.

Why would it matter? he wondered. Despite his lasting
buzz from their promising kiss, Haldane couldn't shake
the nagging guilt. Maybe he wasn't ready yet. As he wrestled those thoughts, Alex Clayton strode into the room
dressed in an entirely black ensemble from jacket to
shoes, which only Clayton could pull off. "Noah." He
nodded. "How are you? Did you have a good dinner?"

Haldane knew that he was not imagining the recognition in Clayton's eyes. "Fine," he said without elaborating.
"You?"

Clayton shrugged. "Dinner alone in front of the basket-
ball game."

They fell into an awkward silence, broken when McLeod burst into the room. Without acknowledging Haldane or Clayton, he called over his shoulder, "Arlene, dear, I'm home."

Soon, the young homely secretary walked in bearing more coffees and a big smile for McLeod.

McLeod winked at her. "Ah, Arlene, if you were ten years older and not American . . ." Haldane knew he added the last few words for Clayton's benefit.

Clayton rolled his eyes.

McLeod looked from Haldane to Clayton. "Where's our gorgeous leader?"

"She must have had a late night," Clayton said and fired a glance at Haldane.

When they had finished their coffees without any sign of Gwen, Haldane reached in his pocket and pulled out his phone. He tried her cell number but reached her voice mail after five rings. "Gwen, we're waiting in your office, give me a call if you get this." He hung up and dialed her home phone number and left the same message for her.

Haldane put away his phone and held up his palms. "Well?"

Clayton checked his watch. "I've got to get back to Langley in just over half an hour. The Director's called an urgent meeting."

"Why?" Haldane asked. "A development?"

Clayton looked from McLeod to Haldane, and Noah had the feeling he was weighing whether or not to trust them. "I was going to wait for Gwen, but . . ." He reached into his jacket pocket and pulled out two folded pages.

Clayton opened the first page and laid it out on the table in front of them. A photocopy, the Arabic letters on it were written in perfect penmanship.

Haldane and McLeod both leaned forward for a closer look. "What is it?" Haldane asked, alarms sounding in his head.

"We heard from the Egyptians late last night," Clayton said. "Apparently, Abdul Sabri sent this letter to his former commanding officer in the Egyptian Special Forces. The one who overlooked him for promotion."

"When?" Haldane tapped the page with a finger.

"It was postmarked the day after Operation Antiseptic, but as best we can assess it was sent the day before the raid."

Haldane took little consolation in knowing that the letter alone did not confirm Sabri lived through Operation Antiseptic. "Where was it sent from?" he asked.

"Cairo."

McLeod picked it up for a closer look. "What does it say?"

Clayton unfolded the second page, which bore an English translation, and placed it on top of the original text.

Haldane read the letter silently.

General,

For twenty years, I served loyally in your army. I performed every order I ever received. I accomplished every mission you or your designates ever set for me. I excelled where others would not have dared try.

Never questioning my orders, I fought the faithful of the Jihad. And on behalf of you and your illegitimate regime, I tortured and killed them. For which I am destined as you are to spend eternity in the fiery lake of hell.

For all of that, you rewarded my service, my sacrifice, with nothing but neglect and shame. Now you will learn that there is a price for your insult.

When your great ally, America, withers and collapses to her soulless knees because of me, you will see what happens. The faithful will rise up and restore Allah to His rightful seat of power in Egypt and elsewhere. They will quickly dispatch you and your kind to your special place in hell. And you will go there knowing that Abdul Sabri played a role in sending you.

Haldane read the letter over, while McLeod whistled. "I'm no psychotherapist, but I think the old major might have a few wee unresolved issues."

No one laughed.

" 'When your great ally, America, withers and collapses to her soulless knees,' " Haldane quoted. "That doesn't sound like someone who ever intended to negotiate."

"True," Clayton said, folding up the pages and tucking them back into his pocket. "Sabri always planned on releasing the virus."

"Or *still* plans to," McLeod said with a disconsolate nod.

"It has been over two weeks," Haldane said, trying to convince himself as much as the others.

"Two weeks, two months, two years?" McLeod banged the table once with his fist. "If he's still alive and has the supervirus what does it matter to him? Shite, the world can't stay on guard forever. He will get his chance."

Clayton shook his head angrily. "Not if we find Major Sabri first."

"A damn good idea, Clayton," McLeod grumbled.

They sat around in despondent silence for five more minutes. Clayton glanced at his watch. "I can't wait for Gwen any longer. I have to go."

"Thanks for sharing the letter with us, Alex," Haldane said genuinely. "We'll update Gwen when she gets here." Haldane checked his own watch, which read 10:15 A.M. "At least, you don't have to worry about getting to Langley. There's still no traffic out there."

As Clayton buttoned up his overcoat, he said, "I don't know about that. Every morning there are more and more cars on the road. People are getting back to their routines."

"Yeah," McLeod agreed. "I even heard that the New Year's celebration at Times Square is on for tomorrow night."

"They're going ahead with it?" Haldane asked.

Clayton stopped buttoning his jacket.

"I heard something on the radio this morning," McLeod said. "I don't think it's the official celebration, but a bunch of New Yorkers are doing their usual, defiant screw-you-terrorists routine. We're going to party in spite of you buggers! They're expecting a big turnout, too."

Haldane looked at Clayton. "People come from all over the States for New Year's Eve at Times Square," he said, not bothering to mask the alarm in his voice.

Clayton nodded gravely. "I know."

"The reason the Spanish Flu took off like it did was because the soldiers from World War I were decommissioned in France right as the virus hit," Haldane said. "They took it back home with them. What if tomorrow at Times Square . . ."

"We won't allow this party to happen," Clayton said definitively. "Simple as that."

McLeod rubbed his beard with his palm. "Just exactly how do you stop an unofficial party?"

"Don't underestimate us, Duncan," Clayton grunted. "Sometimes we can accomplish things without all the usual red tape."

"You mean like the Bay of Pigs?" McLeod grunted.

Before Clayton could answer, Gwen's phone rang. "Maybe that's her," he said reaching for the receiver. "Hello, Dr. Savard's office."

Clayton listened a moment. "No, she is not here." A pause. "Alex Clayton, Deputy Director of Operations for the CIA."

"What?" Clayton's eyes went wide and the color drained from his face. "Where?"

Haldane stood from his seat. "Alex . . ." But Clayton waved him back with a hand.

"Okay," Clayton said. "You call Moira Roberts, the Deputy Director of the FBI, and tell her I told you to. And you call me if you hear anything, anything at all," Clayton said, giving three numbers where he could be reached before hanging up his cell.

Clayton looked slowly from McLeod to Haldane. "The police found Gwen's car this morning at a gas station in Maryland," he said calmly. "There was blood on the backseat."

Gwen felt a vibration against her abdomen under her belt. Nauseous and disoriented, she opened her eyes and squinted through the light. The room smelt musty from mothballs. Springs dug into her back. When she tried to roll over, neither her legs nor her arms would cooperate. With each wiggle, she felt the straps dig tighter into her ankles and wrists.

Anxiety welled in her chest, but she willed herself calm, realizing that panic would be a grave waste of energy.

The cell phone tucked in her waistband stopped vibrating.

She raised her head and looked around the room. The green paint on the walls was peeling. Moldy curtains covered a small row of dirty windows, but the gray light from outside leaked through and around them. The electric radiator hummed loudly.

Though her mind was still bleary from whatever she had been given, she began to put the pieces together. Judging from the metal cot she was bound to, she suspected she was in the bedroom of a cheap motel, possibly the kind with individual cabins.

The sense of orientation helped hold her nerves in check even when she felt the sharpness in her left arm and looked down to see the intravenous cannula sticking out of her elbow's crease. She focused her memory on the face and eyes she had seen in her garage. She had no doubt they belonged to the man whose picture ran constantly on CNN. Abdul Sabri.

She looked up from her arm with a sudden start to see Abdul Sabri standing in the doorway. He took a few more silent steps toward her and stopped by the edge of her cot. In jeans and a collared shirt, he towered above her. His smooth face was blank, but his opaque blue eyes fixed on her intently.

"You have woken, Dr. Savard," Sabri said in a thick but clear Arabic accent.

"Where am I?" Gwen asked.

"It does not matter," Sabri said.

"Why did you kidnap me?" she demanded.

"I wanted to talk with you," he said.

"Why?" she snapped, feeling more violated than scared.

"You are the Director of Counter-Bioterrorism," he spoke the word slowly, cautious with his pronunciation. "I am a bioterrorist. It only makes sense."

"Nothing you do makes sense," she said, and struggled vainly against her bindings.

Sabri seemed to consider her point for several moments and then he nodded. "To you, maybe no. To me, it makes perfect sense."

Realizing how futile her resistance was, Gwen decided to change tacks. "Explain it to me then," she said in a more diplomatic tone.

"I do not think I can," he said, and then his face creased into a very slight smile. "I did not bring you here to talk politics."

"I would really like to know," Gwen said, trying to imagine a way of getting access to the phone tucked under her waistband.

Sabri shook his head once. "I want to know about your new drug. The one the reporters are talking about on the television."

"I wish we had one." Gwen shrugged her bound arms. "It is just a rumor the media has started."

Not a single muscle moved on his face, but his eyes darkened and Gwen could feel the threat as if he were still pointing his gun at her. "I do not believe you, Dr. Savard."

"I am sorry," Gwen said, and swallowed away the bitter taste in her mouth. "What do you want me to say?"

Motionless, he studied her for a long time. His silence was somehow more menacing than anything he had said or done to this point. "It is of no consequence," he said finally. "Let us move on. I would like to hear about your disaster planning."

"What do you mean?" She grimaced.

"A city such as New York, for example," Sabri said. "You must have a plan for dealing with an outbreak. Is that correct?"

"Every city in the country has a disaster plan," she said, calculating how much she needed to share with him to sound as if she was telling the truth. "There are public health officials in each city responsible for nothing but dealing with natural disasters."

"Yes, of course," Sabri said with a nod. "Is there a plan for the Gansu virus?"

Gwen shuffled on the cot, but the ligatures only dug deeper. "You want to know the specific plan for every major city in the States for dealing with the Gansu Flu?"

"No." Sabri breathed slowly, and Gwen sensed the frustration behind his placid exterior. "If the virus comes to New York," he said, "will the ports, roads, and airports be closed as soon as one person becomes sick?"

"We don't deal with epidemics by shutting down a city," she said, though the latest revised draft of the ERPBA called for exactly those measures. "We would send out warnings of course and ask people not to travel. If someone became ill, we would quarantine that person and his or her contacts. The rest is up to local authorities," she lied.

He viewed her for several moments without responding.

Then he looked over his shoulder and called out something in Arabic.

A moment later, a bearded, pudgy man walked into the room. He was dressed in a cheap, ill-fitting gray suit with white shirt and an overly wide black tie. Sweat dripped down from his brow and his exposed shirt had patches of wetness soaked through. He avoided eye contact with Gwen; instead his small dark eyes darted around the room as if looking for a small pet that had escaped.

Gwen's anxiety broke through the tethers of her determination when she saw the long needle and syringe in the fat man's hand.

Sabri said something to the man in Arabic.

The man walked toward Gwen. He stopped at the side of the bed. As he stooped forward to move the needle near the intravenous cannula in her arm, Gwen squirmed wildly on the cot but gained nothing from the effort except more wrist pain. The fat man slid the needle into the cannula, but his thumb rested still on the syringe's plunger.

"This is Dr. Aziz," Sabri said, nodding at the man. "He is going to help us."

"Help us how?" Gwen asked, breathing very rapidly.

"I want to go over your answers again, Dr. Savard," Sabri said.

She fought to control the hyperventilation. "What's he giving me?"

"Something to relax you," Sabri said.

"If you want me relaxed, untie me," Gwen snarled at her captor. "What's in the damn syringe?"

Sabri pointed at the syringe. "That is thiopental sodium. I think you call it truth serum." He nodded to the fat man and said something in Arabic.

Gwen's heart slammed against her chest as she watched Aziz depress the plunger of the syringe.

Her eyelids felt heavy. Seconds later, she felt herself float free of the bed.

CHAPTER

41

Sitting in the passenger seat of Clayton's black Lincoln, Haldane paid no attention to the sights flying by his window or the hooting horns and screeching brakes of the other cars they cut off as Clayton raced them out of Washington and into Maryland. Instead he sat still in the passenger seat, staring at his feet, seething with anger and worry.

Eighteen minutes after leaving Washington, on a trip that normally would have taken forty, the sedan swung into the gas station's parking lot, which overflowed with police cars, crime-scene vans, and other vehicles.

Abandoning the car in the lot's driveway, Clayton jumped out, leaving the door open behind him. Haldane and McLeod piled out after him. They elbowed their way through the throngs of police, technicians, and other government officials to get to where Gwen's navy Lexus sat in the far corner of the lot. A team of crime-scene investigators buzzed around it.

Just before they reached the car, a dowdy woman with a short bob and a plain black pantsuit waved to Clayton. "Alex!" she called.

Haldane and McLeod followed Clayton as he hurried over to where the woman stood by the gas pumps. He pointed to her. "Moira Roberts, FBI Deputy Director." He swung a finger over to the others. "Drs. Noah Haldane and Duncan McLeod with the WHO."

When Roberts flashed Clayton a look suggesting she wasn't thrilled to see two civilians at the crime scene, Clayton said, "They're okay. They work with Gwen. Tell us what you know."

"Of course, I'm only here in an administrative capacity, but I believe I'm up-to-date with the investigation," Roberts said.

Clayton rolled his hand in a get-on-with-it gesture.

"The car was abandoned in the lot some time after midnight when the gas station closed," Roberts said with a troubled frown. "According to the clerk there was another car, a gray sedan, parked in the space right beside it when he closed up last night. We're presuming that whoever abducted her—"

"It's not whoever," McLeod cut in. "It's Abdul bloody Sabri!"

Roberts folded her arms across her chest. "There is no proof that her abduction is even related to the bioterrorist conspiracy."

"Stupid me, jumping to conclusions!" McLeod grunted. "Short of finding a burnt American flag and effigy of the President hanging from the rearview mirror, what sort of proof—"

"Enough," Clayton growled. "You were saying, Moira . . ."

"We believe that the kidnapper or kidnappers must have moved Dr. Savard from her own car into the gray sedan, though we have no eyewitnesses to that effect."

Roberts's by-the-book manner fueled Haldane's impatience. He snapped his fingers. "They said something about blood on the backseat?" he demanded.

She nodded. "There is a blood trail, more of a smear really, along the backseat," she said matter-of-factly. "That's why we're confident Dr. Savard was moved."

Noah wanted to shake Roberts by her lapels. "How much blood?"

"Oh." Roberts waved away his concern with her hand. "Not that much. It's consistent with a cut, for example a scalp laceration."

"Anything else?" Clayton asked.

"We've set up roadblocks over a fifty-mile radius. And we've got our helicopters looking for cars that match the description of the gray sedan." She pointed to the technicians working on Gwen's car and in the field behind. "We're scouring the scene." She paused and viewed them with a look that bordered on sympathy. "It's very early in the investigation. We should have more to go on, soon."

"Okay, who is the lead agent—" Clayton started to ask, when Roberts held up a hand to interrupt him. She reached into her jacket pocket and answered the cell phone without it audibly ringing.

Something twigged in Haldane. Watching her talk, he felt on the verge of a breakthrough, but for several agonizing seconds it refused to surface.

Then it hit him like a slap.

He wheeled and ran over to the three crime-scene technicians working on Gwen's car. Ignoring the bloodstain on the backseat, he tapped the shoulder of the technician kneeling under the steering wheel. "Yes?" the technician said tersely. "What is it?"

"A cell phone?" Haldane breathed.

"I don't have one," the guy said. "There's a pay phone over—"

"No!" Haldane cut him off. "Did you find a cell phone in this car?"

"No. No cell phone in here."

Haldane turned around to find Clayton and McLeod staring at him as if he had lost his mind. "Come with me," he said. He led them a few yards away from the car until they were out of earshot of the others. "Listen, Gwen's cell phone is not in the car."

"So?" Clayton shrugged. "You tried her on it earlier, there was no answer."

"Exactly!" Haldane said. "There was no answer, but it rang. If it was turned off, it would have gone straight to her voice mail without ringing."

After a moment, Clayton's eyes widened. "Son of a bitch! Maybe she still has it on her?"

McLeod threw up his hands. "So it rang? So it's still on her? Big bloody deal! If she can't get to it what help will it be?"

"You explain," Clayton said to Haldane. "I'm going to call Langley to trace it." He pulled his own cell phone out of his jacket and stepped away in search of a quieter spot.

Looking bewildered, McLeod turned to Haldane. "What's going on, Noah?"

"Newer cell phones are all equipped with GPS chips," Haldane said.

McLeod shook his head. "Meaning?"

"GPS chips are ultra-accurate homing devices," Haldane said, tapping the side of his temple with a finger. "So if the phone is turned on, the service provider can track down its whereabouts to within a few feet."

"Shite! That's invasion of privacy!" McLeod said, but his lips broke into a crooked smile. "Haldane, let's pray she hung on to that wee phone of hers."

Without exchanging another word they turned and watched Clayton, who stood twenty feet away with a hand covering one ear and his phone to the other. Arms at his sides, Haldane tried to pump the apprehension out through his fists, but it was of little help. Come on, come on, we need this one! he repeated to himself in what was as close as he came to a prayer.

Two long minutes later, Clayton pulled the phone from his ear and jogged back over to where they stood waiting. "Well?" Haldane asked before the CIA man even reached them.

Clayton flashed a quick thumbs-up sign. "We've tracked the phone. It's at a place called The Quiet Slumber Motel, just outside of Jessup, Maryland."

Noah felt a wave of elation. "How far?"

"About thirty miles north," Clayton said.

Haldane reached over and laid a hand on Clayton's shoulder. "Alex, are we going to tell Moira?"

"We should," he said, but his expression appeared less certain.

"What will they do?" Haldane asked.

"The FBI can be so by the numbers." Clayton shook his head. "They'll want to stake out the place. Organize a coordinated assault."

"Which could take time," Haldane pointed out.

"Hours," Clayton murmured.

Noah squeezed Clayton's shoulder before removing his hand. "Time Gwen might not have, Alex."

"I know." Clayton nodded. "But they have the resources to launch an assault. We don't have three guns between us."

Noah wasn't dissuaded. "But, Alex, we've got the advantage of surprise."

Looking uncharacteristically solemn, McLeod nodded. "The people who abducted her think nothing of taking their own lives. If they got so much as a whiff of a police ambush . . ."

Clayton's jaw clenched and his face hardened into a look of sheer determination. He glanced from Haldane to

McLeod. "If and when we need help, we'll call in the FBI," he said definitively. "Let's go get her."

Clayton drove by the dumpy little motel two miles outside of Jessup without even slowing down. Haldane had seen a thousand roadside motels like The Quiet Slumber, but he had never bothered to study one so intently.

Built backing onto the woods of a campground, it consisted of several individual wood cabins. Haldane counted twelve of them, but it was possible there were a few hidden behind the ones facing the road.

Clayton pulled the car into the gravel driveway of the campground two blocks behind the motel. The campground had been shut down for the winter and theirs was the only car in the lot. Staying in his seat, Clayton pulled out his cell phone and dialed a number.

"Megan, the cell I told you to run," he said into the receiver. "Can you give me exact coordinates?" He paused. "Yeah, the motel complex has twelve cabins, can you pull it up on the map? I need to know which cabin." He waited several seconds. "Okay, from the northeast corner, right?" Another pause. "Megan, there's no room for error. You're certain?" he asked. "Good. I owe you a big one."

Turning to the other two, Clayton frowned. "Okay, they're in the very last cabin we passed. Makes sense. It's the most remote and protected of the bunch." He reached for his door handle. "We're on foot from here."

After they climbed out of the car, Clayton walked around the back of his car and popped the trunk. Reaching under the mat where the spare tire was stored, he pulled out a small metal briefcase. He closed the trunk. He glanced over either shoulder, then laid the briefcase on the trunk and opened the case's latch with a key from his key ring.

Inside, foam padding separated pieces of metal. As

soon as Haldane recognized the components of handguns, he felt the adrenaline leak into his system.

Clayton glanced at the other two. "Neither of you are armed, I assume?"

Haldane shook his head, while McLeod just sighed.

Clayton reached for the smaller gun. He grabbed a cartridge and clipped it into the handle. Then he grabbed the gun by the muzzle and held it out, handle-first, to Haldane and McLeod. "Glock 17. Nine-mm," he said. "Lightweight and idiot-proof. I only have the one extra. Has either of you fired a gun?"

"Point of clarification, I'm from Scotland not bleeding Texas!" McLeod said.

"I've fired a .38 caliber at the range a few times," Haldane said.

"You win." Clayton handed the gun to Haldane.

Haldane swung it in his hand, surprised by how light the weapon felt.

"Straightforward double action, semi-automatic," Clayton explained. "No safety. Squeeze and fire. Clip holds seventeen bullets. If you hold the trigger down, it will fire every two seconds."

Haldane nodded, still amazed at how weightless the weapon felt in his hand.

Clayton turned back to the briefcase. He assembled another gun, which came in more parts than the Glock 17. Just as Haldane thought Clayton was through, he reached for one last piece and screwed what Noah assumed was a silencer onto the tip of the barrel. Clayton pushed his jacket out of the way, and tucked the gun into his belt at the back of his waist.

Haldane did the same.

"The huge advantage we have here is that not only is Sabri not expecting us, he wouldn't recognize us," Clayton said. "But if he or they are watching, and I assume he is, a group of three men approaching the motel would look highly suspicious." He looked to Haldane. "You have your phone?"

Haldane pulled it out of his pocket and held it up.

Clayton reached for his. "Okay, keep my number on redial, I'll do the same with yours. I'll go ahead. Give me a five-minute head start and then meet me on the near side of the third to last cabin. You got it? The third to last!"

Gwen awoke to discover that her mouth was a kiln. She licked her lips and smacked her gums, desperate for saliva. Even before she opened her eyes, the sharp pressure at her wrists and ankles told her that she was still tied to the cot.

When she opened her eyes, everything in the room was encircled by a faint halo. Even Abdul Sabri. Hovering over her, he was shrouded in a bluish white light, making him look like a huge angel. The angel of death, she thought bleakly. She blinked hard, and when she opened her eyes again Sabri had shed his divine shadow.

"What happened?" she asked hoarsely, while trying to focus her thoughts into some kind of plan.

"You were more helpful after thiopental sodium, Dr. Savard," Sabri said in an expressionless tone that matched his face perfectly.

"What did I tell you?" she asked.

He shrugged slightly. "Enough."

She paused and swallowed again against her parched lips. She knew she needed to act soon if she were to stand a chance. "What will you do with me now?" she asked.

"You will know soon." He turned and began walking for the door.

She could feel her cell phone digging into her abdomen below the waistband of her underwear. "Major, I have to use the bathroom," she said.

Halfway to the door he stopped and looked over his shoulder, but he didn't say a word.

"I mean, I really have to go, now," she said.

He shrugged again. "So go."

"That's not very dignified," Gwen said. "I thought you had more class than that."

He started for the door again.

"That is how you would treat a woman?" she yelled after him. "Your religion preaches that as acceptable?"

He stopped at the doorway without turning.

Gwen felt a flicker of hope, as he seemed to vacillate, shifting from one foot to the other.

Then he turned slowly toward her. But when he faced her again, in his right hand she saw the glint from a long serrated blade.

For an anxious moment, standing with his back pressed against the peeling paint of the dilapidated old cabin, two over from the one supposedly housing Gwen, Haldane wondered if they had misunderstood Clayton, or worse, if something had already happened to him. "Where are you, Alex?" Haldane mouthed, making no sound but his breath misted in the cold air.

Silently, Clayton rounded the corner to meet them. "Gwen's alive," he whispered tersely, and Haldane felt a flood of relief. "But she's in four-point restraints on a cot in the second bedroom. There's at least two terrorists with her: Sabri and a squat, bearded guy.

"In the window by the front door, there's a gap below the curtains where I could see in." Clayton bent down and picked up a stick. He scratched out a rough floor plan of the cabin in the dirt. "On the right side the door leads into the living room, which is separated from the kitchen behind by half of a wall and a counter." He marked an X by the line marking the countertop. "The fat one was in the kitchen. Sabri was just coming out of the bedroom." He tapped the left side of the cabin. "The empty master bedroom faces front, but on the back side is the room where they're keeping Gwen. There are two windows high up—I had to stand on an old box to see in—but Gwen was tied to the cot. She looked . . . drugged. But she's definitely alive."

"So what do we do?" McLeod whispered.

"We wait and watch." Clayton nodded. "And if need be, we go in."

"That's your whole plan?" McLeod whispered, unimpressed.

Clayton smiled. "I'm CIA, remember? When we start planning, we end up with the Bay of Pigs." His expression stiffened. He held his phone out for McLeod. "Duncan, I need you to take up the post around back of the cabin. There's no door to get in and out and the windows are too small to climb through, but I want you to keep an eye on Gwen through the window. If anything happens, you call us. Just hit the redial button."

McLeod accepted the phone and nodded.

"Wait here two minutes after we leave and then walk quietly around the back. I left the old box under the window." Clayton turned to Haldane with a confident nod. "We're going to take up the post out front."

"What about the FBI?" Haldane asked.

"I just spoke to Moira," Clayton said. "They're on the way."

Clayton took off his coat and dumped it on the ground, leaving just his black suit jacket on. Waving for Haldane to follow, he dashed around back of the third cabin. Stooped low, he ran below the level of the high windows on the back of the cabin. He stopped at the far corner of the cabin one over from their target and waited for Haldane.

With his hands, Clayton indicated how he wanted them to circle around the far side of the cabin to get to the window in front. He counted down from three with his fingers. Hunched low, they dashed past the box in front of the window to Gwen's room and kept going until they rounded the corner and reached the far wall.

Feeling winded, more from the stress than the short run, Haldane panted while Clayton peered around the corner.

Clayton pulled his gun out from his waistband and nodded for Haldane to do the same, and then he squatted down to his knees. When Haldane pulled the gun out of his belt, it suddenly felt much more substantial and it trembled slightly in his hand.

Clayton crept around the corner of the building and stopped after six or seven feet. He raised his hands off the ground and stared through the lower edge of the window before waving Haldane over to join him.

Haldane crawled forward until he reached him. Slowly, he brought his head up to the same level as Clayton's and stared into the dark living room through the half-inch gap between the curtain and the bottom of the window. The chubby, bearded man paced nervously beside the kitchen counter with a pistol tucked into his waist. Haldane scanned over the rest of the kitchen and living room but saw no sign of Sabri.

Haldane's heart thumped against his ribs. "Where?" he mouthed to Clayton.

Clayton shook his head once.

Startled, Haldane suddenly felt his pocket vibrate silently. He dug a hand inside and grabbed his phone. Recognizing Clayton's number on the call display, he brought it up to his ear. "Duncan?" he whispered.

"A knife!" McLeod whispered hysterically.

"What?"

"Sabri. Knife. Going for Gwen." McLeod rushed the choppy whispers.

Haldane dropped the phone and spun to Clayton. "Sabri's going after Gwen with a knife."

Clayton nodded calmly. "Stay at the door and cover me in the room. Got it?" he whispered.

Haldane nodded.

Clayton counted down again with his fingers. On zero, he took two squatted steps forward and then shot bolt upright in front of the door. Haldane crawled to join him, just as McLeod scurried around the corner waving his arms frantically. "No. No!" McLeod breathed. "It's okay. You don't need to go!"

But Clayton was already in motion.

Elbows locked, he pointed his gun with two hands at the door. The barrel flinched twice, emitting two brief hisses, and then Clayton kicked the door with a heavy blow from his right foot. No sooner had his foot reached the ground than he dove through the now-open doorway.

Haldane scrambled to his feet and stood at the door with his Glock held ready. He peered into the room just in time to see the fat man whirl to face the door. The man reached for his pistol and started to scream something, when suddenly he flew back against the kitchen counter. Eyes open wide, the man slid down against the wall below the counter, leaving a bloodstain behind him, and then toppled forward in a crumpled heap.

As Sabri approached her with his huge knife swaying in front of him, Gwen was overcome with calm. She resolved not to say a word to him. She would not let him cheat her of a dignified death.

He knelt down by her cot, holding his knife inches from her head. His pale eyes burned into hers and she could feel his warm sterile breath on her face. She turned her head away from his and closed her eyes, wondering whether to expect intense pain or nothing at all when the blow came.

She held her breath. Nothing.

When moments later she felt a tugging at her left ankle and her leg suddenly released, she shot her head over to see Sabri cutting through the other bindings.

Before freeing her wrists, he glanced at her. "You cooperate or you die," he said coolly. Then he cut through the last of the ties.

She sat up unsteadily on the bed.

Just as she rose to her feet, she heard the sound of the door bursting open. Before she could react, Sabri grabbed her by the hair and yanked her to her feet in one painful jerk. He wrapped his knifed hand around her neck until the edge dug into the skin just below her jaw. "One move, you die!" he spat as he pushed her forward.

She heard a shrill male scream something in Arabic, followed by a heavy thud.

Sabri carried her by the neck as he ran with her out of the bedroom. As soon as they rounded the corner, Gwen saw Clayton standing in the middle of the shabby living room. His gun was trained right on them.

Sabri stopped.

"It's okay, Gwen," Clayton said evenly, and then he spoke to Sabri. "Put her down, now, Major Sabri. It's over." His gun held perfectly still.

"Yes, over," Sabri repeated and she could feel his breath on her ear. "I will die and you will lose your Director of Counter-Bioterrorism." He jabbed the blade tighter against Gwen's neck, until she felt a sharp sting, realizing her skin had been cut.

"Let her go!" Clayton insisted.

"Put your gun down or she dies now," Sabri said.

Clayton faltered.

"Now!" Sabri hissed.

Clayton backed up away from them several steps until he was near the entryway. That was the first time Gwen noticed Noah at the doorway with only his head, hand, and gun poking through.

The sharp pressure tightened at Gwen's neck. At the same moment, she felt Sabri's other hand digging around behind her back.

Clayton slowly lowered his gun to his side. "I'm putting it down," he said.

Suddenly Gwen realized that Sabri now held a new weapon behind her back. His gun. She opened her mouth to yell, "Alex—" when she was abruptly shoved heavily forward into the wall.

Reality shifted. Everything slowed down for Gwen.

Her shoulder slammed painfully against the wall. She looked up in time to see Clayton spin and stagger backward as a spray of blood arced out of the left side of his chest. He dropped to his knees and then fell backward in the entryway.

She looked over at Sabri. A pistol had replaced his knife. And he fired three more shots at the doorway.

When Clayton swiveled and collapsed at his feet, Noah glanced down for a split second. At the same moment, the wood beside his head erupted in a shower of splinters, and he heard three more loud bangs.

Noah yanked his head back out the doorway. On the other side from him, McLeod was on his knees, risking exposure as he pulled Clayton's bleeding body out of the cabin by his legs.

Clayton's eyes were half-shut and blood leaked between his lips. When his head turned and his glassy eyes found Haldane's, he implored, "End it now, Noah!" He sputtered and the air filled as if his breath had frozen red.

Haldane poked his head out around the corner again. Sabri was wrestling Gwen into a headlock. When Sabri looked up to see Haldane, he fired another shot, and Noah felt the bullet whistle by his head.

Haldane raised his Glock, aiming. His finger froze on the trigger, wavering as to whether he had a clear shot without hitting Gwen. In his moments of hesitation, Sabri dragged Gwen back into the kitchen and down behind the countertop.

Haldane felt a surge of fury rip through him.

His gun leading the way, he strode forward into the living room, moving out to his left.

Just as he penetrated deep enough into the room to see around the edge of the counter, the glass on the painting frame behind him smashed and another bang echoed in the room.

He dropped to a crouch. Not breathing, he inched forward to get another glimpse of the kitchen. Seeing past the edge of the low kitchen wall, his eyes locked on Sabri's.

They both leveled their guns, but suddenly Sabri yelped in pain, as Gwen's teeth bit into his arm. She wriggled free of his grip.

Haldane steadied his aim, struggling for a clear shot.

"Shoot, Noah!" Gwen screamed.

She lunged forward and onto the ground. Noah fired twice. The first shot clipped Sabri in his left arm and the second shattered a water glass above his head.

Sabri's left arm fell limp to his side, but his right hand held steadfastly to his gun. He swung it from Noah to Gwen who was no more than five feet away. His lips formed a grotesque smile, but his gun didn't fire.

Haldane fired two more shots. Sabri's head flopped backward and slammed into the cabinet behind him.

Sitting upright, his body shuddered once and then was still. Sabri stared straight ahead at Noah. Except for the quarter-shaped hole in his left upper forehead, his eyes and expression appeared much the same as they had before he died.

CHAPTER

42

By the time Haldane reached her, Gwen had climbed to her feet. He gently put an arm around to support her without even realizing that he still hung on to the gun with the same hand. "You okay?" he asked.

"Fine." She staggered slightly, but managed to keep herself upright. She gently pushed his arm away. "Go help Alex! He needs you more than I do." And she wiped away the trickle of blood running down from the laceration on her neck.

Haldane turned from Gwen and sprinted across the room to where Clayton still lay sprawled across the edge of the doorway. McLeod had taken his jacket off and wadded it into a ball, which he used to compress the bullet wound in Clayton's upper chest. Every inch of the jacket's green fabric had turned brown from the blood it had absorbed.

Haldane dropped to his knees beside Clayton across from McLeod. "Duncan?"

McLeod shook his head. "He was talking to me." He swallowed hard. "Then he drifted into mumbles. He lost consciousness altogether a minute or two ago."

"You called 911?"

"Twice," McLeod said as he reached the fingers of his free hand behind the angle of Clayton's jaw and thrust it forward in an attempt to better open his airway.

When Haldane leaned in close, he heard the slight gurgle of air and saw bubbles form in the blood in Clayton's mouth. Haldane swept a finger inside his mouth to clear the bloody debris, but it did nothing to improve the breathing. He searched for a pulse at Clayton's wrist and elbow, but felt none. Only when Haldane swept two fingers over Clayton's neck could he eventually find a rapid thready pulse.

"He can't last much longer." Haldane looked up and yelled to no one. "Where the fuck are they?"

Gwen hobbled over to join them. Awkwardly, using McLeod's shoulder to steady her, she knelt down between them and above Clayton's head. She reached her hand down and gently stroked his hair. "Please, Alex," she cooed softly. "Please hang in there."

Clayton's eyelids flickered a few times and then popped open. His glazed eyes looked up at Gwen, and his ashen face broke into a weak smile. Then his eyes closed again.

Haldane heard the faint wail of sirens.

Clayton was still alive when the paramedics loaded him onto the stretcher and screamed off for the Baltimore Trauma Center, sixteen miles away. Haldane knew from their downcast expressions and cautious reassurances that they held little hope for Clayton. The fact that Clayton still had a pulse when they left was more than Haldane expected. He felt a glimmer of optimism.

Haldane walked over to where a paramedic stood beside Gwen, trying to attend to the injuries of her upright patient. Gwen watched as the ambulance carrying Clayton raced off. When its taillights faded, she reached down and yanked the IV cannula out of her elbow. The young paramedic at her side placed a Band-Aid over the site, which matched the dressing she had applied to Gwen's neck.

When the paramedic pointed to her rig, Gwen shook her head. "I appreciate your help." She smiled. "But I'm fine. I'm not coming with you." And, as if to contradict her point, Gwen stumbled a step before catching her balance.

"It's okay," Haldane said to the young paramedic. "We're both doctors." He pointed to McLeod and himself. "We'll watch her."

The paramedic shrugged and walked off toward her truck.

McLeod joined Gwen and Noah. His face, hands, and shirt were still spattered with Clayton's blood. "He's a brave man that one," McLeod said. "If there's any kind of cosmic justice, he'll pull through." He paused. "Then again, I wouldn't count on it. Seems to me God has a pretty sick sense of humor these days."

"It's over now," Haldane said quietly.

"We've thought that before, Haldane," McLeod said, rubbing the blood from his hands. He sighed heavily. "No bloody Lady Macbeth jokes, either. I am going to go find a washbasin."

McLeod strode off in search of a bathroom. Gwen and Noah lapsed into a comfortable silence, watching the traffic gather around The Quiet Slumber Motel. Three helicopters had landed on the road. Vans and trucks filled the parking lot and lined the streets. People in every imaginable uniform, from those of state troopers to the full yellow HAZMAT suits.

Gwen shuffled closer to him and put an arm around his waist. She leaned her head against his shoulder. It felt right to Haldane.

After a few moments, she said, "Noah?"

"Yes?"

"He didn't kill me," Gwen said.

"I'm very glad," Noah said, cupping her face with his other hand.

"That's not what I mean," Gwen said. "He looked right at me and just smiled. He could have killed me so easily."

"Maybe he realized there was no point?"

"Yeah, maybe that's it," she said and fell back into silence.

CHAPTER

43

Gwen awoke late the next morning in a pool of sweat but pleased to discover she was in the comfort of her own bed and not strapped to a cot as she had just dreamed. She felt so achy. She wondered if it was a consequence of the drugs Sabri had given her or just the accumulation of the wear and tear on her body from Somalia to Maryland.

She reached for the bedside phone and hit redial.

"Maryland Trauma Center," the operator said.

When Gwen explained who she was, she was patched through to the ICU where the nurse told her that Clayton was still in critical condition but had "squeaked through" surgery and showed early signs of stabilizing.

Relieved, she hung up the phone but still felt too exhausted to climb out of bed. She couldn't shake the vision of Abdul Sabri's malicious smile. She had a strange feeling, what she imagined might be a form of survivor's guilt, about having had her life spared by him. She couldn't shake the doubt that Sabri was capable of a final generous gesture.

With images of Sabri and collapsing buildings weighing on her mind, she fell back on the pillow and drifted off again.

The ringing phone woke her. Without answering, she turned her head to look at the clock, which read 2:24 P.M. She didn't feel any better for the sleep. And she was beginning to wonder if she still had residual amounts of thiopental sodium or some other drug in her bloodstream.

About five minutes later, the phone rang again. When she lifted her arm to grab the phone, it felt as if there were a dumbbell tied to it. She groped around the nightstand until she found the receiver.

As she dragged the phone to her ear, everything became clearer to her.

"Hi," Noah said. "How are you?"

"Sore," she said distractedly as she wrapped the blankets tighter around her to ward off her sudden coldness. "You?"

"Good." He laughed. "Enjoying my first day off in about two months."

"Slacker," she said, but didn't feel any of the levity she forced into her tone.

"You hear about Alex?"

"I called the hospital earlier," she said. "Any new developments?"

"He's stabilizing," Haldane said cheerfully. "They think he has a good shot."

"Thank God," Gwen said.

"Hey, the FBI hit the motherlode in Sabri's cabin," he said. "They had vials of serum in a small incubator. They also had chicken eggs, very likely inoculated with the Gansu virus."

"No surprise," she said.

"There's more," Haldane said. "Sabri had all kinds of

maps of New York. Two of them had Times Square circled in red. And the FBI found a list of contact e-mails and cell numbers. They've already made twelve arrests—four in Seattle and the rest in New York."

"Good," she said. She tried to share his enthusiasm, but she felt more tired than ever before.

"Gwen," Haldane said softly. "I think it really is over."

"Let's hope." She coughed and then cleared her throat.

"You okay?"

"I'm just getting too old for falling buildings and hostage takings," she said.

"Why don't I come take you out for a late celebratory lunch?" Haldane asked. "That way we don't have to stay up for a New Year's Eve bash."

"I'm not much of a New Year's girl," she said. "Besides, Noah, I'm too drained to go out."

"Tell you what," Haldane said. "I'll bring you lunch. No strings attached."

She swallowed and her throat felt raw. "People never mean it when they say that," Gwen said.

He laughed. "True. There are tons of strings attached. But why don't you let me bring you lunch anyway."

"No, Noah," she said. "I need to take a rain check. I've got weeks of sleep to catch up on."

"Fair enough," he said, with a trace of disappointment. "I'll speak to you tomorrow."

She put the phone back on the nightstand, but deliberately left it off the hook. Despite her wobbly legs and aching lower back, she forced herself out of bed.

She closed all her windows and blinds. Then she locked both deadbolts on her door. When she managed to catch her wind, she stumbled back to the bedroom.

Two days after the shootout in Maryland, the first day of the New Year, Haldane sat at his office in the early afternoon sorting through a huge stack of accumulated paperwork. He had difficulty concentrating on the work; he kept wondering why Gwen hadn't returned his calls. What had changed between them?

McLeod flew through his door and interrupted the ruminations. "Don't tell me," McLeod said, pointing to the pile. "A model of Mt. Fuji, right?"

"Feels like it," Haldane sighed. "What can I do for you, Duncan?"

He looked over his shoulder. "For starters, you could get me a coffee," he bellowed.

Haldane's secretary, Karen Jackson, yelled from outside the room. "I saw two feet on you. Go get your own damn coffee!"

McLeod laughed. "I like that one." He thumbed over his shoulder and smiled. "Hey, I visited James Bond this morning in Baltimore."

"And?"

"Clayton is doing better." Haldane nodded. "He's awake. Fortunately, he's still on the ventilator, so I got to do all the talking."

Haldane leaned back in his seat and laughed. "I'm sure he appreciated that."

"I think so." McLeod nodded earnestly. "He seemed to particularly enjoy our conversation on what a better place the world would be without the CIA."

Haldane shook his head. "Duncan, you're a cruel man."

McLeod stopped smiling. "By the way, I've come to tell you I'm leaving."

"About time," Haldane said. "You're going back to Glasgow for a while?"

"Not for a while," McLeod said. "For good. I'm leaving the WHO. I'm going to take up some lazy-ass hospital post in Scotland. Time to get back on a first-name basis with my family."

Haldane nodded. "No point in me trying to talk you out of it?"

"Not unless you still have that gun Clayton gave you," McLeod said.

Haldane shook his head.

"By the way, I wanted to say good-bye to Gwen, too, but I haven't been able to reach her."

"Me, neither," Haldane said, feeling the niggling worry resurface. "I spoke to her yesterday. She seemed somewhat evasive. She said she was really run-down. Totally understandable, but I thought . . . you know . . . it might have something to do with Clayton and me."

"Ah, love triangles are a mysterious and wonderful thing, aren't they?" McLeod heaved an exaggerated sigh.

Haldane nodded distractedly.

"I even tried the Department of Homeland Security," McLeod said. "She hasn't been to work since coming home either. Apparently, she even stood up her boss this morning for some meeting."

"That's kind of odd," Haldane said, feeling a different kind of concern swell.

"I guess she was traumatized by what happened with Sabri and all." McLeod shrugged. "Maybe she just wants to lock herself away for a while."

The phrase "lock herself away" resonated inside Noah. He rose from his chair. "Duncan, you don't think . . ." He left it unfinished.

McLeod looked up at him with a puzzled frown. "Think what?"

"When I spoke to her yesterday, she was still in bed and it was after 2:00 P.M.," Haldane said as much to himself as McLeod. "She said she was feeling really run-down." He pointed his finger at McLeod. "And Duncan she coughed once, too!"

Both McLeod's eyebrows shot up. "Oh, Christ, Haldane, she wouldn't!"

"She would if she thought she was protecting the world."

Haldane stood outside the condominium, watching the paramedic smash through the door with a portable battering ram.

As soon as the hinges gave way and the door burst open, Haldane, McLeod, and the four paramedics all stormed inside. Haldane ran as fast as his HAZMAT suit would allow toward the master bedroom.

He rushed into the room, but he didn't see Gwen in the bed. The covers were pulled back and lay in a tangled heap at the foot of the bed. A box of Kleenex sat perched on the pillow. Empty wadded tissues were scattered over the sheets. Some were bloody.

Through the plastic face shield of his hood, he scanned the room checking the other side of the bed and even sifting through the blankets.

"Over here!" one of the paramedics called out. "In the bathroom."

Haldane pivoted and ran into the bathroom across the corridor. He had to shove his way between the paramedics, made even bulkier by their biohazard suits, to get to her.

She lay collapsed by the bathtub.

Her color was gray. Her hair was matted in clumps. She wore off-white pajamas that had bloodstains on the tops. At first Haldane couldn't tell if she was alive or dead, but then she coughed with a horrible, harsh rattling sound and her whole body shook.

When he took a closer look at the hand tucked underneath her, he realized it clutched a familiar pill bottle but it was empty.

That's when he noticed Isaac Moskor's little yellow pills had scattered all over the bathroom floor around her.

CHAPTER

44

In his blue rubber biohazard suit, Haldane sat by the bed in the ICU negative-air-pressure isolation room hoping to see some sign of life from Gwen. He had spent most of the past ninety-six hours in the same spot. Much of the time, he struggled to stave off the mental comparisons between this vigil and the previous time in Singapore, sitting at Franco Bertulli's bedside watching him die.

Haldane was particularly anxious this afternoon. The doctors had only weaned Gwen off the life support of the ventilator two hours earlier, but she had yet to wake up through her heavy sedation.

Noah studied Gwen. In a hospital gown with two IVs and an oxygen mask, she looked frail; she carried little fat before the illness, but now the outlines of her hip bones pushed through the sheets. Still, compared to the near corpse they had found on the floor of her bathroom, her improvement in four days had been monumental.

Gwen's eyes began to blink and she slowly rotated her head, first away from Noah and then toward him. As his joy and relief mounted, he couldn't keep the huge smile off his face.

She raised her right hand to him and he took it in his latex-gloved hand and gave it a squeeze. "Welcome back," he said.

"Good to be back," she croaked from having had a tube passed through her vocal cords. She smiled weakly.

With his other hand, Noah shook a finger at her. "Don't you ever pull a stunt like that again!"

"I get that a lot these days." She chuckled. The laugh gave way to a small coughing spell, but it paled in comparison to episodes when they first found her.

"Thank you," she said. "You saved my life. Again."

"No." Haldane shook his head. "You have your friend Isaac Moskor to thank for that."

Gwen's eyes went wide. "His drug?"

Haldane nodded. "When we made the decision to give it to you, there was nothing left to lose." He swallowed away the lump. "We were convinced you weren't going to make it. But once you were started on A36112 . . . wow, what a difference!"

"Where did you get it?" she asked.

"Luckily, we kept all the pills you had spilt on your bathroom floor." Noah smiled. "But as soon as Isaac heard what happened, he flew straight up to Washington himself with a suitcase full of the drug including the IV stuff which you were given."

"And no hepatitis?" She frowned.

"Your blood tests are good so far." Haldane reassured her with a squeeze of her hand.

She nodded. "Remind me to send Isaac a card." She smiled, before yawning.

Haldane leaned forward and ran his other hand over Gwen's brow. "Why, Gwen? Why did you do it?"

"It was so stupid," she said, flushing with embarrassment.

Haldane refused to let it go. "Tell me, please."

"The day after I was freed from the motel, I began to feel so achy and unwell. I just assumed it was some drug Sabri had given me." Gwen paused and took a few deeper breaths of her oxygen. "But when the chills came and I started to cough . . . I knew." Another deep breath. "Obviously, I wasn't thinking straight anymore."

"But . . ." Haldane's hand rested against her head.

She looked away. "I thought if I went into hospital, something might happen."

"Like what?"

"What if the paramedics who found me got sick? Or what if someone poked a finger with a dirty needle? Or what if my mask was faulty and leaked?" Her voice cracked. "I was just so sick of all the sickness this virus had caused. One way or another, I wanted the virus to die with me. No one else." Tears welled in her eyes. "I'm sorry."

"Don't be. You were just being selfless." He smiled and winked. "Once a Bug Czar always a Bug Czar, right?"

She shrugged and wiped away the rest of her tears.

Noah squeezed her hand tightly. "Want to hear the best part?"

She nodded.

"The Gansu Flu virus did die in you," he said.

"Good," she said softly, and then yawned.

"There was only one other potential carrier to worry about, anyway," Haldane said.

"Sabri?"

"Yeah, but his postmortem blood tests showed that the infection was early. He wouldn't have been contagious for another day," Haldane said. "He probably infected himself at the same time as he did you. That way his contagiousness would peak the next day for New Year's Eve at Times Square."

Gwen exhaled heavily. "So that's why he smiled at me and 'spared' my life back in the motel."

"He thought you were going to be his Trojan horse," Haldane said. "At the very least, it was his way of getting in one final shot at us."

She nodded and yawned again. "How's Alex?"

"Doing well," Haldane said. "He might even beat you out of hospital."

"Not if I can help it. I should be home by tomorrow," she said, but her eyelids drooped with exhaustion.

"Gwen," Haldane asked. "When you do get out, do you have any time off?"

"I probably qualify for some sick time," she murmured. "Why?"

"I get Chloe every second week," Haldane said. "So between times, I thought it might be a nice chance to get away somewhere."

"Hmmm," she agreed, though her eyes had closed completely shut.

"Maybe somewhere warm," Haldane said, thinking he was just talking to himself. "It would be nice for us to get away."

"Nice and warm," she mumbled, dreamily. "And no bugs or terrorists."

Haldane laughed. "That's an absolute must!"

Holding her hand, he watched her drift into a deep slumber. Staring at her sleeping form, Haldane realized that he felt something that he hadn't experienced in a very long time.

Peace.

"You've always claimed that no man could replace Richard in your life."

"No man could," Polly agreed.

"Not in your life, then, but perhaps it's a different matter when it comes to your bed."

Polly stared at him.

He continued. "If I'd known, I might have done this much sooner...." His mouth came down on her own with a determination that made her whole body start to tremble.

"Kiss me properly," Marcus demanded rawly against her lips.

"Marcus," she started to protest, but the moment her lips parted his were covering them, devouring them...devouring her.

And the resistance drained out of her body.

PENNY JORDAN has been writing for almost twenty years and has an outstanding record— over one hundred novels published, including *Power Play*, which hit the *New York Times* bestseller list, and more recently the phenomenally successful *To Love, Honor and Betray*. With over 60 million copies of her books in print worldwide and translations in more than seventeen languages, Penny Jordan has established herself as an internationally acclaimed author. She was born in Preston, in Lancashire, England, and now lives with her husband in a beautiful fourteenth-century house in rural Cheshire.

Books by Penny Jordan

Penny Jordan

THE ULTIMATE SURRENDER

HARLEQUIN®

TORONTO • NEW YORK • LONDON
AMSTERDAM • PARIS • SYDNEY • HAMBURG
STOCKHOLM • ATHENS • TOKYO • MILAN • MADRID
PRAGUE • WARSAW • BUDAPEST • AUCKLAND

ISBN 0-373-12189-X

THE ULTIMATE SURRENDER

First North American Publication 2001.

This edition published by arrangement with Harlequin Books S.A.

® and TM are trademarks of the publisher. Trademarks indicated with
® are registered in the United States Patent and Trademark Office, the
Canadian Trade Marks Office and in other countries.

Visit us at www.eHarlequin.com

Printed in U.S.A.

CHAPTER ONE

'HI, MA, guess what? I think I've found the perfect woman for Uncle Marcus. Her name's Suzi Howell. We met her when Chris and I were having dinner with his parents. Suzi's mother is Chris's godmother, and she's gorgeous; tall, blonde—you know, that stylish, elegant type that Marcus always goes for. *And* she's the right age—late twenties—*and* she knows all about the hotel trade because she works for some super-exclusive American outfit in the Caribbean, and—'

'Briony...' Polly Fraser's muffled voice interrupted her daughter's eulogy as Polly emerged from the deep recess of the kitchen cupboard she had been cleaning out.

Why was it one's offspring always chose the most inauspicious of moments to make such announcements? Polly wondered as she gingerly extricated herself from the cupboard and put its contents on the worktop which she was kneeling with one leg whilst standing on her step-ladder with the other.

'You're going to love her; she's just *so* perfect for Uncle Marcus,' Briony continued to enthuse, adding warningly, 'Watch out, Mum,' as she deftly caught the jar of home-made plum jam which Polly had dislodged as she hurriedly stepped down from the worktop.

'Mmm,' Briony remarked, 'my favourite. May I take this back to college with me? Bought stuff just doesn't taste the same.'

'No, it doesn't, does it?' Polly agreed, smartly repossessing the jar and ignoring her daughter's injured expression. 'You know the rules,' she reminded her firmly. 'The customers come first. Which reminds me, if you want to earn a little bit of extra money whilst you're at home that blackberry and apple jelly I made last year from that new recipe has gone down very well...'

'Mum...' Briony protested. 'Can you just stop thinking about the hotel and the guests for five minutes and listen to what I'm trying to tell you?'

Penitently Polly got down properly from her perch and allowed her daughter to lead her towards the kitchen table.

She had been just eighteen herself—Briony's age—when she had met and fallen in love with Richard Fraser. At twenty-two, four years her senior, he had swept her off her feet.

They had met when he had called at the solicitor's offices where she'd worked, following the death of his grandfather, General Leo Fraser, who had left jointly to both his grandsons the large Georgian house which had been in the family for several generations but which neither of his sons, both army men themselves, nor their wives, had wanted to take on.

It had been left to Richard to deal with most of the more mundane aspects of the formalities connected with the will since Marcus had at the time been working abroad for a large multinational oil company, and although Polly had heard a good deal about his slightly older cousin from Richard it had not been until after their own wedding, a breathtaking three months after they had met, that she had actually seen Marcus in person for the first time. Even now, all these years later, she could recall the shock that coming face to face with him had given her. Richard, her own husband, had been good-looking and sweetly charming, with the old-fashioned kind of courtesy that came from a traditional services boarding-school upbringing, but Marcus... To call Marcus merely good-looking was rather like comparing the sweet pleasantness of ordinary milk chocolate to the sophisticated, broodingly rich, dark, addictive flavour of plain.

In other words Marcus was in a class of his own, a man who even now, in his early forties, was just so compellingly male that Polly's mouth still went a little bit dry and her pulse-rate still rose every time he walked into the room. If Richard would have made a classically good-natured and physically attractive hero in the mould of Jane Austen's Mr Bingley, then Marcus could quite definitely have been Mr Darcy—and then some. There was something of a sense of shut-down, controlled male power about Marcus that immediately made one think of a smouldering volcano—a fierce sexual energy which, for Polly, at nineteen and a very, very new and shy bride, had been rather too much for her to contend with.

And it hadn't helped either that in those early days of her marriage Marcus had been so plainly disapproving of her youth and the fact that she and Richard had married so quickly. But, although she had been sensitively aware of Marcus's disapproval of their marriage, Polly had refused to let either him or Richard see it or guess how much it hurt her—for Richard's sake.

Right from the start, when they had met, Polly had sensed how much his older cousin's approval meant to Richard. Both boys had gone to the same school and had grown up more as brothers than cousins—and since Richard was the younger of the two of them, if only by some eighteen months, it was perhaps natural that he should have put Marcus on something of a pedestal.

Because of her own upbringing—she had been orphaned at four and brought up by her father's sister and her husband—Polly had been acutely conscious of not wanting to do anything that might cause a rift between the two cousins. If Marcus's approval was important to her darling, beloved, wonderful Richard, then she was certainly not going to do anything to prejudice it, even if that meant keeping her own unhappiness about the way Marcus was reacting to their marriage to herself.

'For God's sake, Rick, she's nothing but a baby,' she heard Marcus expostulating to her husband when neither of them was aware that she could hear them.

'She's adorable and I love her to bits,' she heard Richard responding happily to his cousin.

Marcus sighed, and she was just able to imagine the tight, reined-in look of irritation that must be on his darkly handsome face. It was hard to believe that someone like Marcus could *ever* understand how it felt to be as deeply in love as she and Richard were with one another.

After their marriage she moved into the small flat that Richard was renting—a tiny place, but with an attic with that all-important north-facing light that artists valued so much. Because Richard was a presently struggling and as yet unknown young artist, who she just knew was one day going to be so famous…and rich…

Right then they were just about managing on the small allowance Richard got from his parents plus the little bits of money he earned from commissions—mostly from his parents' friends. And then, of course, there was the money she earned as a secretary. It wasn't a lot but it was enough...just...and when Richard and Marcus sold Fraser House...

And then it happened...an accident...a trick of fate. During the late wedding gift Marcus had given them— a weekend stay in a very, very luxurious country house hotel—either because the shellfish had not been quite as fresh as they should have been or she had imbibed too much champagne, or both, there was a night when Polly was violently ill. Richard was so generously sweet and loving in the way he looked after her—and soon after she was feeling well again...

But a short time later she totally disgraced herself by dashing into the tiny bathroom of their flat, right past Marcus, who had called to see Richard about the problems they were having in finding a buyer for Fraser House, and it was *Marcus* who first pinpointed the potential cause of her malaise by announcing to Richard in sharp tones of condemnation, 'My God, Rick, if she's *pregnant...*'

'Pregnant...'

As the tears of nausea and shock filled her eyes Polly started to shake with anxiety.

What would they do if Marcus was right? She and Richard couldn't afford a baby. They could barely afford to support themselves.

She was scarcely able to touch a mouthful of the special meal she had prepared for Marcus—trying out ambitious new recipes was her hobby. Her aunt was a good cook, and with neither of her own daughters remotely interested in learning her culinary skills she had concentrated on passing them on to her eagerly interested niece.

Naively, perhaps, Polly had never considered the possibility of becoming pregnant—at least not so soon.

Whilst she was in the kitchen she could hear the two

men talking together, their voices carrying to where she was working.

'For God's sake, Rick,' she heard Marcus demanding sharply, 'what the hell were you thinking about? She's little more than a baby herself...'

'I *wasn't* thinking... You don't when you're in love,' she heard Richard responding simply.

'In love!' Marcus almost snarled. 'You might be *that* but I doubt that either of you knows what *real* love is all about.'

He left shortly afterwards, ignoring the cheek she timidly offered him to kiss, his shark-grey eyes almost black with the intensity of his anger.

'I don't think that Marcus likes me very much,' she forced herself to confess to Richard a little later. They were sitting on their small shabby sofa and Richard was trying to playfully spoon-feed her what was left of the rich chestnut roulade she had served the men for their pudding. Just the smell of it turned her stomach, never mind what the taste would do, but at this stage she was still reluctant to confront the truth.

'Of course he likes you,' Richard told her heartily— too heartily, perhaps, as he avoided looking at her. 'In fact he probably wishes he'd met you first,' he added, before admitting, 'Not that you're really his type...'

'Oh? What kind of girl is?' Polly asked him, more to stop herself focusing on how very queasy she felt than out of any real interest.

'Oh, sort of sophisticated and tall, the kind of girl who looks as though she knows what life's all about, if you know what I mean.'

Polly did, and the kind of girl Richard had just described was as different from the way she was herself as it was possible to be. For a start she was short rather than tall—barely five foot two—and her hair was a soft mousy-brown rather than blonde; and as for knowing what life was all about...

A month later, when it was impossible for her to ignore the fact that Marcus's angry guess had been right and that she was pregnant, Richard walked into the flat to find her in tears and desperately worried about their future.

'Don't worry,' he consoled her as he took her in his arms and held her tight. 'We'll manage...somehow...'

Of course she immediately felt better, comforted by his insouciance and his confidence. Richard had such a warm, sunny nature that it was impossible not to feel buoyed up and infected by his natural optimism and his belief that something would 'turn up'.

A commission for a portrait via Marcus, together with a generous Christmas cheque from Richard's parents, who were living in Cyprus where Richard's father was stationed, helped them to repay the overdraft which had somehow or other built up to alarming proportions despite Polly's excellently thrifty housekeeping. But the flat was damp and cold, and in the new year Richard caught flu, and then Polly caught it from him and was unable to work. The office sent a letter round suggesting that since she would be leaving work anyway when her baby was born it might be as well if she didn't return but concentrated on looking after her health. The letter arrived on a raw, miserable February day when Polly was seven months pregnant and the last of the Christmas money had just been used to pay their rent.

The small sitting room of the flat was crammed with things she had bought for the coming baby—all of them second-hand—including the cot that Richard was cleverly repainting. Polly was sitting there on the threadbare carpeted floor, large round tears running down her face and dripping onto her large round tummy, when the door opened and Marcus walked in unannounced.

In her undignified haste to get up Polly caught her foot in the carpet and pitched forward, giving a sharp cry of protest and fear, quickly smothered against the unexpected warmth of Marcus's expensive cashmere jacket as he caught hold of her, impeding her fall. For a moment, as she stood within the protective circle of his arms her face buried in his jacket, breathing in the raw male scent of him, Polly had the most peculiar and bemusing sense of somehow coming home; of being safe and protected.

It was gone in a second, quickly dismissed by her realisation of just how alien and idiotic her reaction was. She had never felt really comfortable with Marcus, still less as her pregnancy advanced, and she felt sure she could see in his eyes his disapproval of the way their marriage and her pregnancy had taken over Richard's life, forcing onto him responsibilities which did not allow him full exercise of his artistic talents. So how on earth could she possibly have experienced what she *had* experienced? It was her imagination—a *hallucination*—an odd side-effect of being pregnant and poorly. And then Marcus was releasing her, turning his back on her, his face set and unreadable as he headed for the attic and Richard.

It was less than a week later when Richard burst into the flat, full of excitement to tell her of the 'terrific idea' that Marcus had had. He picked her up and whirled her round in his arms despite the bulk of her pregnancy, until she was so dizzy she had to beg him to stop.

'What idea?' she asked him.

'Instead of selling Fraser House Marcus says that we should keep it...'

'But we need the money from it,' Polly protested anxiously. One thing she had learned about her husband was that he was something of a dreamer, prone to wonderful ideas that he painted for her in all the rich colours of his imagination; but, strong as he was on imagination, Richard was rather weak on practicality, and her heart sank a little as she prepared to listen to him.

'We need money, yes,' Richard agreed. 'But Marcus has come up with this wonderful way for us to make some. You know how he's just got that recent promotion which involves him spending more time here in the UK and entertaining a lot?'

Cautiously Polly nodded. Marcus had recently been made the head of his department, travelling daily to the company's UK offices in the city and returning each evening to the luxurious apartment he retained in the small commuter village where his and Richard's family roots were. And she had learned, through listening to his conversations with Richard, that he spent a lot of time having meetings with his overseas colleagues.

'Well, apparently Marcus's boss has just come back from a prolonged visit to their American parent company in the States and he's told Marcus that over there the trend is for visiting execs and their wives to stay as house guests with their US counterparts. Apparently he's very keen to introduce the same sort of system over here. Marcus would get a special expenses allowance to cover all the costs but, as he was saying to me, it would be virtually impossible for him to provide the standard of hospitality that would be needed as an unmarried man living alone in a service flat. That's when he realised what a perfect solution it would be for all of us...'

'*What* would be?' Polly asked him in bewilderment. The baby had started kicking quite hard and her head was still full of flu, and what she really wanted more than anything else was to go to bed—a nice warm bed in a nice warm bedroom…not the horrid, lumpy, uncomfortable bed she and Richard shared in their cold, damp room.

'What I've just said,' Richard told her. 'What a terrific idea it would be if the three of us moved into Fraser House and you and I…well, *you*, I suppose, really,' he admitted a little ruefully, 'looked after Marcus's colleagues…you know…tidied up their rooms, cooked their meals—*that* sort of thing,' he told her vaguely. 'And Marcus would pay us for doing it. Oh, and of course he'd be living there as well, and I suppose you'd have to cook for him too, although he'd still be away some of the time…'

'Richard…' Polly stopped him faintly.

'What is it? Aren't you feeling well?' he demanded anxiously as soon as he saw how pale and shocked she was looking. 'It isn't the baby, is it? It isn't time yet…'

No, it wasn't the baby, although the shock to her system of what he had just outlined could well have caused her to go into premature labour, Polly reflected a little later on as she tried and failed to find the words to tell him how impossible what Marcus was suggesting was. For one thing she just couldn't see how Marcus—immaculate, lordly, impatient Marcus—was *ever* going to be able to live side by side with a small baby…never mind side by side with *her*.

Then, during the night, the ceiling above their bedroom fell in, sending plaster and water cascading everywhere causing Richard to say worriedly that there was no way they could continue to live where they were,

especially since he was having to leave in the morning
to spend the next ten days working on a private commission for his father's regiment. He had been asked to
paint the regiment's mascot—an elderly goat which was
'stationed' at regimental headquarters near Aldershot.

While Polly still wandering round the flat in a daze,
trying to remove bits of fallen plaster from her carefully
washed and ironed inherited baby things, Richard was
on the telephone to Marcus. Marcus arrived shortly after
surveying both the flat and Polly in grim silence before
announcing that the place was totally unfit for anyone to
live in, never mind a pregnant child.

'I am *not* a child,' Polly retorted, flinching as though
he had struck her, reminding him through gritted teeth,
'I am nineteen years old.'

'Like I said…a *child*,' Marcus returned scathingly, before he instructed, 'No, leave those and just go and get
in the car.'

Much as she longed to object to his high-handedness,
Polly thought better of it, which was how she found
herself somehow or other installed at Fraser House, its
'For Sale' sign firmly removed and a team of cleaners
produced from out of nowhere to attack the neglect of
the months it had been empty.

It was the kitchen which converted Polly to Marcus's
seemingly impossible idea. Large and surprisingly well
equipped, considering the age and solitary lifestyle of
the General, it possessed a deliciously warm range and
a central heating system which produced gallons of
scaldingly hot water—something which had been in very
short supply at the flat. And then, of course, there was
the garden, large enough for an army of children, and
the bedrooms—in need of a fresh coat of paint, perhaps,
but each of them with the most wonderfully sturdy coun-

try-style furniture and enough cupboards and dressing rooms for every single one of them to have its own *en suite* bathroom, which Marcus told her firmly was an absolute necessity for his executives and their wives.

The drawing room was enormous, and so too was the dining room, complete with the custom-made dining table and its twenty-four chairs—it seemed the General had never done anything on a small scale and that included entertaining. There was a small library and a pretty morning room which Marcus told her he could remember had been his grandmother's own special domain, and then another sitting room, cellars and an upper storey as well as the attics.

When Marcus told her how much his board were prepared to pay per executive couple per visit, Polly felt faint with shock.

'So much,' she faltered, round-eyed.

'You'll have to feed them for that,' Marcus warned her tersely. 'And proper food, Polly; these people are used to dining at the very best restaurants and they'll expect the same standard here. Not that that will be any problem for you, I know,' he added, totally flooring her both with the unexpectedness of the compliment and his casual acceptance that her cooking skills could rival those of the country's best chefs.

'I...' Polly had begun to feel quite faint. 'I...' she began again. Marcus had been walking ahead of her across the large hallway, which already in her mind's eye Polly could see freshly decorated with a huge bowl of freshly cut flowers on the wooden chest next to her to welcome their visitors. The decorating she knew could be safely left to Richard, who, most unusually for an artist, had no inhibitions or prejudices about turning his hand to such work. The mural he had painted for the

tiny cupboard at the flat which had been going to be the
baby's room had taken her breath away with its delicacy
and imagery.

'Yes, Richard would... Oh-h-h...' The sharpness of
the pain she felt made her catch her breath and stop in
mid-step, her eyes going wide with apprehension and
dread.

'What is it?' Marcus demanded sharply.

'Nothing,' she fibbed, praying that she was right and
that the ominous penetrating pain that was ebbing and
flowing with increasing strength and increasing frequency was simply the false alarm she had learned so
much about at her antenatal classes. It was far too early
for the baby yet. She still had nearly a full month to
go...

And so, reassuring herself, she forced herself to walk
as steadily as she could to Marcus's side, and made to
climb the stairs so that they could inspect the bedrooms
together and decide which ones should be allocated as
guest bedrooms.

It had already tacitly been decided that Marcus would
have the large bedroom which had been their grandfather's, mainly because the bathroom and small sitting
room which went with it meant that he could be reason-
ably self-contained there. Tactfully, Polly had chosen for
them two rooms as far away from him as possible, not
just to maintain their own privacy but also to make sure
that Marcus wasn't disturbed by the baby.

In her heart of hearts she knew the last thing she
wanted was to live in the same house as Richard's
cousin, no matter how much Richard might enthuse
about the idea. But what choice really did they have?

She winced as another pain caught her, sharper this
time, deeper and lasting a little longer, and this time too

there was no disguising what was happening from
Marcus. As the pain gripped her she automatically held
her breath. She felt sick and dizzy and very, very alone
and afraid, and she longed more than anything else for
Richard, or, failing that, her aunt, but Richard was in
Aldershot painting the regiment's goat's portrait and her
aunt was in South Africa visiting her eldest daughter.

As sweat beaded her forehead and her whole body
was gripped by the necessity to deal with what was happening, Polly had no breath left to protest as Marcus
suddenly swore under his breath and started to urge her
towards the front door.

'No… Where…? What…?' she began, and then
stopped as the pain surged again.

She could hear Marcus responding to her question,
telling her tersely, 'Where the hell do you think?
Hospital, of course. Can you walk to the car, do you
think, or…?'

Only the appalling thought of Marcus actually trying
to carry her to the car got Polly there, and she was sure
that Marcus must have broken every speed limit there
was to get her to the hospital so fast.

By then her contractions were coming so quickly that
there wasn't time for her to do anything other than what
she was told as she was whisked from his car onto a
trolley and into the labour ward.

Two hours later, when Briony Honey Fraser made her
way into the world, Polly opened her eyes to look up
into the eyes of the man whose hand she had been grip-
ping onto for dear life all through her labour, and realised, with a bewildering sense of disbelief, that it wasn't
Richard but Marcus. But before she could say anything
exhaustion swept over her, and when she eventually
woke up to find her adorable new daughter tucked into
a little crib at the bottom of her bed and her equally

adorable husband sitting beaming with pride and pleasure at her bedside she told herself that she must have
imagined that Marcus had been there with her during her
labour.

She continued to tell herself until the morning Richard
came to take her and Briony home from the hospital and
commented happily to her, 'What a piece of luck that
Marcus should have been with you when you went into
labour... I've told him that we shall definitely want him
to be Briony's godfather. After all, he was there when
she was born.'

Polly closed her eyes, her skin burning with embarrassed colour. So it hadn't just been a dream...a nightmare more like; Marcus had actually been there with her
all the time. It had been *Marcus* who had wiped the
sweat from her forehead, who had encouraged her to
rest, to push...who had told her in a voice thick with
unfamiliar emotion that she had the most beautiful, gorgeous little baby girl... Marcus, not Richard...

No one would ever know just how relieved she was
to return to Fraser House to find that Marcus was away
on business and that he would be away for almost a
month...time enough for all her disturbing memories
and feelings about the fact that he had been with her
when Briony had been born to subside and be carefully
pushed away into a place where they couldn't cause her
any harm.

But there was one disturbing postscript to what had
happened. By some odd quirk of fate, baby Briony took
one look at her father's cousin and her mother's private
and unacknowledged *bête noire* and openly and determinedly, in that way that only babies could do, declared
her love for him.

It was Marcus she gave her first smile to. It was

Marcus whose name she said first, even if Polly had tried to convince herself that that 'Ma...Mar' had been 'Mama', and Marcus towards whom she took her first faltering steps.

Richard, typically, didn't mind in the least, and in fact was only too pleased that his daughter adored Marcus as much as he did himself, and by the time Briony was three years old even Polly had to admit that Marcus's decision to turn Fraser House into an unofficial very luxurious and comfortable 'home from home' for his visiting executives had worked wonderfully well for all of them.

Polly was in her element in her role as Fraser's chatelaine. Her guests thrived on her warm blend of cosseting and cooking, and Marcus had even remarked dryly to her that his chairman was beginning to complain that he had not, as yet, sampled the delights of a stay at Fraser House, adding that the whole board were unanimous in their decision that this year's official Christmas boardroom dinner should be held there.

As her confidence grew so too did Polly's cooking skills. She devoured new recipe books as eagerly and avidly as her guests devoured her gourmet meals, and as the Christmas preceding Briony's fourth birthday approached Polly was forced to admit that she had never been happier.

Gradually, through his contacts, Richard was getting more work, and he still had dreams of one day being asked to exhibit at the Royal Academy, although privately Polly was beginning to sense that he never would. However, his dreams were precious to him, and she loved him far too much to want to damage them or to hurt him.

The murals he had painted in the house were exciting an enormous number of compliments and bringing in

fresh work, but whilst his portraits were technically excellent Polly was beginning to see that his work lacked
that spark that would have made him great. Still, he was
happy, and if Richard was happy then so was she. But
she often wondered what Marcus, who collected modern
art in a very small but knowledgeable way, *really*
thought of his cousin's talent. She suspected that, like
her, Marcus loved Richard far too much to want to hurt
him.

And then disaster struck. On the way home one night
from working on a commission several miles away,
Richard's car was involved in an accident and Richard
was killed outright. The police brought the news whilst
Polly was tucking Briony up in bed. She was on her
own in the house for once, Marcus being away on business, and she knew what she was going to be told the
moment she opened the door and saw the policeman's
face.

Richard, her beloved, handsome, boyish, loving husband, was dead, and with him too was that special part
of her heart that had belonged exclusively to him.

Marcus had to fly back from Australia for Richard's
funeral, arriving grey-faced and haggard, and not just
from jet lag, Polly knew—just as she knew that he had
never approved of her, and how much he had loved
Richard. But now Richard was gone.

At the funeral her aunt, meaning to be kind, no doubt,
told her firmly, 'Polly, I know this seems like the end
of the world now, but you're young—young enough to
meet someone else and fall in love again.'

'Never,' Polly told her, white-faced and dry-eyed. 'I
shall never, ever love anyone else,' she told her passionately. 'That's impossible. I love Richard far too
much for that and I always will.'

Marcus, who had overheard her gave her an unfathomable look—one which haunted her for a long time after Richard's funeral. Did Marcus, like her aunt, think that she was so shallow, so immature that she *would* forget Richard? If so she was determined to prove him wrong.

CHAPTER TWO

AND that was exactly what Polly *did*, devoting herself to Briony and to her work. So much so that when Briony was seven years old, following a conversation with one of Marcus's colleagues and his wife, who had announced that they were so impressed with the standard of Fraser House's comforts and its cook, they were surprised she didn't consider opening the house as a small, exclusive private country hotel, Polly had taken this idea to Marcus. And, to her surprise, he had agreed.

And so had begun her unexpected career as co-owner and manageress of Fraser House, a small Georgian country house set in its own grounds where the *cognoscenti* could enjoy a true feast of all the senses—or so the restaurant critic who had visited them had proclaimed in the article he had written following his visit.

The years hadn't just brought the addition of an indoor swimming pool and luxury gym area to the hotel's facilities, but a broadening of Polly's cooking skills as well.

Now Fraser House was listed as one of the country's most exclusive small country house hotels, its restaurant ranking with the best of the country's growing stable of to-be-seen-at eateries.

No one as yet might have approached Polly with an invitation to host her own TV cookery series, nor to write a cookery book, but soon after the hotel had opened one of their first clients had asked if it might be possible for their daughter to hold her wedding reception at the house. Then Polly had felt that they had reached a definite landmark.

As joint owner of the house, Marcus had always remained aloof from its day-to-day running, although, to be fair to him, Polly had to admit that he had always been meticulous about giving her whatever assistance and support she had asked for. He was now on the board of his company, one of its youngest directors, and, much to Briony's dismay, had spent nearly two and a half years away from them living in Russia, to help with the newly emergent oil industry there.

More recently he had been spending a considerable amount of time in China, and Briony had already extracted a promise from him that if she graduated with a First he would treat her to a trip to China's Great Wall.

Whilst Richard's death might have deprived Polly of the love and companionship of a husband, Marcus had seen to it that Briony had never lacked the love of a father figure in her life, and Briony adored him in much the same way as Richard had done.

In fact, sometimes Polly felt almost as though the two of them formed a special magic circle from which she, as Briony's mother, was somehow excluded. Because she knew that Marcus had never really liked or approved of her? Because she felt, for some obscure and irrational reason, that in some way Marcus actually blamed her for Richard's death?

Since the beginning of her own first romantic relationship with Chris Johnson, Briony had become increasingly concerned about the fact that her beloved uncle Marcus had no permanent partner to share his life with, and to that end she had been taxing her brain to find someone whom she considered special enough to make him the ideal wife.

Now it seemed, from what she was saying to Polly, she had actually found that someone, and certainly, from the way she was describing her, Suzie Howell did sound as though she was just Marcus's type. Tall, blonde, leggy—the kind of chatelaine who would be perfect for the house Marcus had announced so unexpectedly only six weeks ago that he intended to buy.

'But why? You've always lived *here*,' Polly had protested, white-faced, when he had announced his plans to her. 'This has always been our home. Yours, mine and Briony's.'

'Precisely,' he agreed coolly. 'But Briony is now at college and, as you were saying yourself only a few weeks ago, you are increasingly having to turn away prospective guests. With my rooms to provide two extra bedrooms...'

Polly wasn't able to totally take in what he was saying to her. It had never occurred to her that he might move out of Fraser House.

'I need a home of my own, Polly,' he told her crisply. 'A *life* of my own. And now that Briony is old enough to start making her own life I feel that my duty to her—'

'Your *duty* to her?' She interrupted him, too shocked to be cautious. 'Is *that* why you were living here? Because of *Briony*?'

There was a small, purposeful pause that drove the colour from her face, but it came back again when he told her almost affably, 'Well, of course; you didn't think I was staying for you, did you?'

Staying for *her*? No, of course not! But for him to put into words the enmity she had so often sensed but hoped she had only imagined...

'No. No, I didn't,' she acknowledged in a thick, choked voice. Yet it seemed that with Briony's departure for college both she and Marcus were unanimous in believing that it was time for Marcus to establish a life of his own away from Fraser House. With a wife and family of his own? That was certainly *Briony's* idea...

'Does *Marcus* know that you're planning to marry him off?' she asked her daughter now, as she stood up straight and dusted herself down.

At thirty-seven she still had the same slender, small-boned body she had had at eighteen, although these days it was healthily honed and toned by her three-times-weekly gym workouts, and her once mousy hair was now skilfully highlighted; only the previous week her stylist had finally persuaded her to allow her to chop her smooth, shoulder-length bob into a far more adventurous and modern style which she had insisted was perfect for her.

'Too *young* for you?' she had demanded when Polly had uncertainly raised her doubts. 'Polly, you're thirty-seven, not fifty-seven,' she had scolded her gently. 'Thirty-seven *is* young...'

'Try telling that to Briony,' Polly had commented ruefully. 'She's eighteen, and she won't want a mother who looks as though she's trying to pretend she's her sister.'

'Listen to me,' her stylist had told her firmly. 'There is no way this style is anything other than *absolutely perfect* for you.'

As perfect for her as Briony seemed to think this young woman she had met was perfect for Marcus? This *young* woman. Determinedly Polly reached for a cloth to start wiping out the cupboard she had just emptied.

'Anyway, what I was going to say to you is...' Briony reached to the bowl on the table for an apple—one of their own, which had come from the trees in the small orchard behind the kitchen garden, an old-fashioned

English variety which it was almost impossible to buy anywhere now but which Polly particularly cherished for its unique sweet-tart flavour. You could have a dinner party and invite Suzi to come and then she could get to meet Uncle Marcus and—'

'A *dinner* party!' Polly interrupted her daughter a little explosively. 'Briony, this is a *hotel* and...'

'And it's half term, and you are never busy then,' Briony reminded her. 'And Suzi could recommend you to some of the people she knows and that way you would get more business,' she pointed out craftily. 'After all, when Uncle Marcus goes you're going to have two more rooms to let...'

Polly gave a small sigh. Organising a formal dinner party at short notice was the last thing she felt like doing right now, but, knowing her determined daughter, she suspected that it might be easier to give in now and thus save the time she might otherwise have wasted in trying to reason with her.

Quite where Briony got her determination, her stubbornness from, she wasn't really sure. Richard had had the sweetest nature imaginable and, as Briony and Marcus repeatedly pointed out to her, she had no backbone at all when it came to confrontations.

'I'm not sure that Marcus is going to like this,' she warned Briony. 'You know how he hates being manipulated.'

'Well, yes,' Briony agreed, 'but if I told him that it's a special dinner for me, and that Chris is going to be there...' She made a small face. 'You know how fussy he's always been about the boys I go out with, and he hasn't really had much of a chance to meet Chris yet, since he was away on business when Chris and I first

met and both of us have been away at college ever
since...'

There was a good deal of truth in what her daughter
was saying, Polly had to acknowledge. Whilst Marcus
couldn't exactly be accused of playing the heavy father
with Briony, he certainly was very protective of her.

'So, who exactly am I supposed to be inviting to this
dinner party?' Polly gave in.

Giving her a beaming smile, Briony responded, ticking the names off on her fingers.

'Well, Uncle Marcus of course, and Suzi and her parents. Well, they *are* Chris's godparents,' she reminded
her. 'And Chris *is* staying with them whilst his own parents are away on business. That's four. Oh, and you and
me of course...' She paused and gnawed at her bottom
lip. 'Oh, and I suppose we should really invite Suzi's
boss, otherwise he's going to be left on his own, and—'

'Suzi's boss? Polly interrupted in bemusement. 'But I
thought you said she worked in the Caribbean...'

'Well, yes, she does, but her boss has business interests over here as well, apparently. Anyway it's okay;
you'll like him,' Briony assured her mother sunnily.
'He's younger than you—thirty, Suzi told me—and single. He and Suzi were a bit of an item at one time, but
that's all over now.'

Polly gave her daughter a wry look.

'So that makes eight of us, unless of course there's
anyone else you want me to entertain...'

Briony's forehead pleated consideringly.

'No, I don't think so...' she began.

'No? Not perhaps Chris's great-aunt and uncle, or his
cousin four times removed and her husband?' Polly suggested sweetly.

Briony looked perplexed.

'Chris doesn't have a great-aunt or uncle…' she began earnestly, and then stopped, a rueful smile curling her mouth. 'Okay, so perhaps I *am* being a bit managing,' she agreed. 'But it's in a good cause, Ma,' she wheedled. 'Uncle Marcus *needs* a wife. *You* know that…'

'Do I?' Polly asked her dubiously, adding, 'I don't suppose that it's occurred to you that he might just…just be perfectly capable of remedying his lack of one all by himself? After all, it isn't as though he hasn't had a stream of possible candidates through his life already,' she added a little tartly.

Briony looked at her.

'Do you know, Ma, you almost sound jealous?'

'Jealous of Marcus's women-friends. Certainly not,' Polly declared immediately.

'No, not jealous of *them*,' Briony quickly corrected them. 'No, I meant you sounded jealous of the fact that Uncle Marcus has had someone in his life…'

'Some*one*—you mean *several* someones,' Polly reminded her grimly.

'Oh, come on, you aren't really being fair,' Briony objected. 'There have only been a few, and all of them have lasted for quite a long time. Have you never, *ever* been tempted yourself, *wanted* yourself to…you know…meet someone? I mean, I know how much you loved Dad,' she added hastily. 'Everyone knows that. But there must have been times…' She paused and bit her lip before saying defensively, 'Well, you were only very young when Dad died, and, well, these days it isn't… Women can…'

'If you're asking me if I've ever missed having sex—' Polly stopped her pithily '—then yes, *sometimes* I have, but I've never missed it enough to… I loved your father very much,' she told Briony simply, not wanting to delve too deeply into the exact whys and wherefores of her decision to remain single and celibate.

But then, to her dismay, as though somehow with uncanny and certainly unwanted perception she had actually picked up on her private thoughts, Briony reminded her mischievously, 'I know you're no sexpot—remember the time we celebrated the first year of the hotel being in business and Uncle Marcus gave you that gold bracelet? When he went to put it on for you he started to kiss you, and you backed away from him as though he was the devil incarnate!' She chuckled. 'Poor Uncle Marcus. That must have been the one and only time he got *that* kind of reaction from a woman...'

Remember it...? Somehow or other Polly managed to force her lips into some semblance of a smile, at the same time ducking her head as she made a totally uncoordinated swipe at the interior of the cupboard she had emptied. Of *course* she remembered. But she hadn't imagined that Briony would have done so. After all, she had been very much a child at the time—far too young to have noticed...registered...

'When were you thinking of holding this dinner party?' she asked her daughter huskily.

'Well, it's Wednesday today. How about Friday evening?' Briony suggested. 'You're never very busy at half term, as you've always said this is the kind of place grown-ups come to relax, not to bring their children, and since Chris and I will be going back to college on Monday...'

'Friday it is, then,' Polly agreed hollowly.

'Great. I'll go and give Chris a ring so that he can organise things at his end. What time shall I tell him? Seven-thirty for eight?'

'Yes, fine,' Polly agreed.

As she watched her daughter slide her long legs off the table and hurry to the kitchen door, it wasn't Friday evening's proposed dinner party that was causing her to frown anxiously but the memories which Briony's innocent comment had provoked.

She still had that gold bangle Marcus had given her. He had brought it home with him from the Middle East and the gold was heavy and of extremely fine quality, set with a sprinkling of exquisitely fine small diamonds. It was the kind of gift any woman would have been delighted to receive and to wear, but she had never done so. If she should be foolish enough right now to close her eyes and let her thoughts go back to that warm late spring evening she knew she would almost be able to smell the scent of the freshly mown grass coming in through the open French windows of the small sitting room which Marcus had insisted she retain for her and Briony's own personal use.

'I don't need my own sitting room,' she had protested when their plans for the reorganisation of the house had still been at the drafting stage.

'Maybe you don't, but Briony most certainly does,' Marcus had insisted. 'Fraser House is her home, Polly, and she needs to be able to grow up feeling that it is a proper home. It's what Richard would have wanted,' he had told her firmly, when she had been about to demur. And of course she had given in, and had been glad that she had done so in later years when she had recognised that he had been right to pinpoint Briony's need to feel that at least a small piece of the house and her mother were hers exclusively.

'Oh, Marcus,' she had protested as she'd unwrapped the small gift box she'd held in her hand. 'What...?'

'It's to celebrate our first year in business together,' he had told her coolly.

He had only arrived back in the early hours of that morning. She hadn't seen him arrive since she had been in bed, but she had heard the taxi drawing up outside and then this evening he had come down. All day she had been a little on edge wondering when he would put in an appearance, and then there he was, looking impossibly brown and male, dressed in a white tee shirt that positively hugged his broad male torso and a pair of faded jeans which...

Hastily she had averted her eyes as she'd realised, to her own chagrin and confusion, that for some reason her body was actually responding to the sight of his maleness.

Fortunately Marcus had been too busy hugging Briony to notice what was happening to her but, nonetheless, as her daughter had chattered excitedly to her favourite relative—bar none—Polly had instinctively and defensively wrapped her arms around her own upper body to make sure that Marcus neither saw nor misinterpreted the totally inappropriate provocative little thrust of her hardening nipples against the soft fabric of her top. And then he had given her the pretty gift-wrapped package— after he had given Briony an even smaller one, which had turned out to be exactly the right kind of delicate little gold locket for a young girl of her age.

Who had chosen their gifts for him? she had wondered a little sharply. A woman... And then, as she had thanked him for them, stumbling a little over the words, he had taken hold of her, his hands cupping the delicate balls of her shoulder joints and frowning a little as he explored them, before saying almost accusingly, 'You've lost weight.'

'No, I haven't,' she denied, before admitting as she saw the look in his eyes, 'Well, just a little. I've been so busy, there just hasn't—'

'Mummy gets too busy to eat,' Briony informed him trenchantly, much to her dismay.

'No, that isn't true,' she began, as she turned her head from looking at her daughter to look at him, and then stopped when she realised that he was much, much closer to her than she had imagined. So close, in fact, that his mouth was just near enough...

She tensed and gulped, and then, finding that she couldn't breathe in enough air to her oxygen-starved lungs, she opened her mouth, and Marcus somehow or other totally misinterpreted what that meant. To her shock, he lowered his head, covering her mouth with the warm, firm pressure of his own.

Richard, as a husband and lover, had been tender and gentle, so that sex for Polly had been a happy joyful experience—playful loving in the warm shallows of intimacy and romance, during which she had never once felt unsafe or out of her depth. But instinctively she knew, had always known, that Marcus was not like her husband, that there was to him a much darker and far more passionate maleness.

Sex with Marcus would *not* be conducted in the shallows. No. It would be conducted in the deepest depths, all she would have to cling to if those waters threatened to submerge and overwhelm her would be Marcus himself. As a wife, and then a widow, Polly had deliberately closed her mind to Marcus's sexuality, refusing to admit even to herself that it was there or that she was aware of it; but, as his mouth covered hers, she was suddenly made very potently aware of it—and of him.

She panicked, jerking her head back from his and raising her hands to ward him off.

Just for a second before he released her, Marcus had looked right into her eyes. His own were almost black, obsidian, with an anger he wasn't bothering to conceal, his mouth—the same mouth which had just burned hers—twisting into a dismissive grimace.

'You're a woman now, not a girl, Polly,' she heard him telling her angrily. 'Richard is dead and—'

'I don't care.' She interrupted him wildly, her heart beating in frantic, nervous little thuds as though she was in fear of her life and fleeing from some terrible threatening danger. 'To me he is still my husband and he *always* will be.'

'Such noble sentiments,' Marcus scoffed, 'and so very naive. Richard may have been your *husband*, Polly, but I suspect he never really awakened you as a *lover*, because if he had—'

'How *dare* you?' she almost screamed at him, backing away from him like a threatened hind fearing the approach of the hunter. 'Of course Richard was my lover. How else do you think that Briony…?'

She stopped, almost choking on her own tears, suddenly realising that Briony could see and hear everything they were saying to one another.

'He was your husband, yes, and you conceived his child, yes, but that was a long time ago and in many ways Richard was only a boy,' Marcus agreed flatly, before continuing in a soft, almost mesmeric voice, 'But look at you now; you're trembling like a virgin confronted with her first experience of an adult man and all because I kissed you. Is that how a woman who has experienced a lover's—a *man's*—passion would react?'

He started to shake his head but Polly wasn't prepared

to listen to any more. Reaching out protectively to draw Briony closer to her, she told him shakily, 'You have no right to say such things to me. I loved, still love, always *will* love Richard more than someone like you could possibly understand.'

The look he gave her before he walked past her and out of the room lived with her for a long time afterwards, long after Marcus himself had left again on his travels.

Well, at least Briony had been right about one thing, Polly reflected a couple of hours later, her kitchen cupboards restored to their normal immaculate order: the hotel was relatively quiet at the moment. Not that she minded. They had a very busy season coming up, with Christmas to contend with. They had guests who regularly booked themselves into Fraser House for Christmas and the New Year, and if the conversion of Marcus's room was finished in time for the Christmas season they had a respectably long list of guests already for their occupancy. Christmas at Fraser House was, Polly acknowledged with her customary modesty, something a little bit special.

Yes, she was glad that Marcus had decided to give up his rooms here, she told herself firmly as she glanced round her now immaculate kitchen, and not just because of the extra guests it would allow them to have. The architect they had hired had made the suggestion that the stable block could perhaps be renovated and extended to provide even more rooms, but for once Polly had demurred, explaining that she felt it would detract from the hotel's unique 'feel' if they expanded too much. A little to her surprise, Marcus had actually endorsed her opinion. She hadn't as yet been to see the house he had bought nearby, although Briony had, returning to tell her mother enthusiastically that it was 'ace'.

Built in the early days of Victoria's reign it had originally been a part of the Fraser estate, built to house the widowed mother of the then owner.

Whilst not a dower house in the traditional sense of the word—Fraser House was not a great house in the style of Chatsworth and its ilk—it had been built in a similar if later style to that of the main house and was less than a mile away from it. After the end of the First World War the family had sold off the house, but now the opportunity had arisen for Marcus to buy it back along with the small acreage of land which had been sold with it.

In some ways Polly quite envied him the opportunity to bring the pretty ivy-clad house back to life again—its last owner had been elderly and after her death the house had been left empty for some time whilst her executors decided what to do with it.

Its five bedrooms and spacious ground floor meant that it would make an ideal family house. Was Marcus perhaps thinking of settling down at long last? At forty-two he was very visibly in the prime of his life. His career and financial future were assured, his physical appearance such that no right-thinking, intelligent, heterosexual woman would hesitate to snatch him up as potential-mate material and father to her unborn children. The current scientific evidence was that a woman naturally and instinctively chose the strongest and best-looking mate she could find in order to secure the best genes possible and thus the best chance of survival for her offspring. And no doubt Marcus would be similarly influenced when he chose the woman he wanted to marry. She would be young, intelligent and, of course, stunningly beautiful. According to Briony, her candidate filled all of those requirements.

Lost in thought, Polly made her way slowly to what had always been her favourite spot in the house's grounds— a small dell surrounded by mature trees and with its own natural pond. It was off limits to their guests and could only be reached by a narrow private footpath. It was a spot that Richard had loved, and his last gift to her before his death had been a painting of it done in the spring when the bluebells were out. Now it was autumn and the trees were shedding their leaves, giving the small, enclosed space a haunting, almost melancholy air that was so much in tune with her own mood that Polly could feel her always easily aroused emotions bringing unwanted tears to her eyes.

She had brought so many of her problems and her heartaches, large and small to this spot over the years, but none had come anywhere near the magnitude of the agonising despair she was suffering now.

So much in her life was changing… Briony had already left home and was quickly becoming an adult and no longer in need of her in the way she had once been. Her staff were so well trained that sometimes she felt almost as though they didn't need her either. And then there was Marcus…

Marcus…

She closed her eyes and leaned against the thick trunk of one of the trees.

Of course she had always known that one day Marcus would get married.

Hadn't she?

That he would meet someone…fall in love with them…

'Polly.'

Her eyelids swept up in shock, revealing the tears dampening her eyes as she stared in mute distress at the man who had been the focus of her thoughts.

'What are you doing out here without a coat?' she could hear him demanding disapprovingly. He, of course, *was* wearing a coat—or rather a jacket…the soft, well-worn leather one that she and Briony had bought him together one year for his birthday.

'Marcus,' she croaked when she had managed to find her voice, and then shivered, idiotically justifying his sharp criticism of her.

'You are cold,' she heard him say grimly. 'Here, take this…'

Before she could stop him he was removing his jacket and wrapping it around her. It drowned her, its warmth enveloping her—and not just its warmth. Weakly Polly closed her eyes as her vulnerable senses were assaulted by the unmistakable scent of him.

'No, I don't want it,' she denied, thrusting it off and turning her back on him as she walked quickly away from him.

She could hear the faint exclamation of exasperation he made as he bent to retrieve it, and she wasn't surprised when he told her irritably, 'Don't be so damn childish, Polly. I do realise, you know, how much you resent having to accept anything from me. There's no need for you to reinforce that fact—especially not in such a self-defeating way.'

'That's not fair.' Polly defended herself quickly. 'And it's not true either. I've always been aware of how much both Briony and I owe you, and I'm very grateful for everything that you've done for us.'

When he didn't make any response she added inconsequentially, 'This was always one of Richard's favourite places…'

'Yes, I know,' Marcus agreed curtly—so curtly that Polly turned round to face him properly. His face was wearing that austere, withdrawn expression that made him seem so distant and disapproving.

'He loved to paint here,' Polly continued protectively. 'And…'

'And you keep the painting he gave you of this place in that nun-like cell you call your bedroom…'

'It isn't a cell,' Polly protested, outraged.

'No, you're right, it isn't,' Marcus agreed tersely. 'It's more like a shrine…a shrine to a man—a *boy*—who would have been appalled by your maudlin determination to turn him into some kind of plaster saint…'

Polly could feel herself starting to tremble. Why was it always like this? Why was it always like this between them? Why did they argue so much…fight so viciously? Why, when he obviously disliked and resented her so much, had Marcus done so much for her? But she already knew the answer to that conundrum. First it had been for Richard and then, after his death, for Briony.

'Richard was my husband,' she reminded him with a small quiver in her voice.

'Was… *Was*, Polly,' Marcus emphasised savagely. 'Richard is dead and has been for a very long time.'

'Briony wants me to give a private dinner party,' she told him quickly. 'She—'

'Yes, I know.' Marcus interrupted her shortly. Uncertainly Polly searched his face. What exactly had Briony told him—that she had found the woman she thought would make him the perfect wife? It wouldn't surprise her. Marcus would accept things from Briony that she could never imagine him accepting from someone else. They were on the same wavelength, so much in tune with one another that…that they made her feel excluded, envious… *Envious?* Of her own daughter…? Fiercely Polly resisted her thoughts.

'I have to go back,' she told Marcus jerkily, her body tensing when he fell into step beside her as she headed for the footpath. Just as she reached it she tried to distance herself from him, gasping in shock as a small branch from one of the trees became entangled in her hair.

'Keep still,' Marcus instructed her, immediately realising what had happened and reaching out to free her.

He was standing far too close to her, Polly recognised weakly. *Far* too close. She was beginning to feel dizzy…light-headed…

'Keep still,' Marcus repeated irritably as he tried to tug her hair free. She felt engulfed by him, surrounded by him as he moved closer to her whilst he worked patiently to free her.

Standing this close to him was almost like being in a lover's embrace with him… Polly could feel her skin starting to prickle with nervous tension. She could hardly breathe and if he didn't free her soon and move away from her she knew she was going to panic and do something really stupid.

'There. You're free now.'

Free… For one wild moment Polly actually contemplated telling him how impossible it was for her ever to be free of the unwanted burden she carried, but just in time she stopped herself, her 'Thank you' short and sharp, as though the words hurt her throat.

Her head was beginning to ache, but not because of her pulled hair and no way near as much as her heart.

Marcus provoked her, irritated her, angered her more

than anyone else she knew, sometimes she felt that the hostility between them was such that she could almost reach out and feel it. But only she knew how much, how desperately she needed to cling onto that anger and hostility…how much she needed the defence it gave her.

'There's no need to walk back with me,' she told him tersely. 'I can manage.'

'As you never seem to cease delighting in reinforcing to me,' Marcus agreed curtly. 'Polly, has it ever occurred to you—?' He stopped.

'Has *what* ever occurred to me?' she pressed him. But he simply shook his head and told her grimly, 'It doesn't matter.'

No, she wanted to correct him, *I'm* what doesn't matter to you, Marcus…me. But somehow she found the strength not to do so.

On her return to the house Polly went straight to the kitchen. Polly loved cooking, and its pleasure for her came from a deeply rooted nurturing instinct.

'Ma, you should have had half a dozen children, not just one,' Briony often told her.

Perhaps it was true; perhaps the love she poured into Fraser House and their guests was simply a form of displacement therapy, an outlet for the love and caring she no longer had her beloved Richard to give.

Paradoxically, perhaps Marcus was like herself, someone who, whilst enjoying and insisting on top-quality health-protecting, wholesome food, was not a gourmet, which was probably why, at forty-two, he still had the superbly fit and muscled body of a man half his age— as Polly had good cause to know. The last time he had been home she had hurried down to the swimming pool intent on having her early-morning swim before getting down to prepare the guests' breakfasts, and as she had approached the pool she had realised that Marcus had beaten her to it.

Reluctantly impressed, she had watched as he completed a length in a stunningly effective and fast crawl before turning at the far end of the pool to see her watching him. Quickly she'd started to walk back to the exit but, to her chagrin, Marcus had hauled himself out of the water and come after her, stopping her before she could leave.

'Nice swimsuit,' had been his drawlingly derogatory comment as he had surveyed her. 'What is it—one of Briony's schoolfriend's cast-offs?'

Furious with him for his rudeness, and herself for allowing herself to be provoked, she had compressed her mouth, refusing to make any verbal response even though she'd known her heightened colour had given away her real feelings.

Perhaps her swimming costume *was* a little bit old-fashioned, a plain, serviceable affair which she had originally bought when Briony had been a little girl and she had been taking her for swimming lessons; but the bikini Briony had insisted on her buying for their last holiday together was, in Polly's maternal opinion, far too brief and revealing—little more than a few scraps of black satinised cotton edged in a dull gold, and certainly far too sophisticated for a businesslike early-morning swim.

Distractedly she had watched the downward path of the droplets of water coursing their way through the sleek dark pelt of Marcus's body hair, across the flat, hard-packed muscles of his chest and stomach, and then...

It hadn't been until Marcus had oh, so deliberately wrapped the towel he was carrying around his hips that she'd realised just how hard she had been staring at him, and where, and her face had flushed an even deeper hue of pink as he had asked her, 'What is it Polly? Have you forgotten what a man looks like, or is *this*...' his hand had reached out and touched the hot skin of her face '...because you *have* remembered?' And then, before she could say anything he had challenged her, 'Do you think if your positions had been reversed that Richard would have clung so unnaturally to his widowhood or his celibacy?'

'Celibacy is easy when you...when there's only one man you love—only one man you want,' she had managed to retort; and, after all, it had been and still was the truth.

CHAPTER THREE

'AHA! I thought so. No *way* are you wearing *that*.' Briony pounced, coming into Polly's bedroom just as she was zipping up the plain, faithful black dress she'd decided to wear for Briony's dinner party.

The meal was in the capable if somewhat nervous hands of her young trainee chef, Andrew, and before coming upstairs to get ready she had gone into the conservatory where they were going to be dining to check that everything was in order.

The round table, rather smaller and far more intimate than the long dining table in the dining room, gleamed with crystal and silver, and the conservatory itself was illuminated by the dozen or more heavy floor-standing candelabra which Polly always lit for such occasions.

The simple muslin drapes which had been unfastened to cover the windows added to the wonderful delicacy of the room creating a glimmering, misty, low-lit effect which, as Polly already knew, did wonders for female complexions and—so she had been reliably informed— male libidos!

As she'd come upstairs she had congratulated herself with amused tenderness that Briony was bound to be pleased with her efforts, but it seemed now that she had congratulated herself a little too soon.

'What on earth do you mean?' she responded. 'I always wear this dress for dinner parties.'

'Exactly,' Briony agreed. 'It's the kind of dull, anon-

44

ymous thing that all fifty-something women play safe with.'

'Er…well, yes,' Polly agreed. 'That's why I bought it.'

'But, Mum, you *aren't* fifty-something, and anyway if Marcus sees you in it he will go mad. He told me the last time you wore it that I ought to burn it.'

'Oh, he did, did he?' Polly said grimly. 'Well, in that case…'

'Oh, help, I shouldn't have said that, should I?' Briony yelped. 'What is it with you and Uncle Marcus these days, Mum? You know, when I was little I used to pretend that Uncle Marcus was my father and I used to close my eyes and make a wish that you and he would get married.'

'Never,' Polly told her instantly. 'Never. I…'

'Mmm; that's exactly what Uncle Marcus said too,' Briony murmured, adding, 'Anyway, never mind about all that now… Look what I've got for you.'

Triumphantly she produced the bag she had been holding behind her back and, with a flourish, removed its contents.

'You can't possibly be expecting me to wear *that*,' Polly protested faintly as she saw the tiny tube-like piece of fabric her daughter was holding in front of her.

'Oh, but I am,' Briony grinned.

'It won't fit me,' Polly told her positively.

'Yes, it will; it stretches,' Briony informed her smugly, proving her point by gently pulling out the sheer black fabric with its delicate sprinkling of small jet beads.

'Briony, there's no way I can wear that.' Polly gasped in shock as she saw how see-through the fabric actually was.

'Relax, Mum,' Briony laughed. 'There's an underslip that goes with it. It's perfectly respectable, I promise you. Come on, take that horrid old thing off and let me see this on you.'

Polly tried to refuse but Briony was determined to get her own way, reminding Polly that her boyfriend and his godparents were amongst their dinner guests.

'You want to make a good impression, don't you?' she cajoled. 'And what about Suzi and her boss?'

'I thought it was Marcus you were hoping would impress Suzi?' Polly reminded her through gritted teeth as she saw what time it was and realised that if she didn't get downstairs soon and into the kitchen to calm the young chef's nerves it might be more than her clothes her guests were likely to pull a face over.

And besides, once the dress was on she was forced to admit that Briony had been right and that with the addition of the underslip the dress was discreetly opaque.

'See, I told you it would fit,' Briony crowed as she stood back to admire her handiwork.

'And how,' Polly agreed dryly as she caught sight of her reflection in the mirror. Was she really as slim as that? She looked tiny, fragile, ethereal almost, the black of the dress surely far denser and somehow more...more sensual than any black dress she had ever worn before.

Pulling it on over her head had disturbed the sleekness of her bob slightly, so that her hair was falling round her face in a much more softly tousled look than she normally wore.

'No, leave it,' Briony commanded her as she went to pick up her brush. 'It looks...'

'Untidy,' Polly supplied ruefully.

'Er...not exactly,' Briony told her with a grin, adding

quickly, 'Come on, Ma, we'd better make a move, they'll be here any minute.'

She was right, Polly knew, and with another uncertain look at her reflection she turned to follow Briony.

The dress wasn't particularly short but it did outline her shape, the boat-shaped neckline revealing the creamy skin of her throat and shoulders and the long sleeves emphasising the slenderness of her arms.

When she saw the look of relief Andrew gave her as she went into the kitchen Polly forgot about her hair and her dress. She had just finished calming Andrew down and reassuring him that everything would go well when Briony burst into the kitchen to announce that her guests had arrived.

'Poor guests,' Polly murmured sceptically as she followed her daughter.

It was Marcus she saw first, or rather Marcus her gaze was drawn to first. He was standing by the drinks table smiling warmly at a tall blonde girl who could only be Briony's promised Suzi, and then he saw Polly and his expression changed. Was it because of the dress? she wondered a little self-consciously as she smoothed it down with nervous fingers.

'Polly,' she heard him say harshly as he crossed the floor to join her.

'Do you like my dress?' she asked him nervously? rushing into speech. 'Briony chose it for me. It's...'

'"Like" isn't precisely the word I would have chosen,' Marcus began, and then stopped as Suzi came over to them and determinedly put her hand on his arm.

She was certainly very elegant, *and* very taken with Marcus, Polly decided as she watched the tell-tale way the girl was pushing her long blonde hair back off her face whilst moving just that little bit closer to Marcus as he asked what she would like to drink.

Chris she already knew, of course, and his godparents were a very pleasant couple in their mid-fifties, very much the kind of people Polly was used to entertaining as hotel guests.

Behind them and standing to one side of everyone else, very much as an observer, stood another man who Polly guessed must be Suzi's boss.

Tall, loose-limbed and handsome in that clean-cut, fair-haired way that was so American, as he caught sight of Polly he turned fully towards her, his eyes warming with male interest as he discreetly scanned her face and then her body.

For some reason Polly discovered that she was looking at Marcus. What for? Marcus was far too engrossed with Suzi to notice another man's interest in her, and even if he had done, so what? Since when had she needed Marcus's approval to acknowledge another man's awareness of her?

'Everyone, this is Polly, my mother,' Briony announced, tugging Polly into the centre of the room.

As Briony introduced her to their guests, Polly couldn't help but notice the way Marcus turned his back on her, as though making a pretence of studying the table in front of him, whilst Suzi's American boss, Phil Bernstein, gave her a crinkle-eyed smile and closed the distance between them to shake her hand. He continued to hold it warmly in his own as he told her admiringly, 'Briony warned me that there was no way you looked old enough to be her mother, but...!'

'Please don't tell her we look like sisters,' Briony groaned.

Phil laughed and told her without taking his eyes off

Polly, 'I wasn't going to. Briony doesn't look at all like you,' he continued to Polly in a slow, liquid-honey voice. 'You are—' His chest lifted as his gaze roamed over her with very deliberate but non-threatening thoroughness.

'Phil, you're embarrassing Mrs Fraser,' Suzi cut in, giving Polly a cool, assessing look and putting her very firmly in her place—and her generation, Polly noted—with that formal and distancing Mrs Fraser.

'I'd like to take you up on your offer to show me round the hotel,' she said, turning away from Polly to continue her conversation with Marcus. 'It's nothing like so large as Gifford's Cay, of course,' she added a little patronisingly, 'but nevertheless it would be interesting to have a look. Of course, the English country house style of hotel is getting a trifle passé now, at least at the top end of the market...'

Grimly Polly listened to her slightly acid voice. There was no doubt in her own mind that the other woman was deliberately trying to patronise her, but what she really found annoying was the fact that Marcus had offered to show her round the hotel without checking with her first.

She was, after all, responsible for its day-to-day running, even if financially she and Marcus were joint equal partners.

'Mind you, you're obviously making a very good profit,' Suzi went on carelessly as, at a discreet nod from Polly, the serving staff removed the canapés and started to collect their empty glasses.

'I saw that dress in a Knightsbridge store when I was in London the other day. She isn't a designer I particularly favour. I'm very much a Gucci woman—and besides, it would be a little old for me. It's the long sleeves that give it away as being an older woman's dress, isn't it? And I suppose when I start approaching forty...'

Approaching forty! Polly gave a small indrawn breath of indignation but it was, rather to her surprise, Phil Bernstein who pointed out crisply to Suzi, 'Actually I think you'll find that Polly is closer to thirty-five than forty, Suzi.'

But what was really worrying Polly, however, was how Briony had managed to pay for such an expensive dress.

Five minutes later when dinner was announced she quietly voiced her concern to her daughter.

'Oh, don't worry about that. I haven't blown all my grant money on it,' Briony told Polly breezily. 'Uncle Marcus paid for it.'

'Marcus?' Polly repeated faintly. 'You asked Marcus to buy me a dress?'

'Well, *I* chose it,' Briony assured her. 'I just told him that unless we got together and did something about it you'd end up wearing that frock horror thing you always wear and he agreed that it was high time you had something new!'

There wasn't time for Polly to say anything else, and, after a quick professional look around the table to make sure that everyone was seated and comfortable, she indicated to the staff that they could begin serving the meal.

'Say, this soup is just wonderful,' Phil Bernstein enthused.

'Thank you.' Polly smiled. 'It's my own special recipe and I—'

'At Gifford's Cay we have three top chefs and the menus are out of this world.' Suzi interrupted them rudely. 'We regularly have top film stars staying, don't we Phil?'

'Yes, we do. We had Meg Ryan as a guest during the summer,' he told Polly with a warm smile. 'You have something of the look of her...'

'Oh, no,' Polly demurred. But she couldn't help but be flattered.

'Wow, have you made a conquest, Ma,' Briony chortled a little later on in the evening. 'He's a millionaire, you know, and the hotel is just one of his business interests. Suzi won't confirm it but Chris is convinced that Phil has come over here looking to buy into something to extend his empire.'

'Mmm...well, just so long as it isn't Fraser House he tries to buy into,' Polly rejoined humorously.

'Do you know, Ma, I sometimes wonder which of us you love the most—the hotel or me,' Briony mock complained.

'Oh, there's no contest,' Polly reassured her dryly. 'It's the hotel every time!'

They were both still laughing when Phil overheard them and asked, 'What's so funny?'

'Nothing, really; it's just a mother and daughter joke,' Polly informed him.

'Uh-huh. You know, I still can't take it on board that you are Briony's mom,' he told her. 'You look like a girl yourself, especially with that very sexy hairdo.'

'What?' Self-consciously Polly lifted her hand, realising too late that she had never managed to smooth down her tousled hair.

'No, I like it. Leave it,' Phil pleaded softly. 'It's... It makes you look like you've just got up out of bed—a lover's bed...'

'Oh!' Polly gasped, feeling even more self-conscious.

'Polly, I think we're ready for the next course.'

The harsh sound of Marcus's voice brought Polly abruptly back to reality.

'But there isn't another course,' she told him, frowning. 'There's just the coffee, which I thought we'd have in the drawing room.'

'Oh?' Marcus queried caustically. 'You do surprise me. From the sound of it Bernstein was more than ready to make a meal of you!'

Polly gasped in outrage. 'Just because he was being polite to me?'

'Polite—by telling you that you looked like you'd just crawled out of some man's bed? If that's *polite*...'

'That wasn't what he said at all,' Polly began—and then stopped. What was the point? She knew Marcus in this kind of sharp, critical mood, when nothing she could say or do was right; and besides, although Marcus had turned his head away from the others so that his comments to her would not be overheard, out of the corner of her eye Polly could see that both Suzi and Phil's heads were turned in their direction.

'More coffee, anyone?' Polly invited, reaching for the nearly empty cafetière and smiling as everyone shook their heads.

'That was an excellent meal,' Phil praised warmly, but whilst both of Suzi's parents added their praise to his Polly noticed how Suzi flashed her an angry look.

Suzi commented patronisingly, 'I'm afraid I'm not really in a position to judge. You see our chef has moved on such a long way from this type of food that—' She stopped and gave a small shrug as though she couldn't find the words to describe adequately the huge gulf which existed between the meal she had just eaten and the wonders of the food she normally enjoyed.

Although she could feel her face starting to burn with what she knew to be justifiably annoyed colour, Polly calmly refused to allow herself to be drawn, but she had her reward and her justification, had she needed it, when, quite unexpectedly, both Phil and Suzi's father rebuked together, 'Suzi!'

'It was a most enjoyable meal, my dear,' Suzi's father went on to compliment Polly. 'Much more to my taste than some flim-flam of unidentifiable bits of raw this and that served with uncooked vegetables or, even worse, warm salad. *Warm* salad, I ask you—'

'Dad, you're out of touch,' Suzi interrupted him crisply, whilst Polly, whose own special recipes included several served in such a manner, hid a small smile. Suzi's father was typical of some of their older male guests for whom she always diplomatically made sure there was a very traditional pudding on the menu in addition to something lighter to tempt their wives' appetites.

'You promised me you'd show me round the hotel,' Suzi reminded Marcus as Polly suggested that her guests might like to move into the drawing room.

'Perhaps we might accompany them?' Phil Bernstein suggested.

A little reluctantly Polly agreed. She could see from the looks that both Suzi and Marcus were giving them that neither of them really wanted their company.

And yet, as Phil held open the drawing-room door for her to precede him through it, Polly found herself feeling unusually determined and assertive.

She, after all, had as much right to show someone round the hotel as Marcus, and she also had just as much right to enjoy the company of an attractive member of the opposite sex. Marcus didn't have any sole rights on being allowed to enjoy some flattering attention, and Phil *was* being very flatteringly attentive towards her, Polly had to admit.

Was she imagining it or was Phil deliberately slowing down his footsteps so that they fell some way behind the other pair? He was certainly walking far closer to her than was the norm, Polly knew *that*, his jacket-clad arm brushing hers as he stood even closer to her to admire the elegant architecture of the window halfway up the stairs.

'Phil, what are you *doing*?' Suzi demanded, suddenly turning round to chivvy them, using a tone of voice which privately Polly thought rather inappropriate from an employee to her employer, but it was obvious to her that Phil had a singularly sweet and laid-back nature, not like Marcus, who was standing at the top of the stairs glowering down at them.

'I was just admiring the view.' Phil responded to Suzi's bossy question.

'But it's dark outside,' Suzi told him, frowning.

'Mmm…' Phil agreed, and then turned to look at Polly.

Polly couldn't help it; she could feel herself blushing like a schoolgirl whilst Suzi ground her teeth and then turned on her heel, walking down the galleried landing so fast that she and Marcus had reached the end of it before Polly and Phil had got to the top of the stairs.

As Polly walked faster to try to catch up with them Phil placed his hand on her arm. 'Let them go,' he told her quietly. 'I must apologise for Suzi's rudeness to you earlier…'

'I expect she's still suffering from jet lag,' Polly offered diplomatically.

It was kind of Phil to apologise to her on Suzi's behalf but Polly suspected that the other woman wouldn't be the least bit grateful to him for his tact.

'Chris's parents mentioned that you were widowed very young.'

'Yes. Yes, I was,' Polly agreed.

'And you have never remarried? Not for any lack of opportunities, I'm sure.' Phil smiled gallantly.

'Looking after Briony and running this place hasn't left me much time for...for anything else,' Polly responded.

'Mmm... I imagine that you would also have difficulty persuading your guard dog to allow another man into your life,' Phil commented dryly, nodding in the direction the other couple had taken.

'My...my guard dog?' Polly repeated in bemusement. 'You mean *Marcus*? Oh, but he...isn't...he doesn't...'

'As your business partner and half-owner of this place, of course it is in his interests to ensure that you remain single and put the business first,' Phil continued, taking any edge off his words with the smile he gave her. 'In his shoes I suspect I might be tempted to do exactly the same.'

Polly didn't make any response. She couldn't. Marcus would never try to stop her from having a relationship with someone if she wished to do so. Would he? Just let him dare! She was not answerable to him where her private life was concerned, and so far as the business was concerned they were equal partners. It annoyed her more than she wanted to show that not just Suzi but Phil too, it seemed, appeared to believe that it was Marcus who held the real power.

'No comment?' Phil pressed.

Polly stopped walking to look at him. He was looking back at her with an expression of quizzical but very male interest in his eyes.

'I'm a free agent,' she told him. 'And as for my guard dog…' She paused, and then told Phil recklessly, 'He will soon be moving into a new kennel.'

Heavens, what on earth had come over her? What she had just said was tantamount to… But no, she didn't want to think about what a foolishly dangerous flirtatious step she had just taken. Already she was beginning to regret it and to feel almost breathlessly light-headed— and equally breathlessly light-hearted? If so…

'We'd better catch up with the other two,' she told Phil huskily.

Marcus had already finished showing Suzi the first of their guest rooms when they caught up with them.

Whilst all the bedrooms had had to be redecorated since Richard had originally painted them, when she had had them done Polly had held many a mental conversation with her dead husband. It wasn't just his memory she wanted to keep alive but his whole artistic ethos, and when she saw the look of admiration in Phil's eyes as she proudly showed him their guest bedrooms Polly knew that she had succeeded.

'No. Not that door,' she intervened quickly when they had almost reached the end of the corridor and Phil was striding towards the last room.

'That's Marcus's suite of rooms,' she explained.

Suzi made a small, tantalising *moue* and told Marcus suggestively, 'Oh, what a pity we can't go in… I think a man's bedroom tells you so much about what he's really like…'

What he was really like *in bed* was quite plainly what

she meant, Polly decided, but she suspected that if Marcus had volunteered to show her his rooms she might have been disappointed.

They were very plain and impersonal—but then, of course, Marcus did not spend an awful lot of time in them, being away on business so much, and Polly couldn't remember there ever being a time when, to her knowledge anyway, he had had a woman stay over in them.

She knew there had been women in his life, of course; there had been photographs taken whilst he was away with a variety of stunningly beautiful women posing next to him.

'A friend,' had been his inevitable response when Briony had asked innocently who they were; sometimes she herself had answered phone calls from husky-voiced women asking for him and just giving their Christian name with the confidence of knowing that it would be instantly recognisable to him.

Oh, yes, Marcus was a very heterosexual, very male man.

'The hotel really is very small, isn't it?' Suzi drawled disparagingly. 'More of a guest house, really.'

Anger flashed in Polly's eyes as she listened to her. She herself and her loyal staff had worked very hard to get the hotel deservedly recognised as one of the country's best small country house hotels and to refer to it as a guest house was, so far as she was concerned, not just rude but ill-informed as well.

But, before she could say anything, a little to her surprise, Marcus was speaking, telling Suzi firmly, 'Fraser House is perhaps not a hotel in the larger sense of the word. In fact I suspect that, like others in the rather select grouping it shares, it doesn't easily lend itself to label-

ling. As you've just observed, we are rather short of
bedrooms—so much so that we are increasingly having
to turn potential guests away. Which is one reason why
I've decided to give up my own rooms here!'

'Personally I would much rather stay in this kind of
hotel than one of the larger, more impersonal ones,' Phil
intervened.

'We do have more rooms on the next floor,' Polly
told Suzi crisply, nor could she resist adding pointedly,
'And I rather doubt that you'd find many guest houses
offering the kind of facilities that we offer. Our leisure
complex not only has a first-rate gym but we also have
an Olympic-size swimming pool.'

'Oh, if you're talking about swimming pools you
should see the ones we have at Gifford's Cay,' Suzi
responded smugly. 'One of America's top sports facilities designers designed them for us didn't he Phil?'

'I'd love to see the other rooms,' Phil told Polly pointedly, calmly ignoring Suzi's boastful remark.

The rooms on the upper floor were all well propor-
tioned and decorated and furnished in keeping with their
sloping ceilings and small windows. Polly was rightly
proud of the way they had made the most of the house's
design without compromising either on the kind of luxury their guests would expect or its age.

As they inspected the last one, Phil lingered by the
window, gazing out of it.

'Who owns the farmland?' he asked her conversationally.

'It belongs to me,' Marcus informed Phil flatly, and
as the two men exchanged a look Polly couldn't interpret
she was conscious of a sharp animosity between them
that almost crackled in the still air.

*   *   *

'Mmm… That was a wonderful evening,' Briony told Polly happily as she helped her mother put away the last of the special Spode dinner service they had used for their dinner party. The Spode was Polly's own service—a special treat to herself the previous Christmas.

'You'll miss Uncle Marcus when he moves out, won't you?'

'No, certainly not,' Polly denied immediately.

Briony dipped her head, her mouth curling in a small smile. She had told Chris of her hopes. He had cautioned her against interfering but she just knew she was doing the right thing!

'I'm tired, Briony; I think I'll go up to bed…'

After she had hugged her mother and kissed her goodnight, Briony wandered round the room for a few seconds and then, as her face split into a wide smile, she punched the air and exclaimed triumphantly, 'Yes!'

CHAPTER FOUR

'SO, THE way I see it is that if we put the sitting room between the two bedrooms and each has a connecting door to the sitting room you would have the option of either a double suite, with two double rooms and a sitting room, or a single suite with one double room and a sitting room, plus another double room, and I've also got the provisional drawings here for the small conference suite you asked me about.'

'Polly, if we could possibly have your attention…'

With a small start Polly realised that both the architect and Marcus were waiting for her response.

A little guiltily she looked at the drawings in front of her.

'Er, yes…those are fine,' she agreed.

She hadn't slept at all well for the last three nights—ever since the dinner party, in fact—and for some reason she felt almost permanently on edge during the day even though physically she was so tired. If it hadn't been for the nervous energy driving her she suspected she would not have stayed awake.

Blinking a little, she forced herself to focus on the drawings. The architect, Neil Harland, had done a very good job for them, Polly recognised. His suggestion was an excellent one but somehow her normal enthusiasm just wasn't there. Every time she closed her eyes she kept visualising Suzi deriding the hotel, deriding *her*, it seemed, whilst making no secret of her admiration for Marcus.

The hotel had filled up over the weekend, and because of that Marcus had arranged for them to see Neil at the dower house instead of the hotel, and now, as Neil removed the plans for the rearrangement of Marcus's rooms to show her his drawings for the proposed conference suite, she was sharply conscious of the fact that this house was alien territory to her; that it belonged to Marcus and that it was going to be his home. His and Suzi's—or, if not her, another woman like her.

'You don't seem very enthusiastic,' she heard Neil saying wryly.

'No... Yes... I am... I think you've done a wonderful job, Neil,' Polly assured him immediately.

Mollified, Neil leaned over the plans he had spread out in front of her and Marcus, indicating to them both how the new conference suite could be built onto the existing stable block to make a courtyard effect.

'It looks wonderful,' Polly told him. 'Wonderful but very expensive,' she added ruefully, giving Marcus an uncertain look before adding, 'We'd have to take out a bank loan to finance it, and I'm not sure...'

'We'd need to get the plans passed first,' Marcus reminded her. 'We agreed that this was going to be a long-term project when we first discussed it.'

'I've got your plans here for this house, Marcus.' Neil interrupted the sharply antagonistic silence that ensued.

Polly longed to be able to leave, but she and Marcus had already arranged to hold a meeting to discuss the finances of the hotel after Neil had left, and for that reason she felt obliged to stay.

It was plain to Polly that Marcus was sparing no expense on the house. But then why should he? He was, as she already knew, comfortably well off and he earned a very good salary—Marcus's mother had come from a wealthy family and it was via her that Marcus had inherited some family money. Richard's parents, on the other hand, who were now retired and living in Cheltenham, had only Richard's father's army pension to live on.

Not that she envied Marcus his wealth, not for one minute. The hotel provided her not just with a beautiful home but with a comfortable living as well, and once Briony had finished college she would be even better off. Not that she had needed to finance her daughter's education—Marcus had made it clear that he was more than willing to do so—but Polly had refused to let him. She had her pride, after all—which reminded her: she would have to find out from Briony first how much Marcus had spent on that dress, because she fully intended to repay him.

Neil and Marcus had finished talking now and Neil was getting ready to leave.

'I'll be in touch about the new bedrooms,' he told Polly. 'When do you think the work will be able to start?'

'That's really up to Marcus,' Polly told him, 'but if it could be finished for Christmas—'

'Christmas?' Neil's eyebrows shot up. 'You'll be lucky…'

'Well, in that case it will have to be put off until the new year.'

That sounds more like it,' Neil said, then thanked them both and took his leave.

'Despite the fact that we've virtually been fully booked all year and our profits are holding steady, our actual profit margins have dropped,' Marcus pointed out to Polly after he had finished going through the books.

'Yes, I know,' Polly agreed, adding when he contin-
ued to look at her, 'The cost of food alone has increased,
Marcus.' She spread her hands and gave a small shrug.
'Then there's the heating, electricity, gas, water, the—'

'Suzi tells me that at Gifford's Cay they ration the
guests' bath and shower water, charging an excess to
those who use more...'

'Maybe, but England isn't the Caribbean,' Polly
pointed out sharply. 'And after a wet summer I doubt
that our guests would be very impressed to be told that
they can't have a bath unless they pay extra for it. And,
of course, you're forgetting that the guests at Gifford's
Cay have the extra facility of three swimming pools,'
she couldn't resist adding sarcastically.

'We do our best to keep costs down and profit margins
up, Marcus,' she continued crisply. 'But our guests expect a certain standard of comfort and if we start cutting
corners...'

'I understand what you're saying,' Marcus agreed.
'But our tariff hasn't increased this year...'

'Not *this* year,' Polly was quick to respond. 'But we
did increase it last year and I was going to ask you what
you thought about us increasing it next year. I think our
guests will accept an increase in costs more readily if
they don't feel that it's something they have to expect
regularly every year.'

'Do you? Or is this just an idea you've come up with
after consulting Phil Bernstein?' Marcus asked her ac-
idly.

'I don't need Phil's help in making decisions about
what's best for Fraser House, even if *you* seem to need
Suzi's,' Polly told him recklessly.

There was a long pause that positively bristled with
the anger they were generating towards one another be-

fore Marcus responded silkily, 'Of course, how foolish of me. It isn't Bernstein's professional expertise you want at all, is it?'

Polly drew in her breath, warning herself not to let her fury get the better of her. This wasn't the time or the place to become involved in a full-scale no-holds-barred fight with Marcus, even if she was inwardly itching to retaliate to what she knew was a deliberately provocative and hurtful gibe.

'What I *want* is absolutely and totally no business of yours,' was all she allowed herself to say once she was able to speak past the lump of fury lodged in her throat.

'In one sense perhaps not. But in another...' Marcus paused and then told her flatly, 'We are, after all, business partners, and when your personal behaviour could potentially affect our shared business interests... Suzi was telling me that Bernstein has quite a reputation. And you do realise, don't you, that he's—'

Polly had had enough.

'That he's what?' she interrupted him angrily. 'That he's *younger* than me? Yes, I *do* realise that, Marcus, but it isn't exactly unheard of these days for a woman to... Anyway,' she continued hastily, 'I could point out to you that Suzi is younger than Phil and you are older than me, but of course *that* doesn't matter, does it?' she flung sarcastically at him.

'What is it that's the big attraction, Polly?' Marcus demanded, cutting across what she was saying. 'What exactly is it that he's got that—'

Abruptly he stopped speaking and then began again curtly. 'Have you considered how Briony's going to feel if you become involved with him?'

'How Briony feels is for her to discuss with me,' Polly responded passionately, biting her lip, reluctantly aware that Briony herself probably did consider Marcus to be as close to her as the father she had lost, honesty compelling her not to accuse Marcus of laying claim to a position in Briony's affections which he did not have when she knew very well that he did.

'Well, if you're intent on making a fool of yourself...' Marcus told her savagely. 'According to Suzi he's a womaniser who—'

Making a *fool* of herself? Polly saw red. 'If responding to a man's *very* flattering appreciation of me as a woman is making a *fool* of myself,' she exploded.

'So you *are* interested in him,' Marcus stated flatly. His eyes were hard and black as he told her cruelly, 'I suppose it's to be expected in a woman reaching that "certain age" of her life when she feels that her youth is over...'

Polly gave an outraged gasp, shocked by the unexpectedness of an attack which was so out of character. Marcus was normally far more subtle, far more urbane. Something or someone must really have rattled him to make him speak with such open aggression—unless his antipathy towards Phil was on Suzi's behalf. They had, as Briony had mentioned, apparently been more than merely employer and employee at one stage. It crossed Polly's mind that in many ways the two of them would be quite well suited. Perhaps Marcus thought so as well and was jealous. Even so—

'How *dare* you imply...?' she began breathlessly, and then stopped as she tried to find the right words to deny his implications without descending to his own level of insult. Taking a deep breath, she told him quietly, 'Contrary to what you seem to imagine Marcus, a woman of thirty-seven is neither past it nor *desperate* to use the same crude analogy you seem to prefer.'

'No?' he asked harshly. 'Then why the sudden hurry to crawl into Bernstein's bed when, so far as I'm aware, you've spent the last fourteen years since Richard's death keeping out of *any* man's, but specifically—'

'So far as *you* are aware,' Polly cut in quickly, her head lifting proudly as she dared him to contradict her. 'You don't know everything there is to know about me, Marcus, and just because…' She stopped and bit her lip, not wanting to lie but determined not to let him guess that he was right in thinking that she had remained celibate since Richard's death.

'You've always claimed that *no man* could replace Richard in your life,' he reminded her flatly.

'No more could they,' Polly agreed, unaware of the quicksand she had marched into until Marcus questioned softly,

'Not in your *life*, then, but perhaps it's a different matter when it comes to your *bed*—is that what you're trying to say?'

Polly stared at him. She had meant to say no such thing but she could feel herself sinking so fast into the dangerously unstable ground beneath her feet that she was too unnerved to know how to save herself.

'You should have told me this before,' Marcus continued silkily. 'If I'd known that sexual frustration was such a problem for you I might have done this much sooner…'

And then, before Polly could guess what was going to happen, Marcus had crossed the small distance that separated them. She backed away from him, gasping in shock as she felt the wall against her back. Instinctively she put up her hands to ward Marcus off, but, ignoring them, he replaced his own hands at either side of her on the wall, his body so close to hers that if she hadn't quickly dropped her arms her palms would have been flat against his chest.

'That's better,' Marcus told her savagely. 'After all, we both know that this is what you want, don't we? You told me so yourself...'

'No!' Polly protested. She couldn't believe this was happening, that he was behaving like this. Not *Marcus* of all people. Marcus whom she—

It was too late; his body was already touching hers whilst his hands closed on her shoulders and his mouth came down on her own with a hard determination that made her whole body start to tremble.

'No!' she whispered again under her breath, but her eyes were already starting to close, her body going soft and malleable beneath his touch...beneath *him*.

Behind her closed eyelids she could feel the searing pain of her own hot, shaming tears.

Why? Why had this to happen? Why *now*...why, after all these years of forcing herself not to think, not to imagine, not to dare to dream—?

She was trembling violently and openly now, and she prayed as she had never prayed before that only she would know the reason for the frantic tremors that were racing through her, and that only *she* would know that her reaction to his remorseless determination to punish her was not because she was afraid or angry but because—

'How many men have touched you like this...kissed you like this since Richard?' Marcus asked her thickly as his hands swept down the length of her arms to hold her whilst the hard pressure of his body leaning into hers made her shockingly aware of the physical effect their intimacy was having on him.

Men were so different from women, so easily and

strongly aroused by the sensuality of physical contact, not needing any emotional input. Whereas she...

'Open your mouth. Kiss me *properly*,' Marcus demanded rawly against her lips.

Oh, God, please let me be able to resist, to prevent him from guessing—knowing.

'Marcus...' She started to protest, but it was no use; the moment her lips parted his were covering them, devouring them...devouring her.

Polly could feel the resistance draining out of her body.

'Marcus...'

As she breathed his name her hands lifted to his arms, her fingers curling round them, digging into the hard muscles. She could feel the frantic thud of her heart— or was it his? It seemed to beat into her body in a rhythm that...

Stop it. Stop it! she warned herself shakily as her mind tortured her with all sorts of dangerous images.

Marcus's hands were on her breasts now, shaping them, covering them, his thumbs rubbing against her hardening nipples.

She made a small sound beneath her breath and his fingers worked her breast free of the covering of her bra through her top.

As his tongue thrust between her lips Polly gave a small stifled moan of pleasure and tried to pull away, but he wouldn't let her. He pulled her, taking hold of her shoulders again and imprisoning her tightly against his body whilst he changed their position so that *he* was the one leaning against the wall whilst she was cradled between his splayed legs...

Oh, God, she couldn't cope with this...not now...not ever...no way... She could feel his hard arousal even before his hands slid down her body to pull her even more tightly into his own; another second and he would be...*they* would be...

Distantly Polly was aware of a ringing noise that seemed to go on and on, then abruptly Marcus was releasing her mouth, and then her body, cursing as he did so.

Too shaken and shocked to do or say anything, Polly simply stood where she was, white-faced, paralysed almost.

'That's the doorbell; it will probably be Suzi,' Marcus told her tersely. 'She wanted to see the house.'

Blank-eyed, Polly tried to speak, but found she couldn't. Her body felt heavy and awkward; even breathing required concentration and effort. She couldn't bring herself to look at Marcus. She couldn't *bear* to do so...

As he walked towards the door she looked across the desk to where she had left her bag and her coat. Such mundane articles, so much a part of her equally mundane and ordinary life, but now she was looking at them as though she had never seen them before. Shakily she walked towards them and picked them up. She could hear Marcus walking down the hallway. Her brain was urging her to move more quickly, to escape, to get away before Suzi came in.

Frantically she reached for her things, her hands trembling so much that it took her three attempts before she could pick them up properly. There was a pair of French windows in the room she was in. Blindly she tugged the bolts, managing to wrench them open and breaking a nail in the process as she stumbled thankfully into the fresh air and headed unsteadily for her car.

Let Marcus make whatever he wanted to make of her

unceremonious departure, she thought as she drove away. She imagined that her continued presence would only have been embarrassing to him with Suzi there, unless he actually enjoyed the thought of having two women in his home, both of whom he…

Shuddering, Polly brought her car to a halt at the roadside and forced herself to take several deep, calming breaths.

What on earth was she doing risking everything she had striven so hard to achieve these last years? Bitterly she closed her eyes, willing herself not to cry.

She could still taste Marcus on her lips, smell him on her skin, feel the raw urgency of his sexuality and the heat of his anger.

His anger… *That* was what had motivated him, driven him to behave so…so shockingly towards her, but *her* motivation was…

Tears burned the back of her eyeballs, sharp as acid, painful as splinters of glass in her heart and just as fatal…like her feelings…

Her *feelings*? She couldn't remember exactly how long it had been after Richard's death before she had recognised her feelings towards him and her oddly out-of-character behaviour when she was with him for what they were—just as she didn't know…didn't remember when she had recognised that love could be pain when it was the wrong kind of love for the wrong man.

Her heart had started to beat heavily with anguish and she squeezed her eyes closed to force back her unwanted tears. Loving Marcus had been a fact of her life for so long that she had thought she had come to terms with it, but seeing him with Suzi, listening to Briony whilst she extolled the other girl's virtues, her suitability to become Marcus's wife and the mother of his children, had stripped back the pretence she had cocooned herself in and left her raw and bleeding with the pain of her love.

And for Marcus to have taunted her in the way that he had only made his indifference to her as a woman more plain. But *why* was he so angry? Because he was afraid she was going to make a fool of herself over Phil and he thought that might reflect badly on him?

Well, better by far that he should think her capable of making a fool of herself over Phil than that he should guess the truth.

Her heart started to beat even faster. But what if she had somehow betrayed herself to him just now in his arms? What if he had begun to suspect that it was *him* she…? But no, he *mustn't* be allowed to guess. She didn't think she could bear the humiliation of that. She *knew* she could not bear the humiliation of it, otherwise why would she have been so painstakingly careful all these long years to keep him at a distance?

She could not pinpoint exactly when she had looked at Marcus and known as a woman did know such things that her feelings for him were far too powerful, far too strong, far too intimate for the kind of relationship they shared.

Only she would know just how many times she had watched him in secret whilst he played with Briony and *longed* for him to give her a second child; to hold her, kiss her, possess her. The love she felt for him far, far outstripped the gentle warmth she had known for Richard. That had been a girl's virginal emotion. What she felt for Marcus was…

She opened her eyes, her face white with strain. If he had chosen to, right there and then he could have… She swallowed painfully, her body shaking as though she were having a seizure as it told her how much it ached for the fullness of his possession, the completeness of it. She was thirty-seven, for heaven's sake, she reminded herself fiercely. She was thirty-seven and a woman in her sexual prime, longing for, aching for the man she loved so much...

A ripple of sensation gripped her body causing her to tense against it and hold her breath.

What was happening to her? Perhaps Marcus was right after all, perhaps she was going through some sort of crisis. Just thinking about him with Suzi, with anyone else, made her feel so...

Stifling a sharply indrawn breath of pain she gritted her teeth and restarted the car. She had had many years to get used to the way she felt about Marcus. To get used to loving him whilst knowing that her love, her longing, her *need* could never be answered. So why now was she suddenly feeling this swamping frightening sensation of aching loss?

Carefully putting the car in gear, she started to drive back to the hotel.

The phone was ringing as Polly hurried into her office. It had been a hectic day altogether. She had been up early to see Briony off, the last of their weekend guests had finally left and now she was looking forward to a few days of peace and quiet before the next weekend's influx began.

'Hello,' she said as she picked up the telephone receiver.

'Polly, it's Phil here—Phil Bernstein,' she heard her caller announcing, to her surprise. 'Look, I realise this is probably going to sound a little bit pushy, in view of the brevity of our relationship, but I was wondering if you would do me a favour...'

'A favour?' Polly repeated uncertainly. 'Well, I... It depends what it is,' she answered warily.

'I'm in negotiations to buy a hotel in London and I was wondering if I could borrow your expertise and ask you to cast your experienced eye over the place and give me your views on it.'

For a few seconds Polly was too surprised to answer.

'Oh, goodness!' she finally exclaimed weakly. 'I'm no expert, Phil. You're a hotel owner yourself, and I'm sure you're more than capable of using your own judgement.'

'Not in this instance. This hotel is nothing like the one I already own, and besides...' He paused, and then told her quietly, 'Look, I don't want to go into too many details over the phone but I really would appreciate your input into this, Polly. I was very, very impressed with what you've done at Fraser House.'

'It's very kind of you to say that Phil,' Polly said, 'but—'

'Look, all I'm asking is that you come down to London, have dinner with me; you can stay here at the hotel overnight—at my expense, of course—and...'

'Oh, no, I couldn't do that,' Polly protested immediately. 'If I were to come down I'd prefer to make my own overnight arrangements.'

'But you *will* come down and have dinner with me?' Phil pounced immediately. 'I mean it, Polly; I really do need your advice.'

Polly wavered. Phil was a flirt, and a very accomplished one, and she wasn't so naive that she wasn't aware that if she allowed him to do so he would be more than happy to take their acquaintanceship a stage further and to become personally involved with her. She simply wasn't that type of woman, and had he merely been telephoning to invite her out to dinner... But his plea to her for her professional advice was a different matter, and Polly felt she would be less than human if she wasn't just a little bit flattered.

'Phil...' she began cautiously just as she heard her office door opening. 'Dinner would be lovely but...'

She froze as Marcus came into the room, immediately feeling oddly guilty as well as slightly breathless. 'Phil, I have to go...' she said. But before she could ring off Phil was telling her, 'Look, don't give me your answer now. Have a think about it and I'll ring back later. I really do want your advice, Polly—as well as your company,' he added in a softer, more meaningful voice before he hung up.

'Who was that?' Marcus demanded sharply as Polly replaced the receiver.

'It was Phil Bernstein,' Polly responded automatically, before adding challengingly, 'Not that it's any of your business.'

'What did he want?' Marcus pressed her, ignoring the second half of her answer and the warning glint in her eyes.

'What he *wanted*,' Polly told him with quiet dignity, 'was to ask me to go down to London to have dinner with him.'

'What? You said no, of course.'

It was the 'of course' that did it—that and the high-handed way in which Marcus was behaving, as though she were a child and he somehow had the right to dictate what she did.

'I haven't given him my answer yet,' she informed Marcus shortly. 'He's going to ring back, and when he does...'

'When he does, you'll tell him no,' Marcus informed her sharply. 'The man's a womaniser, Polly, and you—'

They both tensed as her telephone rang, but when Polly went to pick it up she discovered that the call was for Marcus from the oil company. Leaving him to take it in private, she walked out of the room.

'You'll tell him no' indeed...! Why *should* she? Why shouldn't she accept Phil's invitation if she wanted to? Why shouldn't she live a little if she wanted to? *If* she wanted to. That was the problem, wasn't it? She *didn't* want to, at least not with Phil...

She waited until she was sure that Marcus had concluded his call before going back into her office. He was frowning and looking very preoccupied.

'I'm rather busy, Marcus,' she told him pointedly. 'Was there something you wanted to see me about?'

She could tell from his expression that her cool, businesslike manner irked him. Well, let it. Let him have a taste of his own medicine.

Her unfamiliar stubbornness was surprising Polly a little, but it was also making her feel very strong and powerful.

Looking away from him, she started to busy herself with the papers on her desk, but it was obvious that Marcus was not impressed—or going to be put off. Placing his hands squarely on her desk, he leaned towards her and demanded, 'Stop play-acting, Polly; it doesn't work. What's the idea of this?' he added, reaching into his jacket and extracting an envelope.

Polly's heart gave a little anxious skip as she recognised her own handwriting on it. She knew what it was, of course. It was the envelope she had sent to him enclosing the cheque to cover the cost of her new dress.

'It's for the dress,' she told him as calmly as she could. 'Briony told me how much it cost.'

She could see that he was frowning, giving her a searching look as his mouth hardened.

'What exactly are you trying to do, Polly?' he asked her irritably. 'What point are you trying to make?'

'I'm simply repaying the money you spent,' Polly told him, trying to appear casual. 'There's no need for you to make an issue of it, Marcus.'

'And if I say that I'm not going to accept this cheque?' Marcus challenged her silkily.

Alarm flared in Polly's eyes. She knew that tone of his, but she wasn't going to be browbeaten by him, nor turned into a pathetic bundle of female nerves.

'If you don't then you'll leave me with no alternative but to return the dress to you,' Polly told him determinedly.

'But it was a gift,' Marcus responded immediately.

'I don't want your gifts,' Polly retaliated swiftly, only realising her mistake too late as she saw the way Marcus was smiling at her.

'Not *my* gift, Polly,' he corrected her. '*Briony's*. If I were to buy you clothes—'

'Yes, I know,' she snapped, completely losing her cool. 'You'd buy me something much more appropriate for a woman of my age.'

'Oh, yes, it would be something very appropriate,' Marcus taunted her softly. His voice became much harder as he shrugged and told her dismissively, 'Do what you like with the dress, Polly. If you want to get at me so much that you're prepared to trample all over Briony's feelings to do so, then I can't stop you...'

Ignoring her angry gasp of protest, he turned round and walked out of her office. How typical of him that he should have the last word, and such a pointed one, Polly recognised angrily.

And what made it worse was that he was right. Briony would be hurt if she returned the dress to him and refused to wear it again.

She was still seething with resentment over his behaviour an hour later, when Phil rang again.

'Whatever it takes to get you to say yes and have dinner with me, you've got it,' Phil promised extravagantly, his determination to get her consent making Polly laugh.

'No, truthfully,' she began, fully intending to tell him that she couldn't—and then she stopped, remembering the way Marcus had spoken to her. What right did *he* have to tell her what she should and should not do, whom she should and should not see, especially when he himself...? She took a deep breath and, smothering the tiny voice that warned her to be careful, told Phil recklessly, 'There's no need. I'd *love* to see your hotel...'

'And you'll have dinner with me?' Phil pressed. Polly hesitated.

'Very well,' she agreed somewhat reluctantly. 'But I'll make my own arrangements for my overnight accommodation, Phil,' she told him firmly.

'I understand,' he assured her.

What would Marcus have to say when he found out what she had done? she wondered a little nervously when they had concluded their call. And then, very quickly, she reminded herself that she had the right to do what she wanted when she wanted and with whom she wanted...hadn't she?

CHAPTER FIVE

'IT LOOKS wonderful on you.'

'You don't think that it might be a little bit too young?' Polly asked the shop assistant uncertainly.

The girl raised her elegant eyebrows.

'Certainly not,' she assured Polly firmly. 'In fact if anything... *This* designer is in her mid-thirties herself, and designs for her own age group, so if anything I should say it's perhaps a little bit old for you.' She gave Polly a ruefully conspiratorial smile as she told her, 'She's actually one of my favourite designers and I've promised myself one of her dresses as a thirtieth-birthday present.'

The salesgirl's obvious belief that Polly was closer to her own age than the designer's boosted Polly's self-confidence so much that she found herself buying not just the dress but a pair of impossibly spindly-heeled shoes to go with it.

In a matt black thick jersey fabric, the dress had a cut-away semi-diamond-shaped neckline which did things for her *décolletage* and her arms and shoulders that Polly would have thought were impossible. In it she felt as *soignée* and feminine as any film star, and it was worth paying the outrageously extravagant price just for that feeling alone.

Marcus would have hated it on her, of course, no doubt believing that it was far too sensually alluring for *her*, but then Marcus was not going to see her in it, was he? Momentarily her eyes clouded, her pleasure dim-

78

ming. She had bought the dress as a gesture of defiance—and to replace the one Marcus had paid for which she had mentally sworn she would never wear again. And besides, why shouldn't she indulge herself a little? She could afford it, and it wasn't often she got the chance to come to London to shop.

Fortunately she hadn't seen Marcus since she had accepted Phil's invitation, although she had been standing in the foyer when a call had come through for him from Suzi.

She shivered. She still went hot and cold every time she thought about how she had felt the other day when Marcus had kissed her the way he had.

It wasn't just that she hadn't been able to summon the will-power to stop him; it was the longing she had experienced, the overwhelming aching need for him that had swamped her, and was still making her feel hotly aware of her own vulnerability.

No, she hadn't seen him, even though apparently he had called at the hotel a couple of times when she hadn't been there. But she had dreamed about him, about *it*. Only in her dreams things had not been the way they had in reality. In her dreams the physical desire which had burned through her body had reached its natural conclusion and Marcus had...

Hot-faced, Polly reminded herself of where she was and the inappropriateness of her private thoughts.

Perhaps it *had* been too long since she had experienced a man's touch. Perhaps she should think about...

About what?

She caught herself up swiftly. About having sex with someone...anyone...just to relieve her sexual tension? The revulsion that flooded her at the thought was both a reminder of the intensity of her feelings for Marcus and a relief. Little though she liked admitting how much she loved Marcus, she disliked even more having to think of herself as a woman driven by her sexual urges. Perhaps it was old-fashioned of her to feel this way, but then she *was* old-fashioned, and what was more she didn't intend to make any apologies for being so. She was a little bit ashamed of the relief, though, and was thankful that Briony had not been there for her to have to make any explanations or excuses to when she had packed for her brief sojourn in London.

Not that what she was doing was in any way wrong. *No*, positively not. After all, she wasn't even planning to stay in the same hotel as Phil, and even if she had been... No, what she was doing was perfectly acceptable. Heavens, if she couldn't have dinner with a man without...

It was Marcus's fault that she was feeling like this, she decided crossly. It was Marcus who had insinuated that she...that Phil...

The girl had wrapped up her dress and shoes, and as she handed the bag to Polly she told her warmly, 'Enjoy wearing it.'

'I shall,' Polly assured her with a smile as she headed for the door.

As she left the shop Polly glanced at her watch. It was almost four o'clock; she was meeting Phil at seven—she had declined his offer to pick her up at her hotel and had suggested instead that she meet him in the lobby of the hotel where they were having dinner and where she presumed he was staying.

Now she just had time to get to her own hotel and book in, treat herself to afternoon tea, which she knew they did very well, and then get ready for her date.

Her date... A little wryly she smiled to herself as she
hailed a passing taxi.

Her dinner with Phil was a purely business arrangement, she reminded herself. All he wanted from her was
her professional opinion on the hotel. Well, maybe not
quite all, she admitted honestly to herself as she saw the
taxi driver giving her a quick approving look as she got
into the cab and gave him her destination.

The hotel she had booked into was, whilst small, well
patronised by the *cognoscenti* of the travelling world.
What it lacked in modern, large complex facilities it
more than made up for in the warmth of its service—
and its food—so Polly wasn't totally surprised to discover, as she walked in, that the foyer was a hive of
activity, with the receptionist trying to deal with several
new arrivals plus some queries from an existing guest
who was anxious to know how she might best get to the
British Museum.

Patiently Polly waited, using her time on the other side
of the counter to work on where they might make im-
provements to their own service, but at length the receptionist was free to deal with her.

Smiling, Polly gave her name at the receptionist's request and confirmed her address.

'I'm sorry to have kept you waiting,' the girl apologised as she handed Polly her door pass and gave her
her room number.

Thanking her, Polly made her way through the foyer
to the lifts. Her room was on the third floor, one of six
opening off an elegant hallway decorated in the grand
London house style.

After several failed attempts to let herself into her
room with the pass card, Polly was just about to return

to the foyer when the porter came past with some luggage.

Stopping him, Polly explained her problem and, having checked that she had the right room, the porter obligingly opened the door for her.

The hotel was just off one of London's prettier and little-known private squares, part of a terrace of similar Nash buildings, its windows like those of the property on the opposite side of the road which Polly faced: ornate, with subtly elegant window boxes.

The room itself was large enough to accommodate not just the king-sized bed but also the pair of armchairs placed at either side of the fireplace and the table in between them, as well as a pretty writing desk set between the room's two tall, narrow windows.

The bathroom, to Polly's approval, was the very thing that a hotel bathroom should be. Its marble walls and floor would make it easy to keep hygienically clean, the bath was huge, claw-footed and very much in keeping with the era of the house, whilst the shower looked promisingly as though it could deliver a real blast of water.

The toiletries supplied had the discreet logo of a very up-market supplier and were, in fact, Polly was pleased to note, the same ones she bought for Fraser House. But she was equally pleased to see that this hotel, unlike her own, did not supply its guests with the additional luxury of a choice of aromatherapy oils— and candles.

All *their* bathrooms could be candlelit if their guests required it, and Polly knew from the frequency with which she had to replace the candles in their specially designed safety-glass pots that most of them did. Nor did this hotel have the floating bath pillows which she

knew from their comments that her female guests
adored.

She unpacked, which didn't take her long—it was
simply a matter of hanging her new dress in one side of
the large double wardrobe along with her change of
clothes for her return journey in the morning. Then,
stowing her overnight bag on the floor beneath them,
Polly locked the wardrobe door with the small key provided and put it safely in her purse.

Locking wardrobe doors was a nice touch, which she
made a mental note to remember. The hotel would have
duplicate keys, of course, but nevertheless it would give
guests an extra sense of security.

After her afternoon tea, which was everything she had
anticipated, Polly went upstairs to change for the evening.

Once on, her new dress was also everything it had
promised to be when she had first tried it on. Picking up
her bag, she opened her bedroom door just as the maid
was about to knock. Seeing that she was carrying a pile
of clean, soft white towels, Polly smiled approvingly at
her before leaving her to get on with her work.

The hotel Phil was negotiating to buy was on the opposite side of the city, but fortunately, when Polly got
into her taxi, the traffic had thinned out enough for their
journey to be completed without too many delays.

As she stepped into the foyer of her destination Phil
was waiting to greet her. He came towards her and took
the hand she offered him to shake in between both of
his and then pulled her gently but firmly towards him,
so that instead of shaking it he could kiss her briefly
instead.

Polly gave him an old-fashioned look which he had the grace to acknowledge with a rueful smile.

'It's your fault if I'm having a problem keeping my eyes and hands off you,' he teased, and then unexpectedly the laughter died out of his eyes and he told her more seriously, 'I mean it, Polly; there's something about you that...'

Immediately Polly shook her head.

'I'm flattered,' she told him honestly, 'but...'

But what?

But she loved Marcus, had loved him for over fourteen years, would *always* love him, even though she knew that her feelings, her love, would never be returned.

'But what?' Phil prompted her.

'But... I'm older than you, Phil; I've got a grown-up daughter and...'

The sound he made stopped her.

'Older than me? By what, four or so years?'

'According to Marcus—' Polly began.

'Marcus?' Phil had started to frown. 'What's this got to do with him?'

'Nothing. It's just...' Polly stopped. 'I like you, Phil,' she told him honestly. 'But I'm just not in the market for...for anything other than friendship.'

'Markets can change,' Phil told her meaningfully. 'And I wouldn't have got where I have today if I didn't know how to be a good salesman. You have been warned! Would you like a drink in the bar first or would you prefer to go straight into dinner?' he asked her.

'A drink first, I think,' Polly responded. 'After all, you did say that you wanted my opinion on the hotel.'

'Mmm...I did, didn't I?' Phil agreed.

*　　*　　*

Just over an hour later, when the waiter had brought the main course of their meal, Polly acknowledged to Phil that she was impressed with the hotel.

Its decor was a trifle modern and minimalistic for her taste but, judging by the number of sharply suited businessmen and women filling the bar and now the restaurant, it was obviously a very popular place.

The restaurant had been well planned, to allow those who wished to be seen to be seen and those who didn't to enjoy a little privacy. It was clearly a very 'in' place to dine, and she had already recognised several media celebrities. 'What I have in mind is to offer the business guest the option to bring his or her partner with them— all the rooms here are doubles, and the only difference between our rate for their single occupancy or their double is the additional cost of the inclusive room service breakfast.'

'The extras could include such things as seats for the top shows, special guided tours of galleries, buying trips for art works and antiques, with the advice of an expert, the services of personal shoppers, along with the provision of chauffeurs and minders if required.'

'Mmm, sounds impressive,' Polly told him.

'It will be,' Phil replied unabashed.

'Very impressive and *very* expensive,' Polly reinforced ruefully.

'There's a lot of money out there,' Phil pointed out, then suddenly frowned as he muttered, 'What the hell are *they* doing here?'

Automatically Polly turned her head to see who had caused him to look so grimly displeased, her whole body tensing as there, not three tables away from them, Marcus and Suzi were being seated by the head waiter. As yet they hadn't seen them, and as the waiter handed them their menus and left Polly's stomach dropped on seeing Suzi leaning across the table to cover Marcus's hand with her own.

'Very cosy,' she heard Phil snapping acerbically.

'You obviously didn't realise they would be dining here too,' Polly offered, trying to muster a casual lack of concern she didn't feel. Suzi looked so intimately at ease with Marcus. Briony *would* be pleased.

Polly discovered that she had suddenly lost her appetite.

'I didn't realise—' Phil began sharply, and then stopped. 'I have a suite here.' He gave a small shrug. 'As my assistant, Suzi knows she is free to use the empty bedroom—I'm using this place as a base whilst the deal goes through so it makes sense to be here on hand to iron out the inevitable last-minute snags, but if Suzi thinks...' He stopped again and then frowned as he saw the way Polly was pushing her food around her plate.

'Is something wrong?' he asked her in concern. 'If you'd prefer something else...' As he started to look round for a waiter, Polly shook her head.

'No. No, it's...it's fine. I'm just not very hungry.' She gave him a smile and then bit her lip in vexation as he obviously guessed what the real cause of her loss of appetite was and commented brusquely, 'Yes, I know what you mean. Look, we can always eat in my suite if you'd prefer, or go somewhere else.'

'No. No...there's no need for that,' she assured him quickly.

'Hell,' she heard him curse. 'They've seen us.' And then he was pushing back his chair and getting up. As Polly turned her head she could see Suzi advancing towards them.

'Phil...and Mrs Fraser.' She gave Polly a thin smile

whilst Polly acknowledged her greeting with cool politeness. There was no mistaking the challenging way the other woman had said her name. That Mrs Fraser was quite plainly intended to put Polly where Suzi obviously thought she belonged—in a much older generation.

'When you told me you had a *business* meeting this evening I didn't realise it was with Mrs Fraser,' Suzi told Phil. She was standing between them, her back very firmly towards Polly. The dress she was wearing was long, sheer and cut so low at the back it was immediately obvious that it would be impossible for her to wear any underwear beneath it.

As Polly recoiled a little at that knowledge she chided herself for being absurdly old-fashioned. If a modern woman chose not to wear underwear then was that really so very shocking? Perhaps not, Polly acknowledged, but in her book Suzi's deliberate advertisement of it by the way she leaned her weight first on one leg and then the other so that every male within eyesight was watching her with various degrees of discretion—or in some cases an open lack of it—was in Polly's book certainly a little ill-bred.

'When you said you were seeing a *friend* I had no idea you meant *Mr* Fraser,' Phil was retaliating, with a venom in his voice that made Polly look at them both a little uncomfortably—a working relationship?

'My friends are my own concern,' Suzi told Phil sharply, adding outrageously, at least in Polly's opinion, 'But your business associates should, since I am your assistant, be mine.'

Swinging round on her heel, she gave Polly a hard, assessing look before telling her sweetly, 'I don't know about you, Mrs Fraser, but I always feel rather sorry for older women who make the mistake of falling for younger men. They make themselves look so ridiculous, don't you think?'

'Human beings can make themselves look ridiculous in a wide variety of ways and for a wide variety of reasons,' Polly countered quietly. 'Perhaps I'm old-fashioned but it's always been my credo to judge others as compassionately as I would like to have them judge me.' And then, ignoring Suzi, she leaned across the table and told Phil calmly, 'From what I've seen of the hotel, Phil, I'm sure it will make an excellent addition to your existing business, but now, if you'll excuse me, I am feeling rather tired and I think it's time I left.'

Before he could say anything she stood up and started to walk swiftly towards the exit.

Inside she was shaking with a mixture of pain and anger. How dared Suzi speak so insultingly to her? How dared she and Marcus flaunt their relationship whilst implying that *she* had no right to enjoy a similar degree of intimacy with Phil if she chose to do so? And, most of all, how dared fate hurt her in the way that it was doing? She could feel the sharp, searing, burning pain of her jealousy as though it were a living clawing incubus inside her.

Tonight, Marcus would be holding Suzi, kissing her, touching her, whilst she…

'Polly.'

She froze as she felt the male hand grasping her arm and then relaxed as she realised it belonged to Phil. She had been so absorbed in her feelings that for a moment she'd actually thought that Marcus had come after her.

'You can't leave…not like this. I don't know what on earth Suzi thought she was doing, speaking to you like that.'

'Plainly she shares Mr Fraser's belief that I'm an old has-been, a woman of a certain age, so desperate for a man that...'

To Polly's consternation she discovered that she was perilously close to tears.

'You're no such thing,' she could hear Phil reassuring her, his voice thickening as he protested, 'Oh, my God, Polly, please don't cry... If you do... Have you *any* idea how much I want to take you to bed right now?'

'What for?' she challenged him frantically. 'So that you can count my wrinkles?'

'Polly,' she heard him groaning. 'Look,' he told her, 'let's go up to the suite. I'll order us a room-service meal and...'

Polly closed her eyes, ashamed of how very, very much she was tempted to accept. She knew, of course, that what Phil had in mind, what was really on the menu, was *not* a meal but a night of passion, and she was very tempted to take him up on it. Not because she wanted him, not even because she felt she wanted sex; no, the reason she was so dangerously inclined to accept was seated in the restaurant—all six-foot-odd of far too handsome, hunky masculinity for his own good. And certainly for hers.

Marcus... That was why she was even considering accepting what Phil was offering her... Marcus... Oh, how she wanted, ached to prove him wrong, to show him that even if he did not want her, even if he did not believe she was attractive, desirable...loveable...another man quite obviously did. But then common sense and reality came to her rescue.

Over the years there had been numerous opportunities for her to accept the kind of offer Phil was making her right now, but she had never once felt remotely tempted.

No matter how hurt she was feeling now, how angry Marcus had made her, she was going to remain true to her own beliefs and her own moral code, which meant not having sex with a man she didn't love.

Putting her hand on Phil's arm, Polly looked into his eyes and told him gently, 'No, Phil. It's very kind of you to offer, but...' Against her will her glance was drawn back to the restaurant. She could see Marcus from where she was standing. He was sitting with his back to her, engrossed in his conversation with Suzi. Giving a faint sigh, Polly looked away.

'I can see why you're so enthusiastic about this hotel,' she told Phil warmly.

'When the deal goes through I shall be spending several months here in London—if you should change your mind...'

'About dinner?' Polly teased him, her mouth curving into a deep smile.

'About *anything*,' Phil responded firmly.

A little regretfully she shook her head.

'I shan't change my mind,' she told him. 'The *maître d'* will be concerned that you didn't finish your meal.'

'Like you, I've lost my appetite,' Phil said, adding with a shrug, 'I can always have something sent up to the suite later. I've got some work to do up there. I'll see you into a taxi first, though.'

A little to Polly's irritation, when she returned to her own hotel she had the same problem getting into her room that she had had before. The girl on Reception— a different girl this time—summoned the porter to let her in with his pass key, explaining vaguely to Polly, 'It does sometimes happen with these key cards. I'm very sorry.'

It wasn't quite ten o'clock, but Polly felt so drained that all she wanted to do was to go to bed.

Stripping off her clothes, she hung her new dress carefully in the closet before relocking it, and then frowned as she realised that the other key had been removed from the other half of the wardrobe. Not that it mattered; she would not be needing to use it. Still, she was sure it had been there earlier. The maid must have removed it by accident when she had come in with the clean towels. Polly guessed.

Only when she went into the bathroom a few minutes later she was disconcerted to find that a couple of the towels had been used and left to air on the heated towel rail.

How odd! They weren't the towels she had used, and nor were they hung on the rail the way she would have hung them. Perhaps the maid hadn't replaced them after all... She *had* turned down the bed, though—both sides of it, Polly noticed in amusement.

No doubt that was something she did automatically for all double rooms, even when they were only being used for a single occupancy.

A nice long soak in a hot bath and then she intended to go to bed. She had brought a book with her so she could read for a while if she wanted to.

Turning on the bath taps, Polly determinedly refused to allow herself to dwell on what Marcus would be doing now.

They would probably have finished their meal. Perhaps they would retire to the bar afterwards, or maybe they would go straight to Marcus's room.

There were some things, some pains that not even the warmest, most deliciously scented water could ease, Polly acknowledged despairingly.

It was only when she had stepped out of the bath and wrapped herself in one of the courtesy bathrobes the hotel provided that she opened her overnight bag and realised that she had forgotten to bring a nightdress with her.

Not that it mattered!

One of the herbal sleeping tablets she always took with her when she was away from home would soon help her get off to sleep. Padding naked over to the bed, she slid into it and reached out to switch off the lights.

Twenty minutes later she was fast asleep.

CHAPTER SIX

'EXCUSE me a moment.' Marcus apologised tersely to Suzi, getting up from the table and striding out into the hotel foyer hard on the heels of Polly and Phil, coming to an abrupt halt when he realised that there was no sign of either of them. He had guessed right from the moment he had rung Fraser House asking to speak with Polly, only to be told that she was in London 'on business', just what her business was likely to be and with whom... And it gave him a certain sense of bitter satisfaction to know how shocked she had been to see him.

'Can I help you, sir?'

Marcus frowned as the receptionist smiled politely at him.

'Yes. Mr Bernstein and...'

'Oh, Mr Bernstein has just gone up to his suite. He gave instructions that he isn't to be disturbed, I'm afraid.'

Grimly Marcus looked towards the lift. The temptation to go up to Phil Bernstein's suite and physically compel Polly to leave with him was so strong that he had to ball his hands into fists to stop himself from giving in to it. Couldn't she *see* what she was doing? Bernstein might be all flattering attention now, but Suzi had told him about her employer's penchant for brief affairs. It had been providential that Suzi had already invited him to have dinner with her, and although initially he had declined her invitation she had been more than happy to have him change his mind. What he hadn't been prepared for, though, was that Polly actually intended to spend the night with Phil Bernstein. He ached to go after her, to physically separate her from Phil Bernstein if necessary, but he knew that he couldn't—that he didn't have that right.

'Marcus…'

Marcus tensed as Suzi herself came hurrying out of the restaurant in search of him.

'Is something wrong?' she asked.

'No,' he responded. 'I was just hoping to catch Polly. There was something I wanted to say to her.'

'Yes, I should imagine there is,' Suzi agreed, raising her eyebrows as she criticised contemptuously, 'She really is making a fool of herself. She can't possibly imagine that Phil is *really* attracted to her, surely? I mean, he can have his pick of much more glamorous and younger women…' she continued disparagingly. Then saw the way Marcus was frowning at her.

'But of course you're bound to feel you have to defend her. She is, after all, a member of your family.' She gave him a sideways glance. 'I suppose I should really feel sorry for her. She's going to come down to earth with a very nasty bump when Phil drops her. Still, we mustn't let them spoil *our* night, must we?' she asked him. She reached out invitingly towards him as she told him, 'I can't offer to take you up to my room. It wouldn't be… politic…but we could go back to your hotel…'

'No, I don't think that would be a very good idea,' Marcus replied wryly, shaking his head.

The last thing he wanted to do was to go to bed with Suzi when all he could think about was Polly. And Suzi didn't want him anyway; she just wanted a man—any man. Oh, God Polly: What was she doing? Was she all right?

Before Suzi could voice the protests he could see she wanted to make, he released himself from her hold and stepped away, telling her shortly, 'I'd better go. I've got an early start in the morning. I'm flying to China on business.'

His company was engaged in very delicate negotiations with the Chinese about certain explorative mining work, and the last thing he really needed right now was the kind of intensely personal anxiety he was experiencing.

Heading for the exit, he stepped outside into the cool night air whilst the doorman summoned him a taxi. Once in it, he gave the driver the address of the small hotel he had booked himself into. Quiet and well run, it was part of the same informal group of very select small hotels of which Fraser House was also a member and lay on the other side of London.

Fifteen minutes later he emerged from his taxi to head for the hotel's foyer, where the receptionist was in conversation with another guest. Checking that he had his key card, Marcus headed for the lift. His room was on the third floor, one of a small group of six rooms that overlooked the street.

Sliding the key card into the lock, he waited until the light turned green and then went in.

The first thing that struck him was her perfume, so familiar to him that initially he felt he must simply be imagining it, but then, in the dim glow from the entrance light he had switched on as he'd entered the room, he could see her shape beneath the bedclothes and the soft tangle of her hair.

She slept curled up like a child, not quite but almost

hugging her pillow. His heart started to beat very fast and then very slowly. What on earth was *Polly* doing in his room…in his bed?

Frowning, he backed towards the bedroom door and walked back out into the hallway, letting the door close quietly behind him.

Downstairs in the foyer the receptionist tried to be helpful.

'*Mrs* Fraser? Yes, she *is* booked into room number 113.'

Room 113… That was *his* room. There had quite obviously been a mistake. He was just about to say as much to the receptionist when a middle-aged couple came up to the desk.

'We're booked into room 204,' the man explained to the receptionist. 'But there's a street light outside and it's disturbing my wife. I wonder if we could possibly change to another room?'

The receptionist immediately shook her head, explaining regretfully, 'I'm sorry, sir, but we're fully booked. A large party of Americans… We don't have a single empty room.'

No empty rooms. So that put paid to his own as yet unspoken request to book into another room…a room that was not already occupied by Polly, Marcus acknowledged.

Grimly he turned and headed back towards the lift.

Five minutes later he was in the hotel bedroom gazing down at Polly's sleeping body.

Like him, she had obviously booked a room here which meant… Which meant what? That even though he had seen her leaving the restaurant with Phil Bernstein she was plainly not spending the night with him. Had they quarrelled, perhaps? Had he…? Had she...? Jealousy had to be the most damaging, soul-destroying waste of time there could be. It had been bad enough when it had just been his jealousy of his dead cousin he'd had to contend with, but this...

Softly he spoke Polly's name, but she was so deeply asleep that she didn't waken.

The sensible, the right and proper thing for him to do now would be to persist and wake her up, explain the situation to her and then offer to spend the night sleeping in a chair.

But, faced with the prospect of the next day's long flight ahead of him, the thought of trying to sleep upright in an uncomfortable and undersized armchair was not an appealing one.

Quietly unlocking the side of the wardrobe where he had placed his overnight bag, Marcus hung up his jacket and then made his way to the bathroom. The towels he had used earlier had been carefully refolded on the drying rail to make room for the one Polly had used. Smiling at this evidence of her housewifeliness, he undressed and turned on the shower.

It was the noise of the water that woke Polly. At first confused and half asleep, she thought it had started to rain—very hard—and then, as she became fully awake, she thought she must be able to hear the shower in the adjoining bedroom: But then, as she lifted her head from the pillow and saw the bar of light showing under the closed *en suite* bathroom door, the full realisation that someone was actually in the shower in *her* room, hit her.

Without considering that she could be putting herself in danger, she got out of bed, pulling on the hotel robe as she marched purposefully towards the bathroom door and pushed it open.

As he saw the bathroom door opening Marcus quickly grabbed a towel, turning off the shower.

'Marcus!' Polly gasped in disbelief. 'What are *you* doing *here*?'

'What does it look like I'm doing?' Marcus asked her laconically.

'This is my room,' Polly informed him angrily. 'How did you get in, and *why* are you having a shower?'

'Correction, this is *our* room,' Marcus informed her grimly. 'It seems that the hotel has made a mistake and booked us both into the same room—perhaps because we share the same surname and the same address. I don't know, and right now I don't particularly care just how the error occurred. But what I can tell you, before you say anything else, is that the hotel is fully booked and there are no spare rooms.'

'What?' Polly rubbed her eyes sleepily. She felt as though she had strayed into some weird surreal dream. It seemed an impossibly bizarre coincidence that she and Marcus should have been given the same room, but one look at his face warned her that he was in no mood for her to tell him that she didn't believe him. And besides, what possible motive could he have for lying?

And then a horrible suspicion struck her.

'You haven't brought…anyone back with you, have you?' she asked him huskily.

There was a small, sharp silence before Marcus replied curtly, 'No, I haven't.'

'Oh…'

She stifled a huge yawn. Even though the sound of the shower had woken her up she was still feeling the effect of the herbal sleeping tablet she had taken. Her eyes felt heavy and she longed to go back to bed, curl up and go back to sleep. To stifle another yawn she raised her hand to her mouth, and as she did so her overlarge robe fell open revealing the soft satin-skinned curve of her breast.

Marcus felt as though someone had kicked him in the stomach, and the urge to take hold of her and bury his face in the creamy scented warmth of her neck, to slide his hands inside her robe and touch her, feel her naked body against his own, was so acute and overwhelming that he had to remind himself of just what Polly was doing in London to stop himself from giving in to it. And because of that, and his unwanted jealousy, he heard himself demanding angrily, 'Just why are *you* here anyway? I should have thought the least Bernstein could have done was to offer you a room for the night, even if he didn't want you sharing the one he had.'

Polly could hardly believe her ears.

What Marcus was implying about her wasn't just ugly, it was also offensive, and she knew that if her senses, her emotional responses hadn't been softened and dulled a little by the sleeping tablet they would prob- ably have reduced her to shocked, shamed tears.

Holding her head up high, she told Marcus quietly, 'You shouldn't judge others by your own standards, Marcus. Phil *did* offer me a room. In fact—' she gave him a small sad smile, '—he offered me a suite...'

Now her eyes were clouding with tears, and as he read the underlying message in her words Marcus cursed him- self under his breath. What on earth had possessed him to be so stupid?

'*You* might consider me to be some silly middle-aged woman so desperate for sex that I'll grab at any chance to...to have a man,' she told him, scarlet-cheeked, 'but that doesn't mean that I am one.

'I just can't get it right with you, can I, Marcus?

You're either condemning me for being dull and boringly faithful to my husband's memory or you're accusing me of having some kind of mid-life sexual problem.'

'Polly,' Marcus protested, reaching out to stop her as she started to turn away from him, but she had moved too quickly and as she pulled away he was left holding the empty fabric of her robe.

As she felt the towelling fabric slide free of her shoulder and then her body Polly gave an outraged gasp of shock, turning back to try to hold onto it; but it was too late.

For a second neither of them moved, and even though Polly was burningly conscious of the way Marcus was looking at her body, of the tension she could feel emanating from him, the hot male desire she could almost feel filling the distance between them, it was as though somehow she was experiencing these things at a distance. It was as though it could not possibly be happening, not possibly be *her* standing here, her body naked to Marcus's black-eyed burning scrutiny, her nipples taut and full, aching with a sensuality that shocked as well as tormented her, her belly soft, quivering with that same feeling.

And then Marcus moved and she was jerked sharply into reality, crying fiercely, 'No,' as she backed away from not just the physical presence of him but the dangerous heat and scent of him as well.

He might be nearly as naked as she was herself but his was a different kind of nudity—a man's nudity—which somehow, instead of robbing him of control and power, only seemed to reinforce it, just as it reinforced his maleness.

'Polly,' Marcus repeated fiercely as his fingers curled imprisoningly round her upper arm.

He had only meant to hand the robe back to her. That was all. But somehow, once he felt the soft warmth of her skin, that intention was lost, flattened beneath the fierce onslaught of his own desire, and instead of covering her with the robe he was still holding he let it drop to the floor, covering her instead with his own body.

Frantically Polly tried to fend him off, but it was too late. When she had denied any need or desire for Phil Bernstein she had been speaking the truth, but when it came to Marcus himself *then* she was everything he had accused her of being she acknowledged defencelessly. Then she wanted him...needed him...ached for him so much that—

Deep in her throat she gave a small whimper of pain and self-recrimination, but her body, her emotions, her love, didn't want to listen.

This was *Marcus* who was holding her, touching her, wanting her...

No, not here. She tried to warn herself. To him she was just a woman...just a substitute for the woman he must really want... She had no idea why he had returned to the hotel without Suzi. The other girl had been making it plain enough earlier that she wanted him and Marcus must have felt that as strongly as Polly had herself. No wonder he was now so fiercely and angrily aroused. No wonder he was touching her, kissing her with so much starving hunger, she acknowledged as her head fell back under the onslaught of the savage, burning kisses he was pressing against her throat.

From beneath her semi-closed eyelids she could see their entwined reflections in the bathroom mirror. Marcus's arms were wrapped around her, holding and supporting her. The pale fairness of her skin looked femininely fragile in contrast to the darker, more bronzed masculinity of his, just as the raw, male definition of the muscles beneath his skin highlighted the soft, female roundness of her own body. Male to female, female to male—how perfect they looked together.

A sharp shudder went through her and she moaned under her breath, her eyes closing completely as Marcus's hand cupped her breast. Small, intensely violent shudders of pleasure burned through her, almost too intense to be borne.

She was thirty-seven years old and nothing she had experienced, either with Richard or since, in the celibate years of her widowhood, had prepared her for what she was feeling now.

Shockingly, she was suddenly hungry for everything that Marcus could give her, every last drop of sensation and pleasure—all of it. All of *him*.

Her own hands reached out to smooth the taut muscles of his arms, his skin. He felt male and alive, the movement of his muscles somehow so different from her own. Behind her closed eyelids she could picture him mentally as she touched him, but soon mentally visualising him wasn't enough—she wanted to see him in reality. Her eyes flickered open as she spread her hands as wide as she could over his back, which was strong, alien, exciting. His skin felt so hard, and hot. Richard, while tall, had been more angular than Marcus, less heavily muscled, more of a boy still than a man.

'Polly.'

She could hear the raw urgency in his voice and at some deep level her senses recognised the sharp need wrapped in the rough velvet huskiness, and she responded to it, sensually, triumphantly, pleased that she could so affect him. Her hand lifted to his face; her fingertips stroked exploratively along his jaw, which was

excitingly rough where his beard was growing in a betraying dark shadow. A frisson of sensation ripped
through her sensitive body, as intense and betraying as
though he had actually bent his head and rubbed that
faint raspiness against the most sensitive parts of her.

Slowly she traced the shape of his mouth, her eyes
luminous with emotion and expectation. Her lips had
parted, her breathing quick and unsteady.

Mesmerised, she returned the intensity of his concentrated fixation on her, gaze to gaze, ncither of them moving, and yet somehow she felt as though they were moving together in some secret, intimate dance, following a
tune that only they could hear. Her fingers stilled against
his mouth and Marcus started to caress them, delicately,
with little licks and nibbles, until she was moaning out
loud—a soft, keening sound; the sound of a woman.

A woman... Yes, that was what she was now—a
woman, not a girl, and Marcus was her man!

Unable to stop herself, she glanced sideways into the
mirror again. He still had the towel he had picked up
when she'd walked into thc bathroom draped round his
hips.

'Take it off,' she told him thickly, touching it with
her free hand. 'I want to see all of you, please.'

Silently Marcus did as she commanded whilst Polly
drew in her breath, held it and then let it out again on a
slow, shuddering sigh. Automatically she reached out to
touch him, her fingertips sketching the shape of his
shoulders and arms, registering the faint tremor of his
muscles as she stroked delicately along his forearm, and
then the far stronger tremor that shook him when she
touched his waist, his hip, the hard flat planes of his
buttocks...

'Polly!' She heard him grinding out, the fierce, stark

sound of his voice shocking her into immobility as in it she recognised the curtness and the grimness she was so used to hearing from him.

'For God's sake…' His voice was thicker now, not angry as she had first thought but…tortured almost. 'If you don't…'

If she didn't what? She could feel herself starting to tremble as she waited to hear him tell her to stop touching him, reality suddenly imposing itself on her in starkly jagged pangs of self-consciousness. But as she made to move away from him, her face starting to burn with the hot realisation of just what she was doing, Marcus suddenly reached for her, begging her hoarsely, 'Polly, don't stop—look at what you've done to me.' And, as he moved slightly away from her, Polly realised why he had been so careful not to close that final distance between them. Heat scorched through her body as she witnessed his open arousal. *This* was the male form in all its dark, dangerous beauty, she recognised shakily. This was man at his most primeval, his most potent…and just seeing him made her want to…made her feel…

Deep down inside her Polly was conscious of such hungry yearning, such a sense of emptiness waiting to be filled, such a *need*, that she actually felt the intensity of it make her eyes burn with anguished tears. Longingly she swayed towards Marcus, her whole body curving in an arc of supplication and invitation, her eyes heavy with the knowledge of her love and wanting.

Immediately Marcus reached out to take her weight, holding her so that the heat of his body against hers, its power and its arousal, felt like a soothing balm to the aching heat that both consumed her and reinforced some deep inner emptiness.

As he bent his head and cupped her face with his free hand Polly turned so that her lips brushed his hard palm.

'Marcus...please...' she whispered, knowing he would understand just what it was she was pleading for.

'Polly...' She could hear the torment in his voice. 'Have you any idea how long I've waited for this, wanted you like this?' she heard him telling her thickly as he picked her up and carried her through into the bedroom.

'But not even in my wildest dreams, my most intimate sensual imaginings, did I come anywhere near the reality of *this*...' he told her rawly as he placed her on the bed and laid his head on her soft small belly. He kissed her skin, stroked it, both feeding and stoking the hunger she felt for him at the same time. Every touch, every kiss inflamed her even more, pushing her to sensual heights of pleasure she had never known existed.

His mouth against her breast, his tongue, sent little trails of fire running right through her. Twisting frantically underneath him, she cried out in ecstasy as he sucked fiercely on her breast. Pleasure like this was like a forbidden kingdom to her and she was almost afraid of entering it, of giving in, of giving *herself* up to what she was feeling; but to try to stop now, when her body was crying out for him, was impossible.

Mutely she tried to convey to him all that she was experiencing and feeling, reaching out for him and drawing him closer to her.

'It's been so long,' she heard him saying hoarsely as he covered her body with his own.

'Yes. So very long.'

He felt like hot velvet against her. Hot velvet encasing smooth liquid muscle.

Polly sucked in her breath as her body arched for his

entry, quivering, waiting…wanting…eager and yet a little afraid. It had, as he had said, been so long.

It was nothing like her memories of the way it had been with Richard. There was no comparison, nor did she want there to be. This was her first time as a woman. Her first time with a man and not a boy. Each smooth thrust took him deeper into her body, closer to where she wanted him to be, and Polly clung to him in apprehensive exultation as each wave of pleasure took her nearer to fulfilment. His movements were different now—hotter, faster, and then deeper and slower, and her own body was picking up their rhythm, moving in counterpart to it.

It was like singing, soaring, floating, flying, catching the wind and riding with it—a joyful pain of love, an outpouring of it that seemed to burst from every pore of her body.

Polly had no words, no sounds, no thoughts to express the magnitude, the magnificence of what she was experiencing.

She felt the deep climactic shudders wrenching Marcus's body, the hot burst of his completion deep inside her triggering off the seismic quakes of her own fulfilment.

Dreamily Polly tried to bring herself back down to earth. Marcus was saying something to her; smiling, she nestled closer to him, too exhausted, too blissfully content to listen properly or comprehend. It was more than her senses could take on board just to know what had happened, what they had shared. Conversation was completely beyond her, an impossibility.

Marcus could feel his hand trembling as he stroked Polly's damp hair back off her face.

He had waited so long, *loved* so long, but never once had he imagined there would be—*could* be—anything like this. He was not a promiscuous man but there had been women, relationships...pleasure; but none of it— none of *them*—had ever come anywhere near this.

He cupped Polly's face, wanting to tell her how he felt, how much he loved her, how insanely jealous he had felt tonight seeing her with someone else, but as he turned his head to look down at her he realised that she had fallen deeply asleep.

Very gently he lifted her, touching her tenderly beneath the bedclothes, kissing her lovingly before joining her there. His last thought as he switched off the light was one of awed disbelief that they should have shared what they had just shared.

Polly was having the most blissful dream imaginable. In it she was snuggled up in bed with Marcus, close to his body, totally enveloped in its warmth and his love. Euphorically she moved closer to him, murmuring his name, breathing in the warm scent of his skin, nuzzling her mouth into the warmth of his bare shoulder.

'Mmm... Marcus...'

He was moving his arm to draw her closer and she could feel the way his mouth was smiling as she touched it.

'Marcus!'

Bemused, Polly opened her eyes. It wasn't a dream at all; she was actually in bed with Marcus.

As she tried to sit bolt upright he laughed softly, as though her being there with him was so natural and right that they might have been sharing a bed for years.

'Mmm... Now that you've woken me up, what are you going to do with me?' he asked her teasingly. But the way his hand was stroking her naked breast and playing with its hardening tip suggested that he knew very well already what it was he wanted to do with her, Polly recognised, as the final shreds of her dream dispersed and full recollection of the events of the evening brought her eyes wide open and her thoughts into confused shock.

No wonder Marcus was behaving the way he was after what she had said...done...

'Mmm... Nothing to say?' Marcus was nuzzling her breast, her throat, her mouth, his hands sliding over her, stroking her, positioning her.

Polly wasn't naive; she knew, of course, that it was possible to have sex in a wide variety of positions, but she and Richard...well, they had been young, inexperienced and...

She gave a small gasp at what Marcus was doing with her...to her...

'It's nice like this,' he was whispering. 'I can touch all of you as well as...'

Polly gasped again as his fingers stroked her intimately, gently exploring and caressing her. She could feel her body responding to him, reacting to him. Helplessly she closed her eyes and gave in to the surge of desire flooding her.

'Lie still,' Marcus was telling her. 'Let me...please you...like this...'

Polly moaned softly under her breath, unable to silence her pleasure. Marcus moved her again, pushing back the bedclothes so that in the dim light she could just see what he was doing. His body filled hers, fitting her so fully that just to feel him inside her caused her to quiver in a series of tiny convulsions.

'Marcus...'

She clung to him, unable to do anything other than ride the waves of pleasure that were starting to swamp her. Even the smallest movement of his body within hers seemed to trigger them, tremor after tremor, wave after wave until, the tiny movements became not so much a pleasure but a refined form of torture.

She reached for him, digging her fingers into his forearms as she tried to pull him closer, deeper within her. The suddenness with which he acceded to her hungry demand shocked her at first, robbing her of breath as he drove powerfully within her, but then almost immediately she was moving with him, responding to him, opening to him.

This time her orgasm was deeper, longer, and so intense that it flooded her eyes with tears, bewildering her with the complexity of the emotions it released, leaving her shakily and emotionally needy, wanting to cling to Marcus and to be reassured by him that he felt the same way about her as she did about him. At the same time, defensively agitated, she wanted to deny what she was feeling because it made her feel so afraid of her own vulnerability.

'We shouldn't be doing this,' she told Marcus.

'Why not?' he demanded. 'We're both free agents, aren't we?'

When Polly made no response, his grip on her arms tightened.

'Polly...' he began warningly, but Polly had had enough. She had seen him earlier with Suzi, after all. Suzi, whom Briony so much wanted him to marry. Briony! Dear God, what on earth was *she* going to think if she...?

With appalling clarity Polly could see the minefield she had dropped herself into, the emptiness of the life that now lay ahead of her, the deceit, the lies she would have to tell. And for what? A brief taste of heaven which was going to leave her with an aftertaste of the worst kind of hell. How was she going to endure seeing Marcus with Suzi now, after what she herself had just experienced in his arms? How was she ever going to be able to look at Marcus again without thinking...remembering...?

'Polly?' Marcus was demanding.

Resolutely she closed her eyes, holding her body stiff and wooden as she heard him curse under his breath and then release her. The moment he did she turned away from him. She didn't want to stay here in bed with him but her exhausted body was refusing to allow her to move. Tiredly she closed her eyes. Behind her she could feel Marcus's warmth.

Why the hell hadn't she answered him when he had said that they were both free agents? Was there, after all, something between her and Bernstein? Could she be in love with the other man? Had she been using Marcus simply to assuage the desire she felt for him? Marcus was tempted to wake her up and demand to know the truth.

Polly gave a small sob in her sleep. Frowning, Marcus leaned over her. In the dim light he could see her tears and his anger melted. He loved her so much, had loved her for so long, virtually from the very first moment he had seen her—but she had been Richard's then and he had forced down his own feelings for her. He had strong views about loyalty and about commitment, and Richard had been his cousin and there had been a close bond between them.

But it hadn't been either loyalty or concern for his

cousin that had prompted his suggestion to Richard that they keep Fraser House and that he finance its upkeep whilst Richard and Polly—or, more realistically, *Polly* acted as its housekeeper and *his* hostess. Just the sight of her small, too worried, too pale face as she had shivered with cold in that wretched flat of theirs had been enough to make him feel positively murderous towards his impractical cousin. Polly had so obviously needed cherishing and cosseting, and had she been *his* wife and not carrying his cousin's baby...

But at least he had managed to bring some measure of comfort and order to her life—hers and Briony's.

Briony... Marcus blinked fiercely as he remembered Briony's birth. At the hospital they had mistaken him for Polly's husband, allowing him into the delivery room with her.

She had clung so hard to his arm during the most intense of her labour pains that at one point his arm had gone heavy and his fingers had gone white and numb.

He had been so afraid for her and so angry with Richard, demanding that the doctor do something to ease her pain, but Polly herself had shaken her head, insisting that she was all right, so absorbed in what she was doing that she'd hardly seemed to know he was there. And then had come the wonderful, miraculous moment of Briony's birth.

Over the years he had often asked himself whether it was because he had witnessed her arrival into the world that Briony meant so much to him, as though she were his own child.

Perhaps, but that could not explain Briony's own closeness to him; the bond which they shared was a very close one and very special to him.

After Richard's death he had begun to allow himself

to hope, just a little, but that hope had died a swift, merciless death when Polly herself had made it plain on more than one occasion that Richard was the only man she ever could or ever would love.

He had tried to conceal his own feelings by adopting a manner of cool indifference towards her, but sometimes just being with her was so painful for him that he had to distance himself from her, which was the main reason he had decided to move out of Fraser House.

Perhaps at his age his emotions ought to be different, less easily aroused, his need for her tamed and subdued, but if anything the years had only increased his love for her, and with it the sense of anger and helplessness he felt at the waste of her womanhood and his love. But those feelings were nothing to what he was experiencing now at the thought that she might have given another man what she had resolutely always insisted she could never give any man other than Richard—her love.

When he thought of all the times he had held himself back, *pulled* himself back from telling her how he felt, and of all the times when she had vehemently insisted that there was no room in her life for a man who was not Richard, all the years she had clung so fiercely to her love for her late husband...and yet now, within days of meeting Phil Bernstein...

Marcus thought he had accustomed himself to the fact that Polly was so wedded to her widowhood and her memories of her late husband that all she would ever see him as was Richard's cousin.

His eyes felt gritty with tension and lack of sleep. In two hours' time he needed to leave for the airport. The last thing he felt like doing was walking away from Polly right now, absenting himself from her life and leaving the field wide open to Phil Bernstein, knowing the other man would be bombarding her with flattery and attention.

Just what was the attraction the other man possessed that *he* did not? What was it that had made Polly turn to Phil and not to him? Pushing back the bedclothes, Marcus got out of bed. Polly was deeply asleep and he knew that if he stayed where he was the temptation to wake her up and demand to know what made Bernstein so attractive to her and not him would be too much for him.

Wasn't it the female sex that was supposed to need emotional reassurance and close physical contact after sex and not his own? But, when it came to the feelings of longing and insecurity that loving someone who did not return one's feelings provoked, Marcus suspected that there wasn't that much difference between the sexes.

He might as well get dressed and leave for the airport, he told himself; there was nothing to be gained by staying where he was, waking Polly and provoking an argument with her which he knew would result in her defending her feelings for Phil Bernstein.

Half an hour later, as he gently closed the bedroom door behind him so as not to waken Polly, he couldn't help reflecting that another man—a man who did not care as deeply as he did—might have taken a rather macho pleasure in knowing that, whilst Bernstein might be the man Polly had fallen in love with, *he* was the one she had gone to bed with and given herself to... But then it wasn't Polly's body he wanted; it was her love, her commitment, herself—all of her.

Two hours later, when the early-morning call Marcus had booked for himself came through from the reception desk, it woke Polly, who reached automatically for the telephone receiver, listening as the voice on the other end told her brightly, 'This is your early-morning call, Mr Fraser. You wanted to be woken in time to catch your flight to China.'

China... Marcus had gone to *China*? Numbly Polly replaced the receiver.

Blurred images of the evening's events replayed themselves over and over again inside her head whilst she shivered in a mixture of despair and disbelief.

How could she have behaved in such a way; cheapened herself like that? Oh, she knew that the modern view was that a woman had as much right to freedom of sexual expression as a man, but *she* was not a modern woman, not in that respect, and it hurt her to know that she had betrayed herself so badly and allowed her emotions, her *love* to override her normal caution.

Now Marcus must know just how she felt about him. No wonder he had left without so much as waking her up to say goodbye. In just a few self-indulgent, sex-crazed hours she had demolished all the years of careful defences and subterfuge she had hidden her secret behind.

Would he tell Suzi? Would they laugh about it...*her*...together?

Not even Briony, her own daughter, had known how she felt about Marcus.

'I've found the perfect woman for Uncle Marcus,' she had trilled happily, never realising that there was and always had been only one woman Polly could bear to see sharing Marcus's life and his bed: herself.

And now everything she had done to prevent Marcus from guessing the truth had been undermined by her own foolish actions.

Oh, no, there was no need for her to question just why Marcus had walked out on her whilst she lay asleep. No need to ask at all.

CHAPTER SEVEN

AFTER ordering a room-service breakfast, which she'd felt totally unable to eat, Polly was packing for her return journey when the bedroom telephone rang.

Drearily she picked up the receiver, knowing that the only person whose voice she really wanted to hear was Marcus's and, of course, there was no way that Marcus was going to ring her.

'Polly?'

'Oh, Phil, I was just about to leave,' she answered.

'Good; that means I've caught you just in time,' Phil told her warmly, adding before she could say anything, 'There's something I want to discuss with you—a proposition I want to put to you.'

'A proposition?' Polly queried uncertainly.

'Mmm...of a strictly business nature,' Phil assured her, before adding teasingly, 'Not that I would be averse to propositioning you personally if I thought there was any chance you would respond! No, this is strictly business, Polly...but I'll tell you about it when you get here. Just come straight up to the suite; I'll be waiting.'

'Phil—' Polly began, but it was too late. Phil had already replaced his receiver.

Frowning, Polly wondered just what it was he wanted to discuss with her. Beneath that teasing manner he adopted Phil was an extremely shrewd businessman. Was he, perhaps, despite what had already been said, thinking of expanding his operation into the British countryside? Did he have his sights on Fraser House? If

115

so, then it was really Marcus he needed to talk with more than her.

She was very tempted to ignore Phil's phone call and go straight back to Fraser House, where she could lick her wounds in private and brood on the folly of her own behaviour, but it had never been Polly's style to give in to self-pity, and besides, if Phil *was* contemplating making a bid for Fraser House then she owed it to herself to be informed of what was happening.

'Come straight up to the suite', Phi had told her, and Polly did exactly that, knocking a little tentatively on the door, which was opened almost immediately by Phil, wearing a pair of jeans and a casual shirt and looking more than a little preoccupied.

'Polly. Good. You came… Come on in.' He gestured to the table in the centre of the suite's sitting room which was loaded with an appetising assortment of fresh fruit and other brunch dishes.

'Help yourself to something to eat,' he offered, going over to the table himself and starting to pour two cups of coffee.

'Let's sit down,' he added, waiting until she had done so before saying semi-quizzically, 'Polly, let's quit beating about the bush. The deal's going through and I've bought out the hotel's current owners but I can't be here on hand to run a place like this the way it needs to be run, not with my other business interests. This hotel needs a top-class manager, someone who knows the hotel business inside out; someone who combines that experience and intelligence with flair and an intuitive knowledge of what the guests want.'

'If you're asking me to recommend someone…' Polly began doubtfully. She had assumed without knowing how or why that Suzi must be in line for taking over the management of the hotel, but, from the tone of Phil's conversation, it appeared that she had been wrong.

Just how wrong she was about to discover, as Phil shook his head and told her dryly, 'Honey, I don't need any recommendations. I already know exactly who I want to run this place. The *only* person I want to run this place.'

'Oh?' Polly looked blankly at him. If he knew, then why was he talking to her like this, unless it was just his way of using her as a sounding board to confirm his own decision?

'Yes.' Phil turned to look directly at her as he told her simply, 'I want *you* Polly; no one else will do. I've seen what you've done at Fraser House and I've watched you...the way you work, the way you relate to the guests, the way you *are*. You're the best...and the best is what I want for this place.'

Polly was speechless. This was the last thing she had expected.

'Phil... Phil, hang on...' Polly protested a little shakily. 'You can't really mean this. It's—'

'I *do* mean it,' Phil insisted.

'I...I'm flattered that you should think of me,' Polly began, 'but, Phil, I can't. There's Fraser House, for one thing, and—'

'Fraser House?' Phil interrupted her, with a small disparaging shrug. 'You've done wonders with it, Polly, but you're capable of doing so much more, especially now that Briony is off your hands and at college. Come on, admit it; you'd love the challenge of somewhere like this, of something you can really get your teeth into. You must want to spread your wings, Polly, and what, after all, is there to keep you tied to Fraser House now?'

What indeed? Polly reflected inwardly. Briony had

gone and soon Marcus would be following her. All she would be left with would be her memories and her ridiculous, foolish hopes and dreams, her aching what-might-have-beens, whilst not so very far away Marcus began his new life with his new wife and no doubt his new family.

How would she feel seeing them walking into Fraser House as a close-knit loving unit? Marcus and Suzi bringing their children for lunch. Suzi basking in Marcus's love whilst *she* was forced to stand on the sidelines and watch.

Yes. If she stayed she would have to endure scenes like that, and the kind of pain that... But if she left she would be leaving behind so many precious memories—memories of Briony's childhood, of the difficult years when she and Marcus had built up the business together, years when Marcus had been there working alongside her, helping her, being there for Briony. So many memories, all of them bittersweet and edged with the pain of her loving him, yes, but yet, in so many ways, oh, so precious.

She could take her memories with her, of course, but deep down inside Polly knew that she didn't want to leave Fraser House. She was happy there; it was her home as well as her business. Deplorable though it sounded if she admitted it, she wasn't particularly ambitious. Oh, she liked to know she had done a good job, she loved knowing her guests felt happy and comfortable, but the thought of moving on to something bigger and supposedly better held very little real appeal for her. And this hotel, stunning though it was, was too big, too impersonal, too state-of-the-art for her tastes.

'Phil, it's very kind of you to offer me the chance to manage this hotel,' she began steadily, 'but—'

'But?' Phil interrupted her, his eyebrows lifting. 'You can't be going to turn me down?' he said with such obvious astonishment that Polly had to smile a little at his self-confidence. 'There's no way that running a hotel like Fraser House can compare to running a place like this. Apart from anything else, just think about how impressive it's going to look on your CV. Manage this place for me, Polly, and quite literally the world will be your oyster; you'll have every hotel chain in the world beating a path to your door.'

'It sounds very tempting,' Polly agreed. 'But...'

'Go away and think about it,' Phil counselled her.

'Phil,' Polly protested, wanting to tell him that she had already done her thinking and made up her mind, but he was shaking his head and mouthing 'Please' at her as his phone started to ring.

'Look, I've got to take this call,' he told her quickly. 'It's from my bankers in New York. But please, Polly, think seriously about my offer. You don't have to make an immediate decision. I can give you a week or so...'

But what about Suzi? Polly wanted to ask him, but he was already turning away from her, and, sensing that he wanted privacy to speak with his bankers, Polly made her way to the suite door.

As she took the lift down to the foyer her head was buzzing. There was no denying that the offer Phil had made her was one that most people would think she was a fool to turn down.

As she stepped out of the lift she was so engrossed in her own thoughts that at first she failed to see Suzi.

But the other woman had seen her, and was making a bee-line for her, coming to a halt just a little too far inside Polly's own private space for Polly's comfort.

However, as she instinctively made to step back from the other woman Suzi moved aggressively towards her.

'There you are,' she announced. 'I want a word with you.'

'Suzi,' Polly protested. 'I think—'

'Oh, I already know what you think.' Suzi interrupted her savagely. 'You think that just because he spent the night with you, just because he took you to bed, it means he *cares* about you. Well, I've got news for you. I hate to be the one to ruin all those little plans you've been making for happy-ever-afters, but someone's got to tell you the truth. You mean *nothing* to him,' she told Polly cruelly. 'Nothing at all. You're just someone he was using for sex because I wasn't there.' She gave a small, sharp-toothed little smile, her eyes full of angry contempt as she looked Polly up and down disparagingly.

'He is a very highly sexed man, after all, *and* very good in bed...very good.' She gave a small dismissive shrug. 'But there's much more to the relationship *I* have with him than just sex. He and I belong together, and if you think for one moment that I'm going to let someone, *anyone*—but least of all a woman like *you*—come between us then you are very, very mistaken.

'He's already asked me to marry him. Did he tell you *that*?' she challenged, and then smiled triumphantly as Polly's wounded gasp gave her away.

'Well, he has, and not just asked me but *pleaded* with me,' she added. 'And of course I can give him so much more than you can. You are—*how* old? Close to forty—?'

'I'm thirty-seven,' Polly interrupted her shakily.

'So, you're thirty-seven.' Suzi gave a contemptuous shrug. '*I'm* twenty-six. Do you really honestly think he could possibly want you? But then I suppose when a woman is as desperate as you so obviously are she'll tell herself anything,' she added disparagingly. 'And, of course, he is a very wealthy man. I suppose a woman of your age has to think of her future…her pension,' she taunted.

Her *pension*…? Had she not been feeling so shocked and distressed, Polly could almost have laughed. She might be a full decade the other woman's senior, but she was still a long, long way from having to think about her old age. Nor had she ever, or would she ever, look to a man to provide her with financial security.

'He only took you to bed because he feels sorry for you,' Suzi continued. 'He told me himself that you'd been coming on to him, that you were gagging for it,' she added crudely.

Gagging for it! Polly actually felt as though she might be sick. The thought of Marcus even discussing her with someone else, never mind in such crude and cruel terms, tore at her sensitivities as sharply as though her flesh had been raked over by a leopard's claws and each tiny wound was drawing blood, her self-esteem mortally poisoned.

Even so, no matter what her feelings were, she had at least to try to defend herself, and she did so by taking a deep breath and telling Suzi quietly, 'Only a few minutes ago you told me that *he* only took me to bed because *you* weren't available. Now you say it was because he felt sorry for me. Perhaps you'd better make your mind up exactly what it is that *did* motivate him!'

'I know what motivated him,' Suzi assured her sharply, 'and if you hadn't made it pathetically obvious that you were available to him he would never… It's no wonder Marcus has got such a low opinion of you.'

Polly bit down hard on her bottom lip to stop herself

from crying out in pain. She had no idea how the other woman knew about last night, although logically she knew there was only one way she could know. Marcus himself must have told her.

Polly could feel herself writhing inwardly in self-loathing. Was *that* why he had left ahead of his early-morning call? Because he had been overwhelmed with remorse and longing for the woman he *really* loved, because he had wanted to make a clean breast of what had happened to Suzi before he left for China, to beg her forgiveness and—?

'You might think you've been clever,' Suzi went on venomously, 'but you haven't. What you've actually been is incredibly stupid. Men aren't like us. Sex is just a game to them, a challenge and sex with a woman like you…' She gave another dismissive shrug. 'Like I've told you, *I'm* the one he *loves*. The one he's going to marry.'

Polly could feel her head starting to swim. She felt dizzy and nauseous and emotionally battered by the insults and rebukes Suzi had flung at her, as though she had actually physically abused her. The other woman's aggression, whilst it might be understandable in view of her relationship with Marcus, was so alien to Polly's own behaviour that Polly felt completely unable to deal with it.

She had on occasion had to deal with unpleasant guests, but there had never, ever been anything, anyone in her life before like this. Perhaps she was weak and naive, she acknowledged; perhaps her life had been too confined and sheltered; but alongside her own deep shame at what she had done and the way she had succumbed to her love for Marcus ran an equally deep seam of distaste and, yes, even revulsion against Suzi. But Suzi was the woman Marcus loved.

'I appreciate what you're saying,' Polly told her quietly, with as much dignity as she could muster, 'but really, don't you think it's a subject you might be better off discussing with Marcus—?'

'My, my, aren't *we* the ladylike one?' Suzi cut across what Polly was trying to say caustically. 'Ladylike in bed with him as well, were you? All simpering "Yes, please" and "No thank you"?'

'Well, let me give you a piece of advice. In future keep away from him. He's mine, and unless you want me to make what you've done public... I'm sure that Briony would love Chris's family to hear about the way her mother behaves and the kind of moral values she has, for instance,' she threatened.

The mild ache in Polly's temples had become a full, throbbing tension-induced headache of mega proportions, the pain so intense that Polly could barely see straight, never mind *think* straight, but from somewhere she managed to find the presence of mind to tell Suzi simply, 'I know that I ought to be feeling rather sorry for myself, but somehow you're the one I feel sorry for, Suzi...'

And then, without giving the other woman a chance to retaliate, she stepped quickly past her and headed for the hotel exit, her head held high, her body under rigid control as she fought to conceal her trembling legs.

Once outside Suzi's eyesight, though, she couldn't maintain the pretence. Her stomach was churning, her whole body shaking, her face so paper-white that a female passer-by actually stopped to ask her anxiously if she was feeling all right.

'Yes…just a headache…' Polly fibbed before hailing a passing taxi.

She still had to check out of the hotel and collect her overnight case. The room, much to her consternation, actually held a faint, agonising echo of Marcus's scent.

The tears that burned the back of her throat and eyes felt like raw acid.

What was she doing crying over him, a man who had not only been the cause of her betraying every moral cornerstone she had built her life on but who, in addition, had callously and cynically laid bare the intimacy of her feelings to the woman he really loved?

She had never dreamed that Marcus would be capable of an act of such malice and degradation and she still found it hard to believe.

'When are you ever going to learn?' she asked herself out loud as she faced the mirror. 'He was *using* you, *abusing* you, and you let him. You encouraged him. You deserve everything you got. You deserve Suzi's anger and her contempt, and right now, knowing what you know about him, you should be thanking your lucky stars that he loves her and not you.'

'You're just someone he was using for sex because I wasn't there,' Suzi had taunted, and, even though she had known all along that that was what he was doing, having it put into words, hearing Suzi tell her that Marcus felt nothing for her, had torn her apart and left a huge gaping wound within her that she knew would never be properly healed. *Never*.

How was she going to be able to continue to live and work at Fraser House now?

But she didn't *have* to stay there—not with Phil's job offer on the table.

The thought of leaving Fraser House wrenched painfully at her heartstrings, but she told herself that it was a punishment she fully deserved in view of her own folly.

She had, after all, seen Marcus with Suzi, sensed the intimacy between them.

But for Marcus to have made love to her out of nothing more than sexual necessity and spite was so far removed from the man she had thought him to be she could hardly bear to think about it.

By the time she reached home she had made up her mind. She was her own person, and responsible for her own life. What was the point in exposing herself to even more misery and humiliation? Before she could weaken and change her mind she telephoned her solicitor, Richard's family solicitor, who had known her all her married life.

'You want to sell your share in Fraser House,' he repeated when she'd told him what she wanted to do.

'Yes,' she insisted, explaining at least half truthfully, 'Briony is at college now and Marcus is moving into his own house. I've been offered the chance to manage a much larger hotel and—'

'Have you discussed this with Marcus?' she heard Tim Webb asking her.

'Not yet: he's away on business in China at the moment and this offer came up rather unexpectedly, but...'

'Well, I would certainly counsel you to do so, Polly. You and Marcus are, as you know, joint owners of Fraser House but—'

'Yes, I appreciate that,' Polly agreed. 'All I'm asking you for, Tim, is your advice on how, legally, I should go about selling my share and withdrawing from managership of the hotel,' she reminded him gently.

'Well, as to that, the contract I drew up for you when

you became the hotel's general manager is pretty flexible and informal, as you know. At the time Marcus was anxious to make sure that everything was shipshape from a financial point of view. I'm sure I don't need to remind you of the muddle Richard left his affairs in, and I know that Marcus was concerned that you and Briony should be financially secure.'

Sensing that Tim was rebuking her, Polly felt her face starting to burn.

The time of Richard's death had been so traumatic for her that she had only the haziest recollection of the more practical side of things. Marcus had taken charge of everything, and whilst she could remember feeling that his behaviour had been rather high-handed at the same time she had also felt an undeniable sense of relief that he had taken charge for her.

'I'm not planning to defraud Marcus, Tim,' Polly responded sharply. 'I simply want to know what the procedure is, what exactly I need to do to ensure that I'm free to accept this new position I've been offered. With the plans he's got for his own life I think you'll find that Marcus will be only too glad to have any kind of contact with me legally severed.'

Appalled at what she was saying, what she might be giving away, Polly abruptly stopped speaking, but fortunately, either because he was too wise to comment or because he hadn't realised the significance of what she had just said, the solicitor did not take her up on her incautious statement.

He simply said, 'I'm sorry. I'll need to get the file out and go through it. I suspect a formal letter to Marcus should be sufficient to release you from your responsibilities as the hotel's manager. So far as your financial involvement as co-owner goes, though...'

He paused. 'What exactly do you have in mind? If you're planning to sell your share then I have to advise you that, from memory, I think the original documents specified that Marcus should be offered first refusal of any prospective sale of your share. So if you were thinking of putting your share on the open market, or if you have already received an offer you were thinking of accepting...'

'No. No, nothing like that,' Polly hastened to assure him. 'The offer I have received is purely an offer of *work*, and has nothing to do with my co-ownership of Fraser House.'

'Well, in that case, you might find it would be worth your while to think of retaining your ownership in the hotel. You and Marcus could appoint another manager, which would leave you free to take up this new job offer.'

Another manager for the hotel... Polly caught her breath. Suzi was more than qualified for such a position, and indeed already worked in such a capacity for Phil Bernstein, but would Marcus want his new bride to work, especially if they were anxious to start a family? What was she doing to herself? Polly asked herself wretchedly as her mind remorselessly relayed to her taunting images of Marcus enjoying the prospect of becoming a father, his arm curved possessively around Suzi's burgeoning body, pride and tenderness softening his eyes, his body turned protectively towards her.

'No...'

'What? I'm sorry?' she could hear Tim Webb saying to her.

'No, it's nothing, Tim,' Polly said apologetically. 'I was just thinking of something. I'm sorry, what were you saying?'

'I was just suggesting that I could perhaps draft a letter for you to send to Marcus, formally telling him that you wish to terminate your managership, along with another letter offering him first refusal on the sale of your share of the business, subject to a professional valuation, of course.'

'Yes, that sounds a good idea,' Polly confirmed hollowly.

As she replaced the telephone receiver she told herself that she was glad that the decision had been made and there was no going back. That was just the first hurdle over, though. She still had to tell Briony, and to inform Phil Bernstein that she had changed her mind and she now wanted to accept his offer.

She telephoned Phil first.

'Good girl,' he praised her. 'I knew you'd see things my way... When can you start?'

Polly couldn't help laughing despite her misery.

'I still have to formally terminate my managership with Marcus,' she warned him.

'A piece of cake. Tell him I'll pay him whatever forfeit he wants. Anything just so long as he releases you... In fact, give me his number; I'll give him a call myself.'

'I can't. He's in China at the moment on business,' Polly told him. 'But quite honestly, Phil, I'd rather do things legally and properly. My solicitor is drawing up a formal letter for me to send to him.'

'Uh-huh; well, if you have any problems with him, *any* problems at all, just let me know. My legal guys are the best in the business...'

'I'm sure they are,' Polly conceded.

'So if Marcus starts making things difficult, or giving you a hard time...'

'I doubt very much that he's likely to do anything like

that,' Polly sighed. 'In fact, I should imagine he'll be only too happy to terminate our contract.'

'Well, Suzi said something about the two of you not getting on very well, but I thought… By the way, did you happen to see Suzi when you left the hotel this morning?'

'Er, she was in the foyer,' Polly told him.

'Uh-huh. Well, she probably forgot she and I were supposed to be having a meeting.'

Polly was tempted to say that Suzi appeared to have a very relaxed attitude towards her professional responsibilities, but instead she bit her tongue. Briony had hinted that at some stage Suzi and Phil had been more than merely employer and employee, and perhaps it was for that reason that Suzi felt able to behave in a way that she herself would never have dreamed of behaving towards someone who was, after all, her boss.

'How long is it before Marcus gets back from China?' Phil asked her.

'I'm not sure,' Polly confessed, unwilling to admit that she hadn't even known he was going. Not that Marcus had any responsibility to tell *her* what his movements were, but in the past, when Briony had been at home, he had always kept her informed of where he was, giving her a contact number just in case she needed to get hold of him.

Briony…

After she had laughingly refused Phil's suggestion that she drive back to London so that they could have a celebratory meal together whilst he outlined all the plus points of her soon-to-be contract with him, Polly picked up the receiver again and dialled her daughter's telephone number.

The phone rang for so long that Polly was just about

to give up, assuming that Briony must be out, when her daughter eventually picked up her receiver.

'Mum… Hi… I've just come in…'

'Er, Briony, there's something I want to tell you…'

Amazingly Polly discovered that she felt not just a little nervous but also rather apprehensive about telling Briony about her plans. Taking a deep breath, she began to do so.

The silence with which Briony heard her out was distinctly ominous, and Polly knew that her motherly intuition had not been mistaken when Briony demanded sharply, 'Mum, is this some kind of joke? You *can't* leave Uncle Marcus like that. You just can't…'

'Briony—' Polly began but her daughter was obviously in no mood to listen, overriding her with her voice full of passion and accusation.

'Mum, how can you even think of such a thing after everything that Uncle Marcus has done for us…for you…? I thought Suzi was just being a bit bitchy when she suggested that you might be in danger of falling for Phil because of your age, but it seems she was right, and—'

'Briony!' Polly interjected in shock. Why was it that those closest to her had such a low opinion of her and seemed so determined to pigeon-hole her in some kind of potential mid-life crisis area? 'This has *nothing* to do with Phil on any kind of personal level. He has offered me a job, that's all.'

'That's all? But you've always… But you've already got a job… You've got *Fraser House*…' Briony protested.

'The job that Phil is offering me has a lot more scope,' Polly explained as calmly as she could.

'A lot more scope for *what*?' Briony asked her bitterly. 'A lot more scope to go to bed with Phil Bernstein? What does Uncle Marcus think about all of this?'

'He doesn't know. Not yet,' Polly was forced to admit.

'You haven't told him!' Polly could hear not just the reproof but also the shock in her daughter's voice. 'Mum, I don't believe—'

'Before you say anything else, I think you ought to know that the reason I haven't told Marcus yet is because I can't. He's in China and I have no idea when he'll be back.'

'Have you tried asking Suzi?' Briony asked her carelessly. 'She might know.'

'I'm sure she *will*,' Polly agreed tersely. 'Tim Webb is drawing up a letter for me to send to Marcus, telling him I want to terminate my managership. Which reminds me, I don't know how you're going to feel about this, Briony, but I've decided that I want to sell my share of Fraser House.'

'What? Mum, no! You can't do that...'

Polly's heart sank as she heard the distress and the panic in her daughter's voice. She just didn't need this. No way did she need it, but also there was no way she could explain to Briony, woman to woman, just why she wanted to completely sever her contact with Marcus.

'Fraser House is *home*, Mum...*our* home. Ours and Uncle Marcus's.'

'Briony,' Polly intervened. 'I *do* understand how you feel, darling, but please listen. Marcus has already made plans to move to his own house; you know that. You're away at college... Surely you can understand that it's time for my life to move along as well as both of yours?'

'Yes, maybe, but where are you planning to move it to, Mum? Phil Bernstein's bed?'

'Briony, that's enough,' Polly told her sternly. 'I've already told you Phil's offered me a job, that's all. I do understand how you feel about Fraser House…'

'No, you don't,' Briony told her passionately. '*You* don't understand *anything*…' And before Polly could say anything Briony had slammed down her phone, leaving Polly listening to silence.

Shakily Polly replaced her own receiver. Even as a child Briony had always had that little bit of impetuous temper. Polly knew perfectly well that within a very short space of time Briony would telephone her, overcome with remorse and guilt, but her reaction still hurt.

There was no mistaking where Briony's loyalties and sympathies lay.

Wearily Polly massaged her aching temples. Her heart might be aching with desolation and grief but she still had a hotel to run. At least keeping busy would keep her mind off Marcus and Suzi—and off last night.

All day she had been aware of an unfamiliar heaviness, a lassitude almost about her body, a wayward, wilful tendency to remind her very physically and determinedly where its desires lay—not that she needed reminding, not for one minute. There was nothing she longed for more than to be loved by Marcus. *Nothing* she longed for more and nothing she was less likely to get.

Marcus loved Suzi. Suzi herself had told her so. *Marcus* loved *Suzi*!

CHAPTER EIGHT

MARCUS winced, his tense muscles protesting as he bent down to pick up the case he had put on the floor before letting himself into his suite.

The negotiations in China had taken longer than he had expected and, coupled with a long flight, he had been left feeling stressed and tense.

Come on, he derided himself as he pushed the door to his suite closed and put down his case. Who was he kidding? The real reason he was feeling so uptight had nothing whatsoever to do with the negotiations in China. In truth, the source was far, far closer to home.

It was past midnight, and the hotel had been in darkness when he had let himself in, but his body clock was totally haywire, thanks to his long-haul flight, and the last thing he felt able to do was sleep. There hadn't been a day when he had been away when he hadn't thought about Polly. There was nothing unusual in that. There hadn't been an hour when he hadn't thought about her, never mind a day, from the first day he had set eyes on her, but what *had* distinguished these particular days, these particular thoughts from previous ones had been the knowledge of the sexual intimacy they had shared before he had left.

He had always known how much he loved her, but what had surprised him had been the discovery of just how intensely sensually responsive she had been to him. It had almost been as though she had hungered for him, longed for him, *loved* him, with the same longing and

133

need with which he had done for her—with the same *love* he had for her!

Who was he kidding? he scorned again. Polly hadn't been thinking about him, Phil Bernstein was the man she wanted.

As he paced his suite his eye was caught by the pile of post waiting for him.

Automatically he picked it up and started to go through it, his whole body freezing when he opened and read the letter from Tim Webb. Very slowly he read it a second time and then a third.

Polly's room was right at the end of the corridor. Marcus stormed along it, knocked furiously on the door and then opened it, demanding angrily, 'Would you mind explaining to me what the *hell* all this is about?'

It was Polly's habit on quiet evenings to have a relaxing bath, don her bathrobe and then work at her desk, using the time to deal with her paperwork without any interruption. Her first intimation of Marcus's return—and his fury—came when he thrust open her bedroom door, and now, as he strode across the room and came to stand almost threateningly over her whilst he flung down the letter Tim Webb had drafted for her, she could feel herself starting to shake inwardly.

It just wasn't fair that he could affect her like this; that even now, when he was furiously angry with her, she should feel so aware of him, so *aroused* by him, and it was even less fair that she should yearn so much for him to take her in his arms and wrap them around her, holding her tightly, whilst he told her...

What? That he *loved* her? Just how much of a self-deluding fool *was* she?

'Well?' Marcus demanded as he slammed the letter down on her desk in front of her.

Trying to remain as calm as she possibly could, Polly told him quietly, 'I should have thought it was self-explanatory. It's my letter formally requesting my release from my managership of the hotel. I've been offered another job and—'

'Another job?' Marcus exploded savagely. 'Don't you mean it's another *position* you've been offered, Polly?'

'I'm sorry—?' she began in confusion, only to stop, her face burning with outrage and shock, as Marcus explained bitingly, 'A *position* that requires you to be in Bernstein's bed...'

Immediately Polly stood up, pushing her chair away as she turned to confront Marcus and repudiate his totally unfair and humiliating remark.

'Don't you dare to say such a thing,' she cried. 'The *job* Phil has offered me is that of running his new hotel in London, and it has nothing to do with...'

'With what?' Marcus challenged. 'With sex? You're lying, Polly. It has *everything* to do with sex. I must admit I'm surprised that he's willing to go to such lengths to get you into his bed. I should have thought—'

'You should have thought what?' Polly cut across him, hot-faced. 'Just because I made...had *sex* with you, Marcus, that doesn't mean—'

Abruptly she stopped. The last thing she wanted, the last thing she felt able to cope with was this kind of confrontation with Marcus. She had known, of course, that he wouldn't be pleased about her decision; after all, he would have to find someone else to take her place if he wanted to continue—either that or sell his share in the hotel. But surely, with him and Suzi so close to formalising their relationship, that wasn't going to be a problem for him?

'Have you told Briony about this?' Marcus demanded shortly.

'Yes, I have,' Polly confirmed.

'And?' Marcus pressed.

'She…she wasn't too keen on the idea,' Polly admitted, her chin firming as she continued determinedly, 'But she understands that now that she's at college and to all intents and purposes an adult, with a life of her own, it's time for *me* to branch out a little, add to my CV…'

'By doing what? Becoming Bernstein's bed mate?' Marcus challenged her unkindly.

'For the last time this has nothing to do with sex,' Polly protested. 'The job Phil has offered me—'

'Is a piece of juicy bait intended to get you into his bed,' Marcus concluded for her. 'And you must be as aware of that as I am. Well, if you're entertaining some romantic fantasy that he's going to offer you marriage, Polly, I have to tell you Bernstein's got other plans that you obviously don't know anything about. Apparently he's the only male of his generation in his family, and according to Suzi he's almost obsessive about wanting to have a son to pass his business interests on to. When he marries—if he marries—it will be to someone young enough to provide him with the male children he wants so much.'

Polly had had enough, heard enough. She wasn't going to take any more of this—why should she? If Marcus was so determined to think the worst of her then let him. She didn't care. But there was something she *did* care about—something he hated to be told.

'I may have an almost adult daughter, but in modern terms I can assure you that I'm still young enough to give Phil a child—and more than one, if that's what he wants.'

'You'd actually do that…you'd…?' Marcus stopped as though unable to actually say the words. His voice was so hoarse and strained that Polly barely recognised it. Something had gone badly wrong, she knew that; Marcus was reacting as though she'd threatened to destroy someone. Was that what he thought being involved with her would do to a man? Why? Because of Richard? Because she was older than Phil? Because she already had an adult daughter?

Well, if what she had just said had shocked him so much, how on earth would he feel if he knew of the secret longing she had to have *his* child? The dream that had tormented her so often in the early years of her widowhood was that she had had *his* son in the same hospital room where she had given birth to Briony, with Marcus at her side. And they were all there. Marcus, Briony, herself and their new baby…a son.

Such a foolish dream. To match her even more foolish love.

'But what if the child he gives you turns out to be a girl? Have you thought of *that*?' Marcus asked her grimly. 'What would you do then Polly? Bernstein doesn't want female children—ask Suzi.

'My God, I don't know what's got into you recently. Suzi warned me that a woman going through a mid-life crisis can behave…'

Suzi had *warned* him? Polly had heard the expression about seeing red but had never truly appreciated its significance before now. She was by nature a calm, well-balanced type of person, preferring to avoid confrontation and arguments where she could, but suddenly, in a blinding blood-hot flash, it was there, a burst of scarlet, scalding colour that exploded inside her head. It was like an extra charge of adrenalin, rocket fuel to her emotions, blasting them out of the safe orbit they normally travelled in and launching them and her with them into an attack on Marcus's unsubstantiated claim.

'Suzi seems to have been very busy handing out her warnings,' Polly flashed furiously. '*I* was on the receiving end of one of them myself quite recently—but when it comes to mid-life crises *you're* much closer to having one than *I* am, Marcus. After all, you are a prime candidate for—'

'For what?' Marcus interrupted her ominously.

For a relationship with a much younger woman, Polly had been about to tell him, but the idea of any woman of any age *not* finding Marcus irresistibly attractive was so ludicrous that Polly couldn't bring herself to voice it. After all, she had seen the way their female guests looked at him, and she knew just why they had looked as well. No, Marcus was simply not the kind of man who would ever need to find himself a much younger partner simply to prop up his own deflating ego.

Instead, unwilling to give up the argument completely, she demanded pettily, 'Anyway, why shouldn't I have a baby if I want one?'

'You *want* a child?'

Marcus's incredulity and disbelief fuelled her anger.

'Why shouldn't I? Why shouldn't I want to have a man in my life who loves me…a child whom he and I have created together?'

Tears clogged her voice and inside her head she could see both the man she really wanted *and* his child. It had been a long week, and she was physically tired and emotionally exhausted. Just how much more was she supposed to have to take?

'Well, that's a bit of a volte-face, isn't it?' Marcus derided her. 'What happened to the Polly who claimed that she could only love one man and that no one else could *ever* replace him in her affections—or her bed?

'Have you the least idea of what you're going to be getting yourself into with Bernstein, Polly? Aside from the fact that he's younger than you, according to Suzi he uses women like disposable paper tissues, and even she... You know there was a time when the two of them...?'

'I know they were lovers, yes,' Polly agreed tersely. 'But if that doesn't matter to you, why should it matter to me? After all—'

'You *can't* take this job, Polly.' Marcus interrupted her grimly. 'You belong here at Fraser House.'

'I what? No way!' Polly told him furiously, shaking her head. 'I don't belong anywhere, Marcus, nor *to* anyone, *any* man. I'm a free agent, and if I want to work for Phil, if I want to go to bed with him, then I have every right to do so. And if I want to have his child then that's my right as well, Marcus,' she insisted.

He suddenly reached past her, snatching up the letter he had thrown down onto her desk and ripping it into pieces as he told her through gritted teeth, 'You think so? Well, I'm sorry to disillusion you, Polly, but there's no way you are going to be able to accept Bernstein's so-called "job".'

'Marcus,' Polly protested. 'You can't do that. I—'

'You'll what? Make me an offer I can't refuse?' Marcus's mouth twisted cynically. 'Every man might have his price, Polly, but *you* don't have what it takes to meet mine.'

White-faced at his insult, her chest tightening in protest against the savagery of her own pain, Polly whispered shakily, 'I don't understand why you're doing this, Marcus. I thought you'd be glad to have me out of your life.'

'Out of my life maybe,' Marcus conceded coolly, 'but someone has to run the hotel.'

Polly gave a small gasp of pain. She should have expected it, perhaps, but still, to have it confirmed that she meant so little to him as a person, that she couldn't even lay claim to his friendship and affection as a fellow human being, hurt dreadfully.

'Suzi could do that,' she pointed out quietly.

'Whose idea was *that*? Bernstein's or yours? No doubt it would suit you both to have her safely out of your lives, albeit for rather different reasons. Doesn't it bother you at all, Polly, knowing that the position you're being offered, the *job* you're being offered, should more rightfully go to Suzi?'

'I'm not going to listen to any more of this,' Polly told him tersely. 'You can't stop me leaving, Marcus. I have legally given you formal notice of my decision to stop working here.'

'You have,' Marcus agreed cordially, 'but, as I'm sure you'll know, having read our contract, you *are* legally bound to give six months' notice. Six months is a long time in the life of a man like Bernstein, Polly. Are you sure he'll want you enough to wait that long?'

'Six months?' Polly gasped. 'It can't possibly be so long.' But it must be, she recognised; Marcus wouldn't say so otherwise. Six months!

In six months Marcus and Suzi could be married and Suzi could be carrying Marcus's child, whilst *she* would have to stay here and witness their love for one another. Six months! She closed her eyes weakly. There was no way she could endure that kind of emotional torment.

The back of her eyes stung with the tears she was fighting to control, and her throat and chest ached with her tension.

As he watched her, Marcus reflected bitterly that when he had originally had that clause placed in their contract it had been to protect *Polly* and not himself. He had been concerned that if the hotel did not do well her pride might force her to leave and look for another job rather than stay on, suspecting that he might be making up her salary from his own funds, which was exactly what he had planned to do. But as it had turned out the hotel had done so well that there had never been any need for him to do so, and now the clause he had originally devised to protect Polly financially would, he hoped, help to protect her emotionally.

Bernstein had obviously convinced her that he loved her and that they had a permanent future together. Marcus knew Polly, and he knew there was no way she could even contemplate leaving Fraser House, never mind giving Bernstein a child, unless he had. Marcus had learned from Suzi that there was a very different side to Phil Bernstein than the one Polly had seen, and that he was a man who could be as ruthless in his emotional life as he was in his business one. But there was obviously no point in telling Polly that, not when she was so obviously totally besotted with the man.

And Marcus knew better than most just what it was like to love someone beyond all logic or reason.

'*Why* are you doing this to me, Marcus?' Polly asked him chokily. 'What possible reason can you have?'

'You seem to forget that I have a considerable financial stake in this business, and whatever I might think about your other...capabilities...I have to admit that here at Fraser House you would be extremely hard to replace. You own half of the business yourself, and...'

'I intend to sell my share,' Polly told him swiftly. 'If you want... Marcus...Marcus...let go of me,' Polly protested as he suddenly grabbed hold of her.

He was almost shaking her as he demanded in disbelief, 'You're doing what?'

'I'm going to sell my share,' Polly repeated shakily as she felt the tension in his body communicate itself with her own via the hold he had on her upper arms.

'I know I have to offer you first refusal and—'

'Oh, you do, do you?' Marcus interrupted her softly. 'Is that why you went to bed with me, Polly...to offer me first refusal?'

'Oh...!' Polly's shocked indrawn gasp of outrage was flattened in her throat as it threatened to close up with the anguish of what she was feeling. 'I didn't...you weren't...' she tried to explain in shaken self-defence, but Marcus shook his head to silence her.

He knew exactly what she was going to say, of course. She hadn't intended anything to happen. She hadn't wanted *him*. She had wanted Bernstein. He had just happened to be there, to have caught her at a weak moment when her defences were down. But *he* was the one who had held her, touched her, loved her. He was the one she had cried out to, responded to—and suddenly Marcus was tired of playing the 'good guy'.

She had responded to him once. He could show her how good it could be between them...how right they were for one another. He could show her how much happier she could be with him than with Bernstein. He could show her how much he loved her, how much he longed to love her—to love her and protect her and, yes, to give her the child she claimed she wanted.

God, but didn't she know how much hearing that had hurt him? He'd had to watch while she gave birth to Richard's child, wanting so much for it to be his and yet loving Briony for herself in spite of his own feelings. But to see her body growing a second time with another man's child...

No. There was no way he could endure that.

As the hot mist of his jealousy started to settle Marcus told himself that he must have been mad even to consider using Polly's vulnerability to... But then, as he started to release her, his glance fell towards her body, where the thin cotton robe she was wearing was pulling tightly against it. He could see quite clearly the sharp, hard outline of her breast with the taut crest of her nipple pressing against the fabric as though...as though...

'Polly...'

With a muffled groan Marcus reached out to touch her, cupping his hand around her breast, his thumb against her erect nipple, caressing it.

'No.' Polly could hear the sound of her own denial, only the word sounded much more like a long, low plea of craving rather than a rejection. No wonder Marcus wasn't paying any attention to it. No wonder what he *was* doing was stroking her nipple more urgently.

'No,' Polly protested a second time, but she knew that, if anything, her denial sounded even less of a rejection than it had done the first time.

'What is it about Bernstein that makes you want to walk away from here, Polly? You once told me that after Briony, Fraser House was the most important thing in your life because it was a part of Richard.'

Had she said that? She might have done, Polly acknowledged, but she couldn't remember having done so. No doubt it had been a defensive remark she had thrown at Marcus when under attack, but trust him to have remembered it and to use it against her now.

'If it's physical satisfaction you're hungry for,' Marcus groaned hoarsely in her ear, 'then *I* can satisfy that need for you.'

Polly could barely believe what she was hearing—not from Marcus.

'I don't want...' she began huskily, but Marcus wouldn't allow her to finish.

'Yes, you *do* want,' he corrected her savagely, 'and *I* want, Polly; I want very, very much.'

And whilst she was still reeling from the shock of his frank admission he was bending his head and pushing aside her robe so that his mouth could cover the quivering peak of her nipple and draw on it with such fierce sweetness that the whole of her body turned liquid with longing.

It was different now than it had been the first time. Her body knew him now—knew him, wanted him, *craved* him as its lover, remembering and responding to every touch he gave her, every breath he took.

She tried to resist, to summon all her mental powers of logic, reason and self-protection, but such puny weapons were no match for the ferocity of her love-borne desire.

Every charged breath she drew seemed to tell Marcus of her weakness and her longing. His mouth left her breast to cover her lips, sealing her off from the outside world and any means of defending herself, creating such an aura of intimacy around them that it seemed to Polly almost as though she was sharing the air he breathed, as though the blood pumping through her veins came from his heart, so fiercely strong was its beat against her body. She seemed to have no will-power of her own. It was as though in his possession of her mouth he had stolen that away from her, just as his hands were stealing away the covering of her body.

But it wasn't her robe that was making that slithering, urgent sound of impatient removal, she recognised, as she opened her eyes to see Marcus tugging off his own clothes, letting them fall where they stood.

'You look as though you've been on holiday,' she told him dizzily, unable to stop herself from reaching out to touch the warm tan of his skin.

'All those years of working in the Middle East,' Marcus responded gruffly.

'My skin's so pale,' Polly complained, with a small sigh. 'I used to hate it when I was young. I looked so...'

'You looked wonderful,' Marcus told her harshly, stunning her into bemused silence. 'Soft and frail, so feminine that...'

Beneath the hand she had placed tentatively against his chest Polly could feel the increased surge of his heartbeat. It was beating frantically fast as though he was under some kind of strain, as though his emotions...

But Marcus felt *nothing* for her emotionally. Marcus loved Suzi... Marcus...

'Oh, Polly, Polly,' she heard him groaning as he wrapped his arms around her, holding her so tightly that it almost hurt her to breathe.

Her breasts ached where he had nuzzled her nipples, longing for the return of his hot, suckling mouth to their tender, aroused crests, but that was nothing to the ache she could feel pulsing deep within her body.

If she had longed for Marcus down through the years of her widowhood, it had been the longing of a woman ignorant, innocent of the strength of her own female sexuality; but now all that had changed. Now she knew;

now she wanted him so fiercely, so immediately that she was shocked herself by the intensity of her wanting.

Her eyes widened with shock as her brain registered the boldness of her body, urging her to reach out to touch Marcus, unable to resist the impulse to explore the sinewy strength of his bare arm, her breath catching in her throat as she saw the way the muscles contracted beneath his skin and heard his betraying indrawn breath when his stomach muscles tensed and his…

Now her eyes really were wide open with shock. Surely it was not just because she had reached out to stroke him that his body…the most potently male part of him…had swelled and hardened so intensely?

'It's because of the way you stroked my arm; it felt as soft and silkily sensitive as though you had brushed your lips against me intimately,' Marcus explained rawly to her, as though she had actually asked the question that was burning in her mind.

'No,' Polly denied immediately, her face flushing.

'No, what?' Marcus asked her thickly. 'No, you wouldn't ever touch me so intimately? But you did, Polly; the night we spent together, you reached out for me in the darkness and you…'

'No. No, not that; I didn't mean that,' Polly protested frantically, not wanting him to remind her of just how impetuously, just how passionately and wildly she had behaved. 'I…I meant…'

'What did you mean?' Marcus demanded softly. He was drawing her closer to him now, his hand stroking down over her naked back, his breath warm against the top of her head.

'I meant, no, I didn't believe that just because…that you…could…would…'

'You're trying to say that you didn't think I could be

so aroused by such a simple touch; is that it?' he picked up wryly. 'Why not? After all, I can arouse you just as...simply...'

'No,' Polly protested explosively. 'No. I want...'

'You want?' Marcus demanded grimly. 'You want Bernstein—but it's *me* you're with, Polly, *me* your body is responding to.'

'No,' Polly repeated.

'You want me to stop? You don't want me to do *this*?' Marcus challenged her, bending his head to cup her breast and slowly draw its hard crest deep into his mouth.

Polly tried to deny him, to tell him to stop, but instead of forming the words she wanted her lips would only part with a long, slow, tortured sound of female longing.

She might as well have spoken her need and longing out loud, because she recognised how Marcus reacted immediately, picking her up bodily and covering her with hot, slow kisses. Hot, slow kisses that became increasingly demanding and urgent with every step he took towards her bed. Did he touch Suzi like this? Did he make her feel like this...did he...'?

She couldn't bear it, Polly acknowledged; she couldn't endure the agony of what she was thinking, imagining, but she couldn't bring herself to stop him either. She wanted him too much, loved him too much. Why was he doing this to her? To hurt her, punish her, to show her how weak and vulnerable she was, to show her that he had guessed how she really felt about him? Or was he simply driven by male desire, taking *her* out of his need for someone else, simply because she was there and his hunger was so great that it had to be appeased?

'No.' The whimpering sound of agony was drawn

from her throat in a wrenching sob of pain but it was too late; her body was already welcoming Marcus within it, and not just welcoming him but reaching out to hold and embrace him, to hold him possessively within her, drawing him in deeper, urging him.

Helplessly Polly gave in to the desire she could no longer control, everything else overturned and swept away by its pounding tumult. She cried out to Marcus to hold her, clinging to him as the climactic waves of her own pleasure rocked and buffeted her, needing him as her security, her safe place, her haven from their intensity. Needing the sweet, warm balm of his completion inside her to ease the raw emptiness that lay deep within her body.

Whilst she lay beneath him in exhaustion, sexually fulfilled but emotionally empty, so hungry that her need was a gnawing, burning rawness of pain, Marcus removed himself from her, saying thickly, 'Well, whatever else Bernstein *is* doing for you, he certainly isn't satisfying you in bed.'

'How can you possibly know that?' Polly retaliated immediately.

'How do you think?' Marcus taunted her, adding softly, 'Or would you like me to prove it to you—again?'

Her throat ached with the weight of her pain, but there was still something she had to ask him.

'Marcus…the notice period. You have to release me from it.'

'Why? Because you went to bed with me?' He laughed savagely as he shook his head and moved away from her to sit on the edge of the bed with his back to her.

'Oh, no, the time to make that kind of demand was

earlier, Polly…*before*… But then you weren't really in any state to make *any* kind of demand other than the one you made for my body, were you?' he said, with such devastating cruelty that it literally took Polly's breath away.

'That clause stays in place,' Marcus told her softly. 'So you might as well resign yourself to it, Polly. For the next six months you are mine…and you'd better make sure that Bernstein knows it because if *you* don't *I* certainly shall.'

CHAPTER NINE

'Six months? Hell…'

Polly could hear Phil's irritation at the other end of the telephone line. 'What the hell possessed you to give him that kind of power over you, Polly? Your legal advisors—whoever they are—should have—'

'Marcus and I use the same firm,' Polly told him quickly. 'They're Richard's family's solicitors and—'

'Don't say any more. I get the picture. Well, if Marcus is determined to refuse to release you…'

Polly held her breath, half expecting Phil to say that he had changed his mind, that he would have to find someone else to run the hotel, but to her relief instead he said simply, 'I guess I shall just have to be patient. Have you got any holiday due to you? Only that could cut down the six-month period.'

'I don't know. I don't normally take a holiday as such…' Polly told him doubtfully. 'I don't remember putting it in the contract, but it was all such a long time ago.'

'I wish you'd let my lawyers take a look at this contract; they could blow holes in it so big that—'

'No, Phil,' Polly protested. A costly legal battle was the last thing she needed, and despite Phil's confidence she had an uncomfortable feeling that somehow or other Marcus would find a way to win.

'Well, at least you'll be able to spend your time off down here in London setting things up for when you do take over the job,' Phil informed her.

'Yes, I'll come down whenever I can,' Polly agreed obediently.

But, two weeks later, she was forced to admit that the likelihood of her being able to take any time off whatsoever whilst she worked her six months' notice was becoming more and more remote.

The hotel was fully booked, and Marcus had stunned her by announcing that he wanted to have the business professionally valued, and not only that but that he had commissioned a firm of management consultants to evaluate the efficiency of the way the hotel was currently being run as well, so that not only was Polly having to cope with a fully booked hotel, but she was also at the beck and call of two different sets of professionals, both of whose teams seemed to want to go through every tiny detail of the way the hotel was run with a fine-tooth comb, presenting her with list after list of questions which it seemed only she was qualified to answer.

The last straw came one busy Thursday morning, which should have been the morning she worked with the chef to get in their last food orders for the following week and the weekend, but she was finding it impossible to do so because the management consultancy team wanted to know not only how much they paid the gardeners who took care of the formal gardens that surrounded the hotel but also why she had elected to have the beds planted with high-maintenance seasonal plants instead of more cost-effective shrubs.

'The perennial borders were originally planted by my husband's great-grandmother,' she told the earnest young woman who was questioning her, through gritted teeth. 'Our guests like the idea of staying at a hotel that was once a family home: they enjoy reading the history of the house and its gardens, which we commissioned and which we keep in the library, and I don't think they would be quite so interested or enthusiastic if we replanted the long walk with modern, low-maintenance shrubs.

'As I said, the whole point of Fraser House is that it was once a home. Our guests expect those touches which make them feel that they are staying in a private house.'

When the girl raised her eyebrows rather disparagingly Polly began to feel her self-control slipping.

'We are not part of a chain of hotels providing rooms in much the same way as a fast-food chain provides burgers,' she told her sharply. 'If we were…' Taking a deep breath, Polly stopped.

'I'm only trying to do my job,' the girl told her defensively.

'Yes, I appreciate that,' Polly agreed, before telling her crisply, 'But, as I'm sure you'll appreciate, I too have a job to do, and right now I should be sitting with my chef going over the menus for next week, so if you'll excuse me…'

'But we still haven't discussed the cost of having the windows cleaned,' the girl protested.

Polly had had enough.

'We haven't, have we?' she agreed evenly. 'Look, why don't you take that up with Mr Fraser? I'm sure he'd be delighted to help you and to see how painstakingly thorough you are being.'

And with that Polly marched determinedly to her office door, holding it open in such a way that the girl had no option but to leave.

Two hours later, as Polly came away from her meeting with the chef, she saw Marcus walking into the hotel foyer.

'I want a word with you,' he told her peremptorily.

'And I want *several* words with you,' Polly responded with asperity.

'What were you playing at, sending that girl to me to ask about the gardens?' Marcus demanded shortly.

'I might ask you exactly the same question,' Polly pointed out. 'It's Thursday, Marcus, and Thursday mornings I spend with the chef, going through the menus and organising the buying in—you *know* that. It may have escaped your notice but we are fully booked and we also have two members of staff off sick. The last thing I need right now is to have to answer questions about the cost-effectiveness of the gardens.'

Marcus gave a small shrug.

'You say that, but so far as a potential purchaser is concerned the costs of running this place are going to be of prime importance.'

'A prospective buyer? *What* prospective buyer?' Polly demanded.

'There isn't one—as yet,' Marcus admitted. 'But, as in all things in life, it pays to be prepared.'

'This is why you've got these management consultants in—because you're going to sell Fraser House?' Polly pounced accusingly.

'It's one option I may be considering, yes,' Marcus agreed.

'But you can't sell...not without my agreement. I own fifty per cent of the business.'

'I don't need your agreement to sell my own share in the hotel,' Marcus corrected her.

'You'd sell out?' Polly badly needed to sit down. Perhaps it was illogical of her to feel so shocked, as though the ground had been cut from beneath her feet, as though she was being betrayed and abandoned; but, nevertheless, that was exactly what she did feel.

'Why not?' Marcus shrugged again. 'The main reason I had for suggesting that the house be turned into a hotel in the first place no longer exists.'

'The main reason…? You mean now that Briony is grown up there's nothing to keep you here?' Polly demanded.

'I don't owe you any explanations, Polly,' he reminded her starkly. 'You've made your plans for the way you want to live your future, as you've made perfectly plain to me.'

'I have a right to want a life of my own,' Polly protested. 'Whatever you may choose to think, at thirty-seven I'm still too young to sit back and sink into genteel senility.'

'Too young for that, yes,' Marcus agreed, with a bitter twist of his mouth, 'but…'

'But what?' Polly pressed sharply. 'Too old to have a relationship with Phil? Too old to have another child?'

'Mr Fraser, if you could spare me a moment…'

Both of them turned towards the door as the young woman who had been questioning Polly earlier appeared, her forehead wrinkled as she informed Marcus, 'I've discovered that the perennial borders are planted with fresh tulips every year, and I was wondering…'

'You're obviously busy,' Polly told Marcus with a taunting smile. 'Please don't let me disturb you. We can finish our discussion later.'

'Polly!' Marcus called out warningly, but Polly refused to listen. Let *him* explain why the very expensive pink tulips were planted every autumn to flower the following spring. It had, after all, been his idea that they should flower just in time to celebrate Richard's birthday, a reminder to them all that beauty and love and laughter never, ever died whilst there were still those to remember and enjoy such things—and Richard, of all men, had so loved all of those things.

Richard—what would *he* make of what was happening? He had thought the world of Marcus, hero-worshipped him really. Richard. It seemed so long ago now that she had loved and married him, and when she thought of him she thought of him as the boy he had been, a boy of whom she had fond memories—almost, in an odd sort of way, maternal memories now, since she'd had to grow and mature without him. She had never been able to visualise him as the man he might have become, perhaps because really there was only one man for her—Marcus. Right now she didn't know whether she loved him or hated him, he was hurting her so much.

'Hello, Ma. Have you heard the news?'

'*What* news?' Polly asked Briony cautiously. Had Marcus told Briony already that he was looking for a buyer for the hotel? That was *her* privilege, surely, but trust Marcus to pre-empt her role as Briony's parent...

'*The news*,' Briony stressed impatiently. 'Suzi's pregnant and they're going to get married. It's all very unexpected and her parents are quite shocked. Her mother's a little bit on the old-fashioned side, isn't she? I imagine she would have preferred them to do things a little bit more traditionally, but these days plenty of couples have children without feeling any need to get married, and for myself—'

'Briony.' Polly interrupted her daughter stiffly, 'Are you sure? I mean...'

'Of course I'm sure. Chris rang me last night. He was complaining because Suzi is insisting on having a full-blown wedding—bridesmaids, page-boys, the lot. And a big marquee on the lawn. So you'd better prepare yourself. I know you've always refused to do wedding receptions but, according to Chris, Suzi has talked her way round Marcus and he's already given his agreement.

'Ma, are you still there?' Briony demanded. 'You haven't said anything.'

'Yes, I'm still here,' Polly managed to tell her hoarsely.

Marcus was getting married. Marcus was going to be a father.

Marcus...

Marcus...

The pain that tore through her was the worst pain Polly had ever experienced, worse by far than the birth pangs which had torn into her when Briony was born, making her cry out and cling to Marcus so tightly that...

But that pain had heralded the arrival of her new life, a new beginning. It had been pain which had given birth to joy—the joy of becoming a mother. This was the pain of death and loss. This pain heralded the despair of finally having to acknowledge that Marcus was leaving her life. It would never end. This pain would be with her until her life's end.

'Briony, I have to go,' she whispered.

'Ma?' she could hear her daughter protesting uncertainly, but Polly was already replacing the receiver.

'Mrs Fraser.'

Numbly Polly looked blankly at the girl who had stopped her. She recognised her distantly, but the questions the girl was asking her seemed to be reaching her down a long, long tunnel. Something about some towels; what did *she* care about such things now?

Without responding Polly turned away from her and

headed for the side door that led into the house's private garden. Beyond it lay the wood where she and Briony had walked when Briony was little. They had gathered wood there for bonfire night and greenery for Christmas. And when he was at home Marcus had always come with them, holding Briony's hand and making her laugh whilst he teased her. In her memories Polly saw herself as always standing slightly apart from them, alone and unwanted, just as *she* was alone and unwanted by Marcus now.

Marcus had been a wonderful surrogate father to Briony. Soon now he would have a child of his own—Suzi's child.

The pain hit her like lightning, zig-zagging through her mind, her body, her heart, half blinding her as it knifed into her, causing her to stumble against a tree and to catch her foot in its exposed gnarled roots. As she fell Polly could feel the tears starting to flow, but she knew it wasn't the pain of her fall that was making her cry. She could see her tears lying damply on her hand as she lifted it to her face to wipe them away. Odd that they were only water; for some reason she'd expected them to be dark red tears of blood, because that was how she felt—as though her very heart had been wrenched apart and its life's blood was pouring from her.

'Polly? Polly?'

Polly tensed in disbelief and anxiety as she heard Marcus calling her name. What was he doing looking for her? They had both been keeping their distance from one another recently, and so far as she knew Marcus was at his own house supervising the work there.

'Polly.'

She heard the irritation in his voice as he saw her. Quickly she struggled to get up, wincing with shocked pain as she realised that when she'd fallen she had hurt her ankle. Not broken it, thankfully, but wrenched it badly enough for it to refuse to take her weight.

'What's wrong? What have you done?' she heard him demanding as he reached her.

'What does it *look* like I've done?' she responded irritably. 'I've wrenched my ankle.'

'Here, lean on me,' Marcus instructed as he helped her to her feet, ignoring her feeble attempts to push him away.

'You know, then, about Suzi and the baby?' he asked her gruffly, once he was sure she was able to stand.

'Yes…' Polly responded tersely. 'Briony rang. I…' She took a deep breath, heroically intending to do the proper thing and congratulate him, but discovered, to her chagrin, that she just couldn't.

'Yes, I know,' Marcus agreed. 'She rang me too. She was concerned about you. She said you sounded… When I drove over to the hotel they said you'd gone out into the private garden and I guessed you might have come down here. It was always one of your favourite places of retreat.'

Immediately Polly was on the defensive. 'What do you mean? I used to come here with Briony, yes, but…'

'And on your own when you needed to be alone… The anniversary of Richard's death,' Marcus told her. 'I saw you that first year…'

'That was because—' Quickly Polly stopped. There was no way she could explain to him now that she had come here then to ask Richard's forgiveness for loving his cousin. Instead she told Marcus jerkily, 'Briony says you want to have the reception at Fraser House.'

She saw he was frowning as he looked at her.

'That's what Suzi wants and—'

'And what Suzi wants Suzi gets; is that it?' Polly
asked him in what she intended to be a light, carefree
voice but which instead sounded more like one riven
with anguish and pain.

'Look, Polly, I know how you must feel,' Marcus told
her, confirming her fears that her voice had given her
away. 'Believe me, I am truly sorry, but I did try to warn
you.'

'Try to warn me? When? When you were in bed with
me? When you were having sex with me?' Polly demanded angrily. 'Have you told—'

Just in time she managed to stop herself, sniffing back
her tears as she struggled with her emotion.

'I'm sorry. I ought to be congratulating you. No wonder you've been chivvying the workmen on at the house.
It must be nearly ready now, and of course I can understand why you want to sell the hotel,' she told him with
careful politeness. 'In the circumstances Suzi won't be
wanting to take over its management. I know I found it
difficult when Briony was a baby, though of course my
circumstances were different. I was... I had to work,'
she said quietly.

'Suzi won't be having it entirely easy,' Marcus
pointed out sharply. 'Her pregnancy wasn't exactly
planned.'

'No, but you obviously aren't totally surprised,' Polly
said gently.

'No,' Marcus agreed shortly. 'In the circumstances
perhaps it was inevitable, although I'm still sorry that
you had to... Whether you believe me or not, Polly, the
last thing I wanted was for you to be hurt, and if there
was any way I could—'

'If I were you I'd worry more about whether or not *I*
could be pregnant as well rather than how much I might

be hurt,' Polly chided him swiftly, but as she saw the shocked look in his eyes she wished she had not spoken so impetuously. It was obvious that it hadn't occurred to him that *their* unprotected sex could have resulted in a pregnancy. Perhaps he had assumed that she was protected, but there had never been any need.

'What are you saying?' he demanded hoarsely, confirming her suspicion that she had shocked him. '*Is* there any possibility that you could be pregnant, Polly?'

'No,' she denied. 'No…'

'Polly…'

She winced as he gave her a little warning shake, forgetting about the injury to her ankle in his anxiety to know the truth and then immediately checking as he felt her fall heavily against him.

'Polly?'

The urgency in his voice might have made her smile, albeit a little ruefully, at any other time. Right now, though, it made her want to cry. How ironic it was that he should feel anxious and concerned for her—but he wasn't concerned for *her*, was he? He was concerned for Suzi and himself and for their child, anxious that their future happiness together shouldn't be blighted by…

'I don't know,' she admitted heavily. 'It's too soon to know but I… It isn't as easy to conceive when one's older,' she pointed out quietly. 'So I don't think…'

'What will you do if…?'

What will *you* do, not What will *we* do, Polly noticed bleakly, but then why should she expect anything else? She had known all along that he loved Suzi…

'I'll deal with that problem when and if I have to,' Polly told him. 'I'd better get back to the hotel. They'll be wondering where on earth I've got to. I'm sorry that Briony disturbed you, Marcus. You must have more than enough to do without nursemaiding me. No doubt Suzi and her mother will want to come over to the hotel to discuss the reception. Will you be coming with them or—?'

'I don't know,' Marcus told her harshly. 'Perhaps, in the circumstances... Look, this isn't easy for me, Polly.'

'Do you think it's easy for *me*?' Polly couldn't resist asking bitterly as she tried to pull away from him, wincing when the pain lanced through her ankle.

'Keep still,' Marcus instructed her. 'What the hell are you trying to do—make the injury even worse? Lean on me.'

It was pointless trying to refuse. Polly knew perfectly well that without his support it was going to be virtually impossible for her to get back to the hotel. Her ankle had swollen whilst they had been talking and it was beginning to ache very painfully indeed.

It took them fifteen minutes to walk slowly back to the hotel, but once they were there, instead of heading inside, Marcus started to guide her towards his car.

'Marcus, what are you doing?' she demanded tiredly.

'I'm taking you down to the surgery,' Marcus informed her coolly. 'That ankle needs professional attention.'

'Maybe it does, but there's no need for you to get involved. I can—'

'You can what—drive yourself?' Marcus gave her a derisory look. 'I don't think so.'

There wasn't any point in arguing with him, and besides, her ankle was beginning to scream the need for some kind of pain relief—so much so... Polly gave a soft gasp of pain as Marcus helped her into his car.

'You aren't going to pass out on me, are you, Polly?'

Marcus asked her sharply as she closed her eyes and the pain started to wash over her in nauseating waves.

'No, I'm not!' she retorted immediately, gritting her teeth in stubborn determination.

'Good girl,' she heard Marcus telling her with unexpected tenderness as he put the car in motion. 'It won't be long now.'

It wasn't—Marcus was a fast and a good driver—but it was still an agonising ten minutes before he was pulling up in the car park to their excellent local medical centre.

As she reached for the door handle he instructed, 'Stay there, I'll get someone to come out to you.'

CHAPTER TEN

'I'VE got to rest for *a week*? I can't possibly do that,' Polly protested to her doctor after he had examined her, bandaged up her ankle and prescribed some pain-killers. 'I've got a hotel to run.'

'I'm sorry, but in order to get the bruising down you will have to rest,' Dr Jarvis persisted.

'Don't worry, Dr Jarvis, *I* shall see that she does,' Marcus informed him, and, ignoring Polly's irritation, he turned to her to say firmly, 'Until that bandage comes off next week, you will be staying with me, Polly.'

'Staying with you, Marcus? Didn't you hear what I just said. I've got a hotel to run!'

'Yes, I heard you, and you can run it…during the day…just so long as you do so from a chair. But there's no way you are going to be able to work a twelve-hour day the way you are at the moment.'

'And if I can't, whose fault is that?' Polly fumed. '*I'm* not the one who called in those wretched people and—'

'Polly, there's no point in arguing with me. You are staying with me until that ankle has healed, and if I find that you are overdoing things then…'

'Then what?' she challenged him.

'Then you will be staying with me *twenty-four* hours a day if necessary,' Marcus told her softly.

Twenty-four hours a day with Marcus. Polly closed her eyes as she was attacked by a wave of weak longing.

What about Suzi? she wanted to say, but for some reason she just couldn't bring herself to form the words,

163

to ask Marcus what his soon-to-be wife would think
about him moving Polly into the house they were going
to share.

Not that Suzi had any need to feel concerned, as
Marcus had no doubt made more than clear to her, reassuring her with all those tender words and touches that
were the province of the lover.

'What is it? Is your ankle worse?' Marcus asked
sharply as Polly gave a soft sound of pain at the thought
of the loving intimacy Suzi would share with him.

Quickly Polly shook her head before very reluctantly
allowing Marcus to guide her back to his car.

'We'll stop off at the hotel on the way back so that
you can collect whatever you need,' he told her as he
waited to join the traffic.

'I can't possibly run the hotel from your house,
Marcus. I need to be there on the spot,' Polly protested,
trying desperately to find a way to change his mind.

However, the thin smile he gave her as he slid the car
out into the busy main road told her that she had failed
even before he replied acerbically, 'Really? It's odd,
isn't it, how the hotel has suddenly become so important
to you when not so very long ago you announced that
it was so important that you intended to leave?'

'That's different,' Polly insisted. 'At the moment the
hotel is still my responsibility.'

'Mmm… Have you spoken to Bernstein recently, by
the way?'

'Phil? No, I haven't,' Polly admitted, adding, 'He's
away at the moment in the Caribbean.'

'Yes, I know; Suzi flew out to meet him there.'

Suzi was with Phil! There was really no reason why
she should feel so surprised, Polly told herself. After all,
Suzi was still working for Phil. But if she was honest

she *was* rather bemused that Marcus, who had made all manner of unfounded accusations about *her* relationship with Phil, should react so calmly to the fact that Suzi, whom he loved, whom he was going to marry, who was having his *child*, was with Phil in such an undeniably romantic location.

'Phil's secretary told me that he's due back soon,' Polly informed Marcus.

'Yes,' he agreed coolly. As she swung the car off the road and into the drive that led to the hotel, he said, 'You can wait in the car, Polly, to save putting any extra pressure on your ankle. I'll go in and get your stuff.'

Immediately Polly opened her mouth to object, pointing out crossly, 'I'm not an invalid, Marcus. I'm perfectly capable of getting my own *stuff*, thank you very much.'

A little to her surprise he gave in, but still insisted that she lean on him whilst he helped her into the foyer.

Although she was loath to admit it, Polly acknowledged to herself that the pain in her ankle was such that walking was extremely uncomfortable, and she knew too that, if she were to stay in the hotel, without meaning to her staff would probably forget her incapacity and within a very short space of time she would find herself doing exactly what her doctor had told her she must not do.

'There's no need to come with me,' she informed Marcus determinedly as she headed for the lift.

In her room she hobbled from her wardrobe to her dressing table, packing what she thought she would need, reminding herself that it was only going to be for the one night. Tomorrow morning she would be back at her desk. She would soon find a way of convincing Marcus that she could manage perfectly well on her own.

When she walked back into the foyer Marcus was talking to her secretary-cum-assistant, Pat Chorlton.

'Marcus was just telling me about your ankle,' Pat sympathised as Polly hobbled over to them. A kind, motherly woman in her early sixties, Pat was excellent at her job—so excellent in fact that Polly had persuaded her to stay on to work part-time after she had passed her official retirement birthday at sixty.

'Poor you, especially now we're going to have this wedding to organise.'

So Marcus had told Pat about the wedding. Well, she shouldn't be surprised. Like any man in love, he no doubt wanted to sing the praises of his beloved. Trying to ignore the searing pain of her jealousy, Polly assured her assistant, 'Don't worry; I'll be here in the morning.'

'You *might* be here in the morning, provided you are well enough,' Marcus corrected her firmly.

'Marcus…' Polly began fiercely, but he was already picking up the overnight bag she had arranged to have brought from her room, grimacing as he felt the weight of it.

'What the devil…?' he began.

But Polly forestalled him, telling him quickly, 'It's the books. This is my evening for working on the month's accounts and—'

'Marcus, what do you think you're doing?' Polly protested with a small shriek as he put down her bag, unzipped it and removed the heavy account books she had packed into it.

'The doctor said you had to *rest*…remember?'

'He said I had to rest my *ankle*, not my *brain*,' Polly told him trenchantly, adding sweetly, 'You were the one who brought in the systems police, Marcus, and I don't think they're going to be very impressed if the accounts aren't done in time.'

'No—well, if they aren't then they can take it up with me,' Marcus responded equally grittily, while Pat, who was listening, laughed and shook her head.

She said teasingly, 'You two sound just like a long-time married couple.'

Her teasing remark shocked Polly into white-faced silence. Surely Pat, who had always been so tactful and discreet, must know how inappropriate her comment was in the circumstances, with Marcus having so recently made public his relationship with Suzi?

'A marriage made in hell,' Marcus murmured sardonically in her ear as he zipped up her bag and picked it up, but for once Polly felt no impulse to fight back.

Just as soon as she felt strong enough she intended to tackle Marcus again about releasing her from her notice. He couldn't possibly want her either living or working in such close proximity now.

The drive back to Marcus's house was completed in silence. Once or twice Polly snatched a brief look at his set profile, wondering if he was thinking about Suzi and no doubt wishing that she were the one he was taking home with him.

'Wait here,' Marcus commanded Polly as he let her into the hallway of the house. 'I'll take your bag up and then come back for you.'

'Marcus, I'm perfectly capable of walking up a flight of stairs,' Polly protested.

The house had been painted since she had last seen it, and she had to admit that the warm Mediterranean colour scheme Marcus had chosen for the hallway looked very effective and welcoming, as did the heavy plain cream curtains that cloaked the windows and the hand-made light fittings Marcus had commissioned from a local designer. The sitting room she could see through the open doorway off the hall was decorated and furnished with a harmonious mixture of antique and modern, warm rich colours teamed with restful creams and heavy antique country furniture made sturdily of oak married with modern fabrics and designs.

It was easy to imagine Marcus living in this house, but for some reason Polly found it difficult to imagine Suzi here. She would want crystal light fittings, silk fabrics, delicate pieces of porcelain and Regency furniture. This was the kind of home that a child could play comfortably in, the kind of home where friends would feel welcome and formal dinner parties would be abandoned in favour of chatty suppers round the kitchen table.

Heart-achingly conscious of the yawning gap of loneliness there was in her own life, the emptiness she had filled with the make-believe fantasy that they were a family while Briony had been growing up and Marcus had been there on hand to father her, Polly took a hesitant step towards the stairs. When Marcus gave an impatient sigh and came forward to help her she said sharply,

'No. I can manage by myself.'

How symbolic those words were. From now on she would have to manage by herself, without Briony to keep her thoughts busy and occupied, without Marcus to focus her fantasies and yearnings on.

'It's this room,' Marcus informed her curtly, deliberately keeping his distance from her as Polly followed him across the landing. He threw open a bedroom door, flattening himself against the wall almost so that she could precede him into the room, making it plain to her that he had as little desire to touch her as she had to be touched by him. Although, of course, for very different reasons. She dared not allow him to come near her in case she betrayed herself and her love for him, but Marcus was keeping his distance from her to reinforce the fact that he was committed to someone else and that there was no room now in his life for her.

As she stepped into the bedroom Polly came to an abrupt halt, turning to face him as she exclaimed uncomfortably, 'But this is *your* room!'

Even if she hadn't suddenly recognised the room as being the master bedroom from the plan she had seen, the small, intimate details of Marcus's occupation of it would have told her. His brushes were on the tallboy— the ones that had belonged to his grandfather. A towelling robe lay across the huge bed and there were more of his belongings scattered about.

'I can't sleep in *here*,' Polly protested.

'Don't worry,' Marcus assured her laconically, 'I'm not planning to share the room with you. It just so happens that the others aren't quite ready for occupation yet. The painters only left the other day and the carpets aren't being laid until later in the week.'

'But where will you sleep?' Polly asked him in confusion.

'Downstairs. There's a very comfortable sofa in the sitting room. I shall be able to manage in there.'

'Marcus, you're over six feet tall. I'm only just over five feet,' Polly protested. 'If anyone should be sleeping on a sofa it should be me. This is ridiculous,' she added. 'I could have managed perfectly well at the hotel. If I'd known that my being here was going to deprive you of your own bedroom...'

'What is this, Polly—an offer to share the bed with me?' Marcus taunted her.

Immediately Polly went quiet, her face becoming pinched and her eyes haunted.

'There was no need for that,' she told him huskily. 'I can't stay here, Marcus; I—'

'You don't have any other option,' he told her briskly. 'You can't drive and there's certainly no way *I* intend to drive you.'

'I don't want to deprive you of your bed,' she insisted stubbornly.

How could she sleep in it knowing that soon Marcus would be sharing it with Suzi; that a year from now their baby would be curled up in it with them? No, that kind of pain just couldn't be borne. Not by her. Not right now, when the realisation of just how lost to her Marcus was was still hurting her so very, very much.

'You're wasting your breath, Polly,' Marcus told her dryly, glancing at his watch before adding, 'I'm going downstairs to make us both something to eat. If when I come back you aren't undressed and in that bed I'll...'

'You'll what?' Polly challenged him tiredly.

'I'll undress you and put you there myself,' Marcus told her softly, adding, when she changed colour betrayingly, 'Yes, I thought that might be the right kind of incentive. Odd, though, really, isn't it? The last time I removed your clothes you seemed more than eager for me to do so; in fact—'

'Stop it. Stop it,' Polly protested, covering her ears with her hands and turning, hot-faced, away from him.

How could he do this to her? How could he remind her of that now, when they were both standing in the room he was going to be sharing with another woman...with his *wife*? Polly would have thought that what had happened between them would be the last thing he wanted to refer to; that he would feel, if not ashamed of his betrayal of Suzi, then at least anxious to ignore it. In his shoes... But in his shoes she would never have done what he had done in the first place. She would never have been able to share such intimacy with someone she didn't love.

'You've got fifteen minutes, Polly,' Marcus told her firmly as he turned towards the door.

Fifteen minutes. Not an awful lot of time, Polly decided a little breathlessly as she pulled on her nightshirt and emerged cautiously from the *en suite* bathroom into the mercifully still empty bedroom. She had just managed to scramble beneath the bedclothes when Marcus came in carrying a tray.

'Supper,' he told her unnecessarily as he put it down on the bed beside her. Polly's mouth watered as she saw what he had cooked for her: scrambled eggs and smoked salmon...her favourite light meal and one which she normally only managed to enjoy on Christmas Day morning, along with a glass of champagne, whilst she and Marcus watched Briony opening her presents.

'Thank you,' she told him chokily. Had he remembered that it was her favourite, her special comfort food, or had he simply made it because he had the ingredients there? There was no point in asking him, of course.

'Don't forget to take your tablets,' he instructed her as he turned back towards the door.

He was leaving her to eat on her own. Just in time Polly managed to bite back her protest. Of course he was, and she was glad...yes, glad. The last thing she wanted was to have him there with her, extolling Suzi's virtues to her and enthusing about their plans.

After he had gone she started to eat, but, unexpectedly, despite the fact that the food smelled so appetising, she discovered that she simply didn't want it. There was a hot, hard lump in her throat which was preventing her from eating, and an even more intense pain around her heart. Miserably she took two of her tablets and sipped the water Marcus had brought for her.

Her ankle ached and she felt lethargic and drowsy. After putting the tray onto the floor, she sank back against the pillows. The bed had obviously been freshly made and she didn't even have the secret pleasure of having Marcus's scent around her whilst she slept. No, *that* privilege was reserved for Suzi. Tears welled behind her closed eyelids and Polly sniffed defensively. She was not going to cry. She was *not*.

The light was still on when Marcus went into the bedroom later to collect Polly's supper tray but Polly herself was fast asleep, one arm up to protect her eyes from the light. Marcus frowned as he looked down and saw the supper tray on the floor, her meal barely touched.

He had made it especially for her, knowing it was her favourite—had even had to raid the freezer for the smoked salmon.

It was obvious how devastated she was by the news. He had tried to warn her. Suzi had made it plain to him just what her plans were and now that she was pregnant, of course, the baby's future had to come first.

'It will be a boy,' Suzi had told him triumphantly. Marcus hoped she was right, although privately he thought it was still early days for her to be absolutely sure.

Quietly he picked up the tray and headed for the door, closing it gently behind him.

*   *   *

Polly closed her eyes and put her hands to her aching temples. She was having a particularly trying morning. Her sore ankle still hurt if she misguidedly put weight on it, but it had also recovered enough for her to forget this, with the result that every now and again she did so, causing herself to lurch and wince with pain whilst at the same time cursing because she was hampered in her movements. Add to that the fact that Marcus's team of management consultants were bombarding her with questions and that, despite the fact that he had returned from the Caribbean two days earlier, Phil was too busy to return her telephone calls, and it was no wonder that her head ached, she acknowledged wearily.

But the ache in her head nowhere near compared to that in her heart. Now that *was* pain—pain that could not be cured with a pill that could be swallowed. If only…

'Polly? Suzi's here,' Pat hurried into her office to inform her. 'She wants to talk to you about the reception.'

Suzi… Of course Polly had been expecting this, she had been expecting it and dreading it.

'Is Marcus with her?' she asked Pat as casually as she could.

'Yes,' Pat confirmed.

'I'll be right with them,' Polly told her secretary, waiting until she had gone before taking a deep breath and pinning a fragile brittle smile to her lips.

'Suzi…Marcus…' She greeted them both with false pleasure.

'Marcus, I don't know why I need to see her,' Suzi told Marcus rudely. 'You haven't forgotten what I said, have you, about having the marquee opening into the walled garden? I want to have my photographs done in there. The wedding consultant says they can erect a gazebo around the fishpond and, of course, the hotel will have to be closed to any other guests.

'I want to receive my guests in the main hall. The florists will decorate it, of course. I shall be using a top London firm and...'

As she listened to her Polly could feel herself getting angrier and angrier. The walled garden was her domain, a *private* garden, not available to the hotel guests and for Marcus to have given his agreement that Suzi could have access to it without first consulting her felt like a burning brand applied to her bare skin. Such pain should have been cauterising, she recognised, burning away the disease of her unwanted love, but...

'We'll be bringing in our own chef, of course; Phil is flying him in from the Caribbean. Everything in the marquee is going to be colour-themed to tie in with my dress, all the guests must wear black or white, and... Oh, have you told her yet?' she demanded sharply of Marcus as she looked at Polly for the first time.

And then, without waiting for Marcus to reply, she told Polly, 'We'll be taking over the hotel completely for the wedding so it won't be necessary for you to be here. Phil seemed to think you might have some holiday allocation you could use up. We could offer you a room at the Cay but I don't think it would be your style,' she told Polly disdainfully.

She wrinkled her nose as she turned to Marcus, her hand resting possessively on his arm as she said sweetly, 'I did suggest to Phil that we should perhaps think of hiring Richard Branson's island, but he put his foot down...because of my...condition...' She removed her hand from Marcus's arm to pat her stomach complacently. 'He's beside himself at the thought of having a son. Have you seen the earrings he's just bought me?'

As she moved her head the large diamond studs in her ears caught the light, sending dazzling soft lights dancing around the room, but it wasn't that that was making Polly feel so giddy and light-headed.

'You're…you're marrying Phil,' she interrupted Suzi's self-congratulatory monologue huskily. 'It's you and Phil…'

'Yes. I'm sorry, I did warn you that he was mine, didn't I?' she told Polly, giving her a sharp-toothed little smile. 'Phil and I go back a long way, even if we have both let our pride keep us apart for far too long. He admits that he's glad now that my contract meant he couldn't fire me and that having to work alongside me meant that he could never really get me out of his system.

'We're both sorry for any disappointment you've had, but I know you'll understand that naturally Phil wants *me* to take over the running of the London hotel now. He's going to base himself in London for the next few years. It makes sense, of course, especially if we want to get little Philip into one of the top nursery schools. I think the right kind of schooling is so important for a boy, don't you?' she asked Marcus, giving him a flirtatious smile.

'I think the most vital ingredient to any child's well-being is knowing he or she is loved,' Marcus replied quietly, whilst Polly struggled to take on board what she had just learned.

Suzi was marrying *Phil* and *not* Marcus; Suzi was having *Phil's* child and *not* Marcus's… So why had Suzi made that extraordinary verbal attack on her that time in London when she had accosted her as she'd left Phil's hotel?

Phil's hotel! Suddenly Polly understood; Suzi had no

doubt thought she had spent the night with *Phil* and not Marcus, and *that* was why…

At long last Suzi had finished delivering her list of requirements. As she swept towards the exit she turned round and told Polly patronisingly, 'Oh, Phil did say to tell you that if he hears of anything coming up that might suit you he'd be in touch, but I really think you'd be better off staying here… I must go now, otherwise I'm going to be late. We're flying to Paris for dinner. Phil is taking me shopping there.'

Once she had gone the foyer seemed blissfully quiet and empty. Marcus, who had gone with her to her car, came back just as Polly was mouthing the words 'Suzi is going to marry Phil'.

'Suzi is going to marry Phil,' she repeated out loud.

'Yes,' Marcus agreed soberly, telling her quietly, 'Look, Polly, I know you won't thank me for saying this but…if you want my opinion he was never the right man for you.'

'Because I'm too old for him?' Polly asked him dryly.

'No,' Marcus responded fiercely. 'No… Age has nothing to do with it…nothing at all.'

'Oh? That wasn't what you implied to me when—'

'He isn't *good* enough for you, Polly. No way. No way at all… I know how you feel about him, how hurt you must be, how hard this must be for you… God knows, I've been there myself…'

Abruptly Polly remembered that Marcus loved Suzi and that the heady relief she felt at knowing that Suzi was marrying Phil wasn't something he was likely to share.

Impulsively she reached out and touched his arm, unable to hide the warmth in her eyes and her voice as she told him gently, 'I could say the same thing to you, Marcus. She...Suzi isn't good enough for you.'

'What!'

'I know that when you went to bed with me you were thinking about her,' Polly continued quickly, wanting to say what she had to say before she lost her courage. 'I...I should have stopped you but—'

'But it was easier to pretend that I was Bernstein,' Marcus supplied curtly.

Firmly Polly shook her head.

'No. What I said to you about Phil was true, Marcus—he was *never* anything more than a prospective employer.'

'But Suzi said—'

'I don't care *what* Suzi said,' Polly interrupted him. 'I never felt anything for Phil other than the most casual kind of friendship, and I certainly never contemplated having any kind of...of intimacy with him.'

Marcus looked blankly at her.

'Then why...?'

'Look, I think we should just forget the whole episode,' Polly told him hurriedly.

'Forget it? Forget the most important, the most precious hours of my life?' Marcus groaned hoarsely. 'Have you *any* idea just what you're asking of me, Polly? I've waited years to have you look at me...want me...touch me the way you did, and if you think I'm going to forget even a single second of the pleasure you gave me...

'I know you don't love me, Polly; I've *always* known that. God knows I've tried hard enough over the years to provoke an emotional reaction from you, to break through that wall of indifference you've put up against me. Loving you has been so much a way of life for me for so long that...'

Loving her?

'You love me...?' Polly breathed shakily.

Broodingly Marcus looked at her.

'Of course I damn well *love* you,' he told her harshly. 'I've loved you from the first time I saw you, and if I hadn't fallen in love with you then, Polly... Being with you when you gave birth to Briony was the most intensely emotional experience I have ever had. Just as emotional in a different way as holding you in my arms in bed. You will never, *ever* know how much, how very, very much, I wanted Briony to be my child...how much I wanted *you* to have my child.'

'Want*ed*?' Polly asked him cautiously, holding her breath a little as she underlined, 'Wanted as in *did* want, or...?'

'Did want?' Marcus repeated, frowning a little as he tried to puzzle out what she was saying.

And then, as he realised, he reached for her, pulling her bodily into his arms, causing her to tell him in a muffled voice, 'No, Marcus, we *can't*. Not here, where anyone can see us.'

'I don't care *who* sees us,' Marcus retorted masterfully as he kissed her. And then, as he felt her lips soften under his and her body melt, he lifted his mouth from hers and agreed huskily, 'Well, perhaps *some* privacy might be a good idea.'

'A very good idea,' Polly informed him mock severely as she put a discreet distance between them and then hesitated shyly before turning towards the stairs,

'I've got a better idea.' Marcus forestalled her firmly, taking hold of her hand and guiding her towards the door.

'Where are you taking me?' Polly demanded dizzily as he took her towards his parked car.

'Home,' Marcus responded promptly, adding softly, 'I'm taking *both* of you home.'

'Oh.' Polly gave him a pink-cheeked look as he unlocked the door of his car for her.

'Or did I misinterpret that cryptic remark you just made?'

'No,' Polly admitted, shaking her head. 'At least, I'm not totally sure yet, but…'

But she had been very unwell every morning for the past week, and she was so certain herself of what had happened that she had telephoned the surgery just to make sure the pills she had been prescribed couldn't harm the new life she felt sure was growing inside her.

Her doctor had been immediately and thankfully reassuring, but as yet Polly had not been able to bring herself to do any kind of formal test. The symptoms were all there, but knowing or rather *believing* that another woman was also carrying Marcus's child—a woman whom she had thought he loved—had made her reluctant to take the final step that would confirm her suspicions. Was she destined to deprive her children of their fathers? she had wondered despairingly only last night as she had lain, sleepless, in bed.

'Heaven knows what Briony is going to have to say about all of this,' she told Marcus breathlessly a couple of hours later as he smoothed her hair off her face and kissed her gently. He had been a little reluctant at first to make love with her—because of the baby—but Polly had assured him robustly that there was no danger, adding with innocent persuasiveness, 'And I want you so much, Marcus. All this is so new to me… I never knew before… Richard and I… I was just a girl and he was a boy.'

She had told him simply, 'What we shared was good and loving, but it wasn't *love*. It wasn't a *tenth* of what I feel for you. I can't believe how foolish we've both been, wasting so many years. I thought you didn't like me. You always seemed to be so critical of me.'

'So critical that I could hardly bear to let you out of my sight, never mind my life,' Marcus groaned self-critically.

'I thought that was because of Briony.'

'I do love Briony,' Marcus told her. 'And I always will. I hope this new baby *is* a boy, Polly, but not because I share Bernstein's desire to found a dynasty. It's just that Briony has always been so special to me, I'd be worried that another girl couldn't, wouldn't…'

'That you might love your own child more?' Polly suggested softly for him, but immediately Marcus shook his head.

'I couldn't love any child more than I love Briony. No, I was thinking that another daughter, a *second* daughter,' he emphasised with a small smile, 'might feel that she is second best, whereas a boy…a son…'

'Oh, Marcus, I can't believe we've been so lucky…and to think it's all because of Suzi and Phil. How could you think I could possibly want Phil?' she reproached him.

'How could *you* think *I* wanted Suzi?' Marcus retorted.

'But surely you guessed how I felt when…'

'When we made love?' Marcus supplied for her. 'I know you were responsive to me. My God, how I knew that, and you'll never know how much I wanted to capitalise on that, Polly…how much I wanted to steal you away somewhere and keep you there in my bed until you were forced to capitulate and admit that you loved me.'

'You actually contemplated doing something like that?' Polly asked him, round-eyed.

'Well, not exactly,' Marcus admitted, 'But I certainly fantasised about living in a world where I could have done so, although in all honesty there was no way I could ever compel you to do or give anything you didn't want me to have willingly.'

'Briony is going to be dreadfully shocked. She wanted you to marry Suzi,' Polly told him.

'Mmm... She did rather get it wrong, didn't she?' Marcus agreed. 'She warned me that you were in danger of making a fool of yourself over Bernstein and asked me to keep an eye on the situation because she was afraid his intentions towards you weren't entirely honourable...'

'She did what?' Polly protested indignantly. 'So *that* was where you got the idea that I was going through some sort of mid-life crisis, was it? Just *wait* until I speak to her...'

'Briony, darling, how nice. We...*I* wasn't expecting you to come home this weekend,' Polly told her daughter as she went to hug her, hoping as she did so that Briony hadn't noticed how flustered she sounded.

It wasn't that she didn't want to see Briony, it was just that she and Marcus had planned to spend the day shopping for things for the nursery, and then they were going to have dinner out to celebrate their future together, Marcus had told her. They had already decided on a very quiet family wedding and Polly had a sneaking suspicion that tonight Marcus intended to present her with an engagement ring, an old-fashioned courtesy which wasn't perhaps necessary in their circumstances but which she found touching nonetheless.

They had had official confirmation that she was pregnant now. Marcus was over the moon, and so protective of her health that Polly couldn't help but be tenderly amused.

She—*they*—had every intention of telling Briony, of course, but she wanted time to find the right words, the right way.

'How are the plans coming along for the wedding?' Briony asked conversationally after she had hugged her mother.

'The wedding...? Oh, we've...' Guiltily Polly bit her lip. Briony meant Suzi and Phil's wedding, of course. 'Oh well, Marcus has decided that we really can't accommodate all Suzi's requirements and I think they've decided to get married in the Caribbean now after all...'

'And the job—your job with Phil?' Briony probed.

'Oh, that... Well...er... I've decided to stay here.' Polly took a deep breath. 'Briony, darling, there's something I have to tell you.'

'Marcus, I couldn't believe it,' Polly told him in a pained voice as she related the incident to him later. 'There I was, expecting Briony to be so disappointed because her plans to marry you off to Suzi had come to nothing, but when I told her about us she positively beamed from ear to ear. It seems that she'd wanted us to be together all the time but that she'd begun to despair that we ever would be, and so she decided to try to make us both jealous...

'I can't believe she could be so devious. But she told me that it had been obvious to her "for ever" that we loved one another, even if we were too blind to see it...'

'I know; she rang me a couple of hours ago to tell me how thrilled she was—about both our pieces of news.'

'Yes. I thought she might be a little bit shocked about…about the baby, but she was thrilled.'

'Will you please stop looking at me like that?' Marcus murmured softly to Polly as she smiled luminously into his eyes. 'This is a public restaurant, and what I want to do with you right now is a very, very private matter indeed.'

'Marcus,' Polly protested, pink-cheeked.

'Polly,' Marcus teased her back.

He had given her the engagement ring he had bought her earlier, and then he had undressed and made love to her, kissing every inch of her naked body before clasping her ring hand and lifting it to his mouth. Tenderly kissing her ring finger, he'd whispered to her, 'My ring…my baby—' he had kissed her tummy '—and my love…' And then he had kissed her mouth, and Polly had felt as though all the love inside her had turned into the softest and most delicious liquid heat, as if every bit of her was melting with desire and happiness.

'What's wrong?' Marcus asked in some alarm as she suddenly pushed her meal away from her almost untouched.

'Nothing,' Polly told him simply, taking a small breath before she told him huskily, 'I just want to be alone with you, Marcus…now…please…'

EPILOGUE

'HAVE you heard the news? Suzi has had a little girl,' Briony informed her mother breathlessly as she came hurrying into the nursery, pausing to give her mother the briefest of kisses before turning to the crib and cooing with tenderness, bending down to extract her small half-brother from his wrappings of blue-edged white cotton.

'She was so convinced it was going to be a boy. Apparently Phil isn't too pleased at all, because the tests they'd had done all predicted that she was carrying a boy.

'Not that *we* care, do we, my darling baby brother,' Briony crooned as she cuddled him. 'Mum, I'm sure he's grown since yesterday. He *feels* heavier.'

Polly smiled tenderly. The baby had been born pre-maturely, and they had all been concerned about how quickly he would grow and put on weight. But their fears had all been allayed as Alistair proved to be a healthy baby with a keen appeite.

Briony was even more besotted with baby Alistair than Marcus was, and that was saying something.

As with Briony's birth, Marcus had been there with her to share Alistair's, and even to Polly's protective maternal eyes there had been no difference whatsoever in the degree of tenderness with which he had held his own blood child and that which he had shown the newly born Briony.

'I'll always be his favourite,' Briony had told her mother smugly the day Alistair was born. 'Fathers always have a softer spot for their daughters, whilst mothers spoil their sons...'

Their *daughters*...? But, after all, that was exactly what Briony was to Marcus—his precious and much loved daughter.

Half an hour later, after Briony had left, Marcus came into the nursery just as Polly was putting Alistair back into his crib. She smiled up at him and told him softly as she went to kiss him, 'Thank you.'

'What's that for?' Marcus asked in bemusement as he returned her kiss—with interest.

'For being you,' Polly told him truthfully, 'and for giving me...everything.'

'Mmm... Well, if you *really* want to thank me...' Marcus teased her, drawing her towards the door that led to their own bedroom...

MONTANA MAVERICKS

Bestselling author

SUSAN MALLERY

WILD WEST WIFE

THE ORIGINAL MONTANA MAVERICKS HISTORICAL NOVEL

Jesse Kincaid had sworn off love forever.
But when the handsome rancher kidnaps
his enemy's mail-order bride to get revenge,
he ends up falling for his innocent captive!

RETURN TO WHITEHORN, MONTANA, WITH

WILD WEST WIFE

Available July 2001

And be sure to pick up
MONTANA MAVERICKS: BIG SKY GROOMS,
three brand-new historical stories about Montana's
most popular family, coming in August 2001.

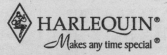

HARLEQUIN®
Makes any time special®